FOX FIRE

THE KITSUNE

BY:
JH DEMOND
&
TJ BERRY

FOX FIRE PUBLICATIONS, LLC 2019

ISBN 13: 978-0-692-12174-0
ISBN 10: 0-692-12167-6

Printed in the U.S.A.
First Fox Fire paperback printing, March 2019

Acknowledgements

JH DeMond,

To my husband and my kits for listening to all of Gwen's adventures. To my parents for their love and support. To my grandmother for giving me a typewriter and plenty of paper. To Dr. Clark for recognizing and encouraging my love of editing. And to TJ Berry for walking into my office six years ago and insisting I come up with the names of two main characters.

TJ Berry,

To my mother, the original storyteller in my life. To my siblings, for putting up with all of my 'odd' behavior. To my friends and friends who became family, thanks for all the support and love. To Dr. Clark and Dr. Bonner, thanks for showing me a different way to view the world. To Dr. Bieniek, you were right, I had to do what I didn't want to do, to figure out what I do want to do. To Dr. Bartlett for giving me the best/worst encouragement ever, "[You're] stupid and you'll never amount to anything." And last but certainly not least, to JH DeMond…for giving me a whole new world to explore.

Fox Fire Publications would like to thank www.SelfPubBookCovers.com/CatT. for our cover art.

The Kitsune Chapters

Chapter 1: Normal

Normal girl…you are a normal girl. You are a normal Japanese girl with an Americanized-Welsh name, blood red hair and green eyes. Funny how nothing about me says normal, but this is my human form. It's not as if I chose it. "Right?" I ask the picture of myself, covering my mirror. It wouldn't do much good to look there. All I'd see is a fox staring back at me. A kitsune…a trickster…the fox spirit named Gwendolyn Elizabeth Frost. I sigh. Not anymore. I'm a normal girl named Gwen Frost…with normal foster parents and this is my first day of normal high school.

"Normal. Shouldn't be too hard, should it?"

"Gwen," my foster-mother, Mrs. Taylor, calls from downstairs. "Are you almost ready? If you don't leave soon, you'll be late." saying

"Coming." I toss my wavy hair (thank you, Mrs. Taylor for helping me style it) and turn away from my picture. I glance around the room. I have to admit, aside from the oversized vanity mirror, I love this room. Pink walls trimmed in white with lots of open wall space for pictures and posters. I pick up my jacket. The mahogany-framed day bed is perfect for lounging since I don't sleep much.

The dresser and nightstand are oak; the smell of them reminds me of the forests near obāsan's…grrr, grandma's estate. Mrs. Taylor picked out the furniture, but she went a step further and helped me fill the closet with the cutest clothes. I even managed to talk her into getting a couple of skirts that are more than two inches above my knees. I walk out of my room and head downstairs.

I take my fluorescently pink backpack from the bottom post of the stairs' rail. I sling it over my shoulder, heading for the door. My foster-mother meets me with a lunch bag, metal thermos, and a small package in paper towel wrapping that I know contains a bagel. Mrs. Taylor always wants to make sure I am well fed. She constantly comments that I look too thin. I wish I were a little older so that I could maybe add a few pounds to my appearance. I'd have to be a fifty-year-old changing her appearance to look like a seventeen-year-old. Wishful thinking, I remind myself. Obāsan…grrr, grandma always shows off her ability to look like anyone.

I take the treasured items. I place the thermos and bag into my backpack and zip it closed clumsily while holding the bagel. She awkwardly wraps one arm around me. Her brown curls hang over my shoulder. I imagine her warm brown eyes closing tight with the corners wrinkling when she smiles. She still doesn't believe that I really care about her and her husband. I wrap my arms around her. She releases me and looks me over. "Now, you have a good day, okay?" I nod. She opens the door and I step outside.

"Bye," I whisper as she pushes the door shut. I walk across the red porch, down the concrete stairs and across the small front yard. I stop. I turn back and…yep; there she is at the window, watching me. I smile and wave. She does the same and then disappears behind the curtain.

At least my first day of school is shaping up to be a good one. Gorgeous North Carolina weather, I'm almost at the bus stop and I've got plenty of time before…I gasp. The feeling that someone… something is watching me interrupts my thoughts. It's not Mrs. Taylor this time. This feels ominous…like Gavin's aura except darker…so, much darker. I peer at the houses behind me but see no signs of movement. I turn back around, but still feel the eerie sense that someone…or something is watching me as I continue toward the bus stop.

I reach the bus stop just in time to see the bus round the far corner. The yellow and black bus with the numbers forty-one dash three on the side stops in front of me. The doors slide open and the driver greets me with a welcoming smile. As I board the bus, I can't help but visually sweep the street one last time…this time with fox magic reinforcing my eyesight. I can practically feel my eyes glowing.

Everything seems to be in its place. I don't sense…anything supernatural. So, I shake the feeling as best I can and move to the back of the bus. It's already in motion again before I fall into an empty seat. I unwrap my bagel so that I can devour it before we reach the school. I tear a piece off and pop it into my mouth. It's still warm and it tastes really good. I smile as I take another bite and mentally thank Mrs. Taylor.

#####

Hoodie? Check. Bag? Check. Black, blue, and grayish-silver spray paint? Check. I cram the paint into the bag, zip it, and hit the door. I have to tip toe past mom's room. Hopefully, working the late shift means she's too tired to get up and rag me about my clothes or…

"Hey, Alex," mom says groggily from her door.

"Hey, mom," I say, pulling my hood lower. She steps closer and pulls it off.

"I never see you anymore, baby. Glad you washed all that black goop out of your hair. Your chestnut brown looks so much better." She ruffles my hair. "Just like your father's." I fake a smile. "You look so much like him. From your pretty brown eyes to your cute little nose, you look just like him."

"Mom, have you been drinking?" I pull my hood back onto my head.

"No." She puts her hand on her forehead. "I'm just really tired."

"Well," I start while turning away. "I gotta get to…" I stop to clear my throat. "…I gotta get to school."

"Wait," she snaps. "I got another voicemail…from the school." I make a cartoonish gulp. "You've been skipping school again."

"No, I…"

"Stop," she snaps this time with an actual snap of her fingers. "I know you have. A friend of mine saw you downtown around nine…and I'm not an idiot, so I know school starts at eight."

"Eight-fifteen," I mumble.

"Do it again," she begins in her 'mom' voice while pointing. "And you're grounded."

"Okay."

"What?" she says, moving her hand to cup her ear.

"Yes, ma'am," I reply slightly louder.

"Okay. Get over here and give me a kiss." She puts her arm around me and kisses me on the cheek. She releases me then disappears behind her bedroom door. "Have a good day," she calls. I hear her bedsprings creaking. She must be exhausted. They have her working twelve-hour shifts again. That sucks.

I can't think about that right now. I pull my bag onto my shoulder, causing the cans inside to knock together. The noise brings Max running over to me. His tail wags behind him. "Best Border Collie ever," I recite to him. He sits and looks up at me. His mouth seems to droop into a smile every time I tell him that. I scratch between his ears. "Take care of mom, okay?" He stands and goes over to her bedroom door. He lies down in front of her door and watches me back away. "Good boy." He lays his head down. "Time to make that money," I whisper.

I pass through our microscopic apartment, with the hand-me-down late nineties furniture and hit the door. Crap. Ma and Max distracted me, and I forgot to take my bike. I head back inside and grab my horrible black spray-painted bike. The handle brake barely works, the tires are perpetually bald and the seat's tearing. I guess if I can still pedal it. I carry the bike down the stairs. I hate living on the second floor. Everything's a pain living on the second floor. Even bringing in groceries feels like a huge deal.

My phone vibrates. Crap, I must be late. I slip it out of my hoodie pocket. "Rex," I say.

"Hey, panna," Rex growls from the other end. "Where you at?"

"I'm running a little late, man. I'll be there as soon as…"

"Tick, tock, panna. Every minute you keep me waiting, that's ten bucks I'm taking off your payday." I end the call and hop onto my bike. I pedal as though my life depends on it. I'm at least twenty minutes out by bike and he's only paying me four hundred. My mom needs that money…we need that money…I can't think about that now. Pedal, Alex, pedal.

I make the trek in fifteen minutes. Thankfully, Rex isn't counting the five minutes I've spent trying to catch my breath against me. The sunlight is already shining off his bald head. He licks his top teeth, showing that horrible gold grill he has in front. He crosses his massive arms, showing the tattoos there. "Puerto," is on his left arm and "Rico," is on his right. He's proud of his heritage. That's about the only thing I admire about him…well, that and the wad of cash he always seems to have.

"Okay, homes," he starts, turning to the side of the Williams Street Bridge. "I want King Rex painted right here…with letters as big as I am. And I want it to be gray with blue trim and a black shadow."

I nod. "You know, Rex and King basically mean the same thing, right?" He raises one eyebrow. "You're basically getting me to write, King King on the bridge."

"I'm not stupid, homes," he growls. He points to himself. "My name means King, but it's not King, got it?" I nod. "Good. Now, get to work. I'll be back in an hour and you better be done by then or that's another fifty off." Rex hops into what has to be the nicest sports car I've ever seen in real life.

I pull the cans out of my bag and find a little piece of cardboard. It takes me twenty minutes to finish the outline for Rex's tag. I rush through the fill-in and smudge the R in Rex's name a little bit at the top. I hope that I can cover it with the shadow and touch up the outline. The cardboard ends up pulling double duty for that and I end up with paint on my hands…but it actually turns out pretty good, when I finish. I toss the spray cans in my bag.

Rex pulls up in a brand-new Cadillac Escalade as I toss the last can inside. He climbs out of the truck and stares at the tag. He crosses his arms, attempting to take in every inch of the design. A girl climbs out of the other side and I have to fight the urge to whistle…she's so hot. Long legs, blonde hair, curves in all the right places and all I can think is…why is she with a guy like Rex?

"Nice, panna," Rex says with a smile, snapping me out of the staring contest with his girlfriend's body. He nods. He turns to the blond. "Eh, Renee…nice, right?"

Renee looks at the tag. Her forehead gets that wrinkle that tells me she has no idea what she's looking at. "It's alright, I guess," she finally says with all the intellect of every blonde stereotype out there. I sigh. There goes all attraction I had toward Renee…thankfully. Rex doesn't seem like the type who would be nice about catching some guy staring at his girl.

Rex rolls his eyes. "So, panna," he starts again. "How long will this be up?"

"Well, I used exterior spray paint so, somebody from the city will probably come by and paint over it before it fades." He looks the tag over one more time with a nod. "So, it's good? We're straight?"

"Yeah, man. We're straight," Rex says while pulling out a huge wad of cash. He counts off two hundred-dollar bills from the outside then moves to the center of the folded bills…where the twenties are. I sigh and look down at the ground between us. He really is only gonna pay me the three and change. "Here, man." Rex slams several folded bills in my hand.

I count out the bills quickly. …two-eighty…three hundred…three-twenty…forty…sixty…eighty… "You're giving me the whole four?" I ask, shocked by his kindness and considering the gun-shaped lump under his jacket, I should consider him for sainthood.

"Yeah, you earned it, man," he says, looking at the tag. "This is good, man. Damn good." I can't help but notice that he stopped calling me *panna*. I shove the bills into my hoodie pocket and reach for my bag.

"Thanks, man. I really appreciate it."

"Yeah, whatever, panna," Rex returns. Well, that didn't last long. "Now, get the hell outta here, before I change my mind. Shouldn't you be in school, anyway?" I check my phone. Crap, it's already after nine. Maybe it took me longer than an hour.

I run over to my bike, hop on, and steal one more glance at Rex's girl. I shake my head. Never mind that.

I gotta get to school. Hopefully, Stephen managed to cover for me in first period, but I don't have anybody to hold me down in second. I pedal. I pedal like my life depends on it…cause according to my mom, it just might.

I'm out of breath as I see the school over the horizon. I shaved two minutes off my estimated time. And I'm pretty good at estimating how long it'll take me to get somewhere on this bike.

I pedal into the parking lot with a whole five minutes to spare before second period. Just before I reach the second row of cars, I hear a loud screech and see a flash of black speeding toward me. I fall off my bike while trying to stop and scrape my elbow on the concrete. I look back just in time to see my bike slide under the front end of an expensive car. I hear a scraping noise and cringe.

"Great," I think. "There goes that money…" I rush back over to the car. I bend down to look at my bike, grateful that I didn't hear a crunching sound.

10

"What the hell's wrong with you?" I exclaim as I hear the car door open. "You could've killed me! Why in the hell were you driving like that in a parking lot? Why don't you watch what you're doing, jerk?" I stand up and see a tall pale guy, scowling at me. His hair is in gelled tufts, which with the anger in his face makes them look like short black nails.

"What am I doing? I think you should be asking yourself that question, idiot," he barks. "You almost got your stupid bike stuck under my car. I mean, who even rides bikes anymore? What are you, four years old?" He points at me. "If that piece of crap scratched my car, you're dead."

I look at him, at a loss for words. Is he serious? Can he really think that this is my fault?

"Got nothing to say for yourself?" he follows. "That's what I thought," he adds before I can answer. "Now get your tricycle out from under my car and pray you didn't do any damage."

I obey, primarily because his uncaring demeanor stuns me. I climb onto my bike as he shuts his door and revs the engine. As I start to peddle, he honks the horn. I shake my head, trying to make sense of what just happened and trying to convince myself not to go back and punch him.

I chain my bike and check my watch. Awesome, I might still be early for my second class. I look closer and see that it's cracked. The hands have stopped. I walk into the school and look at the clock. Not only have I missed first period, if I keep this up, I'll be late for second too. I walk to my locker and hear the bell ring just as I open the door. Just my luck.

Chapter 2: Appearances

I wander the hall, looking up at every room number along the way. I was twenty minutes late for my first class because I couldn't find it. I'm a fox spirit and I couldn't find a stupid classroom…in this stupid school…along these stupid halls that all look the same…and stupid. I take a deep breath. This shouldn't be this hard. At least, I know where my locker is. I walk over to it and enter the combination quickly.

"Nice shoes," I hear behind me.

I open my locker and chuckle. Real high school is just like those television shows about angst-ridden teenagers. Sarcasm-laden compliments seem to abound in this environment.

As I pull my lunch out of my backpack, glad I remembered to put it in my locker this time, I hear one of my pink mechanical pencils fall to the floor. I reach down to retrieve it and as I do, another hand reaches down to pick it up. I pull my hand back instinctively.

"Sorry, I didn't mean to scare you. I thought you heard me," says the girl as she extends the pencil to me. This girl has large blue eyes, long silky blonde hair, and perfect skin. Not only does she sound like the high school girls on television, she looks like them. Can they airbrush people in real life?

"Here ya go," she says as she hands the pink writing implement to me.

"Thanks," I say, giving a subtle head nod as I slip the pencil back into my bag.

She stares at me. I close the locker and spin the dial. I pause and offer her my hand. "Hi, I'm Gwen," I say, hoping that my fake enthusiasm doesn't come across as sarcasm.

"Hi, Gwen. I'm Meghan, Meghan Powers," she adds as she tosses her golden locks over her shoulder. "You're new, aren't you?" Meghan asks with curiosity bubbling beneath the two cobalt marbles that she calls eyes. If I was a little older, I don't doubt that my eyes would automatically faze to that color…I simply adore their color.

I nod.

"I thought so," Meghan utters so plainly that even if it weren't true, I'd be convinced that it was. She hesitates as if contemplating something. She extends her delicate fingers. "Let me see your schedule."

"Why?" I ask cautiously.

"So, I can show you around. You don't want people thinking you're a loser. Especially in those shoes."

As I look down at my pink Converse with the purple piping and laces, I realize that I had been the target of her earlier shoe-related sarcastic comment. No wonder she was staring at me when I dropped my pencil…

After taking several more seconds to think it over, I extend my class schedule. Meghan takes it, scans it quickly before smiling and declaring it "perfect. Our schedules match except for two classes. We even have lunch together. The only divergence in our schedules is our first and last periods of the day." She passes the slip back to me. I barely remembered to get it signed by my first period teacher.

Meghan looks down at her designer watch. "Come on, loser! We've got to get to second period."

Regardless of her opinions on my fashion, I think it might be nice to have someone to help navigate the hallways. Besides, I don't sense any deception from her…well, none regarding me anyway. She definitely has something hidden just below the surface though. She walks away. I follow quickly on her tail…oh, the irony.

If our simple stroll down the hall is any indication, Meghan is wildly popular. Between most of the boys fawning over her and the girls' emotions seeming to run the gamut from idol-like worship to complete revulsion, I have to wonder if she is the best choice of "friend" for me to make since I'm trying to keep a low profile. She doesn't seem to be leaving that choice up to me, however.

"Ugh," Meghan sighs.

"What?" I ask, as I note her eye roll. She glares to her right at two boys, standing by a row of lockers then looks at me.

"DO NOT…TALK TO THOSE TWO, UNDER ANY CIRCUMSTANCE," she demands.

"Why?" I glance back at them.

"The…almost cute one is Stephen…and his skeevy friend is Rich. They are pretty much wastes of space, who have been in love with me since pre-K."

I steal another glance at the pair. One is tall with pale skin and a russet head of hair that falls over his ears and covers his forehead. He has a pointy nose and wire-framed glasses in the shape of little rectangles. He has a small amount of hair on his top lip that looks more like dirt than a mustache. Gross…he just blew a kiss at me. Now, I know who the *skeevy* one is.

The other has a mocha complexion with buzz cut, jet-black hair. His mahogany eyes steal a glance at me, then he smiles and looks away sheepishly. His smile is warm and infectious. Huh, she's right. He is cute.

"Dibs," I hear one utter to the other. I glance back and Stephen has a disappointed look on his face, so I'll have to assume it was Rich, who said it.

I turn to Meghan. "What does dibs mean?" She frowns as we continue walking toward our next class. The hairs on the back of my neck suddenly stand on end. I stop walking.

Meghan turns to look at me. "What's wrong, loser? Our class is right over there," she says and motions to the room on the right. Quick Gwen…think of something fast.

"Oh…um…I just remembered that I forgot something in my locker."

Her face twists awkwardly. "You remembered that you forgot?" I nod.

"I'll be right there." She nods then continues on her way. I head back to my locker to make the lie plausible when just as quickly as it came on, the feeling is gone. I sigh and return to my locker, hoping that the feeling will return and that I'll be able to find its source.

#####

Rich and Stephen, the closest things I have to friends here. "Here"… like I haven't lived here my entire, dull life. I dump another book into my locker. The edges are fraying on both straps of my backpack. Little black hairs stick out from the side like Max's tail. I asked my mom for a new one a month ago. She told me as long as this one holds books, it's good enough. Sounds like everything else in my crap-filled life…good enough.

14

"There she is," Rich exclaims with a relaxed sort of casualness to his voice. I turn to find him pointing down the hall. I smack his hand down immediately. "Ow," he snaps. "That hurt!"

"Good," I return. "What's the matter with you?"

"What's the matter with you?" Stephen poses. I slam my locker door, causing both of them to jump. "He was just pointing out the new girl."

"He didn't have to make it so obvious." I look down the hall to find...gorgeous green eyes, perfect light olive skin, beautiful red hair and pouty full lip...and wait...what was I just thinking about? Stephen smacks me in the back of my head. "Ow."

"You're staring. Almost as bad as pointing," he answers my question before I can even ask. I steal another quick glance at her. "Her name's Gwendolyn Frost, but she goes by Gwen."

"Gwen," I sigh. She smirks while staring into her locker. Whatever's in there can't be that funny, can it? Wait, no...can she...no, no way she could hear us from there.

"Gwen," Rich spouts. "Not Suki or Kikyo or something cute and Japanesey like that?" I smack his arm at the same time Gwen slams her locker door. She seems angry about something now. She frowns and glares in our direction. She lowers her eyes instantly, opens her notebook and stares at it.

"Shut up, Rich," I growl. "Just because she's Japanese that doesn't mean her name has to be. I mean, you're a douche but your name's not... Oh wait, Richmond. Howard. Mortimer...is kind of douchy."

Stephen laughs uproariously. "Yeah, it is," he bellows in agreement. Gwen closes her notebook with a smile on her face. She walks toward us and by the time she reaches us, she's laughing. Could she hear us? I watch her pass in amazement...she's even prettier up close.

"What the hell?" I spit aloud.

"What?" Rich and Stephen ask simultaneously.

They turn to see what I'm looking at. "Aw man, you're staring at her butt," Rich blurts out. "And you called me a douche." Stephen chuckles.

"No, guys...she's...she's got a tail..." ...three of them. I look again and see nothing but her perfect butt. Crap, now I'm really just staring at her butt. She stops and glares at me over her shoulder. She has to be able to hear us...right? "I swear guys. She had three tails." I sigh and touch my forehead. "Or, maybe I'm just going crazy or inhaled some spray paint fumes or something." She's still staring at me. Why is she still staring at me?

"Wait...was it a tail or three tails?" Stephen asks. Rich arches his eyebrows curiously. I shake my head. I look at Gwen again. Her eyes look brighter and...man, it feels like she's looking through me or something. She sighs then turns and disappears into a classroom.

"Whoa," Stephen breathes. "Was...was she staring at you?"

"I think so," I say with a nod.

"No way," Rich argues. "It was all me." Stephen and I laugh and walk away, leaving Rich. "What? It could happen." Stephen laughs harder, but my laughter trails off...with the image of three tails, the same color as her hair, wagging behind her.

I tried to forget about Gwen's tails...or my insane, daydreaming brain playing tricks on me, but I couldn't. All day, I just kept seeing them, moving from side to side behind her. Why a tail? Why three of them? Okay, enough of the crazy talk...uh, thoughts. Focus...on seventh period English... the only thing standing between me and the weekend...and…work…and a stupid Friday. I sigh. Another day of work.

The door opens at the front of the room just as Mrs. Bustamante is about to begin. And then suddenly, there she is again. Gwen Frost...tail free, thank God, but just as beautiful as I remembered. No, even more beautiful than I remembered.

Mrs. Bustamante reads her name off her form and then faces the rest of us. "Class, we have a new student." Why do teachers still do this? It wasn't cool in the first grade and it's a million times worse in the eleventh. "This is," she pauses to read. "Gwendolyn Frost."

Gwen smiles then waves. "You can call me, Gwen. Everybody does." Even her voice is pretty.

"There's a seat open in the back," Mrs. Bustamante says. "Right next to Alex, Alex…raise your hand, dear." I do and she motions to me. Gwen smiles and heads toward the back. Ugh, why do I hear my heartbeat in my ears all of a sudden? Why does she have to be so pretty? Why is she staring at me with those pretty eyes of hers? No, seriously…why is she staring at me? "Gwen," Mrs. Bustamante calls from the front. Gwen looks at her. "Is there a problem, dear?"

"No, ma'am," Gwen says, then slides into the seat next to me. Mrs. Bustamante starts writing on the board. I feel like Gwen's watching me and it's making me nervous. I steal a glance and I'm wrong. She's watching the board. I still can't shake the feeling that she's watching me though. I look again. I'm wrong…again. Maybe I am going crazy. I mean, the thing with her tail…tails. I thought she could hear us but for all I know she could've had a Bluetooth in her ear. And now, I'm imagining that she's…standing right next to me. I look up…and she is…

"What do you see?" she asks in this weird echoing voice. I shake my head. "What…do you see?" she asks again. Suddenly, her shoulders catch fire…with red and orange flames. I gasp. "What do you see?"

I jump out of my seat. "You're on fire!" I shout. I look around and the entire class is staring at me. Mrs. Bustamante shakes her head and motions for me to sit back down. I look at Gwen and she's staring at me, too… from her desk. Her expression is different from everyone else's though. She seems more in shock than like she's about to laugh. Her eyes seem brighter again, too. "Sorry, Mrs. B," I breathe. I sit down slowly.

"Now, if the daydreaming can come to a close," Mrs. Bustamante adds before returning to the board. I steal a glance at Gwen. She has a worried expression on her face although she's facing front. I face the front. Out of the corner of my eye, I see Gwen lean over and pick something up. I try to look but she slides it into her pocket quickly. For a second there, I could've sworn it was a leaf. Great, now I'm adding leaves to the delusion. Ah well, I'm not gonna be able to concentrate now so, I might as well draw. I steal one more glance at Gwen…and before I know it, my pencil's already working.

16

Chapter 3: Observing

He saw it! I didn't think he would…but he saw it. He saw my flame avatar. Does he know what I am? Can he see me as a fox? He keeps looking at me. Why does he keep looking at me? In the hall, he couldn't stop staring at me. I thought it was because he found my human form attractive, but then he saw my tails. Did he see my tails because he can see through fox magic? Or, did he see my tails because I lowered my guard?

Breathe. Breathe. Breathe. Gwen, you're fine. He doesn't know anything. He can't. If he did, he wouldn't have reacted the way he did…either time. He definitely wouldn't have told his friends about my tails if he knew anything. I have to look at him. Try to feel out his aura again. I let the fox magic flow to my eyes. Every aura in the room is dim…little to no magic in any of them…not even Alex. Wait, did I just see a silver spark in him? I shake my head and let my eyes return to normal. Maybe, it's me. Maybe by letting the Taylors bind me, I hurt my ability to see auras. I sigh. I hope not.

"Gwen," Mrs. Bustamante calls from the front of the room. "Had your old class already covered *A Tale of Two Cities*?"

"No, ma'am. We read *Great Expectations* instead."

"Ah, I love *Great Expectations*. I just wish that it were on the curriculum here." She walks over to her desk and opens a drawer. She retrieves a book and slides the drawer shut. "I'm sorry, dear, but you're just going to have to try and keep up as best you can." She walks to the front of my row and hands the book to the dark-haired boy there. "Pass this back," she says. He takes the book and does as she asks.

"That's fine, ma'am," I say as the book makes its way back. "I love to read, and I usually finish books pretty quickly."

"Good, good," Mrs. Bustamante says with genuine excitement. "Perhaps, you can rub off on your fellow student in the back of the class. Right, Alex?"

"Yes, ma'am, Mrs. B, ma'am," he returns, sounding as though she'd just threatened to shoot his puppy.

"Now, where was I…," Mrs. Bustamante says before returning to the board. I steal a glance at Alex's dejected face. He scowls and stares at the piece of paper in front of him as his pencil moves over it feverishly. I lean as much as I can without being noticed and find that he's drawing…me. Not as a fox spirit, but as I am. He doesn't draw any tails or flames…just my human form. He's quite the artist, too.

"Hey," I whisper. He instantly covers his drawing. "I've actually already read, *A Tale of Two Cities*. I liked *Great Expectations* so much that I wanted to read some of Dickens' other works." He arches his eyebrow as if I'd just grown a third eye. "I'm saying…um…if you ever wanted help…or a study partner, I…" His eyebrow doesn't fall. "Never mind," I spurt and face front. He ponders my words then returns to his drawing.

I stare at him occasionally through the remainder of class. He never looks at me to verify any of my features. He just focuses on the drawing. He pays special attention to my eyes. He's putting so much detail on them that you'd swear he'd been staring into them his whole life. I shake my head.

The bell rings. I collect my things, then head toward the door like the rest of the class. Well, like almost the rest of the class. I look back and Alex is still working on his sketch. He finally looks up and realizes that the class is almost empty. He grabs his backpack and shoves his book, notebook, and the sketch of me into it all at once. He peers up and catches me staring at him. I turn away and quickly file out with the rest of the class.

"Hey, loser," Meghan calls as soon as I step out into the hall. I laugh and go over to her. "How was your first day?"

"Not too bad, I guess. There was this guy in my seventh period though."

"Is he a cute guy?" Meghan asks before I can finish my thought.

I bob my head unevenly. "Yeah, he is actually."

"Nice. Did he ask you out?"

I shake my head. "No, no…he could barely look at me," I lie.

"Where's your class slip?" Meghan says quizzically.

"My…my what?" is the closest thing to a response that I can muster.

"Your class slip. That piece of paper that you had to take around to all of your teachers and get them to sign it." I shake my head. "You have to take that back to the office and turn it in." I make an 'oh' face and glance over my shoulder at my last class.

"Mrs. Bustamante still has it. I'll be right back." I go back to the classroom and find Mrs. Bustamante and Alex standing at her desk. She's lecturing him about his grades and how he might fail English. Alex notices me and turns away quickly. Mrs. Bustamante turns to me.

"Yes, Gwen dear?" she says as a question.

"My-my class slip," I squeak out with one eyebrow arched. Mrs. Bustamante finds the slip, signs it and extends it toward me. I walk over and take it. I turn back to the door and prepare to leave, but I don't. I can't. Why can't I?

"Mrs. Bustamante," I say turning back to her and Alex. "I couldn't help overhearing what you guys were talking about…I mean, I wasn't trying to eavesdrop, because who really likes an eavesdropper, but I heard you because I was like standing right there and…"

"Get to the point, Gwen dear," she says impatiently, while miraculously making it sound patient.

"Right, point," I breathe. "English was my favorite subject back at my old school. I excelled at it. So, if Alex needs a tutor, I'd be happy to help."

Mrs. Bustamante smiles and turns to Alex. "That sounds like a wonderful idea. Doesn't it, Alex?" He huffs and stares out the window. "Well, it's not optional if you want to pass my class."

Alex turns to look at me. I freeze for a moment. My forehead furrows. He has some sort of power. I don't know if even he's aware of it yet.

"Whatever," he says, pulls his backpack further up on his shoulder, and hurries past me. He storms out of the room.

"I didn't mean to embarrass him," I apologize to Mrs. Bustamante.

"No, dear, it's not you," she explains. "From what I understand, he's been like this for years now." I peer after him with genuine sympathy filling me. Perhaps that

18

silver spark I felt in him was pain or anguish. "You will have to read *A Tale of Two Cities* if you're going to be his tutor, Miss Frost."

"Yes, ma'am," I say to excuse myself. I walk toward the door and stare out into the emptying hallway.

"'Tis a far, far better thing I do…" comes from behind me, but in a voice that is definitely not Mrs. Bustamante. It sounds dark and frightening. I turn back to see her smiling face still staring at me. I nod and step out into the hall. What was that? And why do I keep getting these eerie feelings in a town with little to no spirit magic?

#####

"There she is," I breathe…aloud, like a moron. There's nobody around to hear me, so why…

"Yeah, she is," Rich spurts from over my shoulder. I nearly jump out of my skin. He laughs as Stephen looks down and shakes his head.

"Dude, there is something up with that, chick," I say, stealing another glance at Gwen standing at her locker. "I don't know what it is, but it's weird."

"What do you mean?" Stephen asks. "Did you see her," he pauses to make air quotes. "…tails again?"

"No," I grumble. "She was on fire this time." Rich and Stephen both laugh. Gwen sighs and continues staring into her locker. She moves her head so that it seems like her left ear is tilted toward us.

Meghan Powers walks up behind her and taps her on the shoulder…Meghan Powers is talking to her…she's talking back to Meghan Powers…they're both smiling. "She's friends with Meghan?" I ask louder than I meant to…causing Gwen's head to snap around to see me. I duck around the corner, Rich, and Stephen quickly do the same. "I swear she can hear us."

"Yeah," Stephen responds to my question and I mutter a 'thank you' to myself that he didn't hear the thing about her hearing us. He looks around the corner. "That's how we first saw her." I can't help but wonder if he's staring at Gwen or at Meghan. Rich and Stephen have both been in love with Meghan since the first grade.

"So, you guys were quasi-stalking Meghan again?" I ask. Stephen's eyes never leave the two girls.

Rich gets that disgusted look on his face. "No, we weren't…"

"Yeah," Stephen interrupts Rich's lie, while he continues looking around the corner. He sighs and his shoulders slump. He turns back to us.

"Are you guys still going to let a first grade 'dibs' stand?" I ask Stephen before moving to Rich.

Rich nods enthusiastically. "Heck yeah," he starts. "I saw Meghan first and I called it. If he wanted her then he should've been quicker."

"I was five," Stephen whines.

"Actually, you were four," I correct him.

"You snooze, you lose," Rich boasts. He makes an L on his forehead. "Loser."

"Yeah, you're still making Ls on your forehead, but he's the loser," I say with a bit of snark behind it. Rich lowers his hand and Stephen snickers. "Besides, you do know she's a human being and not a cow, right?"

"What do you mean?" Rich asks confused by my statement, not that that's hard to do.

"'Dibs' stands for Dealer Identification Book," Stephen adds. "It's what potential customers would use to mark livestock they were hoping to buy."

"Yeah, well that heifer's mine," Rich bellows triumphantly. Stephen and I both groan...and cringe.

"Wow," I sigh. "Why are we friends with you again?"

"You're an idiot," Stephen piles on.

"That's okay, because I'm the idiot with dibs on Meghan Powers," Rich brags. He looks at me. "Oh, and I have dibs on the new girl, too."

"Yeah," Stephen stretches out sarcastically. "She literally turned her nose up at you." I laugh. "Plus, she seems to have a thing for Lex."

"Don't call me that. I told you not to call me that," I moan. "It makes me feel like I should be bald and fighting Superman." Rich and Stephen both laugh.

"I know," Stephen chuckles. "That's why I do it."

I groan again. "What time is it? I think my watch broke when that idiot almost ran me down in the parking lot." Stephen retrieves his phone to check the time.

"Why don't you just use your phone?" Rich asks.

"It's dead," I respond. "Again," I mumble a second later.

"It's three-thirty," Stephen finally says.

"Crap, I'm gonna be late for work. I gotta head," I say extending a fist to Stephen, who quickly bumps it with his. "Catch you guys later," I add before bumping Rich's waiting knuckles. I rush down the hall.

"Hey, do yourself a favor," Stephen calls after me. I turn and walk backward. "Just ignore that girl, man. Every time you see her something weird happens." I nod and continue on my way.

He's right. Every time I've seen her today, something weird happens. So, I'll just ignore her. I won't look at her. I won't think about her. I won't pay her any attention at all. I sigh. Even if she is the prettiest girl, I've ever seen...EVER.

20

Chapter 4: Brother

I sit at the rickety, formerly red picnic table overlooking the soccer field behind the school. From here, I can see the buses filing in to pick up students and shuttle them home. Mine hasn't arrived yet. Home…my foster parents don't feel like home to me…the Taylors are nice, caring and giving, everything that you'd want parents to be. Still, they're not my family. They're not kitsune. As far as I can tell, they're not spirits of any ki…

I feel his presence in the back of my mind before any of my other senses detect anything of him. It's the same as it has always been. His aura is dark; ominous…it feels like a heavy blanket draped over me. Every hair on the back of my neck stands on end. My head feels foggy, my heart sinks and I find it difficult to breathe. I glance only slightly to the left and of course, there he stands, on top of the table. He's dressed in his usual dark colors. His jacket is as black as his hair. The jacket partially covers a gray t-shirt. Black jeans and large clunky boots complete his ensemble. Ugh, he still dresses so Goth.

"Hello, Gavin." I resume scribbling in my notebook. I can feel his eyes moving along with each pen stroke.

"Oh Gwenie, Gwenie, Gwenie," he begins in a low rumble. An eye roll later and I peer up at him. His frost blue eyes scan the students gathered in the bus yard. "Are you still soooooo desperate to fit in with these miserable little secret-filled meat sacks that we dare to call 'human', little sister?"

"Are you still sooooooo desperate to lord your superiority over them, big brother?"

"Tsk. Why not…? We ARE superior to them in every way." His eyes return to me. "And you actually like these sheep." A pair of girls walks by our table, staring at Gavin longingly. He looks down on them…in more ways than one. "Baaaaaaaaaaaah, you're sheep." The two girls scurry away quickly. I glare at him. He doesn't return my gaze. "Don't look at me like that. They are, and you know it."

I close my notebook. "Well, considering how many of them you've bitten, I would've thought you'd compare them to rabbits."

Gavin chuckles. "No, I actually enjoy the taste of rabbits."

"What do you want?"

"…you to come back with me."

"I've given up the spirit world."

"Your crimson aura says differently."

"I can't just stop being…" I look around to ensure that no humans are within earshot. "…kitsune, because I wish it."

"You mean being a fox spirit," Gavin says plainly.

"Keep your voice down," I complain through gritted teeth.

"Why?" He looks around. "You don't want them to know that you're a fox spirit," he exclaims loudly. I quickly collect my notebook and bag and stand. I storm off, which is only fitting because that's how most of our discussions end. "Where're you going?"

"Away from you," I spit. He hops down from the table and appears in front of me instantly. "Are you crazy?" I whisper. "First announcing what we are…then using swift paw in front of humans." The glow fades from his eyes as the effects of his fox magic wane.

"Don't walk away from me," he says coldly. He peers over my head, glancing at the students blessedly not staring at us. "I need to talk to you...seriously." He motions to the back of the school. I roll my eyes. "Please." I huff then turn back to the school.

Alex walks past me. I try to keep my eyes low...and he does the same. I look back at him as he continues toward the parking lot. Gavin takes notice.

"What?"

"Look at that boy," I demand, motioning to Alex. He stops at the bike rack near the parking lot and begins working the combination lock on a black bicycle.

Gavin does as I ask and shrugs. "What about him?" he asks with his usual lack of interest in all things human.

"No," I groan. "REALLY...look at him." Gavin's eyes glow with fox magic augmenting his already impressive eyesight. He looks Alex over once more. Gavin returns to me with a frown and his normal blue eyes.

"So?"

My jaw drops. "You don't see it," I spit incredulously.

"See what? As far as I could tell he's a normal human boy." I shake my head. "Why did you see something different?" My head bows. Gavin chuckles. "What's wrong? Can't you do it? Or, have you actually gotten weaker since you got here?"

I shake my head and turn toward the school building. I walk, and Gavin follows. "No," I finally muster. I know I'm going to regret telling him this, but he has to know. "I've been bound."

Gavin takes me by the arm and turns me around to face him. "You've been WHAT?!?!"

"Bound," I squeak out.

"How could you allow yourself to be bound? What human managed to trick YOU?"

"I did it on purpose," I bark back, trying to regain my strength. I manage to free myself from his grasp, though it takes a bit of fox magic to help. "I decided to bind myself to my foster parents."

Gavin inhales a quick breath through his nose. "What charm did you use and where did they hide it?"

"I used a small golden sunflower from a charm bracelet."

"You literally used a charm as your charm, how quaint." I shrug. "Fine. Whatever. Where did they hide it?"

"I don't know."

"What do you mean, 'you don't know'?"

"I MEAN, I don't know. I gave it to them and told them that it was a symbol of how I accept them as my parents and that they should put it somewhere safe."

"You didn't even tell them what it could do," Gavin grumbles. I shake my head. "If they lose that charm you know what has to happen, don't you?"

"When I turn eighteen, they will release me regardless," I submit.

"You're an idiot, little sister," Gavin says with venom in every word. He steps past me and looks at the soccer field. "And you're going to feel like an even bigger idiot when I tell you what I came here for."

"It's not because you miss me," I prod. He turns to me with a look that should've sliced me to ribbons…and had I truly been human, it probably would've.

"Obāsan wanted to see you."

"Why does Gran want to see me?"

"If I knew that, I would've started with, obāsan wants to see you because dot, dot, dot…but if I had to hazard a guess…I'd guess that it was because of the missing kitsune."

"What missing kitsune?"

"I've heard whispers. There are…other kitsune living in the States. Some of them…just two or three…have gone missing. I'm guessing obāsan sent me to make sure that YOU, little sister, weren't one of them."

"What's been happening to them?"

Gavin shakes his head. "Nobody knows. That's why we have to find your charm and get you out of here."

"And go where? Back to Japan…hide at obāsan's until this 'blows over?'"

"Glad you didn't completely forget your manners." I groan and turn toward the parking lot. Meghan sits in her VERY expensive car with the top down. She spots me and turns in my direction. She comes to a screeching halt in front of me.

"Hey, loser," Meghan says nonchalantly. "You got any plans?" I shake my head absently. "What's wrong? You act like you've never seen a Deep-Sea Blue BMW 35i before. It's okay. Most people haven't."

"No. I…aren't only buses supposed to come this way?"

"Yeah and if I did everything I was supposed to do, I'd be a loser like you," she says with a bit of humor in her voice. I smile. "Get in."

"Give me a minute. I have to talk to my brother."

"Your brother?" Meghan says, peering past me. "Is that him?" Gavin has his back to us.

"Yeah, that's…Gavin, my brother."

"Gavin? Gwen?" she says our names like they're questions.

"Our dad was…Welsh…Frost. Gwen and Gavin are both very…Welsh names."

"I didn't mean anything by that," Meghan recants.

"Yes, you did," Gavin says from the other side of the car. Meghan jumps out of fright. I put my hand on her shoulder to calm her down. Gavin looks her over hungrily…not sexually…as if she were something to eat. I let the fox magic do my talking for me. He starts then stares daggers back over her head.

"Ignore him," I spurt. "He does stuff like that to mess with people."

"I'm sorry," Meghan begins. "I really didn't mean to offend you."

"No need to apologize," Gavin says plainly. "To offend me, you'd actually have to matter to me." Meghan gasps. "I'll be at your house around seven, baby sister. Don't keep me waiting." He glares at Meghan. "Human." With that, he walks toward the parking lot.

Meghan turns to me with a stunned expression. "Ignore him. He's kind of an ass." Meghan sighs. She tips her head toward the passenger side. I smile and walk around the car. I slide into the front seat and before I can even close the door, she speeds away.

#####

I use the chain to lock my bike to the parking meter out front. Stupid cracked sidewalk. Stupid parking meter has stupid gum all over it. Ew, I think I got some on my finger. I look at the clock tower over the courthouse. Crap, I'm already late. I grab my bag and rush over to the store. I push the door open and the bell chimes. Stupid digital chime.

"You're late," Mr. Hamish says from behind the counter. He finishes ringing Mrs. Turnipseed up. Ugh...Mrs. Turnipseed...all gray hair, wrinkles and bad attitude. I actually heard my mom say that she felt sorry for Mr. Turnipseed for having to put up with her-

"What are you staring at?" she barks from underneath her massive, blocking all chances of sunlight hat. I look down at the floor and shake my head, like the good little store employee that I am.

I lift my eyes. "Nothing, ma'am," I return with what I hope is a convincing smile. I look around the store. I know my mom meant well by helping me get the job. She wanted to teach me "financial responsibility and scheduling management" as she put it. The extra income I bring in, doesn't compare to when I tag stuff for people, but it definitely doesn't hurt either. And I don't mind working for Mr. Hamish. He understands about school and...well I don't have much of a life outside of school, work, and making tags for whoever pays me, so there wasn't really an "and".

I just hate the way some of the customers treat me. I hate putting on the fake happy face, smiling and nodding while they say the worst crap to me. Like it's my fault the truck hasn't brought the random cookies they randomly want today. Don't get me wrong, not all of the customers act like I kicked their puppy. It just seems like everyone takes all of the crap from their day and dumps it out on the "merchandise retention assistant" aka stock boy slash customer service representative aka cashier slash whatever the hell Mr. Hamish tells me to be.

"Move," Mrs. Turnipseed barks, despite the fact that she has a clear walkway to the door. I take another step away from her and back into a cardboard candy display. The candy bars spill out in every direction.

"Crap," I spit as I bend to round them up. I hear Mrs. Turnipseed chuckle as I toss the first bars back onto the display. The bell chimes above the door and I look back to see if the old bat's left yet. No such luck. A guy stands in the doorway. He looks familiar, but I can't remember where I've seen him before. Okay, am I crazy, or did Mrs. Turnipseed just hiss at him?

"Nice hat," the man says with a smirk. I forget about the fallen candy bars for a minute as I turn to see them. "It'd be a shame if you...you know, lost it and had to go out into that hot, hot sun without it." What's this guy talking about? It's pretty cool out today. "I mean, you could get a REAL nasty sunburn," he adds with his smile growing. Mrs. Turnipseed hasn't said anything back to him. If it were anybody else, she'd have torn them a new one just for mentioning her stupid hat.

24

"Get out of my way," she says, but she sounds like she's…begging… "I haven't wronged you, trickster." Does she know him?

"If you want to keep it that way, leech," the guy starts with a serious look. "I recommend you leave. Now." With that, Mrs. Turnipseed makes her way past the guy and out of the store. He watches her leave. The second she's out of sight, he turns to me.

"Can I help you?" I grumble as I toss the last candy bar back into the display.

He tweaks his head to one side and looks at me. He cracks an all-new smile. "I know you," he says with so much smugness that I feel like I'm gonna have to clean it up after he leaves. "Yeah, you're the little…thing who almost crammed his bicycle under my car."

"Not to mention the rest of me," I add, rising to my feet.

He extends his hand. "I'm Gavin," he says plainly. I look at his hand and cross my arms. He smiles outright…what is with this guy and his stupid smile? He lowers his hand and looks at my nametag. "And you're…Alex," he says as his eyes rise to meet mine.

"Yeah," I say, taking a step back. "Like I said, what can I do for you?"

"Can I help you?"

"Can you help me?" I ask.

"No, idiot," he starts cutting me off. "You didn't ask me…" His voice drops into a mocking tone. "'What can I do for you?' You asked, 'Can I help you?'" I feel my lips twist up in disbelief at what a phenomenal jerk this guy is being…and after almost running me over.

He steps creepily close. "Okay," he begins with all humor leaving his voice. "What are you here for?"

I tweak my eyebrows. "I'm here to work. What're you here for?"

"Alex, watch your tone," Mr. Hamish calls from the counter.

"Sorry, Mr. Hamish," I reply.

"Are you after my sister?" Gavin growls, even closer to my face…although I didn't think standing closer was possible. "Are you?"

"Who is your sister?" He sniffs me. I lean away from him. He leans closer and sniffs me again.

"You're not lying," he says. I give him my best, 'no, d'uh' face and shake my head. "So, you don't know…" He trails off and takes a step back.

"What…is…going…on…with your eyes?" I ask, taking in the now bright blue eyes staring at me. He pinches the bridge of his nose. He looks away. "Are you alright?" I ask out of courtesy more than anything.

"Fine," he snaps. His eyes are normal. It must be me. I mean Gwen's tails…Gwen on fire…now, his eyes…Is it all connected to Gwen? "What are you thinking about?" he grumbles.

"Wow," I reply. "Very chick-ish of you to ask me that," I poke. He holds a twig up in my face. "What's that?" He uses his thumb to snap it at the top. "Gwen," I blurt and almost choke on her name. I put my hand on my now slightly sore throat. "What the hell?" I gasp. "Why did I say that?"

"Because she's on your mind," Gavin says calmly. I stare at him not believing how insane that was. "Now," he starts again. "Why is she on your mind?" I scowl. He holds up and snaps the twig again.

"Because I think she's cute," I spurt again with that same gagging feeling. He seems patently shocked by this response.

"Anything else?" he poses while holding up the remains of the twig. I extend my hands to stop him.

"I thought I saw her with tails," I volunteer without weird twiggy-coaxing. Gavin scowls in response to this. "And…for a second, I could've sworn she was on fire. But I must've been daydreaming or something." Gavin nods. I look down at the disheveled candy display. "I don't know what it was," I add returning to…nothing. I look around the store, but Gavin is already gone.

The bell chimes at the front door. I look up hoping to see him leaving, but it's Rich and Stephen coming in. Stephen stares at me for a second. "Are you okay? You look like you saw a ghost."

"Or tails on the hot new girl," Rich adds with a laugh. Stephen joins him.

"Did you guys see a guy…tall…dark hair…blue eyes…leather jacket…"

"Why? Is he your latest crush?" Rich jokes. Stephen laughs again.

"No," I snap looking around again. "He's the guy who almost ran me over this morning…" Stephen stops laughing. "…and I think he might be Gwen's brother."

#####

Meghan and I drop our shopping bags into her trunk. She smiles triumphantly and closes it. We walk to the front of the car and then collapse into the seats like a synchronized routine. I let out a large sigh that sounds oddly like a yawn at the end.

Meghan snickers. "Don't tell me that wore you out, loser." She starts the car.

I laugh, "I'm not used to exercising my wallet that much. If I hang out with you, I'm going to have to get a job…or two."

Meghan chuckles. "Please. You look presentable now. You can't put a price tag on that."

I fidget slightly, realizing that I will not only have to explain the new clothes, but also that I spent this month's allowance…already. I don't want to seem ungrateful when my foster parents have bought me so many nice things. I just couldn't resist a few more…pretty things…

Meghan notices my restlessness and changes the subject. "So, you want to grab an iced mocha on the way home? It's my treat," she adds with a gleaming smile that reminds me of sunlight…without the harsh glare, of course.

"Sure," I answer, grateful for a small distraction before I have to explain my outrageous spending and my beautiful purchases.

Meghan takes me to a cute little bistro style coffee shop. We sit near the center for maximum visibility, although, Meghan says it's so that we can see everyone come and go. She makes several comments about the various patrons. "He's cute but a few crunches wouldn't hurt him… She should not wear those shoes with that skirt… She should not wear that top EVER." Oddly enough, her comments don't seem to be mean-spirited, or at least, I don't sense any malice behind them. I think she genuinely believes that these "suggestions" would make these people better somehow.

Her lack of ill will is confirmed by subsequent comments, such as: "She's so pretty, but she should pull her hair back away from her face…" or "That haircut really works for him…" and "Her cheekbones are amazing. I'm actually a little jealous."

I smile at Meghan's blunt honesty. I find her such a breath of fresh air. Kitsune are never this open and honest, unless talking to family members. I'm absolutely certain that humans are not this honest with one another either though.

As the traffic in the shop picks up, I suddenly get the feeling that someone…or something is watching me. I glance around the bistro. I let the fox magic flow to my eyes and still I see nothing. I finish my coffee quickly and focus on my new friend's chatter, hoping that she'll get that I'm ready to go. She does and acknowledges it by bounding out of her chair. She looks down on me with a smirk then tilts her head toward the door. I nod and rise to my feet.

By the time we reach the car, I've completely forgotten my paranoia. But, when we pull into the driveway at my house, my paranoia returns. I assume it's just Gavin, like earlier today, but I don't feel him. This feeling isn't oppressive like my brother's presence. It's just as ominous…no, even more so, but without the warmth that his aura exudes. I'm sure of it now. It's the same presence I felt when I left the house this morning.

"Gwen, aren't you going to get your stuff?" Meghan calls, snapping me out of my focus. "I don't need you dragging down my gas mileage by hauling around your stuff."

I laugh and walk back to the car. She opens the trunk and watches me pull out my bags through the rearview mirror. I catch a hint of her eyes but fortunately, manage to avoid a glimpse of my own. I make my way back to the side of her car with my treasures.

"Now, you won't look like such a loser, loser," she says.

"Thanks for everything," I say.

"No problem," she says looking down at her watch. "Oh, I gotta run. I'm babysitting tonight. I'll pick you up at seven-fifteen, okay?"

I steal a glimpse at my watch. "But it's already after eight," I reply.

"Wow, you are such a loser," Meghan says sympathetically. "No, I mean in the morning."

"Why?"

"So, you'd rather ride the bus?" Meghan poses with her eyebrows raised. I shake my head, floored by the proposition. "Good," she returns with her brilliant smile showing off her flawless teeth. "Later, loser," she taunts. With that, she shifts the car into reverse, screeching the tires as she leaves the driveway.

I head into my foster parents' house, glad that I survived my first normal day of normal high school...and dreading my first normal encounter with my foster parents.

I shift my bags to allow me to open the door while I take one last glance around the neighborhood. Nothing looks out of place. I take a deep breath and push the door open.

"Hello?" I call, closing the door behind me.

"We're in the dining room, dear," Mrs. Taylor calls, where I assume she is getting ready for dinner. "And we have a visitor."

"Oh," I say loudly, contemplating taking my bags up to my room to avoid being seen. I place my foot on the bottom step, making thought action.

"Yes, your brother Gavin stopped by to see you and I asked him to stay for dinner," she sings.

I stop dead in my tracks, arms laden with my treasures. What is he doing here? What has he told them about me? What game is he playing? I return both feet to the floor and turn to the dining room. No, wait...he did say he was coming around seven. I got so caught up in spending time with Meghan that I completely forgot. Another thought sends a chill rippling up my spine a second later. If Gavin really is here...who or what had I felt watching me earlier at the coffee shop?

Chapter 5: Relative

"What's a candy bar doing in the middle of the floor?" I mumble as I bend over to retrieve the dropped Snickers bar. As I stand, another one whacks me on the side of the head. "Ow," I snap and turn to Rich, killing himself laughing. "Dude," I bark and bend over to pick up the other candy bar.

"What?" he poses as his laughter dies down. "You've just been Snickered!" He laughs again…until a Crunch bar smacks him in the ear. "Ow," he yelps and stumbles to one side.

"Crunched," Stephen bellows in a deep booming voice while he 'Hulk's up' at Rich. I laugh. Stephen pounds his chest twice then points at me. "I got your back, dog." Rich straightens up and rubs his ear. He laughs. I join in on their laughter. Stephen grabs the Crunch bar and tosses it to me.

"Boys," Mr. Hamish calls from the front counter. We turn to him at once. "Stop throwing the merchandise."

"Sorry, Mr. Hamish," we apologize in unison. He shakes his head in that 'you're a bunch of idiots, but I still like you' kind of way.

"So," Stephen begins. "Seen anything else weird today?"

"Yeah, didja? Huh?" Rich asks while rushing over to me and throwing a few phantom-punches. I shove him and put the three candy bars back on the shelf.

I shake my head. "Not since that guy Gavin was here earlier."

"You mean the lovely Gwen's brother?" Rich asks.

"What?" Stephen asks through his belly laugh.

"Who talks like that…seriously?" I ask.

"Give you a hint. He has two thumbs," he begins holding two thumbs up. "And has dibs on the hotties that you both want." Rich motions to himself. "This guy," he sings while doing a weird thumb-centric dance. Stephen scoffs.

"Alex," Mr. Hamish calls, which thankfully stops Rich's weird thumb ballet.

"Yes, sir," I say while leaning back to see him around Rich and Stephen.

Mr. Hamish hikes himself up on his toes so that he can see me. "Don't forget to stock that new candy bar on the bottom shelf," he says.

"Which one?"

"You know…the one that's made here in town," he explains. "The local stuff," he adds after realizing I don't know what the heck he's talking about.

"Oh," I say. "You mean that honey-nut thing?" I ask trying not to sound overly disgusted…even though I am. He nods. "Those things are gross Mr. Hamish." Rich and Stephen snicker.

"Well, that may well be," he admits. "But I promised Daphne Baggett that in exchange for twenty percent, I'd keep 'em on the shelf as long as she wanted or until they went bad." Mr. Hamish returns to his paper. "Didn't say which shelf," he adds under his breath. I laugh.

"What's so funny?" Rich asks. I walk to the back where the boxes are. I pick up the top one and return to Rich and Stephen.

"You didn't hear what Mr. Hamish said?"

Rich looks at Stephen. Stephen shrugs and they both look at me. "I didn't hear anything," Stephen says.

"Whatever," I spit and drop the box. I rip the cheap tape off the top and look at the gross handmade packaging surrounding the gross homemade candy bars. I start tossing them on the shelf.

Stephen steps closer and looks at the bars. "I can't believe Mrs. Baggett is Jamie-Lynn's mom." I shake my head.

"Artistic ability is usually passed down," Rich piles on. "…not up." Rich reaches over me and collects one. He looks it over and shrugs. "Hey, Mr. H," he yells. Mr. Hamish looks up. "Put this on Alex's tab, wouldja?" I stand and look at Mr. Hamish, who nods still even though he's looking at his paper again.

"Thanks a lot," I mutter while stocking the gross *candy* bars again. Rich tears his bar, which I bought for him, open and takes a bite of the granola, nut disaster.

I glare as he chews on it and ponders the taste. "How is it?" Stephen asks.

"It's not bad," Rich says before he takes another bite. I scowl in disbelief. I stick out my tongue remembering the taste. How could Rich like that thing? He breaks off a piece and offers it to Stephen. Stephen tries it and moans approvingly while finishing it. Great…neither of my friends have taste buds.

The front door chimes. Stephen finishes chewing and swallows while staring at me stocking the quote-unquote candy. Rich looks at the door. He smiles that weird, 'I see a hot girl' smile of his.

"What's up with you?" I ask.

"I'll answer that question with a question. What has long strawberry blonde hair, full pouty lips, beautiful hazel colored eyes…?" At this point, Stephen turns to the door. "…long gorgeous tan legs and a permanent scowl…oh, oh, and is one of my future ex-wives."

Stephen stifles a laugh.

"What?" I respond.

Stephen shakes it off quickly. "Oh," Stephen starts. "And is usually accompanied by a short blond with blue eyes, crazy white teeth, and is all attitude and aggravation."

I put the last bar on the shelf. "Are we talking about two girls?"

Stephen closes one eye. "One girl…"

"…and one guy that menstruates like a girl," Rich adds. A hand smacks Rich on the back of his head.

"I heard that, butt-face," I hear from a familiar voice.

I stand. "Kai…?" I call with equal parts shock and horror. Sora steps up beside him. "Sora," I add with the same mix of emotions.

"Hey, cos," Kai says.

"Hello, Alexander," Sora breathes.

"Alex," Mr. Hamish calls. We turn to look at him. "Who are these young people?"

"Oh, Mr. Hamish, you remember my cousins, Sora and Kai Garner, from Oregon," I explain. Kai waves and Sora tips her head to him. Mr. Hamish nods pleasantly although his facial expression is anything but. Sora and Kai return to me without paying him any real attention.

"Can we talk to you for a second, cousin?" Sora says. I frown. She tips her head toward the back of the store. She's always so serious.

30

"Fine," I grumble. I walk to the back of the store. Sora follows me. I look back and see Kai glaring at Rich and Stephen. We reach the end of the aisle and I turn to face Sora. "Okay," I start. "I haven't seen you guys in what? Four years…? Not since my dad's funeral and now, you just…"

"Our dad's dead," Sora says so plainly that she might as well have told me the sky is blue.

"He's…?" I look at Kai. His expression says everything that Sora's never would. I return to Sora. "When's the funeral?" I mean, I can't really be sad. I never really knew their dad. I met him twice and both times he looked at me like I was something to eat…or something that was about to make him throw up.

Sora presses her lips into a line. "We buried him two months ago," she says monotonically. Typical…is what I should say out loud, but their dad died and it's not like they're responsible for the way that he and the rest of the family treats me and my mom…well, treated. "We'll be staying at your apartment for a couple of days," Sora says like it's a fact and not a question. I nod. Might as well try to make it look like she asked, right?

Chapter 6: Strange

I round the corner leading to the dining room and find…Gavin politely sitting down to tea with the Taylors. I look at him with wide eyes then those same eyes instantly move to Mr. and Mrs. Taylors' beaming faces. "Gavin," I say trying to compose myself. I realize that it didn't work when I drop my bags.

"Hello, Gwenie," he purrs. "You don't call, you don't write…"

"What are you doing here?" I grumble, wishing I was fast enough to punch him in the face without my foster parents seeing. "How did you find me?" I add.

"Adoption agency," he retorts succinctly. "Once I proved we were related, they were more than happy to help me find my…long-lost baby sister."

"You didn't tell us you had a brother," Mrs. Taylor coos. She's already under his spell.

"We're not that close," I say while subtly trying to see through any enchantments or spells that he might've cast on them. Without being able to really use my fox magic, I might as well be trying to see through mud.

"Is he your half-brother?" Mr. Taylor supposes. He runs one hand over his straw-colored hair as he continues to gaze at me through his brown, horn-rimmed glasses.

"No…same mother…"

"…same father," Gavin finishes. "May they rest in peace." He sips his tea coolly and smirks. The Taylors appear to be completely lost. I mean, what do you say to two teenagers…talking about their dead parents?

Gavin's smile returns as his eyes fall to the bags at my feet. "Oooooo…you've been shopping," he hums. "Did you buy anything…pretty?"

That one word hangs in the air then falls on me like a lead weight. No, it's more like a double-edged sword. It mocks my kitsune side because of our inability to resist pretty objects and my human side because he can sense the guilt connected to these bags. That guilt swells up inside of me and grips my heart.

"Yes," Mr. Taylor concurs moving into a semi-standing state so that he can see. His mahogany eyes count each bag strewn about my feet. "That's a lot of bags you have there," he says.

I try to hold it together, at least, until I see the look on Mrs. Taylor's face when she spots my bags. I crumble. "I'm so sorry," I sob. "I didn't mean to spend so much…my friend Meghan and I went to the mall after school and we got carried away," I ramble. "I promise I'll pay back EVERY cent that I spent…"

"…oooooo, rhymie," Gavin prods.

"Shut up," I spit, hoping that my gaze tells him I want him gone. He smiles through a frown of his own.

"It's okay, Gwen," Mr. Taylor says breaking up the staring match. How can it be okay? The Taylors are in their late-forties…and every cent they have can't be wasted on their foster daughter. Mr. Taylor is a professor at Elizabeth City State University and Mrs. Taylor is an administrator at the local elementary school. They don't have much money and yet he's trying to tell me that… "No worries, right dear?" he asks of his wife.

Mrs. Taylor covers her mouth with one hand. Tears well in my eyes at the thought of how much I've disappointed her. I suffer more regret when her other hand covers here heart. "I'm sorry," I sigh. "I am so, so sorry. I didn't mean to…"

"It's not that," Mrs. Taylor says as tears fall from her eyes. She wipes a tear away. "You…made a friend already," she moans happily. "I was worried that you wouldn't be able to make any friends starting school so late in the year…I thought that coming in this late you would…" She cuts off because of the dam breaking. She cries outright. Mr. Taylor moves to her side and puts his arm around her.

"It's okay, dear," Mr. Taylor repeats his sentiment, this time, directed at his wife.

I inhale deeply. "Honest joy," I breathe. Gavin looks at the floor. The honest joy coming from them right now is almost overwhelming. I put my hand over my heart, mirroring Mrs. Taylor's posture. This is why I wanted to live with the humans…to experience…moments like this. I rush over to them and kneel. They each take one of my hands and stare at me as if I were their whole world. I steal a glance at Gavin, and he moves his hand over his forehead. He pushes his hair toward the back of his head, mocking Mr. Taylor's receding hairline. I grit my teeth and frown at him for making fun of such an honest and sincere man.

"I have always said," Mrs. Taylor begins, drawing my attention away from my idiot brother. "If I had ever had a daughter, she'd be…EVERYTHING that you are." I smile. "Warm, caring, beautiful…makes mistakes, but is willing to fix them." She nods with an eye-crinkling smile.

Gavin grumbles. "Excuse me," he cuts in. We look at him, them with a lot more patience than me. "I hate to interrupt, but…where's your restroom?"

"It's down the hall. Second door on the left," Mr. Taylor explains. Gavin nods then rises from his chair. He gives me that sinister smirk of his that tells me he is up to something. He rounds the corner, leaving his hand on the doorframe sliding it around after him. He's probably going to search the house for my charm.

The wind shifts subtly. I look at Mr. and Mrs. Taylor still delighting in the presence of their foster daughter. Of course, they didn't notice. No human would. Gavin is using his fox magic openly. He's speeding around searching every inch of the house. Another sensation drags me away from Gavin…that ominous feeling returns. It's outside the house again…this time, it's hungrier. It wants something. I rise slowly, looking at the front door.

"Gwen?" Mr. Taylor calls with a puzzled look on his face. I look at him and fake a smile the best way that obāsan…grrr…I mean, grandma taught me.

"I…should put these bags away," I start. "I'll let you have a look at them after Gavin leaves," I add for Mrs. Taylor's benefit. She smiles and nods. I collect the bags quickly and head toward the stairs, or more accurately, the front door.

I reach the bottom of the stairs and Gavin is already there. He puts one finger up in front of his face to shush me. I nod and look at what has his full attention…the front door. His eyes flash pale blue as the fox spirit part of him begins to take over. His lips pull away from his teeth slowly, revealing that they are transforming into fangs. Little flares of blue flames erupt from his shoulders, sleeves and the top of his head. The flames emerging from the top of his head take the shape of two little pointy ears. I reach out and take his arm.

"Gavin," I whisper. He looks at me with that cold, calculating gaze of his. "Not here. Not now," I breathe. And just as suddenly as it appeared, the ominous feeling, with its ravenous hunger, vanishes. I steal a glance at the door, then Gavin, who has already managed to calm himself. His eyes fade to their normal blue.

I release his arm and he sighs. Is he relieved that whatever it was has gone or angry that he didn't get to fight it? "What was that?"

"Not sure," Gavin states plainly, heading back upstairs. "I've never felt anything that…hungry before." He stops on the eighth step. He looks at me over his shoulder, "There is a vampire in this town though. Maybe, she's been starving herself and is out for a bite." He scrambles up the stairs.

"What?" I gasp and follow him as quickly as my legs will carry me at a human pace. Great, Gavin's here, I'm getting a weird vibe from that cute boy, Alex and now a vampire. What else is going on in this town?

#####

I'm at school. When did I get to school? I run my hand over my face, trying to clear the grogginess. My days are starting to run together, I guess. Between working at Mr. Hamish's store and doing odd tags, I must be running myself ragged. Is someone laughing behind me? I wonder what stupid thing they're laughing at this time.

As I walk down the hall, I notice the laughter seems to be increasing and that everyone is turning around from his or her locker. At first, I think they are looking at someone behind me. I steal a glance and there's no one there. I hear giggling pick up behind me as soon as I turn around again. Then as other students hear the laughter, they turn around and join in. A random jock nudges his buddy with his elbow and looks at me. My face reddens and everything around me slows down. I can hear my heartbeat in my ears as the pressure builds. I speed up my pace and head toward the nearest restroom. I push the door open and check under the first stall. The next one and the last one are as empty as the first. I rush over to look at myself in the mirror.

I look normal. Nothing wrong…there's nothing out of place…no nose goblins or dirt or paint or anything weird. I tilt my head to one side and then the other…everything seems normal until I turn to the side, getting ready to leave the restroom. Coming out from my lower back are what look like three tails of fire. I swat at them, trying to put the fire out, but that only fans the flames and makes them spread. The flaming tails flash with a brighter red and the tips' yellow seem to become white as the fire builds.

The flames spread to my hands, but they don't burn. I shake my hands but that doesn't help…well, it helps the fire. I turn on the faucet and try to put out the fire. The water doesn't even seem to reach my hands. I glance up at my panicked expression in the mirror…and notice that I have whiskers and the top of my nose is black. Furry ears sprout from the top of my head. I reach up to touch them and the flames pass from my hands to the ears. Now, they look like two little candle flames sticking up from my hair. The flames spread further up my arms; I notice that they aren't burning my clothes either. I can feel the heat from the flames, but I should be in excruciating pain or at least, getting burned, right? I move my arms around and the flames creep up to my shoulders and along my back. I wake up in a sweat just as the flames crest my shoulders and more fire starts to rise from the tails.

I pant and look around my room. I check my hands, my arms, the top of my head and finally my butt. I sigh. Nothing, there's no fire…no flames…no burning…no tails. I put my hand over my face. What was that about? Does this have anything to do with Gwen? I mean…I saw her with three tails and then she was on fire…then her freakish brother shows up. Not to mention Sora and Kai showing up to tell me that Uncle Flynn died…two months ago. Yeah, that's gotta be it. The day just got to me. That's all…

"JESUS," I snap and almost jump out of bed. Kai is freaking perched on my desk like a cat. I clutch my chest, trying to keep my heart inside. Sora stands by the door with her arms crossed. "What the hell is the matter with you guys?" I snap between pants. "The living room's not good enough for you?"

"We heard you moaning," Kai says as if it's a joke.

"We were worried about you," Sora says as if she's bored.

"I'm fine." Kai looks at Sora. She cuts her eyes to him then back to me. "What?" I snap with more anger than I meant to.

Kai climbs down. "You said a name."

"I did?" I ask them and myself.

"Who's Gwen?" Sora asks moving away from the door.

"She's a new girl…at my school." When would I have called her name?

"Is she hot?" Kai poses.

"Insanely." …and possibly literally. I hear two quick sniffs from Sora. Kai looks at her, too. She tilts her head back toward the living room. Kai nods.

Kai walks over to Sora. "Well…see ya, cos." She opens the door and he walks through it. "We can finish talking about the hot new girl tomorrow."

"Whatever," I say as I grip my covers tighter.

"What was your dream about?" Sora asks. I shake my head. "Were you running through a forest?" I look up at her. "A jungle maybe?" I shake my head again. "Were you…chasing this girl, Gwen, and don't really know why?"

"No," I spit, disgusted by the thought. I don't really know why that would bother me so much. "What…? Why would I dream about any of that?"

Sora thinks for a moment. "So, you've NEVER had any dreams like that?"

I sigh. I can't help but wonder how she knows about that weird dream I had a few weeks ago. Something was chasing me down the hall…but it was weird. I was moving so fast that I was surprised I could see everything going on around me…I could smell everything around me, too. I found Stephen just by his scent and begged him for help. He was so scared of me though. I didn't understand it, at all.

"You have, haven't you?" I open my mouth, but nothing comes out. How can I tell her that the craziness coming out of her mouth…is true? "No worries," she breathes then reopens my bedroom door. "We can talk about it in the morning." She waves dismissively then exits. I nod. "Make sure we get a chance to talk before you head to school tomorrow."

"Whatever," I grumble. I lay down, hoping to get a little more sleep. I stare at the wall and let my mind wander. How does Sora know about my dream? I yawn and my eyes flutter. The wall becomes hazy in the darkness. I look at my hand. And that dream I just had… just like the hallucination that I had with Gwen. I frown and just like that, the frown goes away…and everything goes dark and still.

I jolt awake and sit up to look at the clock. The sun's already up. Crap, I'm late…again. I forgot to set my alarm. I scramble to get dressed and splash some cold water on my face. I rush by the living room, trying to keep quiet and not wake Sora and Kai. I also notice my very smashed alarm clock in the kitchen trashcan. I guess I'll have to go back to using my phone as an alarm clock.

I pick up my bike; drag it out the door and down the steps. Man, I don't even have time for breakfast. I'd love a toaster pastry or even one of those granola things mom got when she was on that healthier foods kick. I'd even settle for one of those gross candy bars that Mrs. Baggett makes.

I pedal to school as hard as I can. If I push myself, I might just make it to first period a few minutes late. I fly down the street, glad I grabbed my hoodie on my way out the door. The air is cool…but moving as fast as I am, it's murder on my eyes. It feels like my cheeks are on fire…my lungs, too. Heh, not like in my dream either. This fire burns and hurts like hell. Good thing I don't have too much further to go. Just one more block and…yep, there it is. School's dead ahead. I can make it. I can make it. Pedal harder.

I pull into the parking lot and ride up to the bike racks. I fumble with my backpack, trying to get my bike lock out and end up dropping the lock…and nearly the entire bag. I pull the pack up, get it set, and groan. Frustrated by my clumsiness and waste of time, I lean down to pick up the lock and cuss under my breath. Just as my fingers close on the lock, I feel my pencils slide out of my backpack and poke me in the back of the head. I left the stupid front pocket open. I guess I'm the stupid one. I scoop the pencils up and cram them back into my pack.

I bend down and lock my bike to the rack. I run to the front doors and then slow up once I see the clock on the wall right inside the doors. There's no point in going to class now. If I went to class, by the time I got there, we'd only have a few minutes left. I sigh. Mom's gonna kill me.

I head toward my locker and before I make it, my phone buzzes. I fish it out, surprised that I remembered to grab it…and not…breakfast. I answer it without even looking. "Hello?"

"Where are you?" Sora barks, sounding, to a scary degree, like my mom.

"I'm at school. Where did you think I'd be?"

"Why didn't you wait for us?"

I roll my eyes. "Because I've been going to school without you guys for the last…" I pause for effect. "…ever since I've been going to school."

"You are so the opposite of funny," she snaps. "We're on our way."

"What? Why? Hello? Hello?" I look at the display. She hung up. Why is she 'on her way?' I mean, them showing up out of nowhere last night, refusing to talk about their dad, watching me sleep and now this…it's just, too…

"Weird," I hear from my left. It's Gwen. She's so cute. I stare at her, trying not to blink. Who knows what hallucination I might miss in the time between my eyes closing and opening?

"I'm sorry…" she says stepping closer. "…I just got a weird feeling to come out into the hall. So, I got the pass…" She flashes it. "…and here you are."

I nod with a deer in headlights expression.

"We have a class together don't…" The bell rings, cutting her off. She looks up at the clock. I take that as a cue to blend in with the people filing out of the classroom behind me as if they were standing at the door, waiting on the bell. I pull my hood up. She looks…but I'm already four or five people away. She frowns and looks down. I scoff and turn to walk away. Man…even that wrinkle she gets between her eyebrows is cute.

Chapter 7: Employment

Where did he go? I mean, he was right here and now I feel…lost. Why do I feel lost? I know my way around. I know that any minute now, Meghan will find me and call me 'loser' in that pleasant way that she does. It's like her way of calling me her new best friend. I lift my eyes again, this time filling them with fox magic. Everything slows. The people…the clock…everything slows down. I still don't see him but, he's here…and he feels…lost, too.

"So, I heard you need a job, loser." I drop the fox magic. *How does she even know that?* I think as I turn to face her. "Here," she says, offering my bag.

I claim it and drape it over my shoulder. "Thanks. What about the pass?"

"They're dated, so at best; you could only use it today, anyway." I nod. "Now, what's this about a job and stuff?"

"Yeah, I told you I was going to need more income to be able to keep up with your extreme shopping skills," I laugh. We walk toward our second class.

"Well, I know the perfect little place for you. I have a friend who owns this cute, little boutique down the street from the square…"

"Let me stop you right there. After our trip yesterday, I definitely don't think I should work at a boutique. Besides, I'm going to that general store in the square this afternoon to see if I can get a job there."

"Gross," she returns without skipping a beat. "No, loser…no, I can't…I won't let you get a job that will make you an actual 'loser.'"

I shake my head, shocked by her continued openness. "I have to pay back my foster parents. I spent a month's allowance," I lie. I actually spent two…and a half. "And doing chores around the house will take a million years to pay them back."

"Ugh, you mean, like, actual manual labor? Don't you have someone to do that for you?" she says with one raised eyebrow. "Like the hired help or something?"

"Not everyone has as much money as you, Megs."

"Megs?" She thinks about her newly assigned nickname. "I like it. No one's ever called me that before." Good. Now, maybe she'll let up about this job thing… "But still, listen to Megs, you CANNOT get a job at that gross convenience store." …or, maybe not.

"General store…"

"Whatever you call it, it's still gross. And I'm gonna have to visit you there."

"Aw," I start in with a mocking tone. "You're gonna visit me?"

Meghan shakes her head. "Don't get all Goth on me, loser. You're like my best friend."

"After one day?"

"Sure, why not?" She smiles with a shrug. She turns and walks into our classroom. I follow her. We file in and take our seats near the center of class. Meghan's phone rings. She retrieves it from her little, pink purse, that looks so small that it shouldn't have anything in it at all. She answers it.

"OMG," she begins. "You will not believe the dream I had last night." She leans over to me. "You should hear this too, loser." She returns her focus to the phone. "My new BFF, who else?"

Meghan continues talking on the phone, but I can't focus on what she's saying because I'm thinking about the dream I had last night. Why was I running through a forest on all fours? I mean, even when I'm in full kitsune form, I don't like running on all fours...not like Gavin does. My eyes drift closed and it's almost like I'm back in that dream again.

I loved it. I feel...free. I don't feel the oppressive burden of my fox magic weighing me down. There's no oppressive 'Gavin' feeling either. I can see perfectly through the darkness without having to focus fox magic into my eyes. My ears pick up every sound as if each one is whispered directly into my ear. I smell the sweet aroma of the moisture clinging to the trees and underbrush. This feels amazing.

There seems to be a clearing up ahead. I rush into it with my senses wide open. In the center of the open area, I see...me. I stare at myself curiously. How am I running through the forest and waiting for myself here at the same time? I just noticed...me. I smirk...well the other me smirks. My...her eyes flash emerald green as she imbues them with fox magic. "Gwen?" Her...my foxfire ears spring up from her head. "Gwen?" She crouches and flicks her three foxfire tails. "GWEN?"

I snap out of it. I look around and everyone is staring at me. I turn to Meghan. "Wh-what happened?" I ask with one hand on my forehead.

"You tell me," she returns, seeming confused and concerned. "Are you alright? I mean, you were kind of freaking out and breathing really hard."

My hand moves down from my forehead until it covers my face. "I was?" I ask, partly out of wonder and partly out of sheer embarrassment. Meghan nods, still staring at me with wide eyes. The rest of the class slowly begins to ignore me, but not her. She leans in closer.

"Are you sure you're alright, loser?"

I shake my head slowly. "I don't know. That's never happened to me before."

#####

I walk out of the double doors, feeling like a free man. I'm so ready to grab my bike and take a nice, laid-back ride to work. I'm out of seventh period on time for once. I swear Mrs. Bustamante might just murder me one day. I'm glad that, for once, I don't have to rush somewhere. As I come down the stairs, leaving the front of the school feels kinda weird. I hit step nine...why am I counting the stupid steps? I swear someone just called my name from behind me.

I turn around and...I don't see anybody. I hear my name again and look back up the stairs. Then I hear it again, only louder. "Alex," I hear coming from just inside the front of the school. I squint and try to get a better look at the guy.

I go back up the stairs and meet him head on. Hmm, he just looks like some random who probably just happened to have a class with me at one point or another. I take a good look at his face. I think his name is Evan. I recognize his constantly pale skin and long black hair hanging down in Goth-bangs across his forehead. Not the kind of dude that I'm used to looking for me, but the more and more tags I do, the more and more that keeps happening.

"What's up, man?" I ask, ushering him to one side to let a couple of girls walk past. They steal a glance at the two of us. They seem to like what they see with one of us, the other not so much. I'm guessing Captain Goth doesn't do it for them.

"Nothing much," he replies in a low voice. I give him a look that tells him I'm not up for chitchat. "Yeah, I should probably get to the point, right?" I have to pinch myself not to groan. "Well, actually...I have a job you might be interested in."

Doubt it. "Well, I only have one rule before I take any job."

He arches his eyebrows and leans away. He twitches his head and the Goth-bangs move to one side. He looks like he's about to laugh. "What's the rule?"

"I have to know what I'm getting myself into before I can agree to it."

"Fair enough," His Royal Goth-ness says. "Look. I got your name from Rex." Rex? "He said you did a tag for him a few days ago."

I nod. "Yeah, so?" is all I manage. How does HE know Rex? They don't look like they would be the kind of people who hung out.

I let that thought pass as he continues, "So, I need a tag done, but not just any tag. This one is special." He takes a picture of himself from his back pocket and some hot Goth chick, looking bored, with a platinum streak down the front of her jet-black hair.

"This color," I say running a finger down that streak.

"I know," he starts again. "I need a special spray paint for it. I got it coming in either tomorrow or Monday. I just need to know if you can get it done for me." He fidgets. He seems like he's antsy for me to agree.

"That depends on how much you're paying."

"I'll give you one hundred now and four hundred more when it's done," he says like it's nothing. I guess being Goth pays.

Still...a hundred now and four more later. I'd be a fool not to take that deal. "Bet. You get me the paint." I tip the picture toward him. "I'll get you a tag." He nods as I slide the picture into my book bag. "Just let me know when it comes in and where you want the tag," I say replacing my bag.

"Great. I'll get the design done by that time, too," he replies.

I frown as he reaches into his pocket and pulls out a small collection of folded bills. "You mean the picture's not the tag?"

"You can do that?" I arch my eyebrows and let the corners of my mouth turn down in an 'of course, I can' kind of way. "Nice, but nah, Bethany and I broke up a few days ago and I had something else in mind. I'll let you know."

I nod. I take the group of twenties from him and slide them into my pocket. "Thanks man, I gotta run to my other job." He nods, backing away. I head down the stairs and look at my phone. Crap. Now, I do have to hurry to get to work.

I rush toward the bike rack. I stop a few feet away. Where's my bike? I rush over to the rack and find what's left of my chain with the lock still attached. It looks like someone tore it off...as crazy as that sounds.

"Alex," Sora says. I turn to her and Kai. "You need a ride to work?"

I look at my shattered chain then back to Sora and Kai. "I guess so."

Kai smirks. "Relax, cos. We put your bike in the back of our rental."

I look at the lock again with a confused expression. "How did you get my lock off? Why did you take my lock off?"

"We were worried about you," Sora says with no emotion.

"I…came…to…school! What is the matter with you guys?" Kai inhales deeply and looks at Sora. She looks at him and he arches his eyebrows. She shakes her head slowly and they both turn back to me.

"We've…" Sora starts. "…been a little on edge, since our dad…died." I frown. She still seems even…but I've never seen Sora, showing anything close to emotions, not since we were little kids. "What's wrong?"

I shake my head. "You guys offered me a ride, right? In your rental car…how did you guys get a rental car? Sora, you're only eighteen and Kai, you're the same age as me."

"That's easy to explain," Kai says, moving toward the silver SUV.

Sora follows him. "We lied…and we're really good at it." Sora retrieves a set of car keys from her jacket pocket. She presses a button on the keychain and the alarm chirps. She smirks, then walks away.

Chapter 8: Eatery

Why am I so nervous about this? It's not even an interview. It's just to check to see if I might get an interview. I should be casual…and calm. Am I dressed ok? What would one wear to a pre-interview interview…? I mean, I'm wearing a long enough skirt and sensible top. I look down at my ensemble. This should be okay…I think I'm making too much of this. Yes, I probably am. Breathe, Gwen. Just breathe.

I push the door open and take a deep breath with my first step. I force myself not to jump as the chime above the door sounds. I freeze in the doorway, look around and then enter. I feel like someone's watching me. It's not the malevolent stare that I felt the other morning. This is different. It's…lustful…no, not quite that far…it's flirty. It's like an infatuation.

"Hello," a voice calls from near the cash register. I start and try to calm myself down.

I straighten my shirt and clear my throat. "Hi," I say meekly as I walk over to the store's counter.

"How can I help you today, miss?" the man behind the counter asks.

Stay calm…stay calm. It was a simple question. Just answer it. "Um, yes…I'm actually here looking to help you…I mean…" I laugh nervously. "A job…I'm here looking for a job. I-I was wondering if you were hiring right now," I manage to say finally. Darn it, Gwen. That was a GREAT first impression. I know I must sound like a mumbling, stumbling idiot.

The man arches his graying eyebrows and looks at me kindly. His expression reminds me of the way obāsan would look at me whenever I lost the lying game to Gavin again. "Actually, I'm not hiring right now. I'm sorry," he says with a voice so tender it makes me blush.

I nod absently and turn away dejectedly as he continues, "But I know that the coffee shop across the square is hiring. They have an opening for a cashier or a barista or something like that. They've had a sign in the window for a few weeks now."

I peer out the glass door, hoping to spot the sign. I motion in the direction of the wooden sign wafting in the breeze across the town square.

He looks over my head. His eyes return. "Yeah, that's the one."

"Thank you," I manage to squeak out in more of a gasp than actual words.

"No problem, good luck," I hear as the bell chimes above my head again.

I look across the street and see the previously unnoticed coffee shop's front window. I remember hearing Meghan mention it before, but she took me to her second favorite coffee spot instead. I make it halfway across the street and sure enough, there is the small handwritten "HELP WANTED" sign. I make it to the sidewalk and halt. I feel eyes on me again. The flirty eyes are staring at me again. I turn back to the general store. Nothing. I sigh. Maybe I'm just on edge because Gavin is here.

I return to the coffee shop. I gather my resolve and walk over to the entrance, reminding myself to breathe again with every step. This shouldn't be too hard. That rejection wasn't as bad as I had imagined, and he was so nice…despite telling me, "no."

"I…SERIOUSLY…cannot imagine you schlepping coffee for money, Gwenie."

"And I...SERIOUSLY...cannot imagine you not being annoying every waking moment of every day of my life," I return to Gavin's arrogant smile. "Why are you here?"

"Oh, I'm crushed that my adorable little sister thinks that I'm here for any other reason than to make sure that she remains safe."

"Lie," I spit instantly.

"I just wanted to see where you'd be seeking gainful employment."

"Lie."

"Ugh, fine. I wanted to know if you had any new ideas about where the Taylors hid your charm yet."

"Truth...and no," I say, turning away from him. "I thought you searched their house, when you," I pause to make air quotes. "...stopped by for dinner last night."

"I did. It wasn't there.

I take the handle. "Can I go now?"

"See that...right there," Gavin says stepping closer. "If you go in there with that confidence, that anger...that fire...no pun intended...they'll hire you on the spot."

I roll my eyes and pull the door open. As it swings open, the bold aroma of coffee mixed with the scent of caramel and vanilla and the tiniest hint of cinnamon hit me immediately. The smells overpower me. The nerves I felt before blow away with that small burst of air conditioning escaping the open door.

Comfortable earth tones decorate the interior of the coffee shop. There are square, two-tone brown wooden tables with rounded corners and chairs around them in the center of the shop and booths lining the walls and partially frosted windows. The tops of some of the tables have abstract designs painted on them. In three of the corners, sit deep plush crimson couches and a coffee table spread with magazines and newspapers with lamps that give these areas a homey feel.

There are wooden-framed chalkboards on the exposed brick walls where customers have written neighborhood events and even makeshift classifieds. Artistically drawn coffee cups and coffee beans are also interspersed along the walls with little flowers and various candies. To top it off, there is a dormant fireplace near the counter. I can just imagine it roaring to life with flames on a fall or winter evening.

A moderate number of customers fills the shop. They sit around reading or chatting and drinking their coffees. I can't see anyone who I think might work here, so I walk over to the counter and peer into the glass display case beside it. Freshly made pastries, cake slices, frosted cupcakes, and small sandwiches fill the space. As I turn my attention to the rows of flavorings behind the counter, a young woman appears from what I suppose is the kitchen in the back. She has long chestnut-colored hair held together in a ponytail, caramel-colored skin, and wears a brown apron. She doesn't look that much older than Gavin.

"Can I help you?" she asks, wiping her hands on her apron.

"Yes, I'm looking for a job. I saw the sign in the window and I wanted to talk to the owner to see if I could work here," I say with a confidence boosted by the intoxicating smells permeating the shop.

"Well, I'm glad you came in then," the girl says. She reaches both hands behind her back and then takes off her apron. She smiles. "Wait just a sec."

44

She leans into the kitchen. "Hey Em, take a break from making those flyers and hold down the shop for me, ok?"

"Ok," calls a female voice from the kitchen area.

The first girl turns her attention back to me. She comes around the counter and sits down at a table near the back of the shop. She motions for me to join her. The olive-colored polo shirt she's wearing says, Jelly Bean Coffee in white letters. It is an odd name, especially for a business that doesn't sell jelly. I steal another glance at the case as I sit. At least, I don't think there's anything with jelly in it.

"I'm so glad you came in today. My name is Jennifer, and I'm the owner of Jelly Bean Coffee. What was your name again?" she says, extending her hand across the table.

"I-I...didn't...I'm Gwen. Gwendolyn Frost," I reply, trying to gather my waning confidence.

"Nice to meet you, Gwen," she says, smiling as she shakes my hand. "So, you're looking for a job?"

"Yes."

"Do you have a resume or any references?"

"Well, I've never had a job before, but my foster parents could be references, I guess," I reply a bit uneasily. I hadn't thought about providing job history until she mentioned it.

"That's ok. Emily didn't have any work experience when she started last year," Jennifer says, motioning to the brown-skinned girl walking out of the kitchen. "But with a little training, she's turned into a great barista for me. Plus, she does graphic design work. She even designed this logo," she adds while motioning to the shop's name on her shirt. "But she'll be graduating this year, so I need to train someone to take her place."

"You wouldn't happen to know anything about graphic design, would you?" she asks as an afterthought.

"No, actually I don't," I reply, starting to feel uneasy again. I'm sure I could learn graphic design, but I don't want to lie to get this job. "I was wondering though, what's with the name of the shop?" I ask, trying to turn the conversation to her. Humans always love to talk about themselves or at least, that's been my experience.

"Well, my name is Jennifer Ellison and my little sister used to call me Jelly because she tried to say my whole name in baby talk. It caught on with the rest of the family, so it just made sense when I opened a coffee shop to name the place 'Jelly Bean Coffee,'" she says enthusiastically.

I nod and smile, hoping my diversion worked.

"Well, the position I'm hiring for starts at five dollars an hour plus tips. You'd be shadowing Emily when she works, so you'd have to start out working her schedule. You two would split the tips from the jar and then keep any other tips you make. Do you have any questions about the position?"

"When does she work?" I ask, hopeful that I still have a chance at getting the job.

"Emily works three nights a week and on Saturday evenings. Friday and Saturday nights are our busiest nights, so you'll get a taste of how busy we get," Jennifer says.

"I think I can handle it," I tell her.

"Great. Then I'd like to offer you the position. You can start next week," Jennifer says as she stands.

"Just like that?"

Jennifer nods. "Just like that." She leans forward. "Perks of being the owner."

"Thank you," I respond.

"No, I should thank you for coming in…that sign's been in the window for three weeks. I've got to get back to work," she says looking at the small line that has formed at the counter. "I'll see you Monday at three-thirty."

"See you then," I say and smile to myself as I walk back out onto the street.

I groan as I shove my straw down into my too thick milkshake. I look at the…people I'm sharing a table with…Sora to Kai to Stephen then Rich. I frown and shove the milkshake away. Sora glares at me with one arched eyebrow. "Something wrong with your milkshake, Alex?" she asks like she can't possibly contemplate deciphering any human emotion. I cross my arms and lean back.

"Nooooooo," I moan. "I'm just irked because my best friends…" I look at Rich and Stephen. "…can't seem to get along with my cousins long enough for me to work a shift. Mr. Hamish sent me home because of you guys. I might get fired."

"It wasn't my fault," Kai complains instantly. "Rich is a jack-hole."

"You're mom's a jack-hole," Rich spits.

"Hey," Kai whines.

"Say it again and get a fork to the throat," Sora says with cold eyes glowering at Rich. Stephen whacks Rich across the arm, saving me the trouble.

"Not cool, dude," Stephen says.

"Sorry. Sorry," Rich finally concedes. "I forgot your mom and dad died…"

Stephen leans back emitting a sound similar to a snake's hiss. He shakes his head slowly. Kai frowns, looks down and moves his mouth as if he's literally chewing on his tongue to stop from saying something. His eyes seem to be looking through the table. Sora looks away. She looks at me…and there are…tears in her eyes. She swallows deeply, and they disappear.

"I have your pizza," our waitress says as she sets up the deck to place the pizza on top. "…one meaty special with extra bacon, sausage and beef topping…" Kai and Sora's moods pick up instantly at the sight of the pizza.

"I'm starving," Kai grumbles.

"I know. That's why I ordered two," Sora says as a waiter brings a second pizza that I had no idea she'd even ordered. By the time, the waiter puts the second pie down; Kai already has three slices on his plate and another half way down his throat. Sora has two on her plate and one in her mouth. Stephen stares at her in shock. Something near the door steals Rich's attention away.

I turn to find out what he's looking at and it's…Meghan Powers. "Dude," I say with a shake of my head. Rich looks at me. "Don't hurt yourself."

"What?" Rich says with his lighthearted tone. He watches her pass by our table with that twisted smile on his face. "That girl's going be my wife one day."

"Pfft," Kai emits, spitting pizza everywhere. Sora leans away and then throws a napkin ball at him. "Sorry," he whines, still with a cheek full of pizza. "But, Richie Mortimer just said he's going to marry Meghan Powers...one day." He laughs uproariously.

"Kai," Sora says like a command instead of his name.

"No, no," Kai continues with his laugh building. "I mean, am I right? Or, am I right?" Rich frowns and leans back in his chair. "I mean, Creepy Richie Mortimer thinks that he's got a shot with probably..." Kai wipes his mouth with his hand. "...still the hottest chick in your school."

"Don't call me that," Rich grumbles into his chest.

Stephen, turning his attention from Rich to Kai says, "Hey man, easy. I know you guys have issues, but now you're just being a jerk."

Kai takes another bite of pizza. He drops the slice on his plate and looks at Stephen. "Really? I mean, you guys have actually gotten into fist fights about this girl and you're defending him?"

"We didn't fight about her," Stephen says softly into his chest. "We'd fight about..."

"Anything," I breathe. Stephen and Rich look at me. "I mean, you guys used to fight all the time about whatever stupid thing and in reality...you'd really be fighting about Meghan." Stephen frowns. "All because," I continue. "She invited Stephen to her twelfth birthday party and not Rich." Rich sighs then rises from the table.

"Where're you going?" Stephen asks looking up at him.

"To prove you guys wrong," Rich says defiantly then walks away.

"Is he doing, what I think he's doing?" Sora asks, still managing to sound monotone beneath her surprise.

"I think so," I return as Stephen nods in agreement. We watch as Rich crosses the restaurant and approaches Meghan and her three friends' table.

"Is he insane?" Kai bellows.

I shake my head slowly. Kai and Sora both turn their heads so that one ear is closer to Rich than the other. Do they really think they can hear him from here with this craptastic music playing?

Rich says something to Meghan. She frowns. Kai snickers. Sora hits him in some way that I can't see because I can't look away from this train wreck. Meghan says something and even though I can't hear her, her facial expression tells me that it is NOT good. She rises from the table with both hands, palms down on top. Kai and Sora both suck air between their clenched teeth simultaneously and return to their original seated positions.

"What was that?" I ask as they both shift their focus back to their plates, although they are not eating. Kai sticks out his bottom lip and shakes head. Sora ignores me completely.

"Rich?" Stephen says as a visibly upset Rich rushes past our table and continues out of the restaurant. He hits the door so hard that it almost flies off its hinges. I glare at Meghan's table again. Her three friends are laughing their damned heads off...but...Meghan actually looks...sad. She sighs and looks down at the table until her friends turn their attention to her, at which point she perks up immediately.

Stephen stands. "I'm…gonna go check on him." I nod. Stephen rushes out the door after Rich. My focus returns to my cousins, who continue staring at their empty plates. I scowl.

"What did she say?"

"She said that he's…" Kai begins before Sora shoots him a fierce elbow to the ribs, causing him to cough.

"Nothing," she interjects. "We couldn't even hear her from here…just like you."

I look at Kai. "Yeah," he concurs in a gruff voice. "Couldn't hear a thing," he continues while taking a slice of the second pie. I inhale deeply through my nose. They're lying. I don't know how I know their lying or even how I know they heard everything, but I know.

Chapter 9: Rarity

"So, how was your weekend, loser?" Meghan asks as we enter the school.

"It was…fine," I return hesitantly.

Gavin spent the entire weekend with me and the Taylors. They dote on him just like most of the kitsune back home do. So, what if kitsune males are usually only born every one-hundred or so kitsune? It does explain why he always seems to get a lot of attention from everyone, everywhere we go. He may be rare, but that still doesn't explain why he's such a jerk face. I frown. I have to get back to the topic at hand, before Meghan starts to wonder what's going on in my head.

"Yeah, it was fine," I repeat, looking at her expectant face. If you don't count the fact that Gavin wouldn't let us out of his sight for very long…unless of course, he thought he had gathered some new piece of information that would lead him to my charm.

"Just fine? Geez, you really are a loser," Meghan returns. "Me and my mom spent the weekend in Elizabeth City with her new boyfriend, on his boat." We round the corner and pick up two girls who follow the story as if they caught the beginning.

Meghan tosses her hair. "He's kind of a cheese ball." She turns to one of the two girls. "Do people still say, 'cheese ball?'"

"Um, I think so," she replies obediently.

"Good." Meghan returns, completely unaware that we've picked up two more girls. "Yeah, like I was saying, he's kind of a cheese ball, but my mom seems to like him, so I guess, he's okay." She turns to me with an excited expression. "But his boat is A-MAY-ZING. It's a forty-foot schooner that he named Queen Anne after my mom."

"How long have they been dating?" I ask, feigning interest in what is possibly the most boring story I've ever heard. Several of the girls following us, reiterate my sentiment, but with sincerity.

"They've been going out for two and a half months."

"What? Really…?" I ask, not believing the short amount of time they've been together with their mutual boat investment.

"Yeah, why?"

"It's just that…"

"Wait." Meghan comes to a stop, stopping the herd behind us as well. She turns to them. "Go away; I need to talk to my bestie." The other girls depart, but not before some shoot vicious scowls and emotions that are even more vicious in my direction. I shrug and return to Meghan.

"Look," Meghan begins. "I know that they haven't been dating long enough for him to name a boat after her, but he makes my mom happy…and I haven't seen that like…EVER. And he really seems to like her, so I'm just glad that they found each other."

Again, I'm taken aback by the sheer honesty coming from Meghan. "I would've never guessed you felt so strongly about it."

"I know, Gwen," she returns nonchalantly. "That's why you're my bestie, because unlike the other lemmings, you actually voiced an opinion that was the opposite of what I was saying. Plus, I could tell that you were REALLY bored with that story." I grimace. "No worries. Only an idiot or a liar would tell me that they weren't bored with that story." Again, her unfiltered honesty throws me for a loop.

Meghan tosses her golden locks and turns down the hall. "Come on, loser. We're gonna be late for class." I pause. I don't know what the other girls see in her...but the veracity that comes from her on a regular basis actually draws me to her. Even if she hadn't claimed me as her best friend, by this point, I'd probably be vying to be.

"Hello? Loser? Are you there?" I snap out of my quiet daydream and look into Meghan's blue-green eyes. "Are you coming to class or not?" I nod. We resume walking the hall, this time free of entourage. "What were you thinking about, loser? Was it that cute boy from your seventh period?"

"No," I mutter, but now I am. He's like Meghan in that respect. Only I haven't figured out what's so compelling about him...other than the fact that he can apparently see through my fox magic.

"Oh." Meghan's voice hints at excitement. "That reminds me, you have to help with the dance decorations."

"I'm sorry...the what now?"

"We're having our fall dance on Friday and we're decorating the gym since there won't be another home game until next Friday. I'm head of the decorating committee and as my new BFF you HAVE TO help."

"Okay," I return sensing the futility in arguing against her. "When are we working on the decorations?"

"Today, after school."

"I can't."

"And why not?" she hurls back with a hint of aggravation.

"I have to work."

"What? Work? You got a job? You didn't tell me you got a job!"

"You didn't ask."

"Ha-ha, very funny, loser...wait...tell me you didn't get that job at that disgusting convenience store."

"General store," I correct her. "And no, the owner said they weren't hiring but directed me to Jelly Bean Coffee across the square."

"Oh, I love that place. I approve and now, we have a hangout spot." She walks away quickly.

"We do?"

"Yeah, we do, loser." She enters her classroom. She sticks her head back out into the hall. "Hey," she begins with the look of a schemer. "What time do you get off, loser?"

"Um...I think Jennifer said she'll let me go earlier than Emily on my first night..."

"I asked for an actual time, loser," Meghan says impatiently.

"Eight?"

"Good. You can come by after work. We start after six anyway because most of the cheerleaders are on the decorating committee and they have practice. We'll be almost finished by then, but you can help out a little at least. We'll be in the gym and if you smell too much like burnt coffee then go home and shower before you come."

Before I can respond, she returns to the classroom. I shake my head, bewildered by how she bosses me around without actually making it sound like bossing.

The bell sounds. I rush down the hall to my class and of course, the first person that I see is Stephen. I look around the room and…still no Alex.

"Hey," I whisper to him across the aisle. He frowns a bit then looks at me with confusion in his eyes. Yeah, Meghan was right. He is cute.

"Hey," he says finally.

"You're friends with that guy Alex, right?" He nods. "Why doesn't he ever come to first period?" Stephen shrugs. He looks at me with an even odder expression. "What?"

"Nothing." I arch my eyebrows hoping that he'll indulge me. He smiles. Got him. "It's just…I think that he kind of likes you and now you're asking about him." I sigh into a smile. "And now you're smiling while thinking about him."

"I didn't say I was thinking about him."

"But here you are talking to me, a guy that you've never spoken to before, about him." I nod. "And you can't seem to stop smiling."

"Well," I drag the word out. "It's just that he was drawing this amazing picture of me and…"

"He does that," Stephen admits. "He's always drawing pictures of things that he finds interesting or pretty."

"I like pretty things, too," I say with a massive grin stretching my face and there goes that look that tells me he thinks I'm a Martian. "I mean," I almost choke over the words. "I really liked the picture he was drawing." Stephen nods. Mrs. Pritchard walks into the class drawing both of our attentions to the front of the room. I wonder if Stephen still likes Meghan as much as she says he does.

#####

"Again," I grumble, running up the stairs toward the school's main entrance. I can't believe that Sora and Kai made me wait for them to give me a ride. My cousin's from across the freakin' country, who I haven't seen in two years…now, won't let me out of their sight. I growl as I pull the double doors open and see that it is already 9:03.

"I missed first period… again." Mom is going to have a cow…slaughter the cow…then force-feed me the steak before slaughtering me.

"What are you complaining about?" Kai asks over my shoulder.

"Argh!" I nearly jump out of my skin. "What the hell?"

"Eh, Sora wanted me to make sure you got in okay."

"Got in where?" He ignores me and looks down the hall. "What are you looking at?"

Kai inhales deeply, ignoring me. He exhales one loud sigh and runs his fingers through his hair. "Nothing," he mumbles in a half-asleep sort of way. "Alright…" He turns around. "…have a good day, dear." He exits the school.

"Jerk," I toss as the doors swing closed. A second later, the bell is ringing. I sigh and head to my locker. Stephen is already there waiting on me. "What's up?" I twirl the combination lock.

"You won't believe this," he starts. "That new girl was asking about you."

"She was?"

He nods. "She said that you were drawing a picture of her and she liked it."

I huff a laugh and smile. I can't help it. Freaky flames or not, Gwen is hot. I laugh again. "Punny," I say under my breath.

"What?"

"Nothing." I pull my locker open.

"I think she kind of likes you," Stephen says.

"Shut up. Now, you're just talking crazy." He laughs, but this thought brings me back to another insane coupling. "Hey, have you…heard from Rich? I tried to call him Saturday, but I got his voicemail."

"He got away from me after he left the restaurant. I sent a few texts, even tried to call him, but I never heard back." I sigh. I toss my biology book into my locker. "Man, Meghan must've slammed him pretty hard for him to go MIA all weekend."

I nod. "It looked pretty brutal. Do you think he'll give up his dibs now?"

"Ugh, too soon, man…too soon."

"Alex," I hear as I fight off a laugh. I turn to find Goth-boy walking toward me. What was his name again? I look at Stephen, hoping that he'll be able to help me out here.

"Evan," Stephen says, making the name sound cooler and less Goth than it actually is. "How've you been, man?"

"I'm good," Evan returns before pounding Stephen's fist with his own, proving how *cool* he is. Evan slips his pack off and unzips it as it touches the floor. "I got the paint, man." He pulls the can out and offers it.

"Be cool," I snap and take it from him trying to hide it. I make sure no teachers are around. Knowing my luck, Mrs. Bustamante would walk up right about now.

"Sorry, man," Evan returns before tossing his Goth-bangs. He stands. "I've never…"

"Don't worry about it," I interrupt him. I put the can in my locker. "Where do you want it?"

"On the side of my house."

"WHAT?" Stephen snaps.

"Are you high?" I ask. "I'm not getting busted 'cause you got a beef with mommy and daddy."

"It's not like that," Evan says. "It's just…my dad is always down on my music, so I wanna make a statement."

"And how is that 'not like that'?" Stephen asks with one tweaked eyebrow.

"Look," Evan says, pulling a piece of paper out of his back pocket. He opens it and reveals the name 'Death Racers' in silver, blue and black letters. "That's my band's logo. I want to have that on the side of the house by the garage where we practice."

I frown. Clearly, Goth-boy flicked his hair soooooooo much that his brain's come out. "Okay, but, you're gonna have to pay me A LOT more money."

Evan digs deep into his front right pocket. He pulls out a couple of crumpled up bills. He gives me one and then another. I unfold them and it's…two hundred dollars! I look up at him. Geez, Goth-boy's parents must be loaded.

"And you're still gonna give me the other four after I'm done, right?" He nods. "Cool. What's your address?"

52

"It's on the back of the page."

I flip it over so that I can see it. Stephen steals a glance. "Alright. When'll be a good time to do it? I don't want your mom calling the cops on me or your dad trying to shoot me."

"Tonight. My parents are dragging my brother and me out to our grandma's in Elizabeth City for dinner."

"Bet," I return, pocketing the two hundred bones. Evan nods and walks past us. "Later." I'm sure he responded but I didn't bother listening. I flip his design over and stare at the address. "Is this right?" I ask Stephen while giving him a better look.

His face goes into 'I'm thinking' mode. He nods. "Yeah, that's his place. I remember going to a sick party at his house during spring break last year." I keep forgetting that even though he hangs out with me and Rich, Stephen is actually REALLY popular. It's probably because he's so friendly. I don't think anybody in the school has a bad thing to say about him…except that he hangs out with Rich and me. Speak of the devil…

Rich walks over to us. "Hey, man," Stephen says, trying to make his voice sound upbeat and not like someone just shot a puppy. It didn't work.

Rich looks at us like the guys who shot his puppy, rode off in his car and took his mom with him. "Hi," he moans and makes it sound more like he's dying.

"You okay, man?" I ask without really needing to. One look at the bags under his eyes with matching dark circles tells me he didn't sleep much. Plus, hard to believe, he actually looks paler than usual. He kind of looks more of a sickly green color. If he doubled over, I'd swear he was about to hurl.

"I'm alright," he lies. I offer him a handshake. His hand feels cool and clammy. I fight the urge to snatch my hand away from the wet octopus feel.

"You sure?" He has beads of sweat forming around his hairline.

"Yeah, man," Stephen says. "You don't look so good. Not that you ever have, but now you look worse than normal."

Rich emits a hiss that I guess should be a laugh. "Nah, nah, I just had a rough weekend. My folks have been arguing again. So, you know…"

"What about that thing that happened Friday night?" Stephen asks, trying to sound neutral. He might as well have called it 'the incident.'

"What are you talking about?"

"You know…you…," I pause to make hand gestures. "…Meghan…talking. Train wreck ensued…you stormed off…and your boys don't hear from you all weekend."

"Oh that. No worries. I handled that," he says with a weird grin. That kind of expression usually gets me in trouble with Mrs. Bustamante. She says it's a smirk and it means more than I'm willing to say and that's usually true.

"What do you mean, 'you handled it?'" Stephen asks, stepping closer to Rich. "Did you do something to Meghan?"

"What? No, I didn't." I arch one eyebrow. "I didn't."

"Okay," Stephen says. "But you shouldn't let what Meghan said get you down. You know it's hard to come down from the ivory tower." Rich hisses again. The bell rings, drawing our attention to the clock at the corner.

"Crap, I'm gonna be late for my next class," I say and make a break for it. "I'll see you guys later." I make it to a full sprint rounding the corner. I knew things were bad with Rich and his parents, but I didn't think it was so bad that he would lose sleep. Reminds me of mom after dad died. She kept dark circles under her eyes all the time. I sigh. "Dad..."

Chapter 10: Work

School flew by today, except that seventh period…was different. Alex seemed so different today. He actually said hello to me first…and he let me see his sketch. Well, "let me" might be a bit of a stretch…he didn't cover it up as well. He's an amazing artist. It looked exactly like me…probably a little better. He even included a little flicker of flame in the pupils of my eyes.

I'm smiling. I'm trying so hard not to, but I'm smiling. I peer out of the passenger side of Meghan's car. I let my hand hang out the open window and catch the air swirling around it. I use a little fox magic and capture some of it. I should do something nice for him. That drawing was so amazing, and he drew it from memory. I inhale deeply and I'm back in class staring at the drawing all over again…no, not the drawing. I'm staring at its creator…so cute.

The car screeches to a halt. "We're here, loser," Meghan says with so much playfulness that I almost laugh. I collect my bag. "Don't forget, we're decorating the gym tonight." I nod. "Do you need a ride after?"

"No. If I'm too tired to walk it, I'll call my brother." Meghan's eyebrow tweaks above her blue-green eyes. I stretch out with my emotions and feel hers. Her openness makes it easy. She…likes Gavin. He was a complete and total jerk to her, but she likes him. It's probably because no one else has ever treated her like that. Who would be mean to someone as beautiful as she is besides my brother?

"Loser?"

"Yeah," I return, shaking my head for continuously responding to 'Loser.'

"You're gonna be late," she says succinctly. I nod. "And I've got things to do. Soooooo, get out." I laugh and climb out. "Love ya, mean it," she chirps before peeling away quickly. I laugh again as her car disappears around the corner.

I turn toward "The Bean" as Meghan called it. I pause. Someone…something is watching me. I look around…infusing my eyes with fox magic. It's still ravenous, angry…but diminished…not as malevolent.

I turn circles, not seeing anything. My vision waivers as frustration sweeps over me. I take a deep breath and close my eyes. I open them again…and just as quickly as it appeared, the voyeur's presence vanishes. Is it after me? Is it after something else? What is it?

"Gwendolyn?" Jennifer calls from the now open door of The Bean. I muster a smile. "What are you doing?" I open my mouth, but nothing comes out. I shake my head. "It's good that you're early. I have some forms you need to fill out before you start working." I nod and follow her into the shop.

I take a seat at the table nearest the cash register and Jennifer places a small stack of papers in front of me. I rush through them as quickly as I can…but I don't have the information she requires on most of them. Being a foster kid from a different country does help me in that regard.

Jennifer collects the half-completed forms and turns to Emily. "Emily? You remember Gwen, right?"

Emily looks me over as she places a rack of cups on top of the counter. She nods then moves the cups one-by-one under the counter. "New girl, right?" Emily says with a much gruffer voice than I expected.

"Right," Jennifer returns. "I'm leaving her in your capable hands. I have to run by the bank before it closes." She puts one hand on my shoulder. "You'll work until seven tonight, okay?" I nod. She looks past me to Emily. "I'll be back around nine to help you close up." Emily nods then removes the empty rack from the countertop.

"Come 'ere," Emily says as the door chimes, signaling that Jennifer has already left. I walk around the counter. "You can put your bag down here." She motions to a cubby under the counter. I toss my backpack inside. She offers…some sort of cloth to me. "Your apron." I drape the loop over my shoulders and try tying it behind my back with little success.

"You're pretty tiny," Emily says. "You should wrap the strings around you twice and tie it in front." She's right. "Okay, first things first…" She turns to a machine behind the register. "…this is the center of our operation." I nod. "This is the espresso maker. I'm gonna show you how to steam a perfect…"

"Um, one thing," I interrupt. She frowns but pauses. "Are we…the only ones here?"

Emily nods. "Yeah, why?"

"I…just…could've sworn I saw someone come in right before me…" I break off with a scoff…or felt some malevolent entity watching me. "Never mind, you were saying…espresso maker…center of operation."

"Good," Emily says. "You actually pay attention. You should've seen the last girl Jen tried to hire." She shakes her head. "Oh, and call me, Em. I feel like my mom's lecturing me every time Jen calls me Emily." I smile as Em collects a metal cup and returns to the espresso maker.

"What are you doing?" I ask Rich, who's been staring out the front window for the last twenty minutes. He turns to look at me…slow…too slow. It's like it hurts his neck to turn his head. The bags under his eyes seem deeper…darker. He stares out the window again.

"Weird," Stephen whispers. I nod…I think… "Am I crazy or does he look like he hasn't been eating, as well as not sleeping?" I nod, this time for sure. "I've asked him about it, but he always says he's fine…no sleep and all."

"Yeah."

"You guys can stop talking about me," Rich groans.

Stephen arches his eyebrows. I roll my eyes, moving back to the counter. Stephen follows.

"Speaking of sleeping…how are you gonna get Evan's tag done if you have to work 'til nine tonight?"

"Who?" I ask, rearranging the candy on the counter.

"Evan…you know…Goth-boy? He wants you to tag the side of his house."

I nod. "Right…him," I say putting the last bag of Skittles back into place. "I thought I was doing that tag tomorrow night."

"No, I'm pretty sure he said he and his folks were headed to Elizabeth City tonight."

I pause. Crap, Stephen is right. "Damn. I gotta get out of here. I can't mess up a payday like that, man."

56

Stephen shrugs his shoulders. "So, what are you gonna do?"

Mr. Hamish walks out of the back. "Hey, Mr. Hamish," I say, moving toward him. "Do you think it'd be okay if I got off a little early?"

"How early?" Mr. Hamish says.

"Like, now."

"Now? How am I supposed to close up tonight without…?" Mr. Hamish trails off. He shakes his head. "What's so important that you have to get off this early?"

I shake my head and open my mouth.

"You know, kid," he interrupts. "I know that sometimes you do stuff that's not exactly…Kosher to make money, but if you're into something criminal…"

"He won't need help to hide a body or anything," Stephen offers.

Mr. Hamish looks at Stephen wearily, then back to me. He points at me and squints his blue-gray eyes, accusing without words. "Lucky for you, the misses is coming up to see me. So, I tell you what. If you go over to that uh…fru fru, coffee place across the square and get me a black coffee and one of them, um…chai teas for my wife, you can leave as soon as you get back."

I nod. "Where's the money?"

"In your pocket, I suspect," Mr. Hamish says, opening a newspaper.

I shake my head, turning to Stephen and Rich. Rich looks like he's about to fall down. I frown. "Hey, I'm heading over to…"

"We have ears," Rich snaps. "S'okay, I got something to do tonight anyway."

"Cool, I'll come with," Stephen says instantly.

"No, you won't," Rich growls and slips out of the store.

Stephen looks at me. "Do you need a ride?" Stephen asks then looks past me over to Mr. Hamish. "Over to Evan's?"

I shake my head. "Nah, I left the paint in my locker. Plus, I finally managed to get away from my cousins long enough to come to work so…" The door chimes, telling me that my current statement is now moot. "Hey, Kai and Sora," I say, hoping that I sound as frustrated as I feel.

"Hey guys," Stephen says, slipping past them and out the door.

"S'up?" Kai chirps and takes a stick of beef jerky from the rack. "Mr. H, Alex will pay for this." Mr. Hamish doesn't even bother looking to see what Kai is holding. He continues reading his newspaper. With that, Kai tears into it and takes a bite.

"Where are you going?" Sora says with that familiar mom-tone. "And why didn't you wait for us to give you a ride to work?"

"Because I'm not a little kid and I've been doing this for two years without you two." Kai stops eating long enough to steal a glance at me. He clears his throat, then continues chewing. Sora looks at him. He tips his head to me and his eyes bulge. She shakes her head subtly. "And why is everything a big secret with you guys?" Sora swallows deeply.

"You know what? Don't bother," I bark. I walk over to the entrance. "And before you ask, I'm just going to get Mr. Hamish some coffee…right across the square." I storm out and I'm across the sidewalk and the street before I even realize it. I stop. Why do I get so angry whenever I'm around Sora and Kai? I have to remind myself that they're not responsible for the way the rest of our family treated my mom and me. On top of that, they're mourning their dad too. I take a deep breath. Still doesn't explain the separation anxiety they seem to get with me.

I look up at the sign across the next street. "Right, coffee and a...chai tea." I shove my hands into my pockets, hoping I have enough to cover it. I step off the curb when I reach the wadded up five and change that I got earlier today. "Gotta spend money to make money, I guess."

Chapter 11: Shocking

"I will master you, you stupid espresso maker. You've made a fool of me for the last time!" I smack it with the hand towel that Em gave me to wipe down the counter…before she threw up her hands and went to the back…after I ruined another cup of espresso…okay, my fourth espresso. I practically growl at this insufferable machine with the odd word "Simonelli" staring back at me.

The door chime sounds. "Welcome to Jelly Bean Coffee," I sing the way that Em instructed. I turn to… "Alex," I gasp.

He tips his head back to acknowledge me. "Hey. Um, a coffee…black and a chai tea," he mumbles just above whispering.

I absently type on the cash register…and $4.57 appears on the display. I arch my eyebrows, confused by this outcome. "Um, does four-fifty-seven sound right?"

Alex shrugs. "I dunno. I don't really drink coffee. This is for my boss and his wife." He offers me six dollars. "Keep the change." I quickly enter 'cash' and '$5.00' on the register. It chimes, then the drawer pops out, startling me. I place the bill inside and collect the appropriate change. I drop the dollar and forty-three cents into the tip jar.

"You're Alex, right?"

He nods. "Yeah…especially since, you just called me by name like two seconds ago." I nod, feeling a little foolish. "Sorry about that. I'm pissed at somebody else…sorry." I nod again feeling less foolish. He points at me. "And you're Gwendolyn 'call me, Gwen' Frost," he recites my introduction from class on Thursday. "You offered to tutor me. We have English together."

"And Biology," I add. His expression becomes perplexed. "I was late to class on Thursday, so I missed roll, but the teacher called your name on Friday and today." He nods again. "She doesn't seem to like you very much."

"Well, you know," he plays off. "Mutual feelings and whatnot." I giggle. Why am I giggling? That wasn't funny, but here I am laughing at it. Okay, stop laughing. You look like an idiot, Gwen. Oh no, he's staring at me as if I'm a freak. Quick, change the subject.

"Hey, the offer still stands if you…changed your mind about me tutoring you." He purses his lips. Uh oh, I offended him. "Not that you need help or that I think you need help or that…"

"Yeah, Mrs. Bustamante has kinda had it out for me since…she, um…found out who my dad was."

Ugh. His heart sank so much that I felt it even though I wasn't trying to. I inhale deeply. He's not lying either. "Oh," is all I manage.

He sighs. "Um, can I get that coffee…and the tea?"

"Oh right…coffee…let me see." I take two cups from the rack under the counter and turn to the espresso maker.

"Hey," Alex says, drawing my attention. "Just three things…" He holds up the appropriate number of fingers. He takes a small packet from the display by the register. "I think all I need is one of these and some hot water for the tea." He points. "You're at the espresso machine and the coffee pots are…" He turns slightly left.

"…over there. And…" He points at the mugs in my hands. "…since they're not here, I'm pretty sure the coffee and the tea need to be 'to go.'"

"Right." I nod.

"Let me guess, you're new here."

"First day actually," I say with my eyebrows arched.

"You'll get it," he says.

I replace the mugs and subtly sniff. He's not lying. He believes that. "You're so sweet."

"Nah, it's just…from everything I know about you and the way you always seem to have the right answer in class…" He pauses. I continue staring at his adorable expression as he thinks of what to say next. "…and you're smart and you pick up on things easy and…why are you looking at me like that?"

"Like what?" I turn away quickly. Too quickly, I catch my reflection next to the "Simonelli" sign on the espresso maker. A red fox face with glowing green eyes stares back at me. I jump back, bumping into the counter. Alex's hand catches me at the shoulder blade.

"You okay?" he asks as a spark comes from his hand. I jolt away from the electric pulse between us. He jerks away, too. "What the hell?" I turn and he's staring at his palm. He looks at me then at his palm again. "Okay, something weird happens to me every time you're around."

I cover my mouth with both hands. "No…I…"

He backs away. "You know what? I'll go to the place down the street. Keep the money." He moves toward the exit.

"Alex, wait…"

"Oh, and tell your brother to stay away from me, too."

"My-my brother…? You know, Gavin?"

"Yeah, he came into the store where I work and threatened me."

"Wait, wait, wait," I say in a fluster and rush around the counter. "You met Gavin? When? How? Why?"

Alex takes two more steps backward. "He asked me all of these weird questions and then he broke this stick thing in my face and…and…it felt like he was choking me."

"HE DID WHAT?" I bark. Apparently, I spoke a little too loud, because Em rushes out of the back. I turn to her. "I'm fine. I'm fine." She nods then returns.

The door chime sounds. I turn just in time to see the door closing behind Alex. I shuffle my feet uneasily and wring my hands. Why did Gavin harass Alex? What was that spark I just felt from him? Why do I keep thinking about how cute he looked in that black hoodie that he was wearing?

#####

What the crap was that? I look back at Jelly Bean Coffee. I check my palm again. It's not bad enough I see things around her, now I feel things too. I sigh. My hand clenches into a fist on its own and shakes…no, it's trembling. "Why does she have to be so damn cute?"

"Who?" Kai asks.

I jump. "Stop doing that!"

60

His eyes lazily half close. He runs his fingers through his hair. He tilts his head back and looks at me. "Sorry." Wait...Kai...just apologized to me. Kai never apologizes to anybody about anything. He opens one eye wider than the other. "Before you get all up on yourself, Sora made me say that. She wanted me to apologize for her too. She understands why you've been so upset with us. We show up, follow you around, and don't explain anything." I cross my arms. "If anything, it's that we 'can't' tell you anything, not that we don't want to."

"Tell me anything about what? And why isn't she here telling me this herself?"

"Some old lady came into the store, gave us the stink eye and Sora went to follow her."

"Follow her? What for...?"

He runs his fingers through his hair again. "Don't worry about it." I walk away. "Hey, where're you going?"

"Away from you." I continue walking and he catches my shoulder. How did...? He caught up to me quick and I didn't even hear him take a step. "What the h...?"

"Sorry, cos." He pulls me back. "Can't let you do that...Sora's orders."

"Your sister might be your boss, but she's not mine." I shrug out from under his hand. "Besides I told my boss that I was going to get him some coffee and that's where I'm going."

He motions to Jelly Bean Coffee. "What's wrong with that place?"

I walk away. "None of your business." I look over my shoulder. He's not following me. He's staring down the street...probably at Jelly Bean. I sigh. Luckily, the Jumpin' Bean is right off the square. I can't help but wonder if the owners of both know how annoying and stupid their coffee shops' names are.

I check to see if Kai's following me again. He isn't, but he's not on the corner anymore either. I shrug and walk in. No way is anybody confusing Jelly Bean with Jumpin'. This place is decked out more like a chain-restaurant. It's all sterile and uniform. Hate to admit it, but I like Jelly Bean better. I walk over to the counter and place the same order with the team of employees behind the counter. Less than a minute later, the boring looking tall guy with the butt-chin behind the counter calls my name.

I collect the drinks after dropping some loose change into the jar. All of them tell me goodnight on my way out. They probably all said hello on the way in, but I wasn't paying attention.

I make my way back to Hamish's store with only one glance in the direction of Jelly Bean. I back into the front door and Mrs. Hamish meets me. "Alex how are you doing, dear?" she asks with arched brownish-gray eyebrows. She cut her hair shorter than I remember, but it's more of a modern style compared to what she used to wear.

I offer her the tea. "I'm alright, ma'am." She nods and takes her drink. She sips it and smiles. I like Mrs. H. She's a lot friendlier than Mr. Hamish and she always says nice things about my mom and me.

"Is something wrong dear?"

I shake my head. "No, I just...have to get going." I pass her the coffee. "Would you give this to Mr. H and let him know I took off?"

"Of course, dear." I turn. "Wait. Before you go...your..." She thinks for a moment. "...cousin, yes, that's what he said he was. He said he'd be right back. He went to get something more substantial to eat, whatever that means."

I nod. Great, this is my chance. I rush out the door. I grab my bike at the curb and work the combination faster than I ever have. I take my new chain off and shove it deep into my hoodie pocket. I pull the bike away from the parking meter and look up...

Gwen's staring off into space. What is she looking at? Why is she looking at me now? What's wrong with her? I shake my head and climb onto my bike. Can't think about that now, I have to get to the school. I'll barely have time to do the tag before Goth-boy and his parents get back.

I pedal as hard as I can, thinking back to the morning I was racing to do Rex's tag. I really work hard just to throw some paint around. I reach the school in no time. Maybe if I used this same determination, I'd make it to first period. "Pfft, yeah right."

I pull into the parking lot and there are still a few cars here...with student parking decals. What are they still doing here? Doesn't matter, but if parts of the school are still open, it'll make it easier for me to get to my locker.

I drop my bike next to the rack and run toward the side entrance. I check for any sign of the night security guard and thankfully, that big jerk is nowhere to be found. He ripped my other hoodie the last time he caught me sneaking around *after hours*.

I pull on the door, not expecting much...it opens. Nice. I run down the hall. If I could do this EVERYDAY, I might actually like coming to school. I reach my locker and turn the combination quickly. I pull out my backpack and check to make sure the paint's still inside. Got it and the sketch. I slam my locker door.

Then I hear it. Something that sounds like nails on a chalkboard around the corner. I frown. I take a step forward and stop. The sound gets louder and closer. "Screw that," I mutter. "I've seen WAY too many horror movies to 'check on a noise.'" I see a large shadow at the corner. "Crap." I freeze...and almost do what I just said.

The shadow gets larger and larger and just when I think I should see what's making it...I see more shadow. More shadow...with two glowing red eyes... "Double crap." The large red-eyed shadow sniffs then turns toward me. It looks like a bear and a bulldog got together to make a large pile of black paint. It takes two more steps out and it's even bigger than I thought it was. It growls and shows the faintest hint of stained white teeth. I take a step back and it takes two forward. "Screw this." I turn and run like my life depends on it...because I don't doubt that it does.

The shadow growls some more, then releases a sound that reminds me of a really bad car accident before I hear four paws pound the floor. I look back and yeah, it's following at a sprint. I push my legs harder. I turn a corner and lose traction, fall and slide into a row of lockers. I scramble to my feet and keep running. The shadow takes the corner, hits the same lockers but doesn't even slow down.

My knee throbs, slowing me down even more than my lack of air. Before I know it, it gives out and I fall again...hard. I manage to get my hands out, breaking my fall. I try to recover, but before I can...I feel hot breath on the back of my neck. Seven hundred bucks is so not worth this...

62

Chapter 12: Corridor

I step outside and peer back in. "Goodnight, Em." Em waves at me from the register. She smiles although she MUST be exhausted from cleaning up my various messes. She's already probably up for sainthood for managing to put up with me and not screaming. I step away from the door and take a deep breath. At least, I made it through my first day.

"How was your first day?" Gavin asks. I sigh and turn to him. "Did you make a lot in tips?"

"Go away. On second thought, I'll go away." I walk down the sidewalk. Gavin follows. He does know how to push all my buttons. I turn to him. He halts. "What did you do to Alex?"

"Who?"

"Alex."

"You're going to have to be a little more specific. All humans kinda look alike to me."

"The one who I asked you to look at with fox magic. The one who you used one of obāsan's twigs on."

"Oh, him." He seems amused. "If you know what I did, then why are you asking?"

"Why did you do it? You said that you didn't see anything when you looked at him."

"No, I asked, 'what about him?' It's completely different." I gnash my teeth, trying to stop my fangs from showing…not to mention stop myself from bursting into flames. "What? Is Gwenie upset because I lied without lying?"

I try to bring down my emotions. "So, you did see something?" He shrugs. "Don't do that," I whine and hit him with an open hand. He laughs. "Did you see something or not?"

Gavin bobs his head unevenly and purses of his lips. "Something." I sniff. He's telling the truth. I arch my eyebrows, waiting on elaboration. "It's…nothing to worry about, but he…" He thinks on how to say it.

"…has a little spark of silver?" Gavin touches the tip of his nose. "I knew it!"

"Yeah, yeah, but do you know what that means?" I shake my head slowly. "Since it's only a spark and not a flame, he's descended from a supernatural bloodline, but anything he would've gotten from that bloodline is…lost." I sigh wondering if that causes him the pain that I sense constantly. "What are you thinking about, little Gwenie?"

"Nothing. I…you still shouldn't have done it. For all you know, he doesn't know anything about his bloodline."

"Well, who's he gonna tell? I mean, odds are if he's descended from a powerful enough bloodline to leave a spark on him, then his family just hasn't told him about their bloodline." I nod, finding no faults in his reasoning. "Besides, he answered all my questions truthfully so, he's not a threat." I nod again while placing my hand over my heart. For some reason, I'm relieved that Gavin's focus is moving away from Alex.

"What about the vampire?"

"I watched her movements today. It turns out she has a steady supply of blood." I frown. "Her 'husband' lets her feed from him every few days…I was lucky enough to catch them on one of those days."

"How? What did you do?"

"Calm down. I'm not a pervert. I just stood in front of their house." His expression becomes distant. "I think she knew I was there, so she did it right there, in their front window for me to see."

"How do you know she wasn't using one of her vampire mind tricks on him?"

"I didn't sense any magic from her and no fear from him." Gavin shrugs. "So, I'm satisfied." I cross my arms and nod. "BTW," he spells out, "I didn't come all this way just to give you a supernatural status report." Gavin's sense of superiority swells.

"Then why did you come?" I ask with a taut spine and a defensive glare.

"Obāsan, called me."

"Obāsan used a phone?"

Gavin holds his closed fist up. He opens it, revealing the remains of a burned leaf. "Of course not." His mouth turns down at the corners again. "She wants me to go and check on an old friend of hers who lives nearby."

"And you haven't left yet?"

"Funny."

"How old?"

"As old as Obāsan old."

"But if she's as old as Obāsan, she should be stronger than you."

Gavin wags a finger in my face. "Uh-uh. See this particular fox spirit is like us. Half-human and spirit…but like you…" He points that formerly wagging finger. "…she decided to live the life of a human. So, her spirit magic got weaker and weaker until it was practically non-existent."

I know he's only saying this because he hopes it'll make me change my mind about the way I want to live my life, but it won't. If anything, the thought of living a normal…human life just became more plausible.

"Long and short of it is, little Gwenie, I won't be able to watch your back for a couple of days."

"Days? I thought you said she lives close by."

Gavin sighs. "She does. As long as you consider the mountain-y hills of Georgia close by." I nod with a silent 'oh.' "It'll take me a few hours to get closer to where her house is by car and from there it's like a day's trek up the mountain."

"Trek?"

"Shut up. Plus, she apparently has several incantations and charms that ward off supernatural beings, so it'll take me a while to work my way through those."

I can't believe I'm going to say this, but… "Be careful." He stares at me for a moment, confused by the statement. "What? You ARE my brother. At least until I can find a way to disprove that." He smiles and musses the top of my hair. "HEY," I shout moving his hand away.

"Later," he whispers. One swift paw later and he's gone. I don't even sense him anymore. He's able to move so far with one push.

I bow my head. "I'd miss that if I were to lose my fox magic." I lift my head and glance across the square. "Alex?" I gasp. He's staring at me with a scowl. I peer in the direction that Gavin left. Did he see?

Be cool, Gwen. Be cool. Right. That's like asking…well, a being that catches on fire to be cool. I wave at Alex. He readies his bike and turns away. My heart sinks. Did he see, or does he still just think I'm a freak? I groan and turn to walk down the sidewalk as he climbs on his bike and pedals away. Why does he have to be so cute?

I wait for him to round the corner while checking the rest of the square. I really hope he didn't see Gavin use swift paw. He's seen more than enough already.

I inhale deeply, just before I feel the electric current of the wind swirling around me. I let the fox magic flow from my core to my legs. I open my fluorescent green eyes and in almost an instant, I'm at the school's parking lot. I sigh. I really would miss this if my fox magic went away.

I take out my cell and call Meghan. "Hello, loser," she sings.

"Hey, where are you guys?"

"In the gym, d'uh."

"No, I mean, how do I get there? The school looks like it's all locked up."

"The main entrance is open and all the hallways that lead to the gym are open, too. Now, hurry up, loser." I end the call. I climb the steps at the main entrance and follow her instructions.

"You made it," she chirps as soon as I enter the gym. I wave sheepishly at her and her followers as I move toward the center of the gym and her golden tresses. Meghan stands from the massive banner that she was painting and puts one arm around me. "I hate these idiots so much, right now," she whispers. "You have no idea."

She releases me and turns back to the idiots with a massive smile. "Grab a brush, pick a decoration, and get to work." I look at a group of girls painting a large pink…something or other. I take a step toward them and stop when they all look at me in disgust. Awesome, it's another group of Meghan's loyal, albeit clingy and overly protective disciples. "Come over here, loser," Meghan calls, having witnessed the non-verbal exchange. "You can help me with this."

I go over to Meghan and she offers me a brush, handle first. I reach for the brush…wait…what is that? I feel something. Something is wrong. The air wafting in from the hallway seems sour. On top of that, I'm getting that weird leery feeling I've been feeling since my first day of school, but for once, not directed at me. I stretch out with my emotions and sift through the jealousy, the bitterness, the whining and complaining and I feel…fear…honest, deep, petrifying fear.

"Um," I begin with my trembling hand still dangling near Meghan's brush. "I have to…to go. I mean, I'll be right back." Meghan looks at me like a Martian as I back away. I rush out of the gym amid whispers and even a few giggles. As soon as I'm out of sight, I use swift paw and push all my senses to their max with my fox magic to zero in on the source of the fear. I round one last corner…what is that?

It looks like a massive shadow-based familiar is about to bite…ALEX? It's attacking Alex! Somehow, I get an extra push from my swift paw and I intercept the familiar just before its teeth make contact. I kick it in the center of its head and it stumbles back before losing its footing and sliding across the waxed floor.

"What the hell?" Alex pants as I land between him and the creature. I offer him my hand to help him stand. "Gwen? Your eyes...?" I turn away from him instantly, hoping that my eyes will stop glowing. "What are you doing here? What is that thing? Why are your eyes glowing?" he asks all at once.

"Calm down." I try to keep my voice even. "I don't think it's down yet." The familiar bears down on us. "Stay back. I'll take care of it." I leap over its head and it snaps at me. I land on my feet and spin with a heel kick to his hind leg, but my foot connects with teeth instead. How did it turn so fast?

This time, my kick had no effect at all. I dart to the right using swift paw, spring off the lockers and try to kick it again. This time not only is it ready for me, but it swings its massive paw, bringing me down...hard. I groan as my shoulder comes down on the linoleum. It places its massive paw on the center of my chest...so heavy.

"Gwen!"

"Run, Alex!" I scream as best I can from under its paw. "Get away from it." He doesn't listen. He pulls something out of his pocket...it dangles beyond his hand with a strange round knot at the end. He swings the object around, then brings it down across the familiar's head. It doesn't react. It seems solely focused on me now. It leans in close and sniffs at my neck. "Argh!"

"Gwen! Get off her!" He hits the familiar again, this time much harder...hard enough to get its attention. The familiar looks at Alex and growls, baring its teeth. Alex stands his ground and prepares to hit the creature again.

"Get down," comes from behind Alex. He turns just in time to see two...tiger people...leap over his head. One appears to be a girl who resembles a white tiger and the other is a boy who appears to be a Bengal tiger. "We'll handle this thing," the girl says calmly. "Grab the girl and get out of here, Alex."

"Sora...?" Alex asks, staring at the tiger people, swatting at the creature.

"Just go!" the boy snaps and makes his way onto its back. He buries his claws deep, causing it to rear up and roar. Alex grabs my arm. He pulls me out from under the familiar before it strikes again. He helps me to my feet.

"Thank you," I whisper. We move down the hall. I walk. He limps. "Here. Lean on me." I put my arm around his waist and he drapes his over my shoulders. I hiss between clenched teeth as his hand makes contact with my bruised shoulder. "We have to get to the gym."

"What? Why?"

"The decorating committee's there. This thing could get away from..." I trail off sensing a massive burst of power behind us. "It's coming." Alex and I hurry into the...empty gym. "Where is everybody...?"

"You're asking me?" Alex complains. I sense the beast seeking us out. I pull Alex across the gym floor. "There's no way we'll out run it with my busted up knee."

I nod. "We'll hide...and if it comes to it, I'll fight it while you try to get away." We reach the bleachers' edge and Alex maneuvers underneath. I try to step away, but he has my hand.

"No way! Neither one of us did much good against that thing. If we fight it, we'll fight it together." I nod, and he pulls me under the bleachers with him. We move back into shadows. "What is that thing?"

"I don't know."

Alex sneezes instantly. He lifts his head again. I feel his eyes searching me. He knows I'm lying. "I'm allergic to bull," he whispers. "So, please don't make my allergies act up." His eyes fill with allegations and fear.

I swallow a guilty lump and nod. "If...no, when we get away from this thing, I'll tell you everything, Alex."

He nods this time, never breaking eye contact. His hand rubs against mine subtly. He collects my hand and I feel the spark that passed between us earlier...but it's different this time. When I bumped into him at the Bean, it was a painful shock. In the hall, when he helped me up, it was there, but there was no pain and now... I hear a loud huff above us. How did the creature get so close without me realizing?

The bleachers groan and quake. It's out there...sniffing around. I put one finger to my mouth and look at Alex. He nods. Small bits of light make their way through the bleachers. A large area of the stands goes dark and the seats bow downward. The large area moves closer and closer. The sniffs and pants intensify.

"I'll protect you," I whisper and amazingly, Alex says it at the same time. We look at one another then return to the darkness just above our heads. The creature stops sniffing and growls. It sets its four appendages, preparing to attack. A loud whistle comes from the gym entrance. The creature heeds this call. It scampers down the bleachers and suddenly all traces of its presence vanish.

I breathe a sigh of relief. Alex looks at me. "It's gone."

"Are you sure?" I nod. We climb out from the stands and look around. "What was that thing?"

"I'll tell you later. First, let's get you out of here so someone can look at your knee."

"I'm fine." I tap his knee. He groans and nearly falls over. I catch him and look into his pain-filled eyes. He stares back into mine. "Maybe a little less than fine."

I drape his arm over my shoulders. "Come on." We stumble to the school's main entrance. "Who were those tiger people?" Alex looks at me with a confused, but stern expression. "I thought I heard you call one of them, 'Sora.'"

"If you don't have to answer my questions, I'm not gonna answer yours."

"Fair enough." I look down the entrance's thirty or so stairs. There may as well be one hundred and thirty given the state of his knee. To his credit, Alex doesn't complain once as we make our way down. He does groan a few times though. "Now, how am I going to get you home?" I hope he has a suggestion. He shrugs.

A horn blares to our right. Headlights flash on, temporarily blinding us. We both put a hand up to block the glare. The sound of a smooth engine rev resonates and a metallic blue BMW parks in front of us. "What happened to you, loser?" Meghan says from behind the wheel.

"Nothing," I lie. Alex turns to me. I hope my expression conveys that I want to keep this from Meghan.

"I…" he begins with a dry voice. "…broke into the school to get something out of my locker. I fell…and banged my knee…" I nod along with his story that is probably coming across more convincingly than anything I could come up. "…Gwen found me and helped me outside."

"You're a little juvenile delinquent, aren't you?" Meghan says. "Get in, loser. I'll give you a ride home."

"What about Alex?" I say in a half-panic. Meghan glares at me. "I mean, we can't just leave him like this."

She releases an exasperated sigh. "Get in." She tips her head toward the backseat.

"What about my bike?" Alex asks apprehensively. She makes a swirling motion with her hand that I can only suppose means 'come on.' I help Alex to the passenger side and help him into the front seat.

"Uh-uh," Meghan spits. "Backseat." Alex pushes the front seat forward and falls into the back with a groan. He drags himself upright. I sit and pull the car door closed. Meghan pulls up to the bike rack.

Alex tries to lift himself. "I'll get," I say. He shakes his head and continues to pull himself by my seat. I smack his hand. He looks at me with almost as much shock as Meghan does. "I said I'll get it." He stares at me, then slumps back into the seat. I climb out and go over to his bike. I lift it easily…and thankfully without fox magic.

"My trunk's not big enough, loser," Meghan says. "So, you'll have to put it in the backseat…with him." I nod. "And please don't scratch my paint or the leather, loser," she adds, although, that time her nickname for me sounded a lot less friendly and playful. I return to my seat and we are on our way. I catch Alex's eyes in the rearview mirror. I have a lot of explaining to do.

Chapter 13: Cousins

The wind slaps me repeatedly over the front seat. It comes free with an occasional aggravated glare…under wavy blond hair. I'm not alone. She does the same to Gwen. Neither of them has said a word the entire way home. In fact, if not for the turn-by-turn GPS, there would only be silence, the wind, and the purr of her engine.

We turn into the apartment complex's parking lot. "Here?" Meghan asks, not even trying to hide her disgust. "People actually live here?"

"Yes," I reply not trying to hide my frustration either. "I live here with my mom." She pulls up to our building. Gwen pushes her door open and lifts the seat. "Thanks." I put weight on my banged-up knee. She tries to smile…but it just looks awkward. She reaches for my bike. "I'll get it."

"No," she says. "You're hurt."

"Yeah, hurt from breaking into the school," Meghan says.

"Meghan," Gwen snaps. "He IS hurt. Be nice." Meghan rolls her eyes and looks around tensely.

"I'm fine." Gwen bends down like she did in the gym and I move my hands to block her hit. "Okay, okay, just help me get it out the back." She nods and walks to the other side of the car. She lifts it easily and I can't help staring at her to make sure that her eyes don't glow. She puts the bike down with a pant then pushes it around to me.

"Thanks," I repeat and try to take it from her. She resists. "I got it."

"No, I'm gonna help you get to your door."

"I got it," I repeat trying to sound tough.

"I still think we should take you to the hospital…so letting me carry your bike to your door is a compromise…and an uneven one at that." I sigh. Gwen is used to getting her way. I nod, run my hand over my hair, and turn toward the building. Gwen follows, pushing my bike.

"I'll be right here," Meghan says softly. "With the engine running," she whispers. "Hand on my pepper spray."

"Which apartment is it?" Gwen asks.

"722," I answer and grab the rail to make my way up.

"22? That means it's on the second floor, right?" I nod. "And how were you going to get up the stairs carrying a bike on that knee?"

"How exactly did you jump over the head of a weird shadow bear with glowing green eyes?" She doesn't answer. Her head sinks. She follows me to my door. "Well?" I ask as she passes my bike.

"It's complicated." She lifts her eyes to meet mine.

"Like my dad used to say, 'Always is.'"

She nods. "Tomorrow," she says. "I'll tell you everything and answer any questions you have…tomorrow." She peers into my eyes, hoping to gauge my response. "I promise." She saw the skepticism.

"Okay."

"I'll see you in school," she says while backing away. I tip my head to her. She waves, turns and runs down the stairs. I fish my key out of my pocket. Before I can put it in the lock, the door opens. Kai stands in the open doorway, looking like he just woke up…as usual.

"Hey, cousin." He sounds like he just woke up too. I wheel my bike inside, using it as a mobile crutch.

"Don't be a jerk," Sora says from behind him. "Help him with the bike. You know he hurt his knee." Kai shrugs and takes the bike, then pushes the door closed with his foot. Sora walks over and leans so that I can put my arm around her shoulders. I do and she helps me to the couch. I sit and she takes a seat on the coffee table. "Here." She puts an ice pack on my knee.

"You were waiting for me?" She nods. "So, that really was you at the school? I mean since you know I hurt my knee?" She nods again as she holds the ice pack in place. "How the…? What the…? You were…?"

"Shhhhh," Sora says before removing the ice pack and putting it on the table next to her. "Your mom's here…but she's knocked out."

"Did you…?"

"Of course not," Kai whines before sitting next to me. He passes Sora a small round tin. "She means, your mom had a long day at work and she's sleeping really hard." I nod. Sora opens the tin and they both lean away from it before the lid is fully off.

"What's that…ugh…," I break off. I cover my nose with my hand, not that it does any good. "That smells…soooooooo bad. It smells like hot garbage mixed with fertilizer and a rotting fish."

"Imagine how it smells to us," Sora says calmly before putting her pointer and middle fingers into the slimy, pale green goop. "Roll up your pant leg."

"Why?"

"Just do it!" Sora commands without losing her composed veneer.

"No."

"Dude," Kai interjects. "Two ways of doing it…her way, which is asking you to do it or my way, which is letting you limp around school tomorrow." I look at him with a confused expression. "What? You thought I was gonna say 'or we make you do it?'" I nod. "Oh, that's implied in her way. She's just asking out of courtesy, you being our cousin and all, but it'd be a lot more fun to watch you struggle." Kai laughs, causing Sora to glare at him.

"This'll help," Sora says in that quiet, explainy way. I sigh and roll up my pant leg until it's over my black and purple swollen knee. She applies a lot…probably too much…of the stinky goop, that feels even more slimy than it looks. "Now, rub that in." She replaces the top.

I do what she told me. "What is this stuff?"

"Some herbs, a little seaweed and some other stuff that grandma put together for us," Sora says and places the tin on the table next to the ice pack. I hate to admit it, but my knee is already starting to feel better. Sora looks up from my knee and into my eyes. "That should be good." Without looking, she drapes a damp wrap over my knee and replaces the ice pack. "You have questions, right?" I nod. "Okay…shoot."

"What was that thing? How did you do what you did? Did you guys really have fur? How did Gwen do what she did? What was that thing? Wait, I already asked that

70

one. Why was it after me?" Sora reaches out and smacks me in the face. "What was that for?" She rears back like she's going to hit me again. "Okay, okay," I say and put my hands up, palms out, to defend myself. Girls are all about torturing me tonight.

Kai erupts with laughter. "First of all," Sora starts, still eerily in control. "I don't know what that thing was. I've never fought anything like it." I look at Kai. He shakes his head, agreeing with her. "We were beating it and then it just sank into the floor and disappeared."

"How could something that big get away from you?"

"Hello?" Kai moans. "What part of 'sank into the floor and disappeared' seems like it would be easy to follow?"

"I don't know? Maybe it's the part where my cousins are freaky tiger people?"

Sora sighs and leans away from me. "We're not 'tiger people.' We're…skinwalkers."

"Skinwalkers…?"

"Yeah," Kai adds. "Think werewolves only much, much cooler."

"What?"

"We're nothing like werewolves," Sora says with an aggravated, disgusted tone. She pulls a small square of fur out of her pocket. She holds it out in front of me. It's a little square of white fur with a patch of black in opposite corners. "Skinwalkers are like humans…but not exactly." I frown. "We are advanced humans. We can take on the characteristics of our totem animal." My left eyebrow arches almost by itself. "Think of it as our 'soul creature' or a reflection of our inner selves."

"What?"

"You say that a lot," Sora says.

"Just show him," Kai complains.

Sora nods. She wraps her fingers around the fur and closes her eyes. Her eyes snap open…her pale blue cat eyes. I jump.

"You're okay," Kai reassures.

I turn back to Sora, covered in a thin layer of white fur with black stripes. Her fingernails turn black and become really long and sharp. She smiles, showing off her mouthful of sharp, pointy teeth. Her formerly blond hair has become white with streaks of black. Her nose darkens to a soft pink color. She stretches, which I guess signifies the end of her transformation.

"See," she says in a voice a few octaves lower than her normal one. I shake my head, still not quite ready to use actual words. "My totem animal is a white tiger so…" She motions to herself.

I look at Kai. He points his thumb at his smug grin. "Golden Tabby," he says, as if that doesn't sound stupid. I almost laugh, which is better than being scared out of my mind…I guess. "Wanna see?" Kai leans closer. I shake my head.

"Stop it, Kai," Sora snaps. He leans back. Sora shakes her head and slowly her normal color returns to her hair and the fur recedes back into her skin. She closes her eyes and then opens them to reveal her normal hazel-colored eyes. "We're skinwalkers, Alex, because our dad was a skinwalker. Just like…your dad. Our dads were skinwalkers."

"Our?" I finally manage a word, yay. She nods.

"Our dad's totem animal was a Bengal tiger," Kai says. "Yours was…well, grandma and our dad never told us what your dad's was."

I can't take anymore. This is crazy. I run both fingers through my hair. I want to stick my fingers in my ear and scream, 'la, la, la, la, la' and try to pretend that I don't hear any of it. I have to settle for getting out of here. I bolt out of my seat and make a break for the door. Sora appears in front of me. I almost fall trying to stop myself. I look back to where she was sitting before turning back to her. "How did you…?"

"Skinwalker trick," she says, still relaxed. "It's called 'hunter's step'. We focus our strength into our legs and move really fast."

Kai appears behind me. "Wh-what are you guys gonna do with me?" Kai snickers. I don't even bother looking at him, since for as long as I've known them, Sora's been the one in charge.

"Nothing," Sora says. "You're our cousin. The only reason we haven't told you sooner is because…" She stops and looks at Kai. I do the same. He looks down at the floor and shoves his hands into his pockets. "…because grandma doesn't think you…have the gift." I frown.

"What's all this fuss?" my mom moans from her bedroom door. She looks exhausted…like she shouldn't be awake right now. "Are the three of you going out?" I step around Kai and shake my head. "Good. It's a school night and you're not going to be skipping anymore classes are you, Alex?"

"No, ma'am,"

"Good. You all have a big day tomorrow," she says, motioning to us. "So, get to bed." She steps back into her room and closes her door. "I love you," she says as if she's already climbing onto her bed.

"I love you, too." Wait…what did she mean by 'you all'?

Deep breaths, Gwen, just take deep breaths. I walk into the school. I slip my phone out of my pocket and examine it carefully. Gavin hasn't called back. I guess he doesn't have a signal in the North Georgia Mountains. It wouldn't hurt to leave him one more message. I put the phone up to my ear. It goes straight to voicemail…again.

"Gavin, it's me again. I've left you like 12 messages already…but I need you to get back here as soon as possible." I pause. "It's Gwen…in case you didn't know." I hate to admit it but even if not for the shadow bear-dog-thing, I'd actually still want him here…to help me explain everything to Alex. I sigh. Alex is going to have so many questions and what if he tells someone, what I am. Wait, he doesn't know what I am yet. If I tell him, he might tell someone and…

"Hey, loser," Meghan calls with that same snarl from last night. I put my phone away. "Who was that? Your loser boyfriend maybe…?"

"He's not my boyfriend," I whine. "He's just a friend…I guess…I mean, I don't really know…he's the guy from my seventh period…"

"Wait," she cuts me off, still sounding annoyed. "Alex Garner is the guy you've been mooning over for the last few days?"

"Mooning?" I laugh.

"Shut up," Meghan whines. "I heard my mom say it once."

72

"I thought it sounded cool," says a girl from Meghan's entourage…that I wasn't aware surrounded us.

"Me too," another adds.

"I'm gonna start using it," a third girl piles on.

"Ha," Meghan barks. "The tribe has spoken."

"The lemmings, you mean," I say just low enough for Meghan to hear. She snickers. "I have to get to class. I'm running late…because someone was in a mood and didn't give me a ride to school this morning."

Meghan smirks with a nod. She puts her arm around my shoulders and turns us in the direction of my locker. "Consider 'the mood' over…" She smiles in that frighteningly genuine way of hers. "I mean, you can't help who you like, right?"

"Right…wait, I mean…no, I don't like him," I emit and follow up with nervous laughter. Why am I laughing nervously?

"Ooooooooooof course, you don't." Meghan winks, which has less subtly than an actual bull in an actual China shop on an actual rampage. I sigh. There's no convincing her. "Oh look," she sings. "There's your boyfriend now."

Alex approaches with a familiar looking blond-haired boy. I'm smiling. Am I smiling too big? Why am I smiling so big? He's too close now to stop smiling…so, I should probably go with it. I lift my hand and wave. Now, I'm waving, too. "Hey, Alex," I say, sounding more excited than I meant to.

"Hey," he says simply and continues on his way. My mood drops with my hand. I stop walking. Meghan already had. She turns me around to watch him walk away.

"What the hell was that?" she asks. "You guys seemed like you were one step away from him giving you his final rose and now he's acting like you're the weird stalker chick who got kicked off after the third ceremony."

I shrug, moving out from under her arm. "I don't even know what that means," I mumble. I walk away, but Meghan catches me and refuses to let go. "I have to get to class," I complain, still trying to pull away gently.

"You have time." I give up. She's not going to let me go. She turns to the lemmings. "Disperse," Meghan commands with a wave of her hand. They comply like the obedient little creatures that they are. She returns to me.

"What?" I moan, avoiding her gaze.

"Walk with me," she says and for the first time EVER, not sounding completely bored. She turns, walks down the hall and I follow. "Okay. I concede…Alex is sorta cute. I just wish he wasn't such a little thug and maybe that he wore something besides a hoodie every day. Also, it wouldn't kill him and Stephen to find someone to hang out with besides that perv Rich."

I frown. "I guess, if…"

"Not done yet," she cuts me off. "My point is this. If you like him, go for it. Don't do like I did and…"

Meghan stares at something, before shaking her head. I follow her line of sight. Stephen walks in through the side entrance with several football players. He sees Meghan and me and offers a wave. Meghan smiles for a fraction of a second and then her face goes expressionless.

"…and let your new found social status determine who you can and cannot date." Meghan turns back to me and resumes walking. "But I will pretend like I hate the idea of you two together if anybody asks." She continues around a corner. I watch her walk away, slightly deflated and then turn back to Stephen…he stops at the corner, peers after her then continues on his way.

"No way," I sigh then follow Meghan who seems to be heading for her locker.

#####

"Where's room 302?" Kai asks, leaning against the locker next to mine. I don't respond. "Okay," he whines. Still sounds like he just rolled out of bed. "Where's the Biology lab?" I still don't answer. I take the silver spray can from my bag and toss it into my locker. Dang it, I hope Goth-boy doesn't ask for his money back. "Okay, can you at least tell me where the 100 hall is? I'm sure I can figure out the rest if you…"

"It's so weird that you and Sora got into school here without a parent!"

"Well, you know how persuasive Sora can be." I glare at him as if he just grew a third eye. "What?"

"Persuasive? What kind of idiot do you take me for?"

He reaches past me and grabs the spray can. "The kind who has silver spray paint in his locker."

I snatch it from him, toss it inside, and slam the door. "You know what I mean."

"Ooooo, scary." I shove him at the shoulder. He doesn't budge; he laughs instead. "We told the school that we live with our grandmother out in Oregon…true…that we're moving out here to be closer to the rest of our family…" He points and mouths a 'you.' "…also, true. Grandma called and set it up with your mom. The school asked if your mom'd vouch for us and…"

I smack myself on the forehead. "My mom signed off on this?"

He laughs a "yeah. Okay, I have to get going…seriously, where is Biology with…" He reads his form. "…Mrs. Pritchard?"

I snatch the schedule away from him. "You're in my first period?"

"Sweet!" He takes it back. "I'll just follow your scent to class." He turns and rushes off.

"That's not creepy or gross at all. Where are you going?"

"I have to find my locker," he says, before disappearing at the corner.

I lean forward until my head bangs my locker. I pull back and ram it again…and again.

"What happened to you last night?" Stephen asks.

I sigh, shove my hands deep into my pockets…and bang my head one more time. Yeah, I should definitely tell him that some kind of mutant dog the size of a bear attacked me. Not to mention the fact that Gwen, who had glowing green eyes, saved my life and then my cousins, who are apparently some kind of weird tiger people, saved us both and go to school here now.

"Nothing, I must've crashed hard last night." His eyebrows arch even higher. "Sorry, man."

"Crashed? Dude, you said you were going by the school to get the paint and then I didn't hear from you." I look at Stephen, with my head still pressed against my locker. He looks worried. "I was worried about you." Bingo.

"Sorry, man, I didn't mean to make you…um…worry." I hope I don't sound as weirded out as I feel. "I mean, there wasn't really a reason to worry." Am I trying to convince him or me?

Stephen shoves me at the shoulder and glares at me. "Yeah, there was."

I frown. "Wh-what do you mean?"

Stephen starts to respond…

"WHAT THE HELL?" Meghan shrieks. Stephen and I run to the end of the hall. Meghan, Gwen, who is consoling Meghan, a couple of dozen other students, the principal and a couple of cops stare at Meghan's locker. We step farther out from the corner, so that we can see…Meghan's mangled locker.

Stephen stares at me. "This. This is why I was worried about you. Were you here when this happened?"

I shake my head, 'cause I don't think I'd be able to come right out and lie to him…Rich maybe, but not Stephen.

"Look at me," Stephen says, tearing me away from the three massive slashes on Meghan's locker and both lockers on either side of hers. My best guess…if I didn't know the truth…would've been that, someone took a chainsaw to it…three times…in a row…at the same angle…perfectly.

I glance at Stephen and then back to the crowd. Gwen's staring at me. I cut my eyes to the lockers. She nods, then rubs Meghan's shoulders.

"What happened here?" Stephen and I turn to find Rich, looking like he slept on his face…after someone punched him in it six or seven times. Dark, puffy circles under his eyes tell me he didn't get much sleep again. I wonder if his parents are still talking about getting a divorce…or more likely, yelling at each other about getting a divorce.

"Um," Stephen starts. "Something happened to Meghan's locker." Rich nods without even batting his eyes or a casual glance in that direction. He looks exhausted and even paler than usual. "I guess the police are here to figure out what went down."

"Yeah," I say drawing out the word. "Are you okay? I mean, you kind of look like crap…or crap that was beaten up by other crap and left in a field to die." He laughs…or at least, I guess that's what that noise was supposed to be.

Stephen and I exchange a glance. Rich looks like he could fall over any minute. "Yeah…nah, I'm good. Just, you know…stuff…" I tip my head back to acknowledge his reply not exactly knowing what he means by 'stuff.'

Stephen is a lot less convinced. "Dude, you've been M.I.A. on and off since Friday, you come to school looking like hell, and then you don't even react to seeing Meghan's locker shredded."

"Heh, maybe she deserved it," Rich says with an awkward smile.

"What?" Stephen replies. "She deserves…? Did you…?" Stephen looks around; making sure no one's close before coming back to Rich. He steps in closer. "Did you do that to her locker?" Stephen asks lowering his voice.

"Noooooooooo," Rich seems to fall asleep saying. "I…," he stretches out way too long and then pauses to snicker. "…didn't do it."

"Alright everybody," Principal Stanford says. His little plaid bowtie bounces up and down around his tiny neck. He raises his arms causing his green sweater vest to rise up just above where his bellybutton probably is. "The show's over," he continues.

75

"The bell's about to…" Before he can finish it actually does ring. "Get to class. Nothing more to see here."

Rich is gone already. Stephen seems just as lost as I am. "You don't really think he did it, do you?"

Stephen shrugs. "I don't know. He's been acting weird ever since…"

"…the incident?" Stephen nods.

"Excuse me, gentleman," Principal Stanford says from over my shoulder. "Can I help you with something? Like maybe…a couple of days detention for skipping class."

"Nope, I'm good," I return, walking toward Bio. Stephen follows with a shake of his head. Stephen and I make our way to class and…I sigh. Of course, I forgot Gwen's in my first period. She looks at me…and raises her hand to wave. I nod and walk into the room. Stephen takes the seat diagonal from her. Which leaves two seats open…the seat behind him…next to Gwen or the seat in front of her.

"Cousin!" Kai smacks me on the back of the head. I groan. He spots Stephen and quickly moves to the seat behind him. Crap. I have to sit in front of her.

"Mr. Garner," Mrs. Pritchard says in that nasally voice of hers.

"Yo," Kai says with his hand raised. Mrs. Pritchard looks at Kai. "Oh." Kai lowers his hand. The entire class stares at him. "I'm new." He shows his schedule. "See…I got a form."

Mrs. Pritchard sighs. "Take your seat." I move to the seat in front of Gwen with her staring at me the entire time. I slide into the seat and drop my bag. Mrs. Pritchard walks to her desk. She points at Kai, "you. Come up to the front and bring your slip." Kai goes up to her desk.

"Hey," Gwen whispers. I lean back. "Did you want to ask me…um…?" She pauses and I actually hear her take a deep breath and follow it up with a gulp. "…anything about what happened last night?" I shake my head. "Nothing…?" I shake my head again. "Nothing at all…?"

"Now, class," Mrs. Pritchard says as Kai takes his seat. "We'll start with the homework from last night." Kai smirks. He steals a glance at Gwen and smiles bigger. Gwen sighs and sits back in her chair.

My hands tremble…what's wrong with me? Why do I feel sad all of a sudden…like…dejected…put off…and a little…angry…?

Chapter 14: Evasion

He totally blew me off. After what happened last night, he just acts as if he doesn't even know who I am. I lose myself in my bitter thoughts as I continue toward my next class. I mean, I wanted to ask him about the weird tiger people...and that new guy in class.

"Hey, loser," almost making me jump out of my own skin. Meghan laughs. "Geez, why are YOU so jumpy? I'm the one with the mutilated locker." When I don't respond to her question, she turns to look at me more closely. "What's wrong? Did something happen in first period?"

"I'm fine," I mumble unconvincingly.

"Sure, you are."

We walk into North Carolina History and sit down. I take my time pulling out my book and pens, making myself seem busy. Meghan watches as I work to free my notebook. "What?" I whine, realizing she's not going to stop.

"Is it your little juvenile delinquent? Is he still ignoring you?"

I try to work up a lie...but even if I could come up with something, I don't think I could manage saying it. "Yes." My head slumps down on my book. I cross my arms preventing light from reaching my face. "He completely snubbed me in first period," I say to my book, hoping that Meghan overhears.

She sighs. I turn so that I can see the sympathetic expression on her face. "Give him time." She reaches over and moves a few red strands out of my face. I hum. Somehow, this simple action comforts me. I smile. "He'll come around." I nod. How can I go from dreading talking to him about...everything...to wanting to talk to him so bad that it feels like my head is going to...?

"Is anybody sittin' here?" a vaguely familiar voice asks. I lift my head to find the new guy...well, the other new student...standing at the desk in front of me. I shake my head. "Thanks," he moans then scratches the spiky, blond tufts on top of his head. He sniffs. "My name's Kai." His eyes close sleepily and a strange smirk crosses his face.

"I'm Gwen." I motion to Meghan, "and this is my best friend, Meghan." She waves with a strange, wary expression.

Kai tips his head to Meghan then returns to me. "You're...foxy," he purrs with a strange tone on the word 'foxy.' "Aren't you?" I sniff. He's not lying, but he's hiding something, covering it up with double speak. Could he know what I am? If so, what is he?

I glance at Meghan's perplexed expression, verifying that she's not looking at me. I come back to Kai with fox magic-filled eyes. He begins to sit and stops as I feel out his aura. Kai slips his hand into his pocket and glares at me. His eyes are just as bright a shade of green as mine have become. I gasp and jump back making my desk scrape against the floor.

"What's wrong, loser?" I look at Meghan as the fox magic flushes from my eyes. I peer between Kai and Meghan.

"I...um...nothing..." I take a deep breath. "I was...just...I just thought about Alex again." I lower my head again. Kai snickers in his seat.

#####

77

I stare at my palm, wondering why I'm not all fur, fangs, and stuff. I mean, they're my first cousins, right? They're skinwalkers. Their dad was a skinwalker. My...dad was a skinwalker. So, why aren't I? If I was...could I have...stopped that thing last night? Maybe...maybe I could've been the one who saved her. I turn my hand and look at the back. I shake my head.

"Do you wanna try it?" Kai asks.

"What?"

He holds a little bright orange and brown square of fur. "Do you wanna try it?" I shake my head, but secretly...yeah, I do. "You'll never know, unless you try," he yawns. I watch the small square dangle in air.

A loud smack sounds. "What the hell is wrong with you?" Sora snaps.

Kai rubs the back of his head. "What was that for?"

"You know how dangerous it is for someone to have their first transformation in a public place." Kai looks like the housecat that someone put into its bath water.

"What do you mean?" I ask. "What? Do you become whatever animal fur you touch first? 'Cause I've played with my dog Max a hundred thousand times and still no wet nose or black and white fur."

"No, idiot," Sora says as if idiot is my new name. "You have to find your totem animal...but let's say for instance a Golden Tabby WAS your totem...the second you touched his fur...you would change."

"Not good in a public place, I'm guessing."

"Yes...but not for the reason you're thinking..."

"Sorry, man," Kai whispers. "I forgot about that part."

"What part?"

"The part," Sora steals the conversation back. "...where you turn into a snarling, snapping, attacking anything that gets too close to you, out of control bundle of destruction." I swallow a lump that won't seem to go past my Adam's apple. "That's right. Once you become the animal...your spirit and its spirit become intertwined and unless you have a strong-willed Alpha nearby, you'd just go insane for a while."

"That's why our dad was the one who showed us the book," Kai says, slipping his piece of fur into his pocket.

"The book...?"

"It's a collection of animal skins," Sora says matter-of-factly. "If you touch a scrap of fur and there's a reaction...we go out and find a true piece of your totem animal and that piece becomes your power token. It is the literal link between you, the human, and you, the skinwalker." I nod as the bell sounds.

"Ugh," Kai groans, while scratching his head. "When will school be over?"

"It's your first...day," Sora growls between clenched teeth, telling me that this isn't the first conversation they've had about Kai's school hating.

"Yeah, but still..."

"Last period of the day, Kai," I try to help him...for once, while heading to English. "Another fifty minutes and you're free."

He nods as I turn to walk away. For me, it's another fifty minutes of being close to Gwen and having no idea what to say. I mean, I was supposed to ask her questions today, not the other way around.

I walk into class and…again…Gwen's already sitting in her seat…next to mine. I drop my bag, fall into my desk, and put my head down. I pull my hood over my head.

"That looks familiar," Gwen moans.

I pull down my hood. "What?"

She shakes her head. "Nothing." I nod and put my head back down. "And you're sure you don't want to ask me…anything?" I nod again. "Can I ask you something?" I lift my head slowly. She seems nervous and a little like she's in pain. "Do you…not want to talk to me…or is this freaking you out or am I freaking you out because…"

"Gwen!" She wears that same pained expression. She was getting more upset with every question. "It's…okay," I reassure her…which is awesome, considering I'm the non-supernatural with a bunch of supernatural people. She watches me. Her eyebrows arch. "I…just need some time to process, you know?" She nods, but that face remains.

Mrs. Bustamante walks into class and dives into Dickens. I don't really pay any attention. I take out my sketchbook and work on a new sketch. It feels like my pencil's moving on its own. I keep trying to picture what I'm drawing, but I'm not getting a mental image.

I keep working, but I guess I won't see the finished product until it's done. Gwen occasionally steals a glance at what I'm drawing. Whatever it is, at least, it doesn't upset her more.

"Mr. Garner," Mrs. Bustamante says. I look up. "What does this symbolize?"

"Um." She sighs and rolls her eyes. "I have no idea, Mrs. B." She puts her hands on her hips. I try giving what I'm getting. "I wasn't really paying attention." Mrs. Bustamante looks like she's about to spit nails. Gwen's hand goes up, stealing her focus.

"Yes, Gwen, dear?" Mrs. Bustamante hums.

"It symbolizes the lengths to which Sydney Carton is willing to go through…" Gwen pauses to think of her next words while Mrs. Bustamante hangs on them. "…willing to go through…to protect the happiness of his unrequited love, Lucie."

"Very good, Gwen dear," Mrs. Bustamante pants, then returns to the board. I return to my sketch and Gwen does too. When I look down, I see it…it's another Gwen sketch…this time complete with flames dancing around her, three fiery tails, and glowing eyes. Gwen scoffs, but when I look at her. She blushes and smiles.

I dive back into the sketch…fleshing it out…adding shading under her cheekbones, helping the glowing eyes stand out. I add a few shadows to the tops of her arms and shoulders to compensate for the fire behind her. The bell rings before I finish. Have I really been drawing that long?

Gwen stands next to me. She puts her clenched fist over the center of the drawing. She opens her hand and a folded slip of paper falls out. She turns, without saying a word, and hurries out.

I sigh, feeling like crap. It's not her fault. The only reason she revealed herself was to save my life and ever since, I've been acting like she's dog meat…crap, did I feed Max this morning? Dang it! Focus Alex!

I pick up the paper and unfold it. It's a note. As my eyes run along the letter's tiny little flames seem to jump off the page. The note says:

If you change your mind and want to talk, stop by Jelly Bean Coffee tonight. I'll be there from 4pm to 9pm. I want to help you, Alex.

~~Gwendolyn~~ Gwen

I sigh. Crap. All she wants to do is help. I shove Gwen's note and my sketchpad into my pack and run out. Mrs. Bustamante says something, but I ignore her. I look around. Gwen's nowhere in sight.

An angry snarl says "Hey, loser." Meghan storms over, managing to stomp in, I'm guessing, six-inch heels. She gets right in my face. "I don't know what your problem is or why you want to remain a social pariah, but…" She pokes me in the chest. "…stop…dissing…my friend, okay? I have no idea why, but Gwen…likes you. She doesn't want to admit it, but she does. And I'm not going to let the first guy she's interested in here, treat her like…like…"

"Have you seen her?" I hope that my tone conveys my urgency.

Meghan seems thrown. She shakes her head slowly. "Not since, before seventh," Meghan says.

"If you see her before I do, just let her know, I got her note and I will." Meghan nods. I turn and walk away. I have to talk to her, let her know, that somehow…amazingly, I'm not freaking. Well, not totally at least. Wait…did Meghan say Gwen…likes me? A smile moves across my face before I can do anything about it. Gwen likes me.

Chapter 15: Answers

"Why wouldn't he talk to me?" I told him that I'd explain everything, but he didn't even seem interested this morning and was almost as bad this afternoon.

The bell jingles as I finish wiping dry the last warm mug fresh from the dishwasher. I turn and am surprised to be face to face with Alex. His eyes are like pools of melted chocolate and his eyebrows arch slightly in amusement, probably at the look of shock on my face.

"Hey."

"Hi," I reply. "What can I get you?"

His face turns serious. "Some answers."

"Yes," I begin, feeling more nervous than I've felt in my entire life. "Yes, answers...you deserve answers." Alex nods and arches his eyebrows...so cute, so cute, too cute... "Okay." I reach over the counter, ushering him toward a table. He retreats from my hand. I sigh.

"Em?" Emily sticks her head out of the back. She has a little flour on her forehead that moves back into her hair. "I'm gonna take a quick break." I motion to my forehead and back through my hair. "Can you watch the front?"

Emily nods, wipes her forehead and checks for flour on her arm. She moves into the kitchen again, while wiping more of it away. She emerges from the back carrying a fresh pan of muffins.

I step out from behind the counter, undoing the knot of my apron. I move over to the table where Alex is already sitting...

"Okay," he says, interrupting my thought. "First question..." I check to make sure that Emily isn't eavesdropping. She's restocking the muffins in the display case. I put my apron on my lap. I look down at the crumpled piece of polyester. "...what was that thing?" I open my mouth to respond. "And don't tell me you don't know. After you saved me, you went at it like you knew you could beat it. You were surprised when you couldn't." My eyes swell with tears. "And you didn't even react to..."

He breaks off as the bell rings above the door. Two girls enter, walk by us quickly, and approach the counter. Emily halts her restocking efforts to help them...efficiently...

I place my hand on the table. It lands on top of Alex's hand. The second we connect, I feel that spark between us again, like the first time we touched here and like at school last night. Just like when we were in the gym...it didn't hurt. This time, it felt better...familiar. His expression softens, then he renews that serious face. He looks away.

"What is it?" I ask.

He shakes his head. "Nothing. You didn't even react when you saw...my cousins..."

"Your...cousins?"

He nods. "Sora and Kai, my cousins from Oregon," he adds, as if 'my cousins from Oregon' is their last name.

"That's why."

"Why what?"

"Nothing. Like I said last night, I don't know what that thing was exactly, but it had the feel of a familiar."

"A familiar...? What's that?"

"It's a summoned creature...they can take on any shape depending on the will of its master." I pause and move my free hand in a circle. "They do their master's bidding, no matter what they're asked to do."

"So, someone was trying to attack me?" I nod. "Why?"

"My guess is...because you're a skinwalker, like your cousins."

"You know about skinwalkers?"

"Yes, my obāsan..." I break off and grit my teeth.

"Your obāsan...?"

"Grandmother," I spit. "She told me all about skinwalkers. She said that they were...are distant cousins, in terms of abilities anyway, of ours."

"And?" He leans closer...holding me captive with those cocoa jewels in his head. "What are you, 'cousin'?"

"Kitsune," I say absently, still lost in the warmth of his eyes.

"What...?"

I pant, working up an explanation. "It means 'fox' in Japanese or more accurately...I'm a fox spirit."

"You mean like a ghost?" he blurts out loudly...too loud. The two girls stare at us. "What are you looking at?" They whisper to each other, giggle and then walk away.

"Not like a ghost kind of spirit. Spirit...refers more to the power that resides inside of us...our fire," I finish with a hand hovering above my heart.

"Is that why I saw you on fire that first day in Mrs. Bustamante's class?" I nod. He runs his fingers through his hair. "Man, you had me thinking I was going nuts."

"I'm sorry," I apologize, realizing we're still touching. The spark remains. I look down at my hand on his and he pulls it away. "I overheard you talking to your friends in the hall earlier that day." I fidget.

"Go on."

"You were talking about my tails." I lift my eyes...just my eyes. "You saw all three of my tails." He nods. "So, I decided to test you." I retrieve the tiny leaf from my pocket. I hold it out to him.

"What is that?"

"A totem. By focusing my fox magic on it, I can create illusions. The more magic I pour into it, the stronger and more visible the trick becomes."

Alex stares at the leaf, probably not believing such a little thing is capable of what I'm telling him. He looks at me. "How much did you pour into it that day?"

"Hardly any." I draw my bottom lip into my mouth. His head bobs repeatedly. "I saw a spark in you the first day we met. It's what I think you felt when you touched me here and it's probably what you felt when we touched at the school last night." I break off to swallow deeply. "It's what I know you felt when I touched your hand just now."

His eyes dart to just over my shoulder and back. "How's your shoulder?" I laugh nervously, completely disarmed by the question. He arches his eyebrows.

"It's…better…I used some…" I lower my voice. "…a little fox magic to make it heal faster." I move my arm. "But it's still a little sore." He tips his head forward and looks down at his clenched fist on top of the table. "How's your knee? I noticed you weren't limping anymore."

He smirks. "It's okay. My cousins…brought a…stinky ointment with them that helped. It felt a lot better right after I put it on."

"Stinky ointment…?" My mind leaps to the obvious conclusion. "Your cousins are herbalist?" He frowns. "Potion-makers. With supernatural beings…there are those who use magic like kitsune and there are those who use potions and herbs to help them like your cousins." Of course, there are those like my obāsan who can do both.

Alex shakes his head. "No, not them. My grandma."

I nod with my mouth agape. "Well, either way, it is a skill to be commended."

He frowns. "Why are you talking like that?"

"Like what?"

"Formal…it's stiff and kind of awkward."

"I am?" I am. He's right. What's wrong with me? Why did I go uber-explainy on him? I look into his eyes…those honest, warm eyes and I have my answer. It's because like Meghan I feel I could tell him anything and that he would accept me…truly. So, what's stopping me?

"I have to get back. I just took a break to come over."

"Wait," I say as he stands. He falls back into his chair. "You said your cousins were the tiger-pelted skinwalkers, right?"

"Yeah…"

"You mean, the cousins who showed up at school today? I heard you talking to them." He presses his lips into a line and nods. "I have class with one of them. Kai Garner is what he told us his name was."

"Kai Garner is his name. My dad and his were brothers…he and Sora are my first cousins."

"But they're so strong. If your bloodlines are that close, then you should be, at least, as strong as they are."

Alex stands in a huff. "Well, I'm not."

I stand as he turns toward the door. "Alex wait, I'm sorry. I didn't mean…"

"I know." He opens the door. "It's okay. I'll see you in school tomorrow."

"Wait…just one more thing." He frowns. "How long have your cousins been in town?"

"Couple of days, why?"

"It's just…even before that thing came after you; I'd been getting a weird vibe. I got that same vibe last night and that's when I found it attacking you."

Alex nods. "Yeah, but my cousins didn't even get to the school until after…"

"Yeah, plus I didn't really feel anything like that from them when they saved us or at school so…" I bob my head around like an idiot. "Okay…"

"Okay," Alex repeats. "I'll see you around."

My mind scrambles with the thought of leaving the next time I talk to him up to random chance encounter. "Or…," I begin with no real plan reached.

I look down at the apron wadded up in my hand. Yes, a plan forms. I search through my crumbled apron until I find the front pocket. I retrieve my felt tipped pen and take Alex by the hand. He frowns. I drape the apron over my arm holding his, while positioning his palm facing up.

"Or, you could call me tonight." I put the pen cap into my mouth and pull the rest free. I quickly jot down my number on his palm and replace the cap. "You know, if you…think of anything else you want to ask me or…or…or, even if you just wanna talk."

He stares at the number scrawled across his skin and for a second…for one fleeting, flickering portion of a second, he smiles. His expression drops as he opens the door wider and steps outside.

"Later."

The door drifts closed. He looks back and I wave at him, feeling a cold chill. I return to the counter.

"Smooth," Emily says with a large smile and, I'm hoping, a sarcastic round of applause.

"What?"

"That thing with the pen. Old school…it was kinda retro…but still a very smooth maneuver, Ms. Frost." She lifts the empty muffin pan from the counter top. "Before you know it, that little cutie will be crushing on you as hard as you are on him."

I'm thrown…again. "I'm not…" I laugh anxiously. "He's not…," I continue with a lack of actual sentence structure. "We…"

"Yep, crushing…and hard, might I add." Emily returns to the kitchen, muffin pan in hand.

I steal a glance over my shoulder as I return to the counter. I slip my apron over my head and circle its strings around my waist. I follow Emily absently. "Do you really think so?" I ask as I push the kitchen door open.

Chapter 16: Death

I reach the center of the square before staring at my palm again. She wrote her number on my hand...she didn't put it in my phone or ask me to put mine in hers...I smile like a goober. I guess playing it cool was well... "Cool," I breathe and then cross the street.

"What's cool?" Kai asks. I jump and turn to him and Sora.

"I told you, don't do that. Geez," I growl between my teeth, while putting my hand over my pounding heart.

Kai laughs. "Sorry, cos." He's still laughing though.

"Why'd you leave without us again?" Sora grumbles. I sigh. "We're here to protect you, Alex."

"And I still have to go to work and try to maintain some vague part of a real life. I wasn't born into this like you guys were, remember...? I just found out about it yesterday."

Sora nods. "Yeah, yesterday when you were attacked by some kind of dark familiar," she completes my thought. I sigh. Sora carefully takes in my demeanor. She glances across the square. "So, what'd your little friend say?"

"We saw you talking to her," Kai adds before I can ask.

"She's...a kitsune," I say, trying to remember if I promised Gwen that I wouldn't tell them about her. I did tell her about them...so I guess it's fair.

"Hah," Kai barks. "I knew it."

"Kitsune," Sora grumbles. "Okay, if that's true...and I'm not saying it is, then that means you can't trust anything she says to you."

"What? Why not...?"

"Those little fox-faced freaks are all a bunch of liars," Kai says. "They're tricksters. They play with people's emotions...mess with their heads for fun." I look at my hand...can't help but wonder if she's playing me.

"What's that?" Sora asks.

I clench my fist. "Nothing. Pen exploded...ink all over my hand." No, I don't think Gwen's playing me. I don't know what it is, but something tells me I can trust her. I take a step toward the store. "I have to get back to work."

"We're coming in, too," Sora says.

I shrug. There's no point in trying to argue, if she's just going to use that 'mom voice' and get her way. I push the door open and step inside...almost running into Mrs. Turnipseed. She stares at me with what I could swear are blood red, furious eyes. She looks at Kai...then Sora. She shoves me out of the way...one handed, but it feels like a linebacker pushing with two.

"Ugh," I groan, falling against the door. She stares at Sora viciously, as if she's about to attack.

"Which one of you did it?" she asks with venom...and a youthful, Spanish charm to her voice.

"Mrs. Turnipseed?" I ask not believing it's her talking.

"What are you talking about?" Kai asks.

Mrs. Turnipseed steps closer to Sora. "I saw you…outside of my house the other night…you and that damned fox spirit with the blue aura." Sora swallows deeply but her expression doesn't change. "It had to be one of you. Did you do it or did he?"

"I haven't done anything," Sora replies, cold and emotionlessly. She crosses her arms and waits for more verbal assaults from Mrs. Turnipseed.

…a fox spirit with a blue aura…? If I had to guess, Gwen's aura, or whatever, would be red or maybe a flaming reddish-orange like her tails so… "Gavin," I pant.

"What?" Mrs. Turnipseed snaps turning to me. I shake my head with my mouth barely open. "What did you say to me you powerless little nothing?"

"Gw…Gwen's brother…Gavin. He…he was in town a couple of days ago." Mrs. Turnipseed scowls, not getting my meaning. "Gwen is…so…" I hold up one finger, asking for a minute that I hope she'll give me. She takes half a step back. I nod and slip my phone out of my hoodie pocket. I look down at my hand and enter Gwen's number quickly.

"Hello?"

"Hey…Gwen, it's Alex."

"Hey. I didn't expect to hear from you so soon…"

"Yeah," I say awkwardly, looking at Mrs. Turnipseed losing patience. "Hey, um…is your brother around?" Silence. "Gwen?"

"Yes, I'm here. Um…no, Gavin's in…he's been out of town since yesterday." I look away from my phone and Sora, Kai and even Mrs. Turnipseed respond to Gwen's reply.

"Okay," I return. "Um, thanks…"

"Is something wrong?"

"No. I gotta go," I spit and end the call.

"How can I trust the word of a trickster?" Mrs. Turnipseed says with anger so intense, I can feel it.

"Don't trust her." I look into her blood red eyes with deep blue pupils. "Trust me." Mrs. Turnipseed frowns. "Gwen wouldn't lie to me and I wouldn't lie to protect her jerk of a brother." Mrs. Turnipseed lifts her hand to me, palm up…a hand that's…missing all its wrinkles and spots.

Sora steps closer. I hold my hand up, letting her know I'm okay…or at least, I think I'm okay. Mrs. Turnipseed holds her hand up closer to my face. I put mine in it, palm down. She closes her eyes.

"Vinam tik daudz varaz." She puts her other unwrinkled, unliver-spotted hand on top of mine. "Tur ir tikai patiesība." Her eyes open…glowing red. "The things I could have told you…only had I known," she says. A tear streams away from her left eye. She trembles as if she's losing her legs. I put my hand on top of both of hers. She lifts her no longer dark blue eyes.

"Are you okay, Mrs. T?" She shakes her head and her entire expression seems to crumble…and so does some of her caked on make-up.

"I have to go." She shoves Sora and Kai apart to walk between them. She steps across the street. I look at Sora, who's still watching her. I turn back to Mrs. Turnipseed and she's gone. I look around, hoping to get some idea of which way she went.

86

"You're handling this a lot better than we thought you would, cousin," Kai says, scratching the back of his head.

"I guess," I say, still checking for Mrs. Turnipseed. "I should call Gwen back and make sure I didn't freak her out." Sora stares at me in a way that tells me she wants to say something. Before I can even get my phone, Sora and Kai stare off in the distance. "What?"

A second later, I hear footsteps, getting closer. "Lex," Stephen yells, running up to us. He pants after stopping between Sora and Kai. "Alex," he huffs. "Mr. Turnipseed's..."

"What about him?" I ask, checking Mrs. Turnipseed again, while Stephen tries to catch his breath.

"He's...he's dead," Stephen manages.

"What?" the three of us ask. I look at Sora and her expression tells me, she's putting it all together too. "How...?" I ask. "What happened...?"

"It doesn't make any sense," Stephen sobs. "My dad said that it looked like a bear mauled him." I gasp and look at Sora and Kai, whose eyes are already wide. "...in his living room."

"I have to go," Sora snaps. She looks at Kai. "Stay with Alex." Kai nods without complaint. "Don't leave his side...FOR ANYTHING." Kai nods again. Sora rushes off. "I'll be back as soon as I can."

"What? Where's she going?" Stephen asks. "This thing...it's probably the same thing that attacked the school. She shouldn't be..."

"It's okay," Kai says, stepping into the store. "Come in, Steve."

"I told you, it's Stephen."

Kai half turns with an annoyed expression. "Fine, Stephen. Why don't you come into the store, Stephen? It'll be okay, Stephen. Trust me, Stephen." Stephen walks past me into the store.

I look over at Jelly Bean Coffee. "Will it...? Will it really be okay?"

#####

I flip another chair over onto its corresponding table. Why did he ask me about Gavin? Why did he sound so upset...? I slip my phone out of my apron and check it. ...and why hasn't he called me back? "Ugh." I actually hear myself whining in my head.

"Don't worry," Emily says while counting the register. "He'll call."

"Stop doing that," I grumble playfully. She laughs, collects the larger bills, and closes the drawer. She walks into the back.

The bell jingles. I turn to the door. "Welcome to Jelly..." The second I see Alex all coherent thought leaves me. "...bean."

"That was weird." I nod absently. "I got off early. Decided to come by and explain the weird phone call and..."

"Oh, you didn't have to..." I try to sound nonchalant. "I mean, I'm sure you were worried about him bothering you again."

"No, that's not it." He steps past me and looks out of the front window at his cousin, standing outside.

"Is that your cousin?" He nods. "What's he doing here?"

"Looking out for me, apparently. Giant bear-dog attacks…people dying…you know?"

"Wait…people dying…? Who died?" I take his arm, preparing to comfort him. "Are Stephen and Rich okay?"

"No…they're fine. It was Mr. Turnipseed. He…um…was the mayor a few years back…" I nod along with his story. "Apparently, he was this big war hero…and when he ran for mayor he won pretty easily." Alex swallows deeply with serious eyes. "His wife came by the store and she was pretty upset."

"His wife…? Why did she…?"

"She…um…" His voice trembles nervously. "She's um…well, Kai said that she's…a…um…vampire."

"A what? She's a vampire?" He nods. Gavin mentioned something about a vampire, but he said that she wasn't a threat.

"Yeah," Alex says. "Apparently, he left for war and when he came back to town…she came with him or at least, that's what Mr. Hamish told me."

"When was this…?" I ask, still letting the shock of a vampire having a human spouse sink in.

"Mr. Hamish says they've been together for more than forty years, so…"

"No. I mean, when did Mr. Turnipseed die?"

"Earlier tonight," he says softly. I look past him and see that Stephen has joined his cousin. He glances out the window too. "I gotta go." I nod, even though I don't want him to leave. He turns but stops. "I…" He comes back. "…I promised my cousin's I wouldn't tell anybody about them…and their…powers…" I nod again. "So…"

"What powers? You have cousins here?"

"Thanks," he breathes. I smile…so does he…for real, for once…I can feel a bit of peace coming from him, which is surprising considering what he just told me. I suppose the tranquility stems from his coming to grips with us being supernatural. A commotion outside draws us away from each other…Kai and Gavin stare each other down.

"Hey," Alex yells at the same time that I do. They look at us. I motion for Gavin to come in and Alex merely stares at Kai. Gavin and Kai glare at each other one more time and then Gavin comes inside.

"Gwenie," Gavin says, stopping in front of Alex and me.

"One sec…" I look at Alex. "…what you asked me, about your cousins who are apparently in town for some reason?" Alex smiles and nods. "Would you do the same for me with my family?" He nods again.

"Are we done with the secret sharing?" Gavin asks. I shake my head, feeling my frustration building. "Good." Gavin glowers at Alex. "Now, beat it."

"Gavin, I…"

"Nah, it's cool." Alex's demeanor is calm. "I'll…see you in school tomorrow. We can talk more then." I nod and Alex walks out with Kai watching.

I turn back to Gavin. "What is the matter with you?"

"Obāsan's friend…" Gavin uses his deadly serious tone. "…was dead."

"What?"

He nods before continuing. "By the time I got there, someone had already destroyed all her traps, protective charms and wards. They practically destroyed her house…and performed some kind of sick ritual."

"A ritual? What kind of ritual?"

"A twisted one," Gavin gripes. "Somehow, it drained her of all of her fox magic…" He lifts cold, disgusted eyes. "It removed her star balls forcibly."

"…but that would kill a kitsune."

"No duh, Gwenie…kinda the point of the story." He wipes his mouth. "The ritual must have just gotten done when I showed…because there was a lot of ambient magic in the air…and I felt that same feeling as when we were at the Taylors."

"That's impossible." He stares at me. "I felt that same presence last night…when I was attacked by a familiar." His expression turns confused. "A familiar couldn't be that far away from its master."

Gavin shakes his head. "No, it couldn't." He swallows deeply. "What the hell is going on with this town?" I shake my head, admitting that I have no idea. "We have to get you unbound and out of this town immediately."

"The familiar wasn't after me."

"Then who…" Gavin starts but thinks it over. "…that kid?"

I nod. "I stopped it, but tonight…it got a man in town." Gavin frowns. "His…vampire wife…stopped by to see Alex." Gavin sparks with a realization. "You know something?"

"Maybe…"

Gavin quickly reminds me of his run-in with Mrs. Turnipseed. I nod along with his narrative. He falls silent and crosses his arms over his chest. He stalks over to the door with his arms falling to his sides.

"I'm going," grumbles Gavin, pushing the door open.

"Wha…wait…," I rush around the counter. "Why? And, how do you even know where she lives…?"

"Why…? Is because I want to know if the master of this 'weird bear-dog' of yours has come out of hiding and how…? I followed her home after she harassed your pet, remember?"

"Alex is not a pet," I snap instantly, defensively.

"Funny…that you knew exactly who I was talking about," he returns, brandishing his smug sense of superiority. "Anyway. I picked up on her instantly…"

"And you didn't think to tell me more about her or her human husband until just before you left?"

"…she's…vampire," he whispers. "She's no threat to you…well, normal you…you know, unbound you." I cross my arms and frown. "But, I figured you'd be upset if she ate your little pet so…"

"He is not a pet," I repeat with anger raising my voice. "He's a person…just like you and me." Gavin scoffs. "He is."

"He's nothing like us," Gavin complains, fox magic causing his voice to echo. "He's one of them…just a human."

"Like our father," I say, hoping to take some of the wind out of his sails.

"Do you always have to bring him up when you argue in favor of the humans?" he asks with venom. "You don't have to remind me that our mother died because she bound herself to our simple-blooded father."

"Don't talk about him like that," I try to declare out of anger, but it comes out more like a plea.

"Then how should I talk about him?"

"...like he was your father, too." Gavin clenches his jaw and looks down. "Mother...our mother bound herself to him...to a human...because she loved him so much that she never wanted to be away from him..."

"...and look where that sentimentality got her." I want to hit him, but instead I build up my fox magic. He lifts his blue eyes, made paler blue by an infusion of his fox magic.

"She died...fighting to stay with him." His power encroaches on the borders of mine. He's trying to influence me. I push back.

"Exactly. If you get too attached to this...pet...of yours...the same thing will happen to you."

"He...is...not...a PET..." A flicker of foxfire sparks around me...shoving the last of his power away. I gasp and let my fox magic wane. I didn't want to have a physical manifestation of my power. Gavin does the same as if reacting to my energy dropping.

"He doesn't belong in our world, Gwen," he tries to convince me with just his words this time. I shake my head subtly...only subtly because at this point my entire body quivers. "No? He has no power. He's nothing." Gavin purses his lips and closes his eyes.

"I saw it," I growl just above a whisper. "You saw it, too. You said so yourself." He releases a cheek-puffing sigh. This argument is wearing on him. There's no better time to tell him everything than when I've already pushed him this far. Gavin has always...will always hate long, drawn out debates. "I felt it," I admit.

"You what?"

"I felt it. The first time he touched me..."

"...he touched you?" he interrupts with anger blending into his shock.

"I was here. I saw my reflection in the espresso maker; it startled me. I jumped. He caught me and when his hand touched my back...I felt an electric shock..." Gavin wipes his mouth. "...it came from him and rippled through my entire body."

Gavin releases the door handle. I hadn't even realized he was holding it until now.

I swallow deeply. "And...when that...thing...attacked him...I felt it again...only that time it didn't hurt." Gavin, in profound contemplation, nods firmly. "But...," I continue. His eyes return to me...just his eyes. "...every time we've come in contact since then...it's felt..." I swallow another lump and stare at my brother trying to prepare myself for his reaction. "...good...like...I'm supposed to have that feeling."

Gavin's eyes swell. "I have to go," he says in a low, but furious voice.

"What is it?" I catch his arm as he pulls the door open.

He looks at me and I expect to see anger, disgust, or possibly more shock...instead, I get his eyes welling with tears. He looks at me...really looks at me.

His eyes flash brilliant pale blue and he just stares at me…like he's memorizing my face or remembering something.

"You look too much like mom," he breathes. My hand releases his arm before I realize it. I…think that's the first nice thing Gavin's ever said to me…even if it wasn't supposed to be.

"Loser…?" draws our attention from each other. Meghan steps into the open door facing Gavin. "Hey," Meghan breathes to his normal blue eyes. "You're Gavin, right?" Meghan says as a question…and as the first untrue thing I've heard her utter. She knows exactly who he is. Judging by her feelings, she's been thinking about him about as much as I've been thinking about…Alex.

"Yeah and…" Gavin looks past Meghan. "…you're not important enough to remember. Excuse me." Gavin steps out, leaving Meghan staring after him. She sighs.

"Under the category, things that you probably don't want to hear…," she says absently still watching Gavin. She looks at me. "…your brother is so hot I have to wonder if he's July." I arch one eyebrow. "July…" I continue watching her. "…because it's really hot in July."

"Oh, no…I get it. It's just…you can do better…" Meghan rolls her eyes and shakes her head. "…on the joke and the guy."

"Whatever, loser." She walks into the shop. "Now, get me a white chocolate mocha latté, extra foam with nutmeg sprinkled on top.

"Wha-?"

"You do work here, right?" I nod and sigh. I hope Gavin doesn't get himself into any trouble checking on Mrs. Turnipseed. I mean, vampires usually keep to themselves and try to avoid other supernatural creatures out of habit…probably because of their constant fights with the werewolves…but still. She's grieving, so…

"Loser." Meghan snaps, pulling me out of my contemplation.

"Oh, right." I rush to the counter. "I'll get your order…"

"Not that," Meghan returns. "Well, that too, but that's not what I wanted to ask you." I make it around the corner and put my apron back on. "What's um…?" She pauses. This is so weird. I've never heard or seen Meghan at a loss. Given the way everyone else reacts to her, I'm sure no one else has either. I inhale deeply and draw her emotions in. She's flustered…her emotions are swirling around…around…Gavin, still…?

"Ugh," I breathe unintentionally.

"Don't rush me, loser." She retreats instantly. "Sorry." She inhales deeply then releases the breath with her cheeks inflating. "I was…just wondering…what the situation…with your brother is?"

"Situation…?"

"Yeah, is he…seeing anyone?"

"He sees lots of people," I joke.

Her head slumps onto the counter as she groans. "Why are you torturing me, loser?"

I put my elbow down on the counter and rest my chin on my hand. "Not as much fun, when the rabbit has the gun, is it?" What in the world made me say that? I grit my teeth…I feel that ominous, ravenous feeling again.

"No, it's not." Meghan lifts her head suddenly. She looks out the front door. She returns with wide eyes that quickly revert to normal.

"What's wrong?" The ominous, frightening feeling leaves all at once. Meghan seems to relax too.

"Nothing," she lies...for the second time tonight. "I...just thought I heard something." Wait. Did Meghan feel it too? Was it so intense this time that even she felt it?

Meghan moans, drawing my attention. "How about that latté, loser?" I nod and turn to the espresso machine, making sure to avoid the reflective surface.

The door's chime sounds. I turn. "Welcome to Jelly Bean..." I trail off. The guy approaching the counter looks...horrible. He looks like he hasn't slept in weeks, his clothes are practically wearing him, and his skin is white paper pale. "...Coffee. Can...I help you?"

"Rich?" Meghan whispers. She tilts to get a better look. "You look horrible."

Rich...snickers. He pushes his glasses up on his face. The dark circles under his eyes seem to deepen. "No meaner than the last thing you said to me." An eerie smile stretches his face. "But the good news is that you're still smokin' hooooottttttttttt."

Meghan leans away, covering her nose and mouth. "Gross. Your breath smells like a cigarette farted in your mouth."

"You're always such a..." He leans in closer to Meghan. "It's okay. I see through you now. I'm not under your spell anymore." Meghan frowns. Rich cuts his eyes to me. "Now, Gwen on the other hand."

"Um," I start. "What other hand?"

He leans on the counter. I step back. Meghan was rude...but she was right. His breath smells horrible. "You have me completely under your spell, pretty lady." He smiles, and his teeth look gray.

"Um...thank...you...?"

"Back off, Captain Creepy," Meghan barks in my defense. "She's already spoken for."

Rich glares at Meghan as if she's an annoying fly. "'Spoken for...?' What's that supposed to mean?" Rich asks with venom filling his voice. "Are you seeing somebody? Already...?" Anger melds with the poison.

Into what did Meghan just get me? I mean, I like Alex...I mean, I think I do...but I don't know how he feels, and we've never really talked about that kind of stuff. I mean, those pictures he's drawn of me always look so pretty, but-

Rich slams his hand on the counter, causing Meghan and me to jump. "WHO IS IT?"

"Alex," I squeak before I can stop myself. His eyes bulge and for what seems like eternity, nothing moves...until his glasses slip down a bit. "Alex Garner is...his name..."

Rich wobbles a bit. He touches his forehead.

"I'm sorry," I whisper. "...if I might have said or done anything that made you think..."

"You didn't do anything," Meghan states. "This little perv just got it in his head that he had some claim on you like property, just because..."

"Shut up," Rich yells, causing her to do just that. He stumbles back, bumping into a table. One of the chairs falls. "Shut your stupid mouth." He turns toward the door. The bell chimes and he steps outside. He peers in one last time and then walks away.

"See," Meghan says. "I told you that he was a skeevy freak." I sigh. Even a skeevy freak has feelings, right? "Don't pity him," Meghan commands after taking in my obviously telling expression.

Chapter 17: Mourning

Stephen hasn't said a word since we left Jelly Bean…since we left Gwen with her brother. I look at him from the fourth step leading up to my apartment. Kai scratches the back of his head, opens his mouth wide and releases the mother of all yawns. "Are you okay?" I ask.

"Yeah," Stephen sighs. "Are you?"

"I never really talked to Mr. Turnipseed." We reach the top step. I take out my key. Stephen nibbles his bottom lip. "He was…like your godfather or something, right?" He nods. "Are you…?" He nods again. I put my key in the lock and the door opens.

Mom steps into the doorway. "Where have you been?" she snaps. "I woke up an hour ago and I was expecting to see you."

"I had to work."

She looks at Stephen's down demeanor, then back to me. "What's wrong? Where's Sora? Is she okay?"

"Mom," I snap before she can fire off more questions. "Mr. Turnipseed died."

"I'm so sorry," she gasps. She practically pushes me out of the way and wraps her arms around Stephen. He slowly, reluctantly puts his arms around her. "I am so, so sorry, baby." She strokes the back of his head. Stephen crumbles. He cries outright. I put my hand on his shoulder and even Kai pats him on the back.

"I have to go," Stephen sobs, taking a step back. "My mom's pretty upset too." He wipes his eyes.

"You shouldn't drive if you're this upset," my mom says. "I'll give you a ride home." Stephen nods. Mom grabs her keys from the hook by the door. Stephen walks down the stairs. "I'll be back soon," mom says, following him.

I nod and walk into the apartment behind Kai. I think back to when my dad died. Stephen was like my rock. He would come by the apartment and just hang out so that I wouldn't just sit around all day…alone. I sigh. I don't have a clue how I'm going to help him get through this.

"We're gonna get him," Kai says from the kitchen with a mouthful of what I can only guess are potato chips. He peeks around the corner holding a bag and confirming my suspicions. "You hear me?" he asks with slightly fewer chips in his mouth. "We're gonna find this weird-bear-dog-thing and kick its shadowy butt." I wipe my cheek and nod. I notice a tear on the back of my hand. I rub both eyes on my sleeve.

Kai goes over to the sofa and sits. He turns up the bag for the last crumbs then crumples it. "We don't even know where to start looking for this thing."

"You don't look for the thing," Kai says. "You look for its master." He tosses the empty bag over his shoulder. It falls into the trashcan by the kitchen door.

"Stupid son of…" Kai bolts over the sofa and runs to the door. He pulls it open before Sora can finish her sentence, which is good since we don't want her to bother our neighbors with a string of profanity. Worse still, I don't need her launching into a slew of cuss words when my mom comes up the stairs. "Hey," Sora barks, storming in.

"What's with you?" Kai asks, scratching his head for the billionth time. I wonder if he has fleas or lice. "And what happened to your clothes?" Mud covers Sora almost completely. The left knee of her jeans is torn. On top of that, her right jacket sleeve's ripped to the elbow and tatters there. Her hair is a mess and full of mud too.

"I don't want to talk about it!" She pulls what's left of her jacket off. "Let's just say that whatever it was that attacked you at the school was definitely around Mr. Turnipseed's house at some point."

"What? It was there…? Did it…you know?"

She shakes her head slowly. "I don't know." She pulls her shirt over her head, exposing her bra, in one smooth motion. I turn away as quick as I can. "What's your problem? We're cousins."

"Yeah, we're cousins and one of us…" I motion to her. "…has boobs and the other one of us…" I motion to myself. "…doesn't want to see his cousin's boobs."

"He's got a point," Kai says.

"Fine. Whatever." She heads to my room. Before I can fully turn my back on her, again…her jeans fall on my head.

"Ew, ew, ew," I whine, throwing her mud-covered pants on the floor.

"Grow up." She emerges a second later with a towel wrapped around her midsection. "I couldn't tell if the bear-dog thing was inside the Turnipseeds' house, but I definitely picked up its scent again."

"Why didn't you go inside?" Kai asks. "You know grandma's hunter rule numero uno…'confirm the kill.'"

"Because…" Sora steps into the bathroom. "I had a run in with a stupid, blue fox spirit." She pushes the door closed with her foot. Before I can even ask a 'what?'… "He thinks he's so cool." If you didn't know her, by her tone, you'd never guess she was pissed. "…with his stupid spiky hair, his smelly leather jacket, and those dumb…piercing blue eyes."

Kai laughs. "That last one wasn't even a put down."

"Shut up." Sora starts the shower.

"Hey," I start. "You might wanna hold it down. These walls are thin, and we have neighbors."

"I know." Sora's voice echoes off the walls. "I can hear them snoring."

She's telling the truth even if I can't verify it. "So…so, you ran into another kitsune?" I ask awkwardly.

"Yes. He smarted off to me and we fought." I nod. That sounds like Gavin all right. "I couldn't help but notice that he smelled just like your little fox-face, Alex." I swallow deeply.

"It had to be him…Gwen's brother…," Kai throws in. He shoves me at the shoulder. "Aw man, that guy's a jerk."

"What guy?" Sora asks.

"Gavin," I say, deciding to come clean. I mean, I'm not really breaking my promise to Gwen. They would've figured it out on their own. "And yeah…" I look at Kai. "…that guy is a jerk."

"Who's a jerk?" mom says, pushing the door closed behind her.

"His girlfriend's brother," Kai says in a mocking tone.

"Girlfriend?" mom asks.

I shake my head and thankfully, mom lets it drop. "How's Stephen doing?" I ask making sure that she's off the whole 'girlfriend' thing.

"About as well as can be expected." She puts her purse down and slips her jacket off. She drapes it over the back of the sofa. "I did find out that there will be a memorial held in Mayor Turnipseed's honor tomorrow at one o'clock in the square." I nod. "You guys get a half day so that any of the students, faculty and staff of the school who knew him can come and pay their respects."

"That's cool," I breathe. Mom nods and walks over to her bedroom door. "Mom, don't you have to head back in to work?"

"Crap," she spits. She walks by me and passes me her purse. She puts her jacket back on. "Be good, you three." She takes her purse and rushes out the door.

The second the front door closes, the bathroom door opens. Sora steps out wearing a towel around her midsection and another one around her hair. "Get some sleep, you two."

"What? Why?" Kai whines.

"...because...we're going to that memorial."

"Okay, my turn," I start. "What? Why?"

"Because whoever killed the old man might stop by to admire their handiwork." Kai and I nod. "Plus...Stephen sounds like he's really upset..." She pulls the towel from around her wavy hair. "...he might need you." She walks toward my bedroom.

"Okay, am I crazy or did Sora just say something...almost nice?"

"Dude, I'm as shocked as you are," Kai returns, staring after his sister.

"I bet," I mutter before falling onto the sofa. She's right though. Stephen'll probably need me...me and...and...why can't I remember our other friend's name? Rich...wow, why was that so hard?

Chapter 18: Dreams

Don't think about him. Don't think about him. Don't think about him. Which him? Are you more worried about your brother, who never came back from investigating a vampire's human mate's death or are you more worried about Alex who was a target of the same creature that was likely responsible for killing Mr. Turnipseed? Both...? Gavin can handle himself and Alex has his cousins to watch his back, right? I yawn. My eyelids feel heavy. Alex'll be fine. Before I even realize it...I'm asleep.

Or am I? Who's that standing across from...it's Alex's cousin, Sora. She's in her tiger form. Why? I must be dreaming. She rushes me with her sharp teeth and sharper claws gleaming in the moonlight. She swings at my face and I duck out of the way. She comes back around and takes a swing at my midsection. I leap out of the way using a small burst of fox magic. She growls something and moves closer hesitantly.

I say...what am I saying...? It comes out in mumbles...completely undecipherable. Whatever I said made her angry all over again. She rushes me, this time she feints toward my body then sweeps my legs. I fall and hit...tiles...no, shingles...we're on a roof.

I tumble and then fall to the ground. I manage to get my feet under me, then land silently. Sora is on me before I can react. She comes down on my shoulders and drives me into the mud-soaked earth. Why are we even fighting? Is this about Alex...?

She draws back and goes for my head. I manage to get out of the way...her claws sink into the mud. I kick her in the back. She stumbles to her left and I grab her mud-covered hand...I rise and drive her face into the mud, accidentally tearing her sleeve. She growls and kicks me in the stomach. I stumble away.

Sora stands; her pink nose and white and black fur now covered with slimy, wet earth. She runs her hand over her face, and for a second her eyes return to normal before going back to pale blue.

Wait...I'm talking again...what did I just say...? Wait, did she just...? If I didn't know any better, I'd swear she just blushed because of whatever I said. Okay, so maybe she didn't blush...but whatever I said threw her off. She shakes her head and comes at me again. This time I go on the offensive. I throw a flame at her and she ducks under it, sliding past on her knees. She rises slowly. A trickle of blood mixes with the mud, covering her left knee...missing all the fabric that once covered it.

I focus on the blood. She looks down at it with a pained expression. She growls and takes a step back, dragging her injured leg behind her. I lift my hands in submission. She bares her fangs. I show her my claws. What am I doing? Oh, wow...I just cut my own hand and...now, I'm using my fox magic to heal it. She watches in amazement but maintains her distance.

I use swift paw and rush her. She...uses it too and evades me. I reach for her and she slips away again. We repeat this dance for a while until...a misstep, probably caused by her wounded knee, slows her down. I grab her and force her to the ground. She struggles but I...release her. I could've held her easily, but I let her go. She sits up and I sit back. We stare at each other for a moment.

I reach for her bloodied knee slowly…that pained expression returns to her face. I move my pointer finger and thumb near the center and…ugh…I pull out a sharp jagged rock. I toss the stone away.

I put my hands on either side of her knee and force fox magic into the gash. She glares then looks down at her healing flesh. The damaged skin knits itself back together…she probably has naturally accelerated healing that is being augmented by my powers.

I finish repairing her injury and lean further away. I look at her face no longer covered in fur. She still looks like she could take my head off at any minute, but now I don't think she actually would. She runs her thumb over her knee, inhales deeply and stares into my eyes.

Okay…now, I just feel weird…because I can't help thinking…how beautiful Sora really is. I take a deep breath. She even smells good. I open my eyes and she tips her head. I still can't make out what she's saying, but it looks like she said, "thank you." I nod, stand and extend my hand. She takes it and I pull her to her feet…and just as quickly I lose my footing and…

…I fall back into darkness. How is that possible? I was just standing on level, albeit, muddy ground. Did I bump my head? And, why do I smell…I sniff…pine trees. I open my eyes again and I am walking through a forest…at night. I can hear mutters on the wind. No, it's not a voice…it's magic…enchantment. The trees have been enchanted with protection spells and charms…but they're broken now. Why are they broken? Who did it? Did I…? I couldn't…I wouldn't destroy someone's protection charms.

I come across a small cabin in the center of a tiny clearing. There are spells etched into the wood of the cabin. I continue, planning to destroy these protection wards as well. I step on a seal…a tetragonal shape overlaying a heptagonal array appears. That's strange…an odd number formation on top of an even numbered one. That would disrupt its target's energy and…this sigil means to destroy. This close to the cabin…it has to be a last-ditch effort. If this spell goes awry, it could easily destroy the home and the person it's trying to protect.

The sigil flashes with a brilliant white light. The intense light surrounds me and then hellfire flares up. I do not even react to the destructive flames. Hellfire destroys things…utterly and completely. It does not cease burning until what it is set upon is gone…until not even ashes remain. It has no effect on me. I sweep my hand over it and the flames douse themselves. No, the blaze isn't dousing itself. The flames draw away…drawn into something embedded in my hand.

I smile and continue toward the cabin. I spot the seal on the door. It is a three-point protective ward over a five-pointed shielding charm. I reach for the seal and tiny blue, electric sparks repel my hand. I clutch my fist defiantly. I reach for the seal again and get the same reaction. This time I power through…my hand moves through the barrier. My pointer finger makes its way to the edge of the tiny, paper rectangle. The tiny blue sparks increase as the electric buzz intensifies. I pull. The seal tears away, leaving the four corners attached to the door.

The electricity and the pain cease instantly. I discard the seal and put my hand flush against the door. It explodes inward. The splinters fly in every direction, the hinges fall to the ground and the doorknob jingles violently as it strikes the opposite wall. The smell of burning oak fills the air as I take my first triumphant step into the dank, tiny little cabin.

I feel the tingle of magic that caused the door's disintegration. My mouth opens. I emit a bark that ripples through the entire cabin. Every floorboard creaks and groans in response. The windows rattle, barely holding onto their frames. The sparse furniture filling the living room flies away from me in a circle, thrown by the force of my will.

A whimper comes from the far corner and my head whips around to it. I track my target in an animalistic way. Being this close excites me. I move my right hand and the kitchen table flies away from...a woman...an older Japanese woman with salt and pepper hair and deep wrinkles along her forehead. She wears a black yukata and simple black house shoes...like the ones for indoor wear...only back home. In many ways, she resembles my obāsan. "Kitsune," a husky, echoing male voice calls her.

The old woman extends a leaf totem. She inhales deeply and blows on it. A stream of fire juts out. I lift my right hand and the fire parts, flying around me, leaving me unharmed.

The woman panics. She scrambles to her feet, but before she can, I use my power to throw her against the wall behind her. Her frail frame collides with the wall and then she collapses to the floor. She is persistent. She tries to rise again. The woman...the old fox spirit lifts trembling frightened eyes.

I say, "Tenetur lumen. Tenetur ex umbra. Tenetur ex Terra. Tenetur ex Coelis. Deligati ab angelis. Deligati per Daemones. Sentit de virtute contudit. Exsequor."

As soon as I utter the last word, the fox spirit's arms wrench and move behind her back. Her legs come together and bend at the knee. I hear bones breaking and she screams out as best she can. I feel nauseous...no, not dream me...actual me...I feel sick at the sight of this. Why am I doing this to this poor kitsune? The incantation that I spoke, it sounded like Latin...but I can't be sure. What I do know is that it just felt...wrong.

I take a step toward the living room. I lift my clenched right fist and red light generates from the palm of my hand. I turn my hand over, kneel and stretch my fingers wide. When my palm comes in contact with the floor, a sigil burns, extending outward from my hand. My three middle fingers generate three lines. Each line spreads wide but eventually curves to the right. A circle surrounds the sigil, starting from the base of my hand. My thumb and little finger begin an eight-sided array within the sigil. Words appear along the inside lining of the circle, but I can't make them out. Once, the seal completes, it is nothing like any seal I've ever seen.

I stand and return to obāsan's doppelganger. She has cried a puddle beneath her weathered head. That's when I notice that not only is she unable to move because of the spell that I recited...all her limbs are broken, possibly some of her ribs as well. I feel the sickness welling up inside me again. How could someone...let alone I...do this to someone else? She tries to utter something, but a trickle of blood tells me that she's punctured a lung and all words are lost to her need for air.

I lift my right hand and move it toward the sigil. Her battered, broken body glides along the floor and stops in the center of the seal, causing her tremendous pain

101

along the way. I lift my right hand and an eerie black smoke surrounds it. The cloud moves to my palm and takes shape. It forms a long black crystal that extends from the base of my hand to a few centimeters beyond my fingertips. I walk over to the sigil and the destroyed kitsune and place the crystal at the point where it originated.

The crystal has no reaction, but the sigil, in turn, comes to life. The words along the rim glow gold. The lines within flash with a pure white light while the circle itself radiates a deep menacing purple.

"Omnia mea tua erunt. Da sursum vestri metas. Da tua voluntas. Da corpore vestro. Da opes. Da mihi omnibus vobis. Divinitus. Inferno. Solis. Luna. Lumen. Tenebrae. Aalligo te ad hoc cristallum. Nunc tibi omnia mea."

The second I'm done, the old kitsune's eyes glow. She trembles violently. The purple light transforms into a living shadow that engulfs her. It makes its way into her mouth, nose and eyes. It fills her completely.

She inhales one last gasping breath…and then the mist returns from her mouth…as it comes out…her eyes grow dimmer and dimmer. Soon, there is no glow of fox magic left, but it does not stop there. Soon, even the soft glow of life leaves her eyes. Her expression eases and her body stops trembling. The smoke fills the circle but does not expand beyond its borders. It hovers around her. The crystal flashes with a frightening purple light. It absorbs the smoke. When all is dark again…it is apparent…she is dead.

I retrieve the crystal. It explodes into a cloud again and reabsorbs into the palm of my hand. I watch as the last of the crystal returns. I look past my hand at this old kitsune and while I…the real me…still feels sick and like the world is spinning…dream me…feels…righteous somehow…vindicated…I feel…

"Ungh," I cry out, falling to the floor, free of the nightmare. I don't even have time to process the pain of banging my head. I leap to my feet and cover my mouth. I run to my bedroom door, throwing it open urgently. I bolt down the hall to the bathroom. On my knees, I slide to a stop in front of the toilet and place my face in the seat…everything empties out of me…the old kitsune's face…her agony…her pain…and everything just pours out of me.

When I am empty, I rest my arm on the seat and my head on it…still tasting the bile and feeling like it's nothing compared to how my heart feels with the thought of the old kitsune. I think of the light fading from her eyes…and I cry…I cry loudly and with abandon…so loudly that soon, my foster mother rushes into the bathroom.

"Gwen?" Her voice is sympathetic, tender. "Gwen, darling, are you okay?" I shake my head as she puts her arms around me. "Are you feeling sick?" Nothing more comes from me. No food…no worries…no emotions…I am as empty a vessel as the old fox spirit. Mrs. Taylor rubs my back, struggling to hold me close. Any words she utters are lost.

I have felt pure evil…it felt so dark…so horrible…and somehow, at the same time, so…familiar.

Chapter 19: Memorial

I sit in the last row in the center of the square. I mean, I barely even knew Mayor Turnipseed...I had more interaction with his vampire wife than I did with him sadly. His wife...Mrs. Turnipseed is a vampire. Yeah, I'm still trying to wrap my head around that one. Sora and Kai take seats beside me. Kai looks around lazily while Sora stares straight ahead at the podium placed next to the memorial tree that Mr. Turnipseed planted during his first term. It's huge now.

"Where's your little fox?" Kai asks. "I didn't see her in school today."

"I know...and she's not 'my fox.'" Kai sucks his teeth. "I tried to call her, but she didn't answer."

"Maybe she's out, covering for her jerk of a brother," Sora says.

"I told you. She trusts her brother and I trust her. Plus, I...feel like I know her well enough. If there was something weird going on with her, I'd know about it by now." Sora looks at me as if she could choke me. "What?"

"So, you're just gonna believe that little trickster?" Sora grumbles.

I spot Gwen and Meghan, both in black, Gwen with a few accents of purple worked in, cross the street to our left. I stand. She spots me and shows me the phone she's holding to her ear.

I turn to Sora. "Be nice. Remember, she can hear you, just like you can hear her." I walk toward Gwen and Meghan. Gwen says something to Meghan that causes the two of them to split up.

"Mrs...," Gwen starts, but breaks off. "But Mrs. Taylor..." She rubs her forehead. "I promise, I'm okay." Her eyes meet mine. She frowns. "My stomach...hasn't bothered me since I woke up this morning." She places her hand over the phone and mouths, 'I'm so sorry.' I shake my head. "I promise, if I feel even the slightest bit queasy, I'll call you or have Meghan bring me home." She smiles. "Okay, I will. Bye." She slips the phone into her pocket. "Sorry about that."

"You already said that." I chuckle.

"Right, I did. Sorry." Her hands snap over her mouth. "Sorry."

"Don't worry about it." She tucks a loose strand behind her ear. "What was that about your stomach? Was that why you weren't in school today?"

"Yeah, I...," she pauses. "I don't even know if I should tell you this...it's kind of...gross."

"Were you...?" I try not to sound too grossed out by the thought of her...on the toilet.

She stares at me, getting my meaning... "No. No, no...I...I felt queasy and then nauseated...and then I spent most of the night with my face in the toilet." Blood rushes to her cheeks.

I nod sympathetically. "Sorry to hear that." She bobs her head unevenly. I check the square for Stephen. I slide my hands into my hoodie pockets. I haven't heard from him since last night. He seemed crushed. Between this and Rich being MIA lately...I wonder how he's keeping it together.

"Is something wrong?" Gwen motions to the podium. "Besides...you know?"

"Mr. Turnipseed was Stephen's godfather. So, he took his...um, death pretty hard. I mean, he's never been good at losing loved ones and he connects with people really fast and really deep so..."

She nods. She extends her hand...and stops just before touching my arm. She inhales deeply and then pats me on the bicep. Even through my hoodie, that tingle feels good. She shutters...but in a good way. She feels it too.

"Hey," Meghan says. She looks at me, then Gwen. "They're about to start so we should..."

"Yeah," Gwen says. "Okay." She looks at me. "We'll talk after?" I nod. She and Meghan walk away together. They take two seats near the middle of the white folding chairs. Gwen looks back at me. She draws her bottom lip into her mouth and faces front.

"Oh, your little fox-face is still keeping you at arm's length," Sora complains. She wears, in addition to her lighter than she should be for this time of year jacket, a smug expression. Kai stands beside her, sipping a milkshake from the generic chain coffee shop around the corner.

I ignore Sora's jab at Gwen and find three empty chairs three rows behind Meghan and Gwen. I move down the row and see Stephen with his mom and dad on the front row. I tip my head to him. He nods with his sad expression dropping.

A curvy woman, wearing a short black dress with long sleeves, black tights, black gloves, and a large black hat covering her face, walks over to Chief Harper. She shakes his hand before moving to Stephen.

Sora growls. I lean closer. "What's your problem?"

She stares daggers at the woman in dark glasses. "Vampire," Sora whispers. "To be more precise...your vampire regular." I look at Mrs. Turnipseed without her old woman make-up and baggy, over-sized clothing, and big floppy hats...well, this hat is almost as big, but not nearly as floppy. She looks...amazing.

"Who is that?" a man says behind me.

"I hear that's their daughter," another man says. "From what I understand, she and her father had a falling out a few years back. She moved away and never spoke to her parents."

"What's she doing here?"

"She flew in on the red-eye as soon as she heard about her father. She's handling all of her father's affairs and funeral arrangements since her mom's pretty much broken down."

"Aw, poor woman...I mean, I can't imagine losing your father and basically your mother at the same time. But, after so many years together, it makes sense."

Sora frowns and looks down. Kai sighs and looks away. It's only been a few weeks since...Sora lifts her head quickly. She turns to look behind us. I follow her eyes and see...Gavin, leaning against a tree with his arms crossed. He doesn't seem sad...just put off. He notices Sora and me staring at him. He smirks. Sora huffs then turns back to the front. She crosses her arms and slumps down.

"What's that all about?"

"None of your business," she spurts.

104

Gavin's attention moves away from Sora because of a man I've never seen before. The man has thick reddish-brown hair and a bushy beard. He looks to be about forty years old and vaguely reminds me of Gavin. The man slips his hands out of his tan jacket and gives Gavin a large open-armed greeting. Gavin's jaw clenches and he glares back. The man says something and offers him his hand. Gavin stares at his outstretched hand before taking it and giving it a good shake.

Gavin talks to the man and the situation between them gets tenser and tenser, or at least, that's the impression I get from Gavin. The man gives long-winded statements with a lot of excitement only to have Gavin respond with one or two-word answers. I watch the man's mouth form word after word and… "…you've gotten so big, Gavin…" he says. Wait…did I just…hear him?

"What…want…?"

"You know…," the man motions to himself. "…picked your name…"

"Alex," Sora grumbles while squeezing my arm. I mouth an 'ow.' "What were you doing?" I shake my head. "The ceremony's over…"

"What?" I find Stephen in tears, his father and mother holding him. "How did I?"

Kai scratches the back of his head. "It was like you were a million miles away. Kinda like…the first time the super hearing kicked in…" He looks at me. "Did it…? Kick in, I mean."

I look back at where Gavin and the man were standing…and they're nowhere in sight. "Nah. I must've been daydreaming."

Chapter 20: Dessert

"I did not just imagine that," I mutter. I just saw my brother talking with…

"Gwendolyn is that you?" I hear behind me. I turn to my brother and…my uncle, Mihangel, walking toward me.

"Look who I found," Gavin says and if you didn't know him, you would actually believe he was happy to see our estranged uncle. "Uncle Mihangel." He tilts his head toward him.

"Uncle Mihangel?" I step into his open arms. He wraps them around me…strange…because I distinctly remember him condemning our father for marrying our mother and having children with her when Gavin and I were little. It was one of my first memories. "What are you doing here?"

"I…"

"He hasn't exactly been forthcoming with that information," Gavin says.

"I just wanted to tell you both together," Mihangel begins. "I…came through this town a few years ago on business. I met Mayor Turnipseed and we became fast friends. His wife opened his rolodex and just started calling all his contacts. I flew out as soon as I could." I inhale deeply and so does Gavin. I sense that he's lying about parts of his story, but I can't tell which parts. Gavin takes a step back. "I never expected to run into my niece and nephew here."

"Yeah," Gavin says skeptically. "What a weird coincidence." Gavin looks at me and his eyes flash with fox magic for a brief second.

"Gwen?" Alex calls. Oh no, I do not want him to meet my…uncle. Alex walks over. He looks at Uncle Mihangel with a strange expression. I sigh.

"Oh, look Gwenie. It's your…little friend," Gavin condescends annoyingly. "This should be…interesting."

"Shut up," I grumble. "And be nice. His cousins can hear you, just like you can hear them," I whisper.

Alex stops in front of me. He looks at Uncle Mihangel, then Gavin, before settling on me. "Hey Gwen, um, can we…go somewhere and talk?" I nod blankly and step closer. Gavin reaches for Alex and before he can …I hiss. Gavin takes a step back. I can't believe neither of them is going to ask about-

"Gwendolyn," Mihangel says and he will probably finish by asking… "…who's your friend?" I swallow deeply. "Well? Aren't you going to introduce us?"

I motion to my uncle. "Uncle Mihangel, this is Alex." I look at Alex. "Alex, this is my uncle."

"Your…," Alex stumbles over. "…your uncle…?" He points at the subject of his question. I nod. Mihangel extends his hand to Alex and Alex reciprocates. They shake. "Mihangel…?"

"Yeah, I know…I know. Me and their father, Delwyn, used to get the weirdest looks when we were kids," he explains. "Comes with the territory…being a traditional Welsh family." I roll my eyes and I can practically feel Gavin rolling his.

I take Alex by the hand, which raises Gavin's eyebrow. I quickly intertwine our fingers and pull Alex closer before he can say something that undoes my ruse. "We…have to go."

"That's fine," Mihangel says. "I'll be in town for a few days on business anyway."

"I thought you flew in for your friend's funeral," Gavin asks, crossing his arms.

"Well, full disclosure, to get a ticket on such short notice, I had to charge it to the company." Mihangel slips his hands into his jacket pockets. "So, I made arrangements with a business contact as an excuse."

I pull Alex away. "I guess we'll see you around then." I look at Gavin and he nods subtly. I nod back and pull Alex toward the street. "Sorry about that," I whisper. "I just really didn't want to be around my uncle."

"It's okay. So, you're not close with him?"

I rub my forehead. The frustration that our father felt the last time they spoke, still lingers. "I…" I search for the nicest way to word it. "He and my dad didn't exactly get along…very well, you know?" I ask, turning one of his favorite phrases back on him.

"Yeah. He didn't seem to get along with Gavin either."

"That's not fair," I snap. Alex looks at me as if to ask if he said something wrong. "Nobody gets along with Gavin." He erupts with laughter…it's real…and honest…and it sounds…amazing. It invites me to join in and how could I deny it.

Alex looks at our hands still clasp together. He slowly lets go and so do I…after another few milliseconds of that remarkable sensation rushing up my arm.

"So, are you hungry?" he asks with an odd expression on his face. "Because I am, I mean, I skipped lunch, you know?"

I nod and fend off a smile at his constant, 'you knows'. "I could eat."

"I've never eaten here before," he says looking at the Bean.

"Well, of course, everything is fantastic," I gush with an overenthusiastic ring that I hope doesn't come across as sarcasm. The truth is that every treat that Jennifer and Emily have allowed me to sample has been delicious.

"Alright, I'll give it a try." We cross the street. I can't help noticing that not only are Alex's cousins staring at us, but Gavin is, too. I hope they stay outside. Given the dream that I had about Sora and the nightmare that I had right after, I don't really feel like talking to any of them right now.

Alex pulls the door open and holds it. As the smells of fine coffee, cinnamon, vanilla and nutmeg wash over me, I wonder what Alex wants to talk about. I take in his half-sincere smile and feel nostalgic for his honest laughter. I smile in earnest and walk into the Bean.

#####

I take the table near the door…the same table from when she told me everything. Gwen stands at the counter, talking to her boss. She looks at me at the same time her boss does. Gwen tries…and fails…to stop her from waving. I wave back, trying not to give her a 'what's the matter with you?' look. She returns to her conversation with Gwen.

I wonder what all the waving and grinning was. Gwen walks over to the table, carrying our drinks. I stand, but she shakes her head. She places the hot chocolate in front of me and sits down with her frou-frou-caramel latté thing.

"She…um…," Gwen initiates. "…she said that she's going to make something 'special' for us." I nod wrapping my hands around my hot chocolate.

"So…" I look at her…her and those eyes of hers that always feel like they're seeing through me. "…what do…kitsune…eat?" She places two dark green cloth napkins on the tabletop. She opens one with a snap. She drapes it over her lap. Is she mad at me? She lifts hurt, watery eyes…but she looks angry too.

"What do 'humans' eat?" She emphasized 'humans' like Gavin would.

"I don't know…I mean you know more about humans than I know about kitsune, so…"

"No. I mean, we…" She takes a deep breath. "…kitsune…are basically, spirits in human form. So, we eat the same, exact stuff that humans eat."

"Like sushi…? …spaghetti…?" She nods on both. "…foods that don't start with an S?" She laughs. Me too. That turned her mood around.

"Yes." She giggles.

"You have a great laugh," I whisper, then swallow deeply. I can't believe I just blurted that out. She probably thinks I'm an idiot.

"Thanks." She lifts her coffee, takes a sip and as she drinks, her cheeks turn red. She's so pretty…at least, I managed to say that one just in my head. She puts her cup down and looks at me with serious eyes. "I have to tell you something."

"Bum, bum, buuuuuuuuummmmmmm," I hum. She laughs again. "That's rarely good."

"I…I don't know if it's good or bad. It's about these weird dreams…nightmares really…that I had last night." I nod as she tells me about fighting Sora in her tiger form. I stop nodding and try to close my mouth that won't stop hanging open as she scares the hell out of me with the nightmare she 'fell' into next. "…and that's when I woke up and…vomited…a lot."

"I'm sorry," I whisper, not being able to come up with anything better. She musses her bangs and folds her arms as if she's hugging herself. She's putting up a defense between us, thank you mom for making me go see three different therapists after dad died. I remember one part of the story that she told me…'her' fight with Sora. "Hey. Weird, but true…Sora came home last night covered in mud and with a hole in her pants…over her left knee."

"Really?" I nod. "Do you know what this means?" She stretches both hands across the table. I take her hands. "It means that my obāsan was right…I'm an empath like my mom."

"An empath?"

"An empath is a person who can read emotions and, in some cases, use those emotions to read other peoples' minds or thoughts or maybe…even see things that the other person saw."

"Your brother?" She frowns. "Sora came home grumbling about a stupid fox spirit with stupid blue piercing eyes."

"That sounds like my stupid brother." She laughs but stops abruptly. "Okay, that settles one dream…but…"

"Whose nightmare did you live through?" She frowns and nibbles her bottom lip. "It might have just been a nightmare, you know?"

She nods and looks down at our hands. She lifts them slightly, her palms facing up. She smiles. "Thank you."

"You're welcome." She nibbles her bottom lip again and caresses the backs of my hands with her thumb. It makes that tingling sensation I get whenever she touches me...feel...even better.

"Hate to break this up." Goth-boy walks over to our table. I lean back and look at him. Gwen takes her hands out of mine. Goth-boy grabs a chair from the next table, turns it backward, and sits. "But I need to talk to you."

"Right, um..." I stretch out, trying to remember his name.

"Hi," Gwen says. "I'm Gwen Frost..." She offers him her hand. "...and you are?"

"Evan." He shakes her hand for about a second and then flips his Goth-bangs. "I can't help but notice that my house didn't get painted."

"Yeah, sorry about that. Something...um...came up."

"Well, I still expect the job to get done," Evan growls.

Gwen frowns. I shake my head. She rises from the table. "I'm gonna go check on our snack." Gwen walks over to the counter.

"Look, Goth-boy," I say before I can stop myself.

"No, you look." Another hair flip. "My brother has a piano recital tonight. I expect the job to be done or you can kiss the rest of that money bye-bye." Evan stands, takes my hot chocolate then walks out the door.

Gwen comes back with a dish that has a big brownie with a scoop of ice cream on either side and chocolate and caramel sauce all over it. She puts the plate down in front of me with a napkin and two spoons next to it.

"You heard?"

She nods and sits. She motions for me to take one of the spoons as she takes the other. I do. She takes a little piece of the brownies' corner and then adds some ice cream. She eats the scoop.

"So, what are you going to do?"

"I guess I have to do it." Gwen nods and repeats her action with the brownie and the ice cream. "Wait a second..." She stops mid-bite. "No, not that." She takes the bite. "The weird-bear-dog-thing attacked me at the school, right?" She watches me, hoping to get my meaning. "Well, I went to the school to get the spray paint that Goth-boy gave me to do the tag for him."

"You think he's behind it?"

"Well, he is paying me a sick amount just to do a tag."

"Sick...? Tag...?" She arches one eyebrow.

"'Sick'...a lot...and 'tag' think...graffiti, but more artsy."

"Yeah, well you are a really good artist." She smiles.

"Not as good as the sick amount of cash he's paying me." She nods. "I think maybe we should tell my cousins...maybe even your jerk of a brother."

"Not before you..." She scoops some brownie and ice cream and offers it to me. "...try this." I almost choke trying to figure out what to do. She moves the spoon closer to my mouth. "Come on. Just take one bite. Jennifer made it special for us." I take the bite...and it is really good. The brownie is warm and melts the ice cream just

110

enough…or is it the girl feeding it to me? "See?" I smile. I take a few more bites just to make sure. Definitely, the girl.

"Come on," I mumble with a mouthful of brownie. "Let's go find Sora, Kai and Gavin." Gwen nods. I stand and so does she. She collects the plate and both spoons. She hurries over to the counter, passes the plate to…Jennifer…right, her boss's name is Jennifer, and offers a quick thank you. I move over to the door and Gwen runs to me. I hold the door and she steps outside

Sora and Kai practically meet us. Sora frowns. "Wait," I say. "I think we've got something."

"That guy who just left," Gwen starts. "Alex thinks he might be controlling the bear-dog-thing."

Kai scratches the back of his head. "Well, he did peel outta here pretty fast."

"Not enough to go on," Sora complains.

"His spray paint was the reason I went back to the school. I got it out of my locker right before that thing attacked." Sora holds her fist up in front of her mouth. She nods. "I'm…supposed to go to his house to do a tag for him…tonight."

"Will he be there?" Sora asks.

"He said something about a piano recital for his brother," Gwen says. Sora nods again. She looks at Gwen's right hand.

"Is that his scent?" Gwen nods and holds her hand up. Sora sniffs it lightly and so does Kai. "We'll go check it out."

"If we both go, who's gonna watch Alex?" Kai asks. "I mean…" He looks at Gwen. "…no offense, but you weren't strong enough to take that thing." Gwen sighs. "So, why don't I go check out, Mr. too-much-hair-product and you go watch out for our cousin?" Sora nods.

"No," Gwen says. "You both should go. If it is him, he might be able to summon the bear-dog anywhere." Sora clenches her jaw. That's her 'you're right, but I kinda hate that you're right' look. "Gavin and I will watch Alex's back."

"Absolutely not," Sora snaps. "Your brother doesn't give a damn about Alex."

"You're right," Gwen says…less convincingly than she probably thinks. "But he cares about me. I'll protect Alex and he'll protect me." Sora looks at me. I nod.

"Fine," Sora concedes. "But if anything happens to my cousin…"

"…it'll have to have happened to me twice," Gwen says. Sora smirks, which is the closest thing to a sincere smile I've seen from her since I was eight years old.

"Hello, Alex," says a beautiful, songlike voice with a hypnotic Spanish accent. I turn to…Mrs. Turnipseed. Sora and Kai step between us. Gwen takes my wrist and holds it tight. "I mean him no harm."

"Guys," I say. "I'm fine." Sora and Kai step aside but don't move away. Gwen's grip on my wrist eases, but only a little. I guess vampires are bad for humans…normally. "Hey, Mrs. T." She moves closer. She pulls down her oversized sunglasses, showing her deep blue eyes. "How are you holding up?"

"You really aren't afraid of me, are you?"

I shake my head. "If you wanted to hurt me, you could've done it anytime." Gwen's hold tightens again. She pulls me closer and puts her other hand on my arm. She inhales deeply.

Mrs. Turnipseed smiles and bows her head. "You remind me so much of him," she sobs. She lifts her tear-filled eyes. "He was brave like you. I met him in Italy. I thought that he was just another soldier to feed on when he came back from the battlefield injured. That was, until the day he risked his life to save some civilians." Gwen wraps both arms around mine. Kai looks down. Sora's expression is as blank as usual, but at least, she's not scowling.

"I saved his life before I even realized it. One look…one look into that man's eyes…and I was in love with Jordan from that moment on."

"Impossible," Sora snaps.

"No," Gwen says. "From everything my obāsan…I mean, my grandmother told me about vampires, more often than not, when they fall in love, it's…instantaneous and life-long." Gwen cuts her eyes to Mrs. Turnipseed. "But, I've never heard of a vampire loving a human."

"But I did love my Jordan," Mrs. Turnipseed says.

"I know," I return.

Mrs. Turnipseed smiles again. "I wanted to change Jordan so badly. I wanted to be with him forever, but I made it his choice. He would always say, 'my darling Marisa, I know and accept you as you are. It might change me in some way that would make you love me less…and I couldn't live with that.'" Gwen nods along with her story and I feel a tear fall on my arm. "He was wrong though. There was nothing that he could do to make me fall out of love with him."

"So, Mrs. T," I ask. "What are you gonna do now?"

"I don't know. I really don't know. I've been thinking about what I'd do after Jordan passed away for the last decade…but I never came up with anything." I nod. She looks me in the eye again. "But I'll tell you this. After my Jordan is committed to the ground, I'll be leaving this town…forever."

Gwen reaches up and wipes her eyes. Kai sniffs. Sora just crosses her arms and looks away.

"Thank you, Alex," Mrs. Turnipseed says. "For being nice to me, no matter how badly I treated you." I laugh. "You are truly one of the good ones." With that, she takes a step back and replaces her sunglasses. She turns and walks away.

"You too, Mrs. T," I say. "Had I known what a hard time you were having…I'd've been even nicer."

"She's right," Gwen says. "You are one of the good ones."

112

Chapter 21: Tag

Alex gathers his bag and shoves several spray cans inside. I look around his tiny bedroom with his unmade bed and clothes…EVERYWHERE. There are even a couple of bras and panties. I hope those aren't his. That'd be a little weird.

"So," Alex says. "I think I got everything. Have you heard from your brother?"

I shake my head. "I hope he's not still…spending time with my uncle."

"I doubt it," Alex breathes. "He doesn't seem like the 'family friendly' type."

I stifle a laugh. While drawing in air to help with the stifling, I catch a scent and cover my nose instantly. What is…that…God-awful smell…? It's familiar…it makes the hairs on the back of my neck stand up…it smells like…

A growl sounds. I turn…slowly…and there it is. A small bundle of black and white fur with two beady little greenish-blue eyes…sharp teeth…so many teeth. "Eek!" I jump behind Alex. I grab at his hoodie feverishly as the growling little monster stalks into the room.

"Wha-," Alex starts. "What are you doing? What's wrong with you?" He awkwardly tries to look at me, but I bury my face in his hoodie.

"Beast...monster...scary…" I take two steps backward and pull Alex with me. I sneak another peak at the little fiend. He walks toward us. "Teeth…growling…"

"What…? Monster…? Max…? You mean, Max? Max, stop it!"

"Eeeeeee!" I stumble onto Alex's bed. "Get him. Get him. Get him." Max approaches and puts two paws on the bed. He growls again.

"She's a friend." Alex pets Max on the head. Max looks at Alex then at me. Max growls again and I almost fall off the bed. Alex catches my hand and stops me from toppling over. "MAX…STOP IT…NOW!" The dog whines and backs up. Max turns and scurries out of the room. "Sorry."

"Yeah, you didn't have to yell at him like that. He's…"

"Not him." Alex pulls me toward him. "You. I'm sorry Max is being such a butt to you."

"It's okay," I say still slightly panicked. "He's a dog. It's what dogs do, right?" I sigh, stepping down with Alex's help. "I mean, I wouldn't know…being deathly afraid of them and all."

"Awwww," Alex breathes and puts his hands on the top of my head. He smooths my hair down and then his palms move to the sides of my face. I look into his chocolate-colored eyes with little flecks of jade. I swallow deeply. Is he going to kiss me?

"Sorry," he whispers. "Had I known, I would've put him in my mom's room." I breathe in acutely…his scent…is all over the room…it's surrounding me…it blankets me…it smells so…

"Good," I breathe absently.

"Wha-? Good…?" Alex releases me.

"Sorry. No, not good. Sorry. I mean, it's kind of a natural occurrence for kitsune." He shakes his head with arched eyebrows. "We're…all afraid of dogs."

"You fought that weird-bear-dog-thing…which was the size of an actual bear and looked like a dog made out of shadows…and you're afraid of my…puppy…Max?" Alex made a baby voice at the end. My mouth falls agape and I

113

push him at the shoulder. He takes a step away and laughs. "No, no…I'm just saying." I shove him again. This time he catches my hands at the wrists and pulls me toward him. "Let's…um…try to fight against your nature."

"What? What are you talking about?"

"Max, here boy." He's calling the beast? I jump behind him again, but he manages to hold my wrists.

"WHAT ARE YOU DOING?" I grumble through clenched teeth. "Let go! He's going to eat me!"

Alex laughs. "No, he won't."

"Yes, he will."

"Come 'ere, boy." The dog appears; his head still bowed. "Come on, boy. Don't move." He stares at me. I try to speak, but instead…I hyperventilate. Alex takes my hand. "Breathe, Gwen. Breathe. You're okay. I won't let anything happen to you." I believe him.

Alex maneuvers my hand so that it rests on top of his. He slowly moves our hands toward Max. "Be good, Max," he breathes. Max, in turns, looks up at him. He looks to me and his lip curls away from his teeth. I squeak.

"You're okay," Alex whispers. I nod with my head resting against his arm. His hand caresses the top of Max's head. I inhale deeply. He slowly moves his hand from underneath mine. I continue with the same motion. Max sniffs me several times as I stroke his head. His fur is soft and smooth…it feels good.

Alex squats in front of Max and I move along with him. Max steps closer and my heart flutters. My pulse races. Max bounds at me. I fall back and Max climbs on top of me. I KNEW IT. HE'S GOING TO EAT ME…HE'S GOING TO TEAR ME INTO LITTLE TEENY, TINY PIECES…HE'S GOING TO…lick me…again…and again. I laugh because his tongue tickles my cheek.

"What kind of dog is he?" I manage between laughs.

"He's a border collie." Alex pulls Max off me. Max stares at me with his tongue hanging out and his tail wagging. I stand and pet Max on the head. He walks behind me and rubs the side of his head against my leg. I laugh again.

"Alex," a woman's voice says from the living room. "You forgot to walk Max again. He went all over the mat by the door."

"Crap. That's my mom," Alex whispers. I nod with a frown. Why would he be so concerned about his mother coming home? "Wait here." Alex rushes out of the room.

Max looks at me with his ears tweaked upward. I put one finger in front of my mouth to shush him. He lowers his ears and wags his tail again. He rushes out of the room as he hears a conversation pick up between Alex and his mom. "But ma," Alex whines. "I have to go back to work."

"I stopped by the store on the way home and Mr. Hamish said you have the night off," his mom counters. "So, what other excuse do you have?" I decide that if Alex and I are going to go out to do the 'tag' that I'll have to be his excuse. I grab Alex's bag and walk to the door.

I slowly step out of Alex's bedroom, not knowing what to expect. I find a woman who looks vaguely familiar with wavy shoulder-length jet-black hair. She's a little shorter than Alex and it's evident that he takes after his father more than her. Although, I have to admit she is a beautiful woman with skin almost the same tone as mine. She looks past Alex to me with a scowl.

"Hi," I breathe. Alex turns with panicky eyes and a nauseated, pale expression. "I'm Gwen, Mrs. Garner."

"Alex," she says between clenched teeth. "Why is there a girl coming out of your bedroom?"

"She…," Alex begins.

"…came over to help him with his English homework," I explain. His mother arches her eyebrows and glares at him. "Mrs. Bustamante suggested that Alex get a tutor and…" I motion to myself.

"Is this true?" she asks. He nods. "So, you're having trouble with English too?" He nods again. "Fine, but from now on, do ALL of your studying in the living room." Alex nods again.

"Yes, ma'am, Mrs. Garner," I say as politely as I can.

"It's Ella," she says, stepping past him and offering me her hand. I shake her hand and get that same spark that I got from Alex. I frown and quickly wash it away. "Gwen? Gwen? Gwen? Where have I heard that name?" She holds my hand in both of hers. "Oh," she sparks with recognition. "You're the girlfriend?"

"Ma," Alex nasally whines.

"What? Kai said that she was your girlfriend," Mrs. Garner explains. Alex returns her gaze with wide eyes and makes a cutthroat motion. "Oh," she breathes. She returns to me. "And you're so pretty too." She breaks off to think while still staring at me. She looks me over again. "Yes, definitely do ALL of your studying in the living room." I nod.

She returns to Alex. "I can see why you were trying to head out again." Alex shoves his hands deep into his pockets. "Alright, walk her home, but be back before I have to leave for work." Alex nods. I step past Mrs. Garner and follow Alex over to the door. "It was very nice meeting you, Gwen."

"It was nice meeting you, too, Mrs. Garner…I mean, Ella." She smiles. Alex holds the door and I step outside onto the landing. He slips his bag off my shoulder, waves to his mom, and pulls the door closed. "Wait a sec." I move the hair away from my right ear.

"What?"

"Your mom's talking to herself. 'Okay, yeah…,'" I repeat what she's saying for Alex. "'She's way too pretty to be a tutor let alone a tutor that teaches him in his bedroom…'" Alex laughs. "Aw, your mom thinks I'm pretty. That's so sweet."

"She's not the only one," Alex says in low voice that I'm sure he doesn't think I heard. I look at him and he flushes.

"Hey," I start as we approach the stairs. "I thought you said that your dad was the skinwalker in your family."

"He was," Alex says sadly.

"But, I just…got a sensation from your mom. Like the one I got the first time we touched each other."

"By sensation, you mean shock?" I nod. "What does that mean?"

"I don't know...but your mom could be descended from a supernatural bloodline, too."

#####

"You're sure this is the place?" Gavin asks, staring at me in the rearview.

I maneuver around his tiny backseat and pull Goth-boy's sketch out of my pocket. I check the address. "Yeah, this is it." Gwen peers at me around her headrest. 'I'm so sorry,' she mouths. I shake my head to let her know that I don't need *her* to apologize.

"Alright," Gavin growls. "You two get out and do whatever it is that humans do. I'll circle the block and find a place to park." Gwen throws her door open and slides out. She reaches back in and pulls the seat forward. She offers me her hand, I take it, and she pulls me out. I miss the curb and stumble. Gwen catches me. I stare into her lime-colored eyes. She parts her lips and then swallows deeply. "Aw, that's so sweet," Gavin sings.

Gwen lets go, then bends over so that she can see Gavin. She says something to him in Japanese. Gavin responds in kind. Gwen says something angrily. Gavin replies with glowing blue eyes. I step to Gwen's left and her eyes are glowing, too. I take her by the arm and pull her away. I push the door closed and Gavin barks a "HEY!" He shakes his head, revs the engine, and speeds away.

Gwen closes her eyes and emits a closed-mouth scream. I put my hands on her shoulders. "Sorry," she breathes, then opens her normal, beautiful green eyes. "He just gets to me sometimes…"

"All the time," I say. She frowns, but nods. "What'd he say to you?" She walks toward the house. I catch her hand and stop her. "Gwen, what'd he say?"

"He told me…to have fun…" She rolls her eyes and anger streams off her. "…to have fun…with my pet."

"Meaning me?" She hugs herself and nods. "What'd you say back?"

"Alex," she whines.

"Fine," I snap, feeling her frustration. I walk toward the side of the house. I put my bag down on the ground next to the largest stretch of wall without a window. Gwen steps up beside me. I glance at her and she continues holding herself with that same irritated expression. "I didn't mean to push…you know?"

Gwen smiles and bows her head. "I told him that you weren't a pet…that you're my friend…and that you're kind of awesome."

I smile and pull the spray cans out of my bag. "What'd he say after that?" I ask looking at the sketch. "He really irked you with that one." I start working on the outline. She watches me closely. "Gwen?"

"Ugh. He told me not to get too attached to my simple-blooded pet like I'm already too close to my simple-blooded foster parents."

I finish the outline quickly and take a step back. I look at the sketch again. I think I'll do the shadow next since this silver was special ordered.

"What did he mean 'too attached'?" Gwen opens her mouth to respond but looks away. She's blushing. I laugh softly. "With your foster parents, I mean."

"Oh," she returns. "It's stupid. He knows I can't leave until they give me permission to leave."

116

"What do you mean?" I finish the shadow. I can't help but think that if this were one of my designs, I'd take my time with it…well, more time with it. I look at Gwen. She fidgets. "If you don't want to talk about it, that's cool." I don't like it when she gets that worried wrinkle between her eyes. It goes away.

"Thank you. I'll…I'll tell you…" She hugs herself. "Just…not now…I'll tell you all about it later." I nod, working on the fill-in. Gwen watches carefully as I move from letter to letter. She examines it closely as I finish the last letter with Goth-boy's 'special silver paint.' I have to admit, the texture that this silver paint creates definitely makes the letters stand out from the shadow. I start creating the shine with the white paint I brought.

"You…are so talented." Gwen has a contemplative frown. "This…looks amazing."

"Well, it's not really my design, but…"

"You don't have to be modest." She steps closer. She inspects the logo as I polish off the shine. "You do beautiful work. This…'tag' is great."

"You should see some of my original stuff."

Gwen smiles. "You should show me some of it some time." She sounds like she's…flirting with me.

I turn and she gives me a subtle smile. She looks down, tucks her hair behind her left ear, and comes back. Our eyes meet. "I will. Promise." I take a couple of steps back and examine the finished product.

She kneels. "Amazing. It even looks the same from this angle…even with the ridges on the house." I smirk and collect the spray cans. I drop them into my bag, zip it, and sling it onto my back. I grab the cardboard I brought with me.

"Yeah. I had to figure out a way to keep the design intact with the siding on the house. I used the cardboard at different angles to…why are you looking at me like that?" She tries to wipe the smile away. She shakes her head, tossing her shiny red hair from side to side. Man, she's so freakin' cute.

"No reason." She puts her hands behind her back and balances on the balls of her feet. "It's just…it's good to hear you being so passionate about your work."

I carry the piece of cardboard over to one of Goth-boy's trashcans. "So…" I take the lid off. "No, weird-bear-dog-thing, huh?" I drop the board and replace the lid. She shakes her head. "Guess I was wrong about Goth…I mean, Evan."

"No," Gwen whispers.

"You already said that…" I turn to see her…and she looks like Max just walked up to her growling, showing teeth, and drooling. I swallow deeply. "Gwen, you're scaring me." She runs over to me and grabs my hand. She pulls me away from the trashcan and the shrubbery, surrounding the property. "Gwen?"

"GET DOWN!" She pulls me down…hard. A rustle comes from the bushes and a second later, I lose track of Gwen. I look around as best I can. I hear her yell. "GWEN?"

"Stay down, Alex," she shouts back. I rise to my hands and knees, hoping to catch a glimpse of her. She lands, plants her feet, and crouches beside me. Her eyes glow bright green and reddish-orange flames cover her shoulders, hands and the top of her head…in the shape of two little fox ears. She wraps her arms around my waist.

I put my arm over her shoulders. She jumps and carries us over the hedge before I can process what she's doing. We land, and she pins me down on my back. She lies on top of me with panicked, wide eyes.

"Are you…?"

"Shhhh." She holds one flaming finger against my lips. I nod. A growl comes from the hedge. Gwen slowly lifts herself off me. I grab her by the arm. She shakes her head. The hedges part and…there it is…the shadow-bear-dog-thing peeks its head through.

Gwen jumps to her feet and pulls me with her. She wraps her arms around me and skips backward. The bear-dog darts at us. "Gavin," Gwen yells as we land. She stumbles and we fall. I tumble to the right and she goes left. It bears down on us. I crawl over to Gwen and cover her. She looks at me with a thrown expression.

A bang sounds. The bear-dog falls and whimpers…like a regular dog. It shakes it off and starts toward us again. Two more bangs ring out and a big hand wraps around my arm. "On your feet, panna!" Rex pulls me up.

"Rex?"

"No time to chat, panna!" Rex takes aim at the bear-dog again. "Grab your chica and get out of here." I'd argue…but I need to not die today. I grab Gwen and try to pull her to her feet. She wobbles and almost falls again. I put my arms under her legs and scoop her up. I run as best I can. Two more shots fire behind me. Footsteps…human footsteps are on my tail.

I round the next house and check on Gwen. She's unconscious. Did she hit her head or…?

"Back here," Rex says, waving his gun toward the side of the house. I run with him right behind me. I kneel and sit Gwen down. Rex stares around the corner. He pops the clip out of his…Glock 19…? How can he even afford something like that? "Damn, familiars!" He replaces the clip.

"You know about familiars?" He nods and glances around the house again. "How do you know about familiars?"

He glares at me then goes back to keeping watch. "Your dad told me all about 'em, panna."

"My…my dad?"

Rex puts a finger in front of his mouth. "Check on your chica, panna," he whispers. "She looks like she took a pretty nasty hit for you." Gwen doesn't seem banged up, bruised or any…why is my right hand wet? I hold her up with my left hand and take my right arm from behind her back. I gasp so loud that Rex looks at me. My arm…blood covers my arm from the elbow down to my palm…

"Gwen," I moan, trying to stop myself from crying, but I can't…I can't…she's dying because of me…because she saved me. I press my forehead to hers as tears fall down my face…but even more than that…I feel how cool her skin is.

"Hold her up," Gavin says.

Rex cocks his hammer and points his gun directly at Gavin's forehead. "He's okay, Rex. He's her brother." Rex nods and goes back to keeping watch again.

"It's gone," Gavin says calmly as he takes a knee. He looks me in the eye. "Hold her still," he says so seriously that I obey him like the lemmings obey Meghan. I lean her forward, holding her shoulders. Her head rests on my collarbone. Gavin moves her hair away from her back. He places his hands close to her and a blue flame covers her back.

"Madre de Dios," Rex says. Gavin focuses on Gwen, pouring his fox magic, I think Gwen called it, into her. He keeps it going for a few minutes. He relaxes, the flames disappear, and he lowers his hands. He looks at me and nods. I slip my arm under her legs again and pick her up. "Come on," Rex says. "You guys can rest...and clean up inside."

"Inside where...?"

"Inside my house, panna," Rex says, motioning to the house we've been using as a hiding place.

Chapter 22: Rex

Did I die? I don't feel pain anymore. Did Alex die? The last thing that I remember was trying to save Alex...I lost my footing and fell. He tried to protect me...and then...what happened after that...? Wait, where am I? I look around...hardwood floors, white walls and all the lights are out. Whose house is this? Is this another nightmare, because if it is I can't...?

I hear...sobbing. Someone's crying nearby. I walk through the house, carefully...on the quietest of tiptoes. I round a corner and head into what appears to be a study. A woman dressed in all black with long dark hair hanging around her face sits in a green leather chair. She has her back to me. Various degrees, awards, certificates and...military commendations line the vanilla-tinted walls. The woman cries uncontrollably and pays little attention to me...if she does in fact hear me.

"If you've come to kill me," a familiar voice says in a melodic tone. "Go ahead." She turns and reveals herself as...Mrs. Turnipseed. She has her arms wrapped around something. It's a framed picture of Mr. Turnipseed. "Without him, I have no reason to exist." She places the picture on the small table near her seat. She stands. "It was you who killed him, yes? You killed him to get to me?"

I shake my head slowly. She looks at me with a hopeless expression. "Then why did my Jordan have to die?" Tears fall freely. "Why did my Jordan have to die? If you wanted me, why did you kill my Jordan?" She falls to the floor. I hold my right hand up and the palm teems with a bright light. I open my fist and place it face down on the floor in front of Mrs. Turnipseed. That...horrible seal forms again...just like with the old kitsune.

She can't do this. She can't just give up. If something happened to...to Alex...if I let something happen to Alex, I would find who did it and I would make them suffer. She...gave up. She's going to allow me to kill her. Maybe, I can stop this.

Mrs. Turnipseed slams her hand on the floor. She looks up with piercing, glowing blue eyes and her fangs fully exposed. She hisses, rising to her feet. I jump back as she steps out of the circle.

"Castigo," I say in an echoing, booming voice. Her arms fall to her sides and seem unable to move.

She struggles. "Contego," she utters and her arms free themselves.

I look down at my palm and the crystal appears. I hold it out to her. "Igneum globum." The room erupts in searing flames. No. Vampires are weak against fire. It destroys them. Mrs. Turnipseed screams. I approach the room with the crystal in front of me. "Suffoco." The flames douse themselves.

In the center of the room lies Mrs. Turnipseed. Severe burns ravage her arms and her legs. She grimaces in pain. I feel nauseated again. She tries to rise but her arms won't obey.

"Cohibeo," I say, and she moves into the fetal position. I move my hand and her with it back toward the seal. She glares defiantly. I walk over to her with the crystal.

"T-t-tetigerat...," she whispers. My brow furrows. "...Deus Creator omnium..." Is she praying? Is she saying her last rights? "...Angeli lacrymas...fudit, ipsi...largiri..." I place the crystal at the top of the seal, but that doesn't break her spirit. "…nobis. Corde. Anima." The circle glows in purple, gold and white. "Spiritus. Corpus. Mentis."

I begin the evil chant, but that does not stop her prayer. "Omnes…sicut…unum…para mi Jordan…" I reach the end of my incantation. "VIVE!" she shouts.The room fills with a blinding white light. Brighter than the last time…she's dying. And, I can't do anything about it.

"Noooooooooooooooooooooooooooooooo…" I spring forward and…into Alex's arms. He stares into my eyes and his become two pools of shimmering coffee. "Alex, you're alive." I throw my arms around him and give him a squeeze. We part.

"I should be saying that about you." A tear rolls down his cheek. He wraps his arms around me…and it's gone. The nauseated feeling…it's gone but the nightmare-generated fear isn't.

"Mrs. Turnipseed," I whisper. He relinquishes me. He looks into my eyes. "Remember the dream I told you about…with the old kitsune?" Alex nods. "I just had a similar dream about Mrs. Turnipseed. We have to save her." I try to stand. The room spins and Alex holds me in place.

"You're not going anywhere. Gavin's orders," Alex says firmly. "And for the first time since I met him, I agree with him." I shake my head and try to speak, but it takes a few seconds to gather my thoughts. "Look!" Alex shows me his right sleeve, steeped in something red. "That's all you."

"Right. Bear-dog clawed me in the back." I reach for it and my tattered shirt. "Proving conclusively that he's more bear than dog." I try to laugh but it just comes out as a stuttering exhale.

"Not funny." Alex's face is grim. "I thought I lost you…I-I mean, I thought we lost you."

I smile and wrap my arms around him again. Over his shoulder, Gavin stands in the doorway of this…house that I don't recognize.

"What's this about the vampire?" Gavin asks.

"She's in danger. You have to help her."

"I don't have to do squat," Gavin snaps.

I look at Alex. He nods. "Gavin, the same person who went after the old kitsune in the woods, is after me and is after Mrs. Turnipseed." Gavin uncrosses his arms and steps forward.

"How could you possibly know that?"

"Because I dreamt it," I admit. "I dreamt about this person killing the old kitsune, I dreamt about you fighting Alex's cousin, Sora, and I dreamt about this same warlock attacking Mrs. Turnipseed." Gavin frowns. "I'm having dreams, nii-san. Just like mom used to have."

Gavin scowls outright. His eyes flash bright blue. He points at Alex. "Watch her." He walks away. A man with a baldhead walks in as Gavin exits. "Keep them in the house," he orders this man. "I put up some protective wards, so that thing shouldn't be able to get in." The man nods and continues into the room holding a glass.

He kneels next to Alex and offers me the glass. "How you doin', chica?"

"Fine, I guess." I take the glass from him.

122

"It's OJ. I figured with the amount of blood that you lost, you'd need something a little stronger than water." I nod and take a sip.

"Gwen," Alex starts. "This is Rex. Rex, this is Gwen."

"Nice to meet you."

Rex collects my free hand and kisses the backside. "Es una mujer muy atractiva," he whispers.

Alex takes my hand out of Rex's with a frown. "No." Alex shakes his head. "No, no. None of that." Rex laughs.

"What did he say?"

"Don't worry about it," Alex grumbles, glaring at Rex. "How do you know about my dad?" Rex stands and crosses his arms. His shoulders slump.

"What about...your father...?" I ask. Alex shakes his head slowly, but never takes his eyes off Rex.

"Back when I was a little kid," Rex says. "You remember, I told you I lived with mi abuela, right?" Alex nods. "Well, one night, when I was about seven or eight, me and mi abuela were coming home from the carneceria..." Rex smiles absently. "...she was gonna make my favorite dinner. Well, this guy...came up to us. I thought nothing of him, but mi abuela...she sees angels and demons and stuff...she knew what he was right off the bat. She pulled me behind her as soon as he got close."

"What does this...," Alex interrupts, making a circle with his hand.

"Getting there, panna," Rex returns. "Anyway, this old guy asked mi abuela for 'the pendant.' She told him she didn't know what he was talking about and he called her a liar. He stepped closer and then I saw it," Rex breaks off and motions to his eyes. "Demonio had completely blacked out eyes...and his teeth looked like little nails...sharp and pointy.

"He came at us...but he never made it." Rex points at Alex. "Tu padre...tu padre, Riley Garner...tackled the guy...dragged him into the bushes nearby. It was over in a second. Riley came out of the bush..." Rex moves his hand over the center of his shirt. "...covered in...black blood."

"A ghoul," I breathe, commenting on the color of the creature's blood. Alex looks at me. "They're nasty under beings...think...familiar that always has a corporeal body...except they have a...little bit of free will. They smell terrible though."

"Believe me," Rex adds. "You don't have to tell me. Riley smelled like he rolled around in fresh fertilizer with that thing's blood on him. I was scared out of my mind. Mi abuela...it didn't even faze her. Riley sniffed that thing out and figured it was up to no good, so he followed it. He told mi abuela that he'd be watching her back from then on...and he made good on that promise.

"Nothing ugly ever got that close to us again," Rex explains with a degree of pride. "When I got a little older, Riley started telling me all about the supernatural stuff...ways to sniff 'em out...how to protect myself...even how to kill 'em."

"You know how to kill supernatural beings?" I ask. Rex verifies with a nod.

"And how do you kill a familiar...?" Alex asks. "...with a gun?"

"You don't panna. You kill its master and the familiar goes poof," Rex explains accurately. Alex nods. "After a while," Rex says while looking down. "Mi abuela moved to Boca...left this...pendant thing with me."

"Where is it?" I ask without thinking.

"Not tellin' you, little trickster fox," Rex snaps. "I promised mi abuela that I'd keep it safe until…" He thinks about what to say next. "…until a certain somebody needs it."

"Me?" Alex supposes.

"Nah, panna." Rex waves him off. "You're a skinwalker…like your dad…you got all the juju you need." Alex frowns. "Or, at least, that's what your pop kept hoping for. The older you got…the less likely it seemed that you'd get your fur and fangs or whatever. Your pop started to lose hope, panna. He made me promise to watch your back, in case anything ever happened to him."

Alex stands. "That's why…I started running into you…all over the place after his funeral?" Rex crosses his arms. "And, why you've been hooking me up with odd jobs for extra money…the tags and stuff…?" Rex nods. Alex looks to our left with a scowl. "…and Goth-boy, Evan…he's your neighbor…did he get the seven bills from you to hire me?" Rex nods. Alex swallows deeply, sweeps one trembling hand over his mouth and bows his head.

"It's not that you're not good, panna," Rex exclaims. "'Cause you really are…good. I just figured if I over paid you for a few jobs…it'd build up your confidence…and you'd…you know, keep at the art thing, panna."

"You lied to me," Alex grumbles, pointing a quivering finger at Rex. "You've been lying to me this whole time, panna."

"On your dad's say so, Alex," Rex responds apologetically. "Plus, you're as stubborn as he was. If I'd tried to give you the money…you wouldn't have taken it."

Alex seethes angrily, shaking his head. I focus my fox magic into clearing my head. I reach for…and get his hand. He looks at me. "Alex," I whisper and see my glowing eyes reflected in his. "Come 'ere." He shakes his head. "Please," I beg softly, motioning for him to come to me. I take his other hand and I pull him down to sit next to me.

He positions himself so that we face each other. "You're not angry at Rex." He nods defiantly. "No, you're not…I'm an empath…and I feel everything you're feeling." Alex fights back tears. "You're angry at your father…and you think that that's not fair because he died." Alex sheds a tear. I release his hands and put my hands on both sides of his face. I wipe the tear away with my thumb.

"It's okay," I sigh, knowing that it's more of a wish than fact. He cries. "It's okay." He wraps his arms around me and I return the favor. I hold onto him as tightly as I can, given how weak I feel. Like my earlier nausea, the anger slowly melts away from him. My heart feels warmer…knowing that I have the same effect on him that he has on me. I caress the back of his head as Rex excuses himself.

#####

"It's going to be okay," Gwen whispers. Her hand, on the back of my neck, feels so good. Every caress soothes me. She saw through me. She knew I wasn't mad at Rex. I'm mad at dad…mad at him for keeping all of THIS from me. It'd been building since Sora and Kai told me what they are…what I'm supposed to be.

"I know what you did," I whisper. She giggles. "You dirty little empath, you." She laughs again. It's warm and so infectious that it causes a tingle in the back of my

124

head. She eases her grip on me. I lean away and look into her eyes. She smiles. It's just as mesmerizing and contagious as her laugh. I smile.

"There it is."

"What?" She closes her eyes and shakes her head in several quick jerks. She opens her eyes. I look deep into her emerald eyes…little flecks of brown…and…a little gold, but that seems to flicker and disappear like tiny fires in her eyes.

Gwen's eyes dart down for a fraction of a second, then come back up to mine. She pulls on my hoodie. Her tongue moves across her bottom lip quickly and disappears again. Either I'm crazy or she wants to kiss me. I lean…her left hand makes its way up my arm, landing on my right cheek.

"I…" I start and…my stupid phone rings. I pull it out of my hoodie without even looking at it. "Hello?"

Gwen sighs. I watch her carefully, as if she's not real…or she could disappear at any second. She adjusts so that she can reach the half-empty glass of orange juice sitting on the floor.

"You're alive," Kai yawns. Gwen looks at me over the glass and frowns. She finishes her sip and shakes her head. "Bangs McGhee here hasn't done anything remotely supernatural. Sora hasn't sensed anything from him either. How are things on your end?"

Gwen arches her eyebrows, letting me know that she heard him. She inhales deeply. "We saw it again," I confess.

"The bear-dog…?" Kai asks.

"No, grandma Dottie, what do you think?" I return to the sound of rustles and awkward movement.

"Where are you?" Sora snaps.

"We're at the house next door to Evan's." Gwen arches her eyebrows again and holds the glass of orange juice like it's a Faberge egg.

"Alright," Sora says. "We'll be there as soon as we can. Stay put and we'll sniff you out."

"Sora," I bark before she can end the call.

"What?"

"Don't worry about us. We're safe, but Gwen thinks that Mrs. Turnipseed might be in danger."

Kai groans in the background. "Why would we care about a vampire?"

"Tell Kai because whoever's coming after me almost killed Gwen, DID kill Mr. Turnipseed, and Gavin believed her enough to go on ahead without us to check on her," I yell.

"He heard you," Sora replies. "So, it's just you and your kitsune there? Her brother went on ahead?"

"Yeah. Gwen got nailed pretty badly by that thing and needs rest, so he went on without us." I can practically see Sora's contemplative face and hear her nodding.

"Okay. I'm sending Kai to you and I'll go back up Gavin."

"Thanks, Sora…" I get cut off by the phone's beeping. Sora's already ended the call. I suck my teeth and slip my phone back into my pocket.

"Alex," Gwen says in that soothing way that I'm starting to like.

"Yeah, Gwen…?"

"Um…I don't know how to say this, so I'll just say it." I lean forward, not knowing what to expect. Is she going to tell me she wanted to kiss me before, that she likes me…that she…loves me? "I have to use the bathroom."

"Oh! Oh, yeah…okay…" I stand and give her space. She seems a little out of it and wobbly. "Can you stand up?" I ask her, expecting her to lie for my benefit.

She turns and places her purple Converse on the floor. "I think so," she breathes, then touches her forehead. Her eyes drift closed. She pauses way too long. She inhales deeply and moans on the exhale.

"Liar." She opens her eyes and shakes her head. "Just like I can't fool you, you can't fool me either, Gwendolyn Elizabeth Frost."

She smiles. "Wow, my whole name."

"Yeah, yeah. Come on. I'll help you."

She stares at me with a little bit of apprehension. "When you say help me…?"

"Get to the bathroom…not in the bathroom."

She laughs. "Thank you." She reaches for me with both hands and I take them. I pull her up and she still wobbles, even with my help.

"Come on." I move to her side, putting her arm over my shoulder. For some reason, I can't help thinking that for all the power she has, she's really light. Now that I think about it, she described her power as the *fire* inside of her once. Fire doesn't weigh anything.

I turn toward the back of the house and move slowly. "I'm not an invalid," she complains.

"Then stop moving like one." Her head bows forward. "Sorry, I didn't mean it. Really, I didn't."

"I know. It just…sucks feeling weak."

"Are you…your powers, you know?"

She shakes her head and sulks a bit more. "My fox magic is fine, but I'm so physically weak that it's hard to focus them, even on healing."

"I didn't know you were physically weak. I thought it was just your injuries." She shrugs as best she can. I bend down and put my other arm behind her knees.

"What are you-" Before she can finish, I scoop her up. "Put me down." I shake my head. "I just told you, I'm not an invalid…"

"…and you just told me that you were physically weak. And since I can't help you IN the bathroom, we might as well save as much of your physical strength as possible. So there." She looks at me with sad, defeated eyes. She frowns. The left corner of her mouth twitches and she looks down. She releases a sigh and stares at me.

"Arigato," she whispers softly into my ear.

"You're welcome." I put her down in front of Rex's half-bath. I pull the door open with my left hand while supporting Gwen with my right. She moves into the tiny room with its slanted ceiling and odd floral print walls. She holds on to the knob the entire way in.

126

As the door closes, I see her take hold of the sink in place of the doorknob. "Okay, I'm gonna go back up front…because standing outside of the bathroom while you pee seems a little…a lot…creepy." She laughs. "Call me when you're done."

I walk back through the darkened hallway with its stained hardwood floors, pale walls and ceiling that surprisingly matches the floor. A massive iron chandelier hangs from the ceiling near the center of the walkway and looks like it's comprised entirely of ivy-shaped iron. Rex's floral accented living room is even odder with its deep burgundy couches and brown stone fireplace.

Rex walks in. I look at the couch that Gwen bled all over. "I'm sorry about your couch."

He waves me off. "No worries, panna. I've been looking for an excuse to get rid of mi abuela's old furniture."

I look around. Yeah, I would've been looking for a reason too. As I complete my inspection of the understandably old-fashioned decorating style of the room, the doorbell rings.

Rex looks at me and puts one hand behind his back, no doubt on his gun. "You expectin' somebody, panna?"

I shrug. Rex frowns and removes his gun. "Wait," I snap. He glares at me from the doorway. "It's Kai…my cousin, Kai."

Rex nods. He walks toward the front door and I follow. He replaces his gun. "You mean that little blond kid from Oregon?" I nod. He huffs a laugh. "You know, I always wondered how your *other* cousin turned out."

"Gross."

"Double gross," Kai yells through the door. Rex opens it. "Pizza Hut!" Kai smiles into a yawn.

"Come in, panna," Rex says, pushing the screen door open.

Kai grabs the screen door, opens it wider, and steps to the threshold. He stops. "What the hell?" He glares at the doorframe.

"What's your problem, panna? I said come in, before that damn thing comes back."

"I would if I could." Kai lifts his hand and tries to move it across the threshold. It stops. Not only does it stop but it looks like the palm of his hand pushes against a clear window.

"Madre de Dios," Rex breathes.

"What gives?" Kai asks, looking flippant. He slips his hand into his pocket and slowly his features shift to the Golden Tabby that I saw the other night at the school.

"Kai," I growl. "You changed in front of Rex. You had no idea if I told him about you guys or not."

"Of course, you did." Kai pushes his shoulder again the invisible barrier. "You're you, aren't you?" I scowl. He examines the threshold again. "Besides, one of the few times your dad talked to grandma, he told her all about the little Puerto Rican brat and his grandma that he saved."

Rex cocks the hammer of his gun with the barrel right next to Kai's head. "Call me a brat again, panna. We're gonna have some problems, yeah?"

"I already have one," Kai grumbles still trying to force his way in. "I can't get past this stupid doorway."

"It's the ward," Gwen says. I rush over to her side.

"When did you come out? Why didn't you call me? I was gonna help you," I say sounding like it all ran together. "If you're still tired…"

"I'm fine. I was able to focus a little more and I got some of my strength back." She cuts her eyes to Rex. "Thanks for the orange juice, it was yummy." Rex tilts his head back.

"Why can't I get in?" Kai asks in his normal, non-tigery voice.

"My brother said that he put up wards to protect the house from the weird-bear-dog-thing, but I guess he made it to keep out anything supernatural that wasn't already in the house," Gwen explains. Kai rams his shoulder into it again.

"Will you stop?" I grumble. "You can't come in."

Gwen steps forward. "Yes, he can."

Kai tries to ram the shield again and stumbles inside, almost knocking Rex over. "What the hell, panna?" Rex shouts, shoving him off. Kai rights himself and looks around.

"You had to invite him in," I suggest.

Gwen smiles and nods. "My brother's incantation…we're of the same bloodline…I took a shot."

"Nice one," Kai says, scratching the back of his head. He releases a yawn. "Why do I smell blood?"

"Like I said, the bear-dog clipped Gwen across the back and we would've been toast if not for Rex…and Gavin…eventually." Gwen huffs a laugh…sort of.

"You okay?" Kai asks, sounding like he's falling asleep. She nods but leans against me. Her eyes half-close like Kai's usually are. She yawns.

"We should get you home," I whisper. She shakes her head defiantly, but weakly and emits a sort of humming negative response. "You're still tired and you were up early this morning," I add using her early morning nausea as an excuse. She glares at me with accusing eyes. I guess she didn't want anybody to know about that. I mouth, 'I'm sorry.' She shakes her head again before resting it on my shoulder.

I lean closer to her. "You're too weak to even argue with me," I whisper. She laughs…or did she snore? I think she's fallen asleep on her feet.

"I'll take her," comes from the door. Gavin and Sora stand on Rex's porch.

"Damn," Rex spits, staring at Sora. "How you doin', chica?" Kai and I faux-vomit simultaneously.

"I'm doing 'completely not interested.' How are you?" Sora responds, sounding more annoyed than normal. Rex lifts his hands in submission. Thank God. I don't think I could've listened to another minute of him hitting on my cousin. "Let's go, you two." Kai marches out without question.

"What happened with Mrs. Turnipseed?" I ask, holding Gwen up and moving toward the door. Gavin steps into the house, looking sullen. He takes Gwen from me but keeps his eyes low. "Sora…?"

She sighs loudly. Uh-oh… "When we got there, her place was already up in flames," Sora explains.

"We tried to sniff around," Gavin continues.

"But fire makes that nearly impossible," Sora finishes.

I nod and turn my attention to Gwen. She's gonna be crushed when she finds out. Gavin takes in my expression. He looks down at Gwen. His eyes flash bright blue to the point of looking silver. Suddenly, pale blue flames engulf his entire body and by extension, Gwen. I step forward and Gavin glares at me in a way that makes me stop cold.

"I have her," Gavin grumbles.

"Let's go," Sora says again. I look at her and the light coming from Gavin vanishes…and so have Gavin and Gwen. "He used Hunter's Step."

I continue looking around absently, half-expecting to see some trace of them. "I think they call it 'Swift Paw,'" I explain. She nods, then tips her head back. I turn to Rex. "Rex, I…"

"Don't, panna," he interrupts. "Don't thank me. Don't even mention it." He holds his fist out to me. "Somos hermanos." I smile and tap my fist against his. I step out and look at him over my shoulder. He jerks his head upward then pushes the door closed behind me.

I sigh, thinking about how tragic the Turnipseeds' end was. The door opens. I turn to Rex. "We might be brothers, panna, but that doesn't mean you guys don't owe half on my new sofa." He slams the door.

Chapter 23: Ask

I pull my hair into a ponytail...I'm feeling lazy today. I steal a glance at Gavin...leaning against my bed. He holds the stuffed ragdoll that Mrs. Taylor gave me when I moved in. He tilts her to one side, then the other, causing her red mop of yarn hair and her blue and white plaid dress to sway with each movement. He tosses it aside, then catches me looking at him in the mirror. He smirks. He peers at himself and smiles outright.

How can he do that? I look at the picture of myself. Then, I look down at my laptop and see myself in real time. "Do they ask you about that?" I look at him with a puzzled expression. "Do your humans ever ask you about the picture on your mirror?"

I shake my head and return to my screen. "No." I touch up the makeup on my pale cheek. "Mrs. Taylor thinks that I use it as an expression of how confident I am in my own appearance. Mr. Taylor thinks it's just a 'cute, quirky thing' that I do."

Gavin scowls and stands. He goes over to the window and stares outside with his arms crossed. The leather of his jacket tenses, as he flexes his muscles.

"Gwenie," he says, regarding me in a non-condescending way. He looks sad. "I have something to tell you about your dream last night. I..."

"Mrs. Turnipseed is dead," I whisper. Gavin sighs and nods once firmly. "I know. Even if not for the dream repeating itself this morning, Alex called. He thought it might be easier coming from him."

"Was it?" Gavin asks.

I nod, thinking of how Alex stayed on the phone with me through twenty minutes of crying without saying a word. It was as if he knew that I wasn't ready to speak. I look at my brother. Knowing him, if this were the first time I'd heard it, he would've harassed me until I spoke about my feelings...only to act as though he doesn't care.

"Gwenie?"

"Yeah." A bit of the southern twang takes root in my vernacular.

"How long...have you been having dreams like that?" I shrug. The truth is that I don't know. I can't remember when it began, but I do know that they have never been as vivid and true to life as they are now. Usually, they have been realistic but with an element of fantasy or my own personality thrown in.

These dreams are odd...leery...creepy. I felt like I was this mystery killer when he slaughtered that poor kitsune and when he attacked Mrs. Turnipseed. I scoff aloud, drawing his attention away from his silent reflections. I felt like I was Gavin when he fought Sora. I wonder if how I felt about her was true as well.

"You know what this means, don't you?" he asks as I take my purple cardigan from my chair's backrest and drape it over my white, backless top that Meghan told me I 'had to have.'

"No." I toss my hair to make sure that none of it caught in my cardigan. "What does it mean?"

Gavin groans with annoyance, frustration and anger streaming off him in increasing waves. "It means that we have to find your charm now more than ever, Gwenie."

My charm…? I've been so focused on protecting Alex that I haven't given it any thought. "I'll be fine." I collect my pack from the bed. He catches my wrist. I resist, but to no avail. He squeezes. "Ow," I pant and release the pack.

"No, you won't," he whispers in a menacing voice. "You should be able to mop the floor with this familiar, but as it stands, you've barely survived two fights with it." I focus a little fox magic into the muscles of my arm and yank my wrist free. He glares with his eyes glowing. "And to make matters worse, you put this human's life before yours."

"He's my friend and an innocent…"

"We're kitsune. We don't have non-kitsune friends and we don't give a damn about innocents."

"Well, I do," I yell, inadvertently causing my voice to echo with fox magic.

"Gwen?" Mrs. Taylor calls from the hallway. Her last footfall sounds outside my door. "Is everything alright, dear? I heard you yell."

"Yes, ma'am." My brother's face goes from angered to amused in a flash. "I was…"

"…just rehearsing for a play," Gavin says…in my voice. Anger swells up so fast that I have to struggle to contain it. The repeater game was never more annoying or infuriating than when Gavin would repeat my words in my voice. Just one of the dozen ways that he likes to show me how far advanced he is.

"Oh," Mrs. Taylor exclaims with excitement. "You didn't tell us you were in a play."

I place my hand over Gavin's mouth. "I'm not." I try to work up an explanation. "It's…an audition. I doubt that I'll get the part."

"Don't say that, dear," Mrs. Taylor says, letting her voice drop at the end. "I'm sure you'll be amazing. Let us know if you get the part, alright?"

"I will." I glare at my brother, who I'm sure if I had the power, I'd be trying to rip apart right now. Mrs. Taylor walks away. Gavin erupts with laughter. "What is your problem?"

"Right now?" He chuckles. "I have an idiot sister who bound herself to two humans and doesn't even know what they did with her charm."

I sigh. I'm angry, because everything he's been saying is true. I did bind myself to them. I did lose to the bear-dog-thing…twice…I nearly died the second time…and worst of all, I almost got Alex killed in the process.

"That's okay. I'll show myself up," Meghan says.

I look at Gavin in a panic. He frowns. "You have to go," I snap and push against his chest, netting no result.

"Why…? Because your idiot human friend has a crush on me?"

"Exactly. I know you, nii-san. You'll lead her on…get her to the point where she'd be willing to do anything for you and then you'll destroy her." Gavin flashes that sinister smirk of his. I hate that smirk. It's the smirk of a true kitsune. One who would play with a human's head and heart and then discard their plaything when they were done with it…I mean, them.

A knock comes from the door as it swings. "Knock, knock," Meghan reiterates as she steps inside. "Are you ready to go, lo-" Meghan spots Gavin standing near the window. He hits her with the full force of those cobalt blue eyes that he got from our mother. He strikes…and the blow lands so hard that Meghan seems physically affected. "-ser," she finally finishes.

Meghan plays with her hair as she moves closer to Gavin. "Hey, Gwen's foster-mom didn't say you were here."

"That's 'cause she doesn't know," Gavin responds. His voice dropped into a low octave. "And we're kinda keeping it a secret so…" He places one finger in front of his mouth. "…shhh, okay?"

Meghan giggles absently and nods. I roll my eyes before I realize it…it's as if my eyes were even tired of hearing this already.

I take my pack in one hand and grab Meghan with the other. "Let's go," I command her for the first time. "We're going to be late for school."

She nods as she stumbles backward. "Bye, Gavin," Meghan sings. I look back just in time to see him issue a finger-wiggling wave while wearing that same sinister smirk. I follow Meghan into the hall.

"I forgot something," I say. "Wait…right here." I peer back into my bedroom and find Gavin looking through the pink wooden jewelry box that Mr. Taylor picked up for me the last time he was in Elizabeth City. I have yet to put any jewelry in it. "Get out of my room," I snap. He laughs my order off. "I mean it."

He nods, then walks to the window. He opens it, pushing the lower portion up. "Not through the front…" A burst of bright blue fire cuts off my words. He's gone and worse, he made a spectacle of himself.

I turn and walk into the hall. Meghan leads the way downstairs. "He is so annoying," I whine.

"And hot," Meghan adds looking back. I tweak one eyebrow and give her my very best 'are you insane?' look. "Well, not so much for you, but for me…"

"Meghan, listen to me." She stops at the bottom step and turns to me, looking ambivalent. "Listen," I repeat in a sterner voice. She nods. "Don't date my brother, okay? He's…a liar and a manipulator…and…I don't want to see you get hurt. So, just don't date him, okay?"

"What makes you think I won't hurt him, loser?" She turns toward the front door.

I sigh and let my shoulders drop. "History," I breathe and follow her.

#####

Kai yawns so hard that he has to throw his head back, which doesn't make him drop the subject he's been droning on about since he woke up. "Why in the hell are we at school this early?"

"I told you," Sora says again tugging at the sleeves of her new, tear-free, form-fitting leather jacket that stops just above her belt. "We staked out Goth-boy…" She grits her teeth. "…I mean, Evan, while Alex and the kitsunes mixed it up with the bear-dog." She cuts two accusatory, hazel-colored eyes at me. "I want to find out what your little fox face knows about this thing."

"She knows it almost killed her while she was protecting me," I grumble, pulling my worn pack farther up on my shoulder, glad that we grabbed it from Evan's yard after leaving Rex's. "She knows that if not for Rex and her stupid brother neither of us would be alive today."

Sora shoots me an elbow that feels like I've been stabbed minus the benefit of blood as proof of stabbing. I rub my newly bruised ribs. Her eyes bulge and cut to two girls staring at us...wait, no...they're staring at Kai. Sora and Kai follow me all the way to my locker.

"That hurt." I put my bag down. Sora leans on the locker next to mine with her arms crossed. She frowns. "What's with you?"

"I'm..." She clenches her jaw and looks at me. "...I'm kinda pissed." I open my locker and she slides to her right. I push the door wide so that I can see her. "If grandma were here, we'd've found whoever's controlling this thing, thumped him and been on our way back to Oregon by now."

"So, you don't like sleeping on the living room sofa?" I ask her, knowing that I'm poking the bear. She literally growls...and I think I see fangs.

"Here comes your girlfriend," Kai says, tipping his head toward Sora. She and I turn to Gwen, Meghan and Meghan's entourage of lemmings walking down the hall. "Do those chicks follow them everywhere? Like even to the bathroom and stuff?"

I shrug and shake my head. "And she's not my girlfriend." He snickers. Sora just keeps watching them getting closer and closer. "What are you doing, frowny-bear?"

"Who's the blonde?"

"You mean, besides you two?"

She glares and growls again...and I think I see fangs...again! "I know, I've seen her somewhere before." Sora looks at Meghan and Gwen again.

"That's Meghan Powers. Remember?"

"Powers...?" Sora huffs in their direction. "That's just funny." She laughs at her own private joke. "I gotta go." She pushes off the lockers. "Watch the blonde," she whispers to Kai. He nods.

"What was that?" He frowns and shakes his head, then his eyes dart to my right. A hand touches my shoulder and I feel that familiar spark that comes from her touch. I turn to Gwen's hand still lingering...yes, lingering...on my shoulder. She smiles. I smile back.

"We'll talk later," she whispers as she passes. I stare after she moves on, hanging on to the slight tingle of her touch...wow, I sound goofy.

"Man, you look goofy," Kai confirms.

"Thanks, Kai." I close my locker and head to Biology with Kai on my heels.

"So, what do you think your girlfriend wants to talk to us about?"

"First, she's not my girlfriend. Second, she didn't say she wanted to talk to us...she said she wanted to talk to me. And third, why are those girls still following us?"

"Girls...?" Kai glances behind him. "Oh...them. Dance."

"What?"

"The dance tomorrow," Kai explains. "It's a...what'd that flyer call it...Sadie Hawkins style dance."

"So, girls have to ask guys?"

134

"Don't be so literal," Kai complains. "Girls could always ask other girls." I stop in my tracks and stare at him. "Or for that matter, what about the poor guys who wanna go with other guys?"

I laugh. "Never really thought about it, but I guess they don't get to go, because the girls have to ask."

"That sucks," Kai says, scratching the back of his head.

"Never knew you were so supportive of lesbian and gay rights, cousin."

"I'm not…I mean…it's just…," he breaks off to slump down into his desk. "You should be able to take whoever you wanna take, you know?"

"Yeah, I know what you mean." He nods, crosses his arms on the desktop and puts his chin on his forearms. If I didn't know any better, I would swear this is REALLY bothering him for some…

"Alex," Gwen calls from over my shoulder. She looks pale. I probably shouldn't tell her that, but she does. I think she's doing worse than she let on last night. "What?" she asks as I continue staring with my mouth hanging open a bit. I shake my head. "You were staring. Is something wrong?"

"No, no…I was just…thinking about the dance Friday."

"Yes. That's what I wanted to talk to you about."

"Oh, yeah?" I shove my hands into my pockets, trying to play it cool, even though I really want her to ask me to go to the dance.

"Yeah. See I was thinking…that we should go together." I smile. "You know, in case, the weird bear-dog comes around again."

My smile drops away. "Oh, no…yeah…yeah, I was thinking that too," I lie.

"Pfft, I bet you were," Kai mocks.

"Shut up."

"That was supposed to be my line," Mrs. Pritchard says from the doorway. "…except I wouldn't have said it so rudely. Take your seats please." Gwen and I hurry to our desks. As Mrs. Pritchard makes her way to the front, Gwen taps me on the shoulder.

"You never answered," she whispers. I frown. She shakes her head before I can refute her claim. "You just said that you were thinking that too. You never confirmed."

"Mr. Garner," Mrs. Pritchard calls. "Ms. Frost do you two have anything you'd like to share with the rest of the class?" I shake my head and I can only assume that Gwen is doing the same. "Very well…" she stops abruptly. "Yes, Mr. Garner…" I frown. I didn't say…then I look to my right. Kai has his hand raised.

"Why can't guys ask other guys to the Sadie Hawkins dance?" he asks, causing a lot of laughter from the rest of the class. "Oh," he continues as the laughter starts to die down with some scowling from Mrs. Pritchard. "And if you wanted to know what they were talking about…she just asked him to said dance and she was asking about his answer." He offered helpful thumb pointing at the appropriate pronouns. The class explodes with laughter again. I pull my hoodie over my head and put my head down.

"Well," Mrs. Pritchard says sounding closer. I lift my hood and she's standing right next to me. "Don't keep us in suspense, Mr. Garner. What is your answer?" she says sarcastically.

I look at Gwen's bright red cheeks. She looks at me for a fraction of a second before looking away and putting her hands over her mouth then bringing them together like she's praying. I sigh. It's time to put up or shut up.

"Look at her," I exclaim to the whole class. "I'd have to be nuts to say 'no' to her…and I'm not nuts." Every girl in class offers a simultaneous 'aw' while every guy gripes some version of complaint ranging from 'nobody's asked me' to 'I'm not nuts either.'

"Well done, young Padawan," Kai whispers. I chuckle and look at Gwen. She's practically beaming. The red disappeared from her cheeks, although they haven't gone back to being as pale as they were when she walked into class.

Gwen bounds up and gives me a quick kiss on the cheek. "Thank you for making this less awkward," she breathes as she sits back down.

"No problem," I whisper so low that only she and Kai can hear me. I turn back to the front and Mrs. Pritchard has already returned to the board, shaking her head the entire way.

Chapter 24: Superior

"Is it true?" Alex's friend, Stephen, asks as he rushes over to us.

"Is what true?" Alex asks.

Stephen motions between Alex and me. "This. Is this true? Are you guys a couple now?"

"What?" Alex says.

"It's all over school," Kai explains. "The latest version is that Gwen got down on one knee and proposed and Alex took off his gold chain and gave it to her with the promise of replacing it with an engagement ring."

"What?" I laugh at the same time Alex does.

"Well, you know that's how it spreads," Kai yawns.

"The version I heard was a little tamer," Stephen explains. "I heard that you…" He points to me. "…asked you…" He points at Alex. "…to the Sadie Hawkins dance and then you both said that you loved each other and made out in the middle of class."

Alex and I laugh all over again. This time Kai joins in. "How is that tamer?" I ask.

"Nah, nah, it wasn't like that," Alex explains. "She asked me…as a friend…Kai made it a bigger thing than it was…I accepted…peck on the cheek ensued."

"Peck…?" Kai prods. "I think I got to at least a three count…and I'm pretty sure she got a little lip too."

"Kai!" we snap at the same time. He chuckles obnoxiously and holds his hands up in surrender.

"What happened?" Sora says in a voice that could give an ice cube brain freeze. ALL the laughter that developed drains away. "WHAT…HAPPENED…?" Oddly, she's starting to remind me of Gavin when he's angry.

"Nothing," Alex says. "We just decided it'd be best if we went to the dance together. You know, in case of weird…" I put my hand over Alex's mouth, knowing what's coming next and also knowing that we have no way of explaining what a weird-bear-dog thing is to Stephen.

"…okay, I'll say it," I say to Stephen's waiting, anxious expression. "Alex noticed that a lot of the attention I've been getting here was…" I pause. I move awkwardly to signify the awkwardness of what I'm about to awkwardly say. "…of the Pixie, fan-girl, anime loving type." Oh, now that I say it aloud, I hope that that doesn't describe Alex, too. He nods along with my narrative. "So, we figured that if we went to the dance together, there would be fewer awkward turndowns."

"…or, you just could've gone by yourself and surrounded yourself with that Powers-girl's minions," Kai says.

"No. They're stupid." My hands instantly snap over my mouth. Was that too mean? All three boys erupt in laughter, so I guess not. Sora is decidedly NOT laughing. She turns toward the cafeteria.

"Good idea," Stephen says between chuckles. "It's lunch time." Stephen puts one arm over my shoulders and the other over Alex's shoulders. "Time to go turn the rumor mill." Alex groans and I smile as best I can. Kai laughs again before yawning.

The lunch line moves quickly. We get our food. I'm not very fond of the school's version of *pizza*, but at least I have French fries to supplement my meal. I look around and, of course, the lemmings already surround Meghan. They've filled her lunch table to the point that some are standing nearby holding their trays as they eat. Meghan spots me and waves me over. I frown and shrug, motioning to the hordes framing her. She shakes her head and waves me over again. I nod.

"Maybe, we should all sit together," Kai suggests. "Living the lie," he sings.

I laugh and so does Alex. He shakes his head and prepares an alternative suggestion.

"That sounds like a good idea," I say before I can stop myself. Alex's eyebrows come together...so cute...as if he wants to ask me something. "It's fine. Really." He nods. I make sure that Sora and Stephen are still behind us. Once Sora appears from the end of the lunch line, I turn toward Meghan's table and walk in that direction.

I can't help wondering if I'm right. That it really will be fine. "Don't be mad."

Meghan looks at me with her best-puzzled expression. "...don't be mad about what, loser?" Then, as if they heard me, Alex, Kai, Sora, and Stephen walk over to our table with their respective lunch trays. Meghan eyes each of them then looks at me and I actually feel her call me, 'loser,' (in the bad way) with her eyes.

"Meghan...you know Alex and, of course, Stephen..."

"Why 'of course, Stephen,' loser?" Meghan says between clenched teeth, all the while her eyes convey, 'shut up, shut up, shut up.'

"...no reason. And these are Alex's cousins...Kai..." Kai nods. "...and Sora." Sora looks at Meghan and her eyes narrow. "They're...um...going to eat with us."

"Ugh. Fine," Meghan says as a complaint, but her emotions tell me she's a little happy about it. She turns to the girl sitting on her right. "Go away. You're sitting in my beastie's seat." The girl obediently rises and walks away.

Sora's jaw clenches as the girl leaves. "That's okay. I don't think...we'd be comfortable sitting here." She looks at Kai, who seems to be delightfully oblivious to whatever Sora feels. "Come on. There's an empty table open over there." Kai frowns but follows.

Alex watches them apprehensively. "I'm...gonna go sit with my cousins." I nod. He leans in closer. I swallow deeply, wishing he'd stay. "And maybe I'll find out what's up with the rude behavior," he whispers. I can't help but take in his scent. He smells so good I could actually bite him.

"Okay," I say breathlessly as he steps away.

Chapter 25: Nervous

I walk away from Meghan's table as Gwen takes the seat next to her. Stephen follows me. He looks around constantly.

We walk over to Sora and Kai's table…that they apparently shooed everyone else away from because I know this table wasn't 'empty' a second ago…I sigh.

"Hey," Stephen says. "Have you seen Rich?" I shake my head. "Crap. He's still avoiding us…well, you since Gwen's been paying you so much attention." I nod. "And the rumors flying around about you two can't be helping that." I can't believe he's still mad about that whole dibs crap. If he knew what was really going on with Gwen, he'd… "I'm gonna go try and find him." Stephen puts his tray down. He walks away quickly, and Kai pulls the abandoned tray closer.

Kai makes a sandwich of his and Stephen's pizzas and wolfs it down. Sora stares daggers at me. I literally drop my tray and before it hits the table Kai has snatched my slice of pizza and my apple.

"What was that?" I grumble. Sora's eyes move from me, to Meghan and Gwen, and back again. I look at them. Gwen's looking at us. She turns to Meghan quickly. "I get it…okay? You don't like me spending time with Gwen because she's…" I look around. "…a kitsune," I whisper. "But that doesn't mean you have to…"

"It's not her," Sora says. "…not this time, at least."

"It's her 'bestie,'" Kai chimes in between bites of my pizza. "There's something weird about that chick."

"Meghan? What about her? Is she supernatural or something?"

"I don't know," Sora complains. "I don't think so, but when she talked to that girl…I felt…something."

"Disgust, maybe? I mean, the way 'the lemmings' obey her blindly is kind of disturbing to anybody who hasn't seen it before." Gwen looks at Meghan with a weird, worried expression.

"Can you hear us?" Sora says. Gwen nods subtly. "Did you sense something from Meghan, too?" Gwen nods again. "Are you going to find out what's going on with her?" Gwen sighs, her eyes drift closed, and she bobs her head again. "Good. The sooner we find out who's the master of this shadow familiar the sooner Alex is safe."

Gwen looks at me. Her eyes glow. "It's okay," I reassure her. "I'm sure it's not Meghan. If she wanted to kill me, she's had a long time to try…and aside from nasty looks, she's never tried anything…or at least, nothing weird's happened before now." Gwen nods once.

"I'm sure he's right," Sora says. "But it never hurts to be certain." Gwen smiles. "See," Sora breathes. "Me and your little fox face can get along just fine."

Sora and Kai tweak their heads as if a pin poked them at the same time. I turn to Gwen outright. She's talking, but it doesn't look like she's involved in the conversation at her table. I sit down, keeping my eyes on Gwen.

"What's she saying?" I ask. Sora shakes her head subtly, but several times.

"Tell him," Kai says absently, which causes Sora to give him her 'I will kill you' stare. Is Kai trying to tell Sora what to…? "Tell him. Tell him. Tell him," Kai continues.

"Tell me what?" I ask Sora.

She sighs and rolls her eyes. "That's what she's telling us," Kai responds. "To 'tell you...tell you...tell you.'"

I look at Kai then Sora. She presses her lips into a line. "Fine." She locks eyes with Gwen. "She wanted me to tell you that she's going to do whatever she can to protect you for as long as...we'll...let her." Sora frowns. "I'm not telling him that," she snaps. She rolls her eyes again and turns away from Gwen.

"I'll tell him," Kai cuts in with a scratch of his head. I look at Gwen and she tips her head toward Kai. I guess acknowledging that she heard him. I turn back to Kai and he reaches across the table with both of his hands and grabs mine.

"Whaaaaaaattttttttt are you doing there, Kai?"

"Shhhh," he utters with...his eyes closed...? "This needs to be said with the care and delicacy that she put into it." He swallows deeply and my face twists awkwardly.

"You're kind of weirding me out, cousin."

"Alex," Kai starts making his voice sound more awake and lively. "I will...you know? I will protect you no matter what. I care about you and I wouldn't want anything bad to happen to you...because...I..."

"I don't want anything to happen to you because of me, Gwen."

"Dude," Kai starts looking down at our hands. At some point, I pulled his hands closer to me. "I'm not your girlfriend, so I'm not gonna make out with you." I shove his hands away and turn to Gwen. She's laughing. She quickly waves Meghan off then comes back to me. She tucks a strand of hair that didn't quite make it into her ponytail behind her ear and smiles...as if...she's flirting with me. I smile back.

"Okay, see now you're sending mixed signals," Stephen says taking the seat next to me. "You can't hold Kai's hands one minute then turn around and make googly eyes at Gwen...who 'isn't' your girlfriend." Kai laughs.

I pick up a few of my remaining fries that Kai hasn't eaten and toss them at him. "Jerk was just screwing around with me."

"Hey man, if you're gay or bi or whatever, I just want you to know that I'm happy for you, for not being afraid to be yourself," Stephen says. "...but I do have to draw the line at incest." He points at me. "'Cause that's just gross." Kai laughs uproariously. Stephen looks at Sora, who is still wearing her serious face. "Come on, Sora. Where's the chuckle, girl?"

"Better question," Sora says. "Where's your creepy friend, Rich?" Her eyes dart to me then Stephen. "We haven't seen him in a while."

I look around...weird...I didn't even think about Rich today...before Stephen mentioned him...and I didn't give him another thought until just now. I don't remember thinking about him at all yesterday either...except when Stephen brought him up then too. I look at Stephen's puzzled expression and frown. I wonder if it's the same for him.

"I don't know," Stephen admits.

"You said you were going to go check on him and then you came back without him," Sora explains.

"I...," Stephen drags out. "...guess I didn't see him." How could he have forgotten? He just did it. Mr. and Mrs. Turnipseed must be bothering him more than he's willing to admit.

140

The last of the lemmings depart and I turn to Meghan. She closes her locker and looks into my eyes. "What's wrong, loser? You look like you have something on your mind."

She takes one hand in the other and leans with her back against her locker door. I sigh. How can I pose this to her? How could anyone ask someone if they're a supernatural being with magical powers that may or may not manifest in the form of a weird-bear-dog-creature with sharp teeth and an appetite for cute boys…well, a cute boy who I might be crushing on…hard.

"Do you…?" She arches her perfectly manicured eyebrows a bit more. I decide to redirect. "Why did you become friends with me?"

"What?" She laughs with genuine shock streaming off her. Then again, if she's as clever as I think she might be, she might be able to lie well enough to trick even me. "Where's this coming from, loser?"

"I mean, you could've chosen any girl at this school to be your 'bestie,' but you picked me…me, the weird new Japanese girl with red hair and the pink Converse with purple piping." Meghan smiles in a way that tells me she thinks either I'm the 'cutest thing' ever or I'm the biggest idiot ever' or both.

"Is that all, loser?" She maintains that flawless beam of hers. "Well…" She sighs. Her mood and demeanor seem to change in an instant. She steals a glance to her left and then her right. Once she's certain no one's within earshot, she returns.

"What?"

"Gwen…ever since I turned ten years old," she starts with a solemn ring to her voice. "Everyone in my life has done everything I ask them to do." I frown, finding this difficult to accept…until I recall how the lemmings so obediently follow her around…how she dismisses them with little regard to their feelings only to have them come back for more. "At first, I thought it was just because I'm…pretty, but there are lots of pretty girls in this school. And the older I got, the more noticeable it became." She looks down. "Can you imagine what that's like?"

Lonely. "No."

"And then…you came along…" She sounds relieved. "If I had said, 'nice shoes' to any other girl in this school, I wouldn't be able to get rid of her…but you…practically ignored me." She shakes her head. "At first, I thought maybe you just didn't hear me…so I came back around. When I figured out that you did…it…was…AWESOME." She smiles. "And then…then you disagreed with me." She finally lifts her eyes to me and they're filled with tears.

Loneliness…that's why I'm her best friend…she's lonely. She may be supernatural and just doesn't know about it…but it's left her feeling isolated.

"Well?" she asks. "Does that answer your question?" Her feelings overwhelm her and by extension overwhelm me since I synchronized with her emotions.

"Yeah." Tears fall from my eyes.

"Awwwww." She laughs and gives me a hug. "It's okay, loser," she purrs, stroking my hair. Suddenly, I feel like she's exactly right. It is okay. Everything is okay. Everything will be…wait, no…that's not how I was feeling a second ago. What's going on? I take a step back from Meghan and she releases me.

"What was that?" I snap.

"What was what?"

"That. You were trying to manipulate me…put me under a spell or something."

"What are you talking about, loser? Did you NOT take your meds this morning? We were having a moment and then you went a little psycho." Anger swells inside me. I take her by the wrist and pull her toward me. "Ow, you're hurting me."

"Admit it," I bark. "You're a dark witch or a siren or something." She whines and tries to pull away. "What do you want with Alex? Why are you after him?"

"After him…? I thought you liked him," she sobs still trying to pull her wrist free. "Is this about your brother?"

"No, because whatever you are, my brother would crush you the second he caught wind of it. So, what are you, *Meghan*? Are you a dark witch…? A siren…? Some kind of succubus…?"

"No, she's not," a girl says calmly behind me. I turn to two cocoa brown eyes, trained on me from underneath an explosion curly, light auburn hair. Her honey skin tone seems to reflect light, giving her a soft glow. She pushes a pair of thick, black, horn-rimmed glasses back up her small round nose.

"Jamie-Lynn," Meghan starts, sounding comforted. "Can you please tell me what drug is making my soon-to-be former bestie act like this?" I release Meghan.

"I'll explain it to you later," Jamie-Lynn says, stepping past me and over to Meghan's side. She puts her hand on Meghan's back and moves it in a circle. She whispers something and ushers Meghan past me. "You know, you should probably head to 5th period, Meghan. Gwen'll catch up to you later."

"Okay," Meghan chirps happily then turns to me as if nothing happened. "Catch you later, loser." She said it in the good way. I frown. Meghan practically skips away.

Jamie-Lynn's head bows as Meghan rounds a corner. "Ugh. I hated having to do that to her…again." She turns to me. "Can't have her asking too many questions, you know?" I stare at her, taking in her casual manner and not getting any read from her emotionally. "That was so weird. Usually, kitsune are the ones being accused, not doing the accusing."

"H-how…"

"How do I know what you are?" I nod absently; suddenly, I feel like the wind has been knocked out of me. "Because I AM a Witch of Light." I gasp. "Yeah." She chuckles, telling me that she's aware that I know exactly what that means. "And yeah, I know about you, your brother, and Alex's cousins, too."

I swallow a massive lump, knowing that most likely, if she's as powerful as I think she is…I wouldn't be a match for her if I was at full power. Crap, that means Gavin was right again. I really do need to find my charm. "Wh-what are you going to do to me?"

"Nothing."

I frown. "Nothing…?"

She shakes her head. "As long as you keep doing what you're doing." She points at me. "By that, I mean keep protecting Alex from whatever weirdness I've been sensing for the last few weeks and we won't have a problem."

142

"Why Alex…?" I ask slightly apprehensive and not-so-slightly jealous, taking in her beautiful skin and gorgeous cheekbones and amazing full lips.

"Because, I've known him since his dad first moved here with him and his mom." She looks into my eyes and I feel like the rest of the world turns to blackness. "His father was a good person and so is Alex. If anything were to happen to him on my watch, I'd hold you…and that strangely aura'd brother of yours responsible." I nod, and color and sound return to the world.

"Toodles," Jamie-Lynn chirps, then walks away with her hands buried in her overall pockets and her curly ponytail, bopping behind her. I breathe deeply. I feel like I was suffocating until only a second ago…as if someone was holding my head under water…only I wasn't aware of it until I nearly drowned.

"She's a witch," I puff. "She's a very powerful, white witch."

#####

My phone buzzes in my hoodie pocket. I check the message and move toward the front of the store without even looking up.

Kai follows me. "Where're you g…" I extend the phone and continue walking. "Dance emergency," he reads, making it sound more like a question. "I don't think she's using 'emergency' right. What could possibly constitute a *dance emergency*? I mean, especially after what we've been through…? Unless, of course, she found out the weird-bear-dog-thing started taking tap dancing lessons and wants to show us its old soft shoe?"

"I don't know. That's why I'm going to check it out. Mr. Hamish, can I take my break a few minutes early today?" I pause at the door.

"Sure, Alex. Let me know when you get back," he replies from the back.

"Thanks." I head over to the Bean, Kai in tow.

I cross the square as fast as I can. What could Gwen possibly have meant? I feel like I burst through the doors. By the looks on their customers' faces, I probably did.

"Gwen…" I try to catch my breath and appear calmer than I am. "…everything ok?"

"You got my text." Okay, something's bothering her.

Kai laughs, and I turn to him. "Could you give us a minute?"

"Sure, cousin." He takes a seat at a booth near the front window.

"What's going on, Gwen?"

"Alex, I…uh…I don't have a dress," she blurts out, but sounds like she's trying to convince herself not me.

"You what…?"

"Well, I just haven't had time to go shopping, plus I'm still trying to save my money so that I can pay my foster parents back the money that I spent." Her cheeks turn red at the end.

"Make the coffee, Cinderelli; sell the pastries, Cinderelli," Kai sings, reminding me that he can hear every word we're saying.

"Well, that doesn't mean you can't go, right? You know, girls always have something they can wear, right?"

"You can't just wear anything to a dance, I mean…it's gotta be special, I mean…" She's getting flustered. She shakes her head.

143

"Well, it's not like it's Prom." I regret saying that instantly.

"What do you mean *it's not like it's Prom*? This IS my first high school dance…EVER…why are you brushing this off like it's nothing? Especially since it's…" Her lower lip quivers. "…it's *our* first dance…together." Kai exhales loudly…great; even he realizes I'm the d-bag here. Gwen sighs and tries to keep the tears from spilling. Crap. Now, I feel even worse.

The door bell chimes and I can practically hear Kai's teeth grinding…Gavin stands by the door. Crap, now I'm gonna feel worse. He walks over to us, focusing on Gwen. "What's going on? What did your pet do to you this time?"

"Nothing," she lies, wiping tears away. "I'M FINE."

"You always know just when to show up, don't you, Gavin?" I grumble. "And by that, I mean the worst possible time."

"Yeah, I know when to come by and put my sister's pet in his proper place." He towers over me…looking taller than normal. A chair scrapes the floor and I throw my hand out, letting Kai know to sit back down. He replaces the chair that he nearly knocked over and does.

Gwen sniffs. "It's okay, Gavin. I was upset because I don't have a dress for the dance."

"Don't you have something you can wear to this thing, Gwen?" Gavin asks. "I've seen your closet."

"Seriously," Kai says as if he's yelling at a TV show.

"No and I don't have time to go buy something, I'm closing tonight," Gwen explains.

"But you should think about the safety of your pet. I mean, your pet's going…don't you have to protect, your little pet? I mean, we wouldn't want anything to happen…to your pet."

My face gets hotter with every mention of the word "pet."

Gwen sighs, "Fine. I guess I'll work something out. I guess I could borrow something from Meghan, but she's so much taller than I am. I guess if I borrow a short dress, it wouldn't really matter…"

"Yay!" Kai shouts, still watching his invisible TV program. "I think Meghan read your mind."

The door chime sounds and Meghan walks in carrying several bags. "Gavin," she says as if no one else is here. "What are you doing here?"

"Well, I was waiting for a gorgeous woman to walk into the coffee shop and oh, look…my wait is over," Gavin says. She responds with a giggle and red cheeks. Meghan sets the bags down on the nearest table, her eyes lingering on Gavin.

"What is all of this?" I ask, trying to break the awkwardness.

"What?" Meghan snaps. "Oh this…? I just felt like doing a little shopping today."

"Or every day?" Gwen says. "What did you buy?"

"This." Meghan says, whisking a big, white box with a pink ribbon out of one of the bags.

"Maybe you should be a little more specific with your questions," Kai says, standing behind me and looking over my shoulder.

"What's in the box, Meghan?" Gwen asks.

144

"What's in the box? What's in the box?" Kai says, overdramatically reenacting a movie scene.

Meghan shakes her head. She returns to Gwen. "Open it and see," she says, bursting with excitement. Gwen frowns. "Just do it!" When Gwen hesitates, Meghan sighs dramatically. "It's for you, loser, just open it."

Gwen's eyes light up with understanding and excitement. She tugs gently on the ends of the ribbon and it comes off easily. Gwen gingerly lifts the lid, almost as though she thinks it might disappear in her hands. She reaches into the mountains of gift paper and pulls out a small bundle of glittering pink. Gwen finds the top of the dress and pulls it out.

"Oh, Meghan," she gasps at the strapless dress with a fitted top covered in sequins and then a flowing skirt made of several layers of thin pink fabric.

Meghan opens a smaller box and pulls out a pair of flats the same color as the dress. "And I got these." The shoes are simple except for a little flower on the toes. The whole outfit seems perfectly...Gwen.

"They're so pretty!" Gwen almost squeals. "How did you...?"

"Know your size?" Gwen bobs her head. "I make it a point to pay attention to my bestie," Meghan says nonchalantly. "Well, I was out shopping for my dress and this one was screaming 'Gwen' when I walked by it. And I knew you wouldn't have time to come down and see it yourself. So, I just went ahead and picked it up." Meghan extends her arms toward Gwen. "Come on...you know you wanna," she exclaims. Gwen smirks and then slowly moves into her arms. They hug.

"So, it's settled?" They look at me. "You're going, right?" Gwen nods slowly. Did she change her mind...? "If you don't wanna go..." I walk past them.

"No." She catches my arm. "I want to...will you go with me?" She stares at me with soulful, emerald eyes...not fair. How could I stay mad at that? I nod. She smiles and leans into me.

"Well," Meghan says. "That settles things for you two, but...I am still dateless." Meghan turns to Gavin. He arches one eyebrow and smirks. "Gavin, would you like to..."

"Meghan," Gwen snaps. "A word." She grabs Meghan's wrist and drags her away. They conference near the counter with Gwen making large sweeping hand gestures in a pleading manner, while Meghan makes smaller, dismissive gestures. Gavin laughs.

"What?"

He shakes his head. "Nothing, pet."

"Gavin," Meghan snaps, ignoring Gwen tugging on her arm. "You...me...dance...tomorrow night?"

"Sure, why not?" Gavin returns, dripping with overconfidence. Meghan smiles. Gwen releases her and her shoulders slump with a sigh.

Chapter 26: Dance

"It's weird," I say to Gwen, not looking at her. "That's all I'm saying. That it's just a little weird."

"Why?" She dumps another book into her locker. I pick my bag up from the floor and lean against the locker next to hers. "The fact that we're going to the dance together and suddenly the entire school thinks we're..." She looks at me, while working to fish something out of her little pink backpack. "...how did Stephen put it?" Gwen makes an 'oh' face and says, "...coupled up..."

I laugh and take her pack. "Gimme that." I hold it open for her.

"Thanks." She searches through it with both hands. She tucks a stray strand of hair behind her ear. Two girls that I recognize from Meghan's group of lemmings pass by us. One whispers to the other, and girlish giggling ensues. I sigh and roll my eyes.

"Alex," Gwen says from what feels like the bottom of a bag twenty times deeper than her actual bag. "Do you...know a girl named, Jamie-Lynn?"

What a weird question. "Um." I think, tilting my head back. I almost take my hand away from the bag to scratch my chin, but the zipper reminds me that that's how I tore my last pack. "The only Jamie-Lynn I know is Jamie Baggett." Gwen nods, then returns to her bag. "Why?"

She looks at me and the corners of her mouth turn down. She shakes her head. "No reason." I arch one eyebrow, letting her know that I don't believe her.

She nods unevenly, and her thin deep red eyebrows rise and fall. "I ran into her right after I talked to Meghan..." I nod. "...she..." Gwen breaks off to cough. She covers her mouth and it only gets worse.

I put her bag down. "Gwen, are you okay?" She looks at me with panicked, completely freaked out eyes. "GWEN!"

Her hands move up to her throat. She inhales deeply and coughs twice, clearing away whatever was... She stands upright. She looks behind her with one hand still on her throat, completely ignoring the crowd of onlookers. She comes back and stares down the hall past me.

"What is it?" Her eyes swell and she looks...scared. I turn around expecting to see the bear-dog. The only thing I see is a mob of students, staring at us...and a head full of reddish-brown, curly hair walking away.

"Is that Ja-," before I can finish my question, Gwen pulls me back around to her by the arm. She slips hers over my shoulders. "Gwen?"

She shivers. "Just put your arms around me." I do, and she rests her head on my chest. The shivering doesn't stop. "Don't ask," she says before I can. "Just...I needed a hug, okay?"

I nod and stroke the back of her head. She purrs and inhales deeply, pressing her body against me. The shivering slows, and that familiar tingling sensation replaces it. She knits her fingers together on the back of my neck. I inhale deeply...taking in a deep whiff of her hair. I sigh. Are we really faking being a couple or are we actually a couple? Whenever we're close like this...I just don't want to let her go...I mean, she's so strong, but when I hold her like this...it feels like she could break at any minute. How can someone be sturdy and fragile at the same time?

"Loser," Meghan says. We part and Gwen looks past me. "You'll have plenty of time for that at the dance tonight." Gwen nods and wipes her eyes. Was she crying? "Come on. Let's go." I nab Gwen's bag and pass it to her.

"Thanks." She steps past me to Meghan.

"Gavin and I will be by to pick you up," Meghan says to me. "And then we'll go and get Gwen." That doesn't make sense. Gwen lives closer to Meghan than me and… "You have to see her in the dress, Loser-boyfriend," Meghan says in a light-hearted way.

I open my mouth to respond, but before I can, Gwen steps over to me. She places one hand on my chest while holding her bag with the other. She kisses me on my left cheek. "Thank you for putting up with her and my brother," she whispers. I smile. My eyes drift closed as the sweet perfume of her lavender and jasmine scented hair flows over me. She steps away and she and Meghan move down the hall toward the student parking lot.

"What was that?" Sora demands. I turn to find her and Kai waiting.

"Meghan was just telling us about our ride to the dance tonight."

"Not that," Kai grumbles.

"I got a vibe that made the hairs on the back of my neck stand on end," Sora clarifies. "What was it?" I shrug. "How could you not know? You were standing right here when it happened!"

"Sora," Kai whispers. His eyes dart to the left at a few students, staring at us from across the hall. She inhales deeply.

"Look. Something…happened to Gwen. She started choking and seemed scared. I tried to ask her about it, but she wouldn't tell me." Sora thinks for a moment.

"Good enough for me," Kai says casually and earning a scowl from Sora. "We should go and get ready for the dance." He motions to Sora's face. "You know, it's going to take a couple of hours to make this presentable."

"Presentable?" Sora snaps. "Screw that. I'm gonna look as hot as all hell." She marches toward the parking lot. Kai shrugs. He scratches the back of his head and follows her. I secure my bag and follow them.

Once we get home, Kai and I rush through showering and anything that would qualify as manly grooming. Then we spend about an hour waiting for Sora to get "hot as hell." I look down at my suit and tie. It's a black suit on black tie with a white button up. Suits aren't my style, but at least Sora knew me well enough to keep it simple. Kai's not wearing a suit though. He's wearing black slacks and a black button-up shirt with a red tie.

He catches me taking in his outfit. "What?" I can't help noticing that behind his tie, his top button's undone. If he weren't so lazy all the time, I'd guess that that was by design not forgetfulness.

"Nothing. So, which girl finally convinced you to go with her?" I pick at the tweed couch that my mom has had since I was a little kid…sitting in front of the coffee table that she's had just as long.

"Nobody." Kai tilts his head back, checking the odd paint patterns along our ceiling. "I'm going tric-style."

"What?"

"Tricycle…I'm gonna be a third wheel." I nod. "I figured that since Sora and Stephen aren't going on a real date, I might as well tag along with them." I shrug. "I mean, she is my ride after all."

A horn blares outside. Why does it feel like I'm always being interrupted before I can say anything? "I guess that's my ride." I stand. "Tell Sora I'll see her at the dance."

Kai tugs at his earlobe. "You just did." I nod, knowing he's right. Max rushes out of my bedroom and runs over to me. Kai rolls his eyes. "Man, I hate that little guy. He makes the tiger in me uncomfortable."

"Well, he lives here." I pet Max. "You're just visiting." Kai chuckles. I continue petting Max. "Yeah, boy…" His ears go back, lying flat against the top of his head. "I'm gonna see Gwen." He barks once and wags his tail. "Yeah, I'll tell her you said, 'hello.'" Max barks again and runs back to my room. I shake my head. Sometimes I swear I really understand what he's saying.

The horn blares again. Crap…just remembered the jerk I'm keeping waiting. I rush out the door without even saying goodbye to my mom. I'll pay for that later. Gavin parked behind two other tenants' cars with the top down. He wears a black suit with no tie. He revs the engine as I approach.

"You almost got left, pet." I frown and slip my hands into my pockets. He leans over and whispers something to Meghan. She smiles flirtatiously and opens her car door. She steps out, showing of her golden dress. It has two thin straps under its matching small jacket. It has horizontal layers of fabric moving down the top portion until it reaches a belt that seems to be an arrangement of small flowers that are a deeper yellow than the rest of the dress. Below that, the layering continues until it reaches a small horizontal ruffle near the top of her thighs. It finishes with two more layers that end a few inches above her knees.

"You're staring, pet," Gavin complains.

I ignore him. "That dress looks really nice on you," I attempt to compliment without sounding flirty.

"I know, Loser-boyfriend, but thank you for saying it," she adds while moving her pressed, straight hair away from her shoulder. I climb in behind Meghan's seat. She sits back down and before she can even close her door, Gavin peels away with a squeal of his tires.

I try ignoring the flirtations from the front seat. *Your eyes are so blue. No, your eyes are so blue. …so pretty this… so sexy that…* I groan and catch Gavin's disapproving eyes in the rearview.

"We're here, pet," he says, still staring at me. "Fetch my sister, pet."

I smirk. "Arf," I emit, putting my feet up on his seat so that I can hop out. He grumbles something, but I'm already across Gwen's tiny front yard…that I really shouldn't be commenting on since I don't have a yard at all…and climb the red steps up to her porch. I pull open the storm door with my left hand and lift my right to knock. The door opens abruptly. Gwen appears where it once stood.

"Are you ready for me?"

I take in every inch of her and gasp. Clearly, I wasn't ready. The dress looked nice in the box…nicer in her hands…but on her…my words are lost. She has a thin, pink sweater draped over her arm. Her hair cascades down her back and over her right shoulder. Her skin is flawless and…she looks at me with concerned eyes.

"Is…is something wrong?" I shake my head absently. "You're staring…I feel like something's wrong." She looks at the sides of the dress, causing it to fan out as she twirls. "Has something come loose? Am…am I showing too much skin?" I shake my head again, still not quite able to form words. "What's wrong…?"

"Nothing," I finally say. "You're perfect." She gasps then pants a sigh of relief. "I-I mean, you look perfect…" She giggles. "…I mean, you look perfectly fine…"

"It's alright, young man," a woman's voice says. She steps into sight behind Gwen. "She does look perfect, doesn't she?" I smile and nod.

"Alex," Gwen starts. "This is my foster-mom…THE best foster-mom ever…Mrs. Taylor." Mrs. Taylor blushes with an eye-crinkling smile. She mouths a humble 'oh' and puts an arm around Gwen's shoulders. "Mrs. Taylor, this is Alex…"

"So, he's the one you're…"

"Sshhhhh," Gwen issues immediately. I laugh. I guess, actual mom or foster mom, they'll embarrass you no matter what. "We should go."

"Wait," Mrs. Taylor says before we can walk away. We turn and from somewhere she's produced an SLR camera. "Smile." We do. "No, no," Mrs. Taylor whines. "Put your arm around her, dear." I put my arm behind Gwen's back and my hand wraps around the side of her tiny waist. Gwen swallows deeply…she still feels the tingle, too.

"Say cheese," Mrs. Taylor commands.

"Cheese," we say in unison. Mrs. Taylor snaps the picture. She looks at the camera. Gwen looks at me with something behind her eyes…something deep and meaningful.

"Memories, huh…?" Mrs. Taylor says. I take Gwen's hand in mine and nod. She nods in return with a subtle flirtatious smile.

"Soooooooo, this…*Sadie Hawkins* dance…is in your school gym?" Gavin asks, not hiding even the smallest bit of his disdain. Meghan steps closer, her three-inch heels almost bringing her up to his height. She pulls on the hook of his arm.

"We went to a lot of trouble to decorate the gym for this," Meghan exclaims. "Right, Loser?" she adds, peering at me.

I nod firmly. "Yeah, Gavin. Meghan was the head of the decorating committee for this dance and they did an amazing job putting this together." He doesn't look at me, but I can feel the frown on his face. I have to assume that that's true because, in truth, the only day that I actually made it in to help them was on Monday…only to have that time cut short by a strange shadow bear-dog attacking my date.

"Really…?" Alex poses. I shrug before Meghan and Gavin notice. He huffs a laugh that draws their attention. Alex's smile melts quickly. He shakes his head, telling them it's nothing. He even makes Gavin believe him. "Are we ready to go in?" Alex asks.

"Not…quite yet," Sora says. We turn to her…and I suppose Kai and Stephen are with her, according to plan, but I can't seem to tear my eyes away from her…and her amazing…albeit…overtly revealing outfit.

150

The black, heart-shaped bodice of her tiny dress stops just above her hips and is covered in beautiful, twinkly sequins. At the waist, the dress billows out in a collection of pleats culminating in shimmery, silken purple fabric, overlaid with lacy, semi-transparent black material on top. The bottom of the dress ends well above her knees.

Sora's hair is pulled up into a bun, which accentuates her long, slender neck, and dangly curls hang from the back of the bun. Three-inch black peep toe...or at least, that's how Meghan described a similar pair of shoes...heels wrapped in purple satin with crystal accents complete the ensemble.

I had always thought of Sora as a curvy girl, but she is surprisingly tone and firm...everywhere...and that's made apparent by her revealing dress. Her skin is perfectly tanned and absolutely flawless. If Alex wasn't her first cousin, my ego would have taken a massive hit upon seeing her. Meghan, however, is not that lucky.

"Hey guys," Sora says, confidently placing her hands on her hips. "Hey Gavin," she sings to his slightly agape mouth and laser-focused eyes. "Do you like the dress?" She pounds a double meaning into her words. Gavin nods blankly. Meghan cringes as if someone just punched her in the stomach.

"We should go inside," Alex says, trying to cut the tension. I nod and pull him toward the doors. Stephen bobs his head and motions for Sora to go ahead of him. Kai darts through our group and rushes through the open door that Alex holds. I glance back over my shoulder and notice that while Gavin's eyes have never left Sora, Sora's eyes have never left Meghan and vice versa. "Should we...?" Alex starts.

"No. I warned him, I warned her, now they're each other's problem." Alex nods and guides me into the gym. I sneak one more glance and sigh. I did warn her, but it doesn't stop me from feeling bad about how this is going to end. Alex leads us to a table. I place my purse on top and pull out a chair to sit down. Alex collects my hand. I look at him with a bit of shock.

He shakes his head. "You did not dress like that to sit at a table all night." I smile. We walk onto the dance floor hand-in-hand. He gives my hand a little tug, pulling me into his arms. We dance to the pop-slow song played by the DJ. I drape my arms over his shoulders and his hands rest on my hips. Before I realize it, Alex and I have danced through three songs. "You're a good dancer," he whispers.

"I've had practice." ...lots and lots of practice. He smirks. "Oh, wait...you wanted me to say something like, well it's because I have a good dance partner, right?"

He laughs. "Only if it's true."

"It is." He nods.

"I'm gonna get us some punch," he suggests as a not so slow pop song begins. I nod. He makes his way toward the area highlighted by the large sign that simply says, "SNACKS" in red letters. As soon as Alex is out of sight, I feel ill at ease. I rub my palms together and slowly make my way back to our table. Before I get there, I stop...feeling the same rush of emotions that I felt earlier at Alex's locker. I turn.

Jamie-Lynn saunters over to me confidently. Her reddish-brown dangly curls bob as she moves toward me and they catch the tiny flashes of the strobe lights around the room. I freeze. Even if I wanted to move, I can't...no spell required to limit my movements. Fear paralyzes me. She moves over to my side.

"I hope you got my little warning earlier today," she says softly. I pant and shiver. My hands grow cold, clammy and the hairs at the back of my neck stand on end. I tense so badly that I feel pained in the small of my back. She looks at me and smirks. "I'll take that fear I see in your eyes as a yes."

Jamie-Lynn steps around me so that we are face to face. She reaches up, moves the hair away from my right shoulder, and brushes more from my collarbone to just over my shoulder. I feel an intense heat emanating from the tips of her fingers. I tremble. I want to run away from her, but my legs still refuse to allow it. For the first time in my life, I want to scream out for my brother to save me. Although, if she is as powerful as I believe she is, it would not matter.

"Remember what I told you," she says forcefully, but in a deceptively sweet and innocent voice. I swallow a dry lump that will not dissipate. "You will protect Alex, but nothing else." She frowns. "When I told you to protect him…that meant his feelings too, got it?" I nod, though I can't feel my neck or any part of my head any longer, just the intense heat covering my body. "This farce of a relationship…" She shakes her head and holds one finger up in my face. "…if you hurt him, I will end your little trickster life. So, if you don't have genuine feelings for him…LEAVE…HIM…ALONE."

She walks away. The heat subsides quickly…it rushes back to the initial point of contact and then that point on my shoulder feels colder than the rest of my body. I breathe heavily. I hadn't been able to for the past minute. I bow my head to stop tears from escaping. I look up again in time to see Alex making his way back over to me with our punch. I can still hear her last words echoing in my head…*if you don't have genuine feelings for him…LEAVE…HIM…ALONE.*

What if she's right? What if I don't have real feelings for him? I look at him. I drink in those warm brown eyes of his and that adorable smile…no, my heart didn't just skip a beat for its own benefit. However, what if his feelings for me aren't real…? What if his feelings stem from some lingering feeling of debt from me saving his life? Perhaps, he's not the one who is going to be hurt in this *farce of a relationship.* Maybe, it's me.

#####

"Hey," I say softly.

"Hey," she returns even softer and with a quiver to her voice.

I tilt of my head. "Are you alright?" She nods…I never knew a nod could be unconvincing. I put our drinks down. She takes her left hand in her right and plays with her fingers. I reach for her hands. She moves away. I catch her left hand in my right. Our eyes meet.

Her emotions ripple through me. "You're not okay." I take her other hand and pull her closer…until both of our arms angle straight down. "You're shivering."

"It's nothing," she whispers and tries to pull away. I hold her…and intertwine our fingers for good measure. She sighs before lifting bright green, glowing eyes with a flicker of yellow flames whipping behind them. "Please, let me go."

"No." I pull our hands up near my chest; they rest against my heart. She inhales deeply and does a stuttering pant on the exhale. "Tell me what's wrong." She stares

152

into my eyes and shakes her head. "Gwen, we've saved each other's lives...we're 'fake' boyfriend and girlfriend...the least we can do is be honest with each other."

"I saved you," she whispers. "Twice," she adds as she waves both of our hands around in a circular motion.

"I saved you right back." I lean closer. "Remember...my sleeve covered in blood..." I scrunch my nose. "Somebody carried you to safety...that was me." She shutters and looks down at our intertwined fingers. "It's okay. It's okay. That's our thing. Weird-bear-dog attacks...you save me...I save you and then we wait for the next weird-bear-dog attack. Although, you're up two-one so..."

"And that's enough for you?" Her voice cracks with an on-coming cry. "That we just..." She swallows and lifts her tear-filled eyes. "...keep playing savior to each other until..."

"No," I snap, keeping my voice low. "It's not enough for me." She nods in a huff. "You are," I admit without thinking about it. She frowns, pants a weighty breath, and then smiles. "You're enough for me." Her smile falls away and she steals a glance at my lips. And suddenly, we're back on Rex's couch again...our skin, our emotions, our thoughts and this insane tingle that comes from us just touching each other...all laid bare. I want to kiss her. I need to kiss her. I move closer to her. "You're...more than enough for me," I sigh as my lips come closer to hers.

"Yes," she returns in what just barely qualifies as a whisper and tilts her head back...her eyes drifting closed.

"Romeo...Juliet," Kai snaps. We both open our eyes and take a step back from one another. "Sorry," he says simply. "Really, I am, but Sora and Gavin are both getting serious bear-dog vibes."

Gwen swallows deeply then nods. She wipes the tears from under her eyes. Kai rushes off and we follow, still hand in hand. I stop. She stops two steps later. I pull on her fingers entangled with mine. I pull her back to me and she lets me. Our bodies connect and I put my arm around her waist.

"To be continued." She smiles with a nod of agreement.

We turn to follow Kai and Stephen stands in our way. He looks at us with an awkward tweak of his eyebrow. "Are you guys alright?"

Gwen inhales deeply and checks her eyes for tears. I turn back to Stephen and nod. "Yeah, man, we're fine."

"If you say so," he spits. "Have you guys seen Sora...? Or Meghan...?" I look at Gwen. "They kind of...got into it..." Stephen shakes his head. "...I couldn't really tell if it was because of me or because of your brother...he's that Gavin guy, right?" Gwen nods. "Yeah, Meghan said something about him...and Sora said something about me...and then they just started yelling."

"Oh no," Gwen groans and steps past Stephen, heading back toward the dance floor. She turns to look back, causing her flowing red hair to whip out like the bottom of her dress. "I have to find Meghan," she says. "Whatever my brother told her...whatever he's promising her...he's lying and he's just going to hurt her." I've never heard her sound this angry.

"I'll go with you," I add. She nods and extends her hand. I reach out and take it as I move to her side.

"Me too," Stephen adds.

"No," Gwen practically yells. Stephen takes a step back. He readjusts, recovers, and frowns as his eyes dart from her to me. He's looking for an explanation. I still can't bring myself to lie to him about all of this.

"She means…um…maybe you should find Sora? I mean, if they aren't somewhere fighting it out maybe you can calm Sora down…you know, in the special Stephen way you do." He smirks then nods. I don't think he could find any fault in my logic.

"Okay, but if you can't find Meghan or I can't find Sora, we'll meet back here in like twenty minutes, okay?" I nod, and Stephen walks away.

I look at Gwen with wide eyes. "He's going the same way Kai left."

"It's okay. Whatever's going on…" She pulls me in the opposite direction. "I'm sensing my brother toward the back of the school and if he's there…"

"Then so are Sora, Kai and the bear-dog." She nods and pulls me through the crowd. Several of the guys pat me on the shoulder as we make our way across the dance floor, even more try to pat Gwen everywhere they can get their hands. I actually have to shove Kyle McGivney off her. He looks at me, frowns then disappears into the mob of people.

We make it to the outer edge of the mob. "Come on," Gwen says with an urgent tone. She looks around then pushes the fire door open with her hip while pulling the alarm cord. We step outside and the door slams shut behind us. She puts her hand on my chest and freezes. She forces me back against the door. "You should go back inside."

"Can't." These doors don't have handles on the outside.

She lifts her hand and it catches fire, then dies out a second later. Her fingernails are long and sharp. She reaches around me and buries her nails into the small gap between the two faded red doors. The metal bends as she grips one side.

I grab her wrist and she looks at me desperately. "There's something wrong," she explains. "The bear-dog seems stronger than before. I have to get you to safety." She bends the door back, taking my hand on her wrist back with her.

I squeeze her wrist as best I can. I don't think she even notices the change in pressure. "No." She looks at me again. "If you're in danger, it's better if I'm right next to you."

Gwen lets her fingers slip from between the torn doors, leaving a small hand-sized gap between them. "THAT'S INSANE," she snaps. "IF I'M IN DANGER, NEXT TO ME IS THE LAST PLACE I NEED YOU TO BE." Tears well in her eyes. "Don't you get it, Alex? If you're in danger…I can't think straight. I lose my mind and then…I can't fight, let alone protect you, if all I'm doing is worrying about you."

I put my arms around her, completely taking all the air out of her. "How do you think I'd feel knowing you were risking your life and I had no way of knowing what was happening to you?" She shakes and begins to cry. She wraps her arms around me.

A growl comes from the side of the building. We part. Gwen looks at me, then the corner. She moves so that she stands between it and me. The head of the shadow bear-dog peeks around. If I didn't know any better, I'd swear it was smiling…instead of just showing all its sharp, shark-looking teeth.

"This isn't right," Gwen says, stepping back and pushing me with her.

"What do you mean?"

She looks at me with completely panic-stricken eyes. "I mean…this thing is in front of us…but…I still sense Gavin, Sora and the original bear-dog…behind us." I swallow deeply and look at this new creature…whatever it is.

Chapter 27: Three

I have to keep him safe. I have to get Alex out of here. I steal a glance at the door. I'm too weak to get him back inside quickly. It took too much energy to get it open that far. The new bear-dog takes a step toward us. I take two more back. "Alex." I let fox magic flow through my arms and legs, producing a small amount of ambient fire around them. "When I tell you to…"

"Don't even think about telling me to run, Gwendolyn." I hate when people call me by my full first name…except him. It sounds like music when he says it…even though I doubt he could carry a tune to save his life. No…saving his life, my fox magic surges, that's why I'm here.

"Then…stay behind me." My fangs descended…I didn't mean for that to happen. My fiery ears and tails are likely showing too. "And if you see a chance to help me…" I look at him. He nods. I smile showing him the slightest hint of my long, sharp canines.

"You're so hot," he breathes, then moves away. I turn back to the bear-dog…I feel…stronger somehow. Probably because this time I'm not holding back…even with my fox magic halved…I feel like I can do this.

The bear-dog follows Alex with his eyes. I spring forward. "You're mine!" I jump upward using swift paw. I bound off the wall and spin in mid-air…tiny flames flicker and dance around me as I twirl. The bear-dog stares at me. Good. Pay attention to me and leave Alex alone. I dive…preparing to deliver a heel kick to the top of its head…or possibly…

The bear-dog's head bends downward again. What is he…? Alex throws something and hits it. Now's my chance…I bring my heel down, focusing all of my fox magic on the strike. The kick lands in the center of its head, generating an impressive thud that vibrates up my leg…through my spine. This bear-dog is solid. I jump back and stumble…my ankle twinges with pain, causing it to roll. Thankfully, Alex is there to catch me.

"You hit him!" He pulls me back, pressing his right palm against my stomach. Breathe, breathe…and not because of the bear-dog or the ankle pains.

"Yeah, but I think I sprained my ankle in the process." I glare at the bear-dog, lying on the ground; all four appendages sprawled in different directions. Alex bows under my left arm, then sweeps my legs out from under me. "It's okay…"

"Nope," he returns. "I'll carry you…" I open my mouth to object, but I don't know why. I actually don't mind him carrying me. "…at least, until you can heal enough to walk on it." He remembered…he remembered everything I told him about my fox magic and how I use it to heal myself. I nod and place my right hand on his chest as I drape my left arm over his shoulders. I blush, realizing that his left hand touches my thigh. Snap out of it, Gwen. Catch your breath.

"Thank you." I return to the bear-dog…its eyes snap open. "Alex!" My hand clutches at his tie desperately. "Put me down." He shakes his head and holds me closer. He takes a step back. "You can't run with me and this thing…this bear-dog is stronger than the other one." The bear-dog lumbers to its feet. It inhales deeply and shakes its head, clearing the cobwebs. It opens its mouth…as it exhales…it emits flames frighteningly similar to mine.

I squirm in Alex's arms until he puts me down. I land on my good leg and focus all my fox magic into it. If I can get enough swift paw out of this one-step...I throw both arms around Alex and push off as hard as I can. We come to a rest in the trees just off the school grounds. "Dang it. If I were stronger, I..."

Alex wraps his arms around me and throws us to the ground. We land on the leaf-covered earth as the tree behind us explodes. I right myself and look at the splinters that used to be a North Carolina pine tree. I turn and gasp. The bear-dog followed us...just as fast as I moved. I try to stand but my ankle reminds me that's impossible. It stopped healing...I focused all my power into my swift paw.

The bear-dog breathes fire again, my fire...I'm sure of it. He sets all four of his paws as if preparing to hurl another fireball. "Alex," I whine, clutching at him. "I'm sorry." He wraps his arms around me. "No!" I push at his chest. "You have to try to get away."

"I'm not leaving you. Get that through your thick skull...okay? I won't leave you, Gwen." I stop resisting and allow him to pull me closer. He smells so good. I suppose there are worse ways to die than in the arms of someone that you care for...I hope Gavin will tell obāsan I love her. I hope that he'll at least come up with some story to tell the Taylors and Alex's mom...that he won't just leave without explaining anything...either way, they'll be so heartbroken.

"Gomenisai," I whisper.

"Unda," a woman's voice calls behind us. A wall of water erupts from the ground. It forms a well-defined barrier between the attacking familiar and us. The bear-dog's fireball collides with it and both explode into a mass of steam. Alex and I look back and find Jamie-Lynn wandering through the trees; her shawl sways around her as if she were moving through water. The emerald shimmer of her dress catches the moon at just the right moments and make her appear to be covered in tiny, twinkling jade stars. "Well, I guess that secret lasted all of about one day."

"Jamie?" Alex says, sounding astounded.

Jamie-Lynn watches the dissipating steam cloud between the bear-dog and us. "Yeah. We'll have to play catch up in a sec..."

The cloud separates as a massive fireball flies through it. Jamie-Lynn lifts her hands with her pointer and middle fingers extended. She draws a triangle in mid-air before spreading her arms, her palms facing outward. "Concustodio," she says with a powerful echo.

The fireball collides with some unseen shield...but it doesn't explode. It merges with the shield, causing it to flash like a window showing bright yellow headlights. It throws the fireball back at the bear-dog. The redirected attack hits and flames engulf it. The familiar emits a sound that is less than a scream but more nails on chalkboard. It folds in on itself, taking the fire with it until there is nothing left of either.

"Thought so," Jamie-Lynn says.

"Thought what?" I ask.

"That familiar fed on magical powers. So, I used my redirecting shield on it." She looks to where the bear-dog was. She inhales deeply and wobbles, as her eyes drift closed. She cuts her eyes to me. "Well, it's good that my first spell worked, too."

"First spell?"

158

She nods. "Yeah." She turns to us with her arms folded over her…ahem…mostly exposed chest. "I cast a spell that made it so that the next time you used your little quick step trick, it'd bring you right to me." She smiles smugly. Her forehead has a bit of sweat beading around her hairline. Perhaps, she isn't as powerful as I thought.

"Now, my little kitsune…" She steps closer. "What am I going to…?" What's wrong with her? Why'd she st…?

Alex still has his arms wrapped around me…protectively. He pulls me in closer and glares at her. "Her name is Gwen. Not kitsune, not fox face…but Gwen. Who are you?"

Jamie-Lynn smiles after her shoulders slump. "I'm the same girl whose hair you poured sand into when she told you she was tired of being a 'curly carrot-haired freak'…sand…because you said…"

"…you'd probably make a really cute blonde."

"Cute?" I ask Alex.

"It's really me, 'Lex," Jamie-Lynn says reassuringly.

A leaf drifts between us. She reaches out and catches it. "Crap. I have to go. Keep my secret, you guys and I promise, I'll tell you everything." She takes a step back and the wind picks up around her. Swirling leaves envelope her. "Come by my house tomorrow and I'll tell you everything." The leafy tornado ends, and she's gone.

"She's gone?" Alex says what's evident. Why am I angry with him? Is it how harshly he spoke to me or is it that he thought Jamie-Lynn was…cute at some point. I'd prefer to think that it's the former because I can't be as petty as to feel angry with the latter.

I feel it; I feel why she left so urgently. I sense them coming. Gavin arrives first; his entrance marked with a burst of blue flames, illuminating the darkened trees and leaf-covered ground briefly. Sora appears next as though out of nowhere with black and white fur covering every inch of her exposed skin…and there is a lot of visible fur. Kai shows a few ticks later, looking more like a lazy house cat than a Golden Tabby Tiger. The three of them search the immediate area with their senses stretched to the limits.

"What happened to you two?" Kai asks.

"Bear-dog," Alex says, rising to his feet. He gives me his hands and pulls me to my feet. Much to my embarrassment, I wobble on my twisted ankle and clench my teeth.

"You're hurt…?" Gavin asks. "AGAIN…?"

"Wait," Kai says before I can muster an anger-inspired response to my brother's question. "We just put the stomping on that bear-dog thing. When did you guys fight it?" Gavin looks at Kai then places his hands on either side of my ankle.

"There were two of them," I say. Sora and Kai release their respective animal forms at the same time.

"Impossible," Gavin snarls then drives his foxfire into my leg… I groan. …painfully. Alex slips one arm around my waist and takes my nearest hand in the other, balancing me. Gavin stares at us. His eyes are frigid…and a bead of sweat rolls down his temple.

"She's telling the truth," Alex confirms. "Gwen fought it and…"

"...and surprise, surprise," Gavin interrupts. "She got beat again."

"This one was stronger than the other one," Alex protests. "He shot fire out of his mouth...and..." Alex looks at me and I return his gaze. We never actually promised to keep Jamie-Lynn's secret until tomorrow, but he intends to, I can tell. "...and I think it absorbed some of Gwen's fox magic." Gavin finishes with my leg and stands.

"What's wrong with you?" I ask because I've never seen Gavin as tired as he is now.

"Captain Wonderful decided to take on the bear-dog all by himself," Kai explains. "He crushed it, but Sora thinks he over did it."

"He DID overdo it," Sora groans. "...because he's an idiot." Gavin jerks as though pricked by a pin. Sora growls and digs her fingernails in the tree behind her. She sees me and relents.

"Gavin," Alex breaks the tension. "You shouldn't fight the bear dog alone...that's why we..."

"Well, I guess if Gwen's pet says so," Gavin starts smugly.

"He's not..."

"Don't call my cousin 'a pet,'" Sora growls before I can finish. "My cousin is nobody's pet...damn, lying trickster fox..."

"Tsk," Gavin emits, his face twisting awkwardly. He crosses his arms and turns his back to her.

"What's going on with you two?" Alex poses. "You've been acting weird around each other since the first time you met." But, that wasn't the first time they met, Alex. Gavin peers at Sora. She notices, hurls a 'humph' at him, and then turns her back to him.

"I have to get back to my date," Sora says with a fresh wave of anger whipping around her...oddly matching Gavin's feelings.

"You seem like the type to date boring little humans," he grumbles.

"And you like the type to date bleach blond Barbie dolls," Sora retorts. She turns her back again, uses swift paw and vanishes.

"That was weird," Kai submits. I bob my head then return to...the spot that Gavin once occupied.

"This whole night's been weird," I return, putting my arms around Alex. He looks into my eyes.

He nods in agreement. "...even for us."

"We should get back...to check on Stephen and Meghan." I flood my legs with fox magic and a second later the trees, as well as the white witch that inhabited them, are a distant memory.

#####

Kai crouches behind us. He lifts his eyes, fading from a golden honey color to his normal blue. He stands, then walks past us. "You're fast, fox face."

"Why do you call her that?" I bark. "She's been nothing but nice to you and..."

"Sorry." Kai holds his hands up, palms facing us. "Gwen, you're really fast...and I mean that as a compliment."

"Thank you, Kai," she says.

160

He lowers his hands. "Allow me." He reaches between the faded red doors, where Gwen started, and pulls the door open. He steps back and motions for us to enter. Gwen smiles warmly and walks in.

"Thanks, cos," I add, then follow her inside. I look around as the door closes behind Kai. The dance seems to be dying down, but thankfully nobody noticed that we were gone. I wonder if anyone noticed Jamie leaving. "We should find…"

"Stephen and Meghan," Gwen breathes.

"Yeah."

"No." She points to the dance floor, at Stephen and Meghan, dancing together, his jacket on her shoulders. Her head rests on his shoulder, even though the song that's playing isn't very slow. "Yeah, I see them."

"What?"

Gwen shakes her head subtly. "It's Sora. She's talking to me. She told me that I should get my friend, because she's dancing with her date." Gwen's eyes move across the dance floor. "Well, where's Gavin?" she asks Sora, who's staying out of sight. "What do you mean, he left?" Gwen barks angrily. "I know what *left* means, I mean…" She pauses. "Oh." Gwen moans sadly.

"What's going on?"

Gwen swallows deeply and faces me. "Gavin abandoned her…and us, but that's not really important right now." I nod. "He told her that he was ditching her. Didn't give her a reason or anything…he just said that this dance was boring and that he was leaving."

"Crap."

"Yeah," Gwen adds with a nod. "Meghan tried to get him to wait until she found us, but he took off." She wraps her arms around me. "We should go. Do you think Sora would give us a ride home?" Gwen tilts her head back. "Please…" She begs Sora. "I really appreciate it."

"So, she's…?" Gwen nods before I can finish.

"Do you guys want me to get the discarded dates?" Kai asks. "Or do you guys want to?"

"We'll get 'em," I say. "Just…head out to the car and figure out how we're all gonna fit."

"Oh, I've already got that figured out," Kai says confidently. I look at him. He nods. "Yeah, it's easy…shotgun!" He walks away.

"Shotgun…?" Gwen asks.

"Yeah, it means he calls the front seat." She bobs her head and makes the 'oh' face. "Come on…from the look of her, it looks like you're gonna have to talk Meghan off the ledge."

"Odd expression."

"I just remembered it. It's something Jamie used to say all the time."

Gwen nods and steps away from me. She pauses when she realizes I'm not right beside her. She looks back and extends her hand. I take it. She guides me through the people still on the dance floor.

"Meghan!" Meghan takes a step back from Stephen. She huffs as if she's trying not to cry and holds her arms open. She steps into Gwen and wraps her arms around her. "I'm sorry," Gwen whispers while rubbing Meghan's back under Stephen's coat.

"You tried to warn me," Meghan returns in a low, shaky voice. "You tried to warn me about him."

"He's a jerk," Stephen snaps.

"He IS a jerk," Meghan moans into Gwen's shoulder.

"Yeah, he is," Gwen agrees. "Come on. Alex's cousin will give us a ride home." Meghan sniffs and nods against Gwen's shoulder. Gwen turns Meghan and guides her toward the exit. Stephen and I follow.

We make it outside and Gwen looks around. Meghan bends awkwardly to keep her head on Gwen's shoulder. "Where's Sora?" Gwen asks.

A second later, Sora brings the Range Rover to a literal screeching halt in front of us, startling Meghan and Stephen. I don't know if it didn't bother me because I know my cousin or because I'm getting used to all of this.

"Get in, kids," Kai sings from the passenger seat.

"Shotgun," Gwen whispers, then guides Meghan to the back door. I rush past them to open the door and Stephen's already there. He holds it and motions for them to climb in. Meghan does, and I step closer to Gwen.

"You...girls should probably sit in the middle," I whisper, looking at Stephen staring at Meghan.

"Stephen," Gwen says. He turns, and she tips her head toward the car. Stephen purses his lips then climbs in after Meghan. I push the door closed as Gwen walks around the front of the car. I follow, while slipping my jacket off. I drape it over her shoulders as she reaches for the door handle. She pauses and smiles at me. I pull the door open.

"Such a gentleman," she sighs before climbing in. I slide in behind her, but not before catching her subtly sniffing the lapel of my jacket. Her eyes swell. She caught me catching her. She smirks...until I try to close the door behind me. "Oh," she pants as I squeeze her between Meghan and me.

"You guys are gonna have to get a lot cozier than that," Kai laughs.

"Fine," Meghan whines before anyone else can manage a response. She lifts herself and comes down...on Stephen's lap with her legs toward the center. She drapes one arm over his shoulders and leans her back against the door. "I hope this is, okay?" Stephen nods with a smile threatening to break out. "Not you," Meghan snarls. She glares at Sora. "I was talking to your date."

"S'not like he's my boyfriend," Sora says, putting less thought into it than she put into checking her make-up in the mirror. "He was only my date for the night."

"Thanks," Stephen snips, adjusting to the new seating arrangement with Meghan moving in-sync with him. "Are you okay?" he breathes, while staring into her eyes. She maintains that same eye contact with him and swallows deeply. "I-I...mean, with the...um...seat...I mean."

Meghan doesn't look away, even for a second. "I'm good."

"Come on, now…you're better than that," Stephen adds in a way that only someone as cool as he is could get away with. Meghan smiles and places one hand on his chest to balance herself.

"Alex," Sora says with no emotion. "Close the door. It's hard to drive with the back door open…or you know, knowing that I let my idiot cousin fall out of the car."

I look at Gwen…who…actually looks awkward. She smiles into a little laugh then holds herself up. I slide into the car more and pull the door closed behind me. Gwen comes down…in my lap…and the wind flies out of me with the thought that…GWEN IS SITTING IN MY LAP. I gulp…actually, gulp. Think about anything, but Gwen in your lap. Like the dance or the fact that there are two bear-dogs now…or…the fact that Gwen is SITTING…IN…YOUR…LAP.

"Are you okay?" she whispers as Sora maneuvers us around a corner. I nod. "You're lying," she sings into my ear. I smile, probably the most awkward smile ever. "What's on your mind?" Her lips accidently grazing my ear. I bite the inside of my cheek trying not to think about the amazing girl…sitting in my lap. I taste blood. Good, I should focus on the gash in my cheek, not on the gorgeous redhead with amazing green eyes, breath as sweet as honey, and beautiful olive-tinted skin. Nope, don't think about that at all.

"Are you two making out?" Meghan asks. Gwen lifts her eyes. She starts to say something, breaks off, and just shakes her head. "It kind of looked like you were. I mean, if you were…gross, but good for you." I laugh. "I meant you…loser-boyfriend." Gwen giggles and presses her forehead against my cheek.

"Sorry," she whispers. Her eyelashes tickle my skin when she blinks. "Why can't we be like this all the time?" she murmurs softly at the same time I think it. "Well, not exactly like this," she adds. I smile.

"And it's right here," Meghan says to Sora. "It's the third house on the right." We pull up to a massive, two-story, old school white house with four ridged columns in the front and a terrace facing the street on the second floor. White curtains cover all the windows, all of which have the soft glow of pale yellow light behind them.

"Nice," Kai pants.

"Thanks," Meghan returns as she pushes the backdoor open all the way. She lifts herself and Stephen slides out from under her and out of the car. "Thanks for the ride," Meghan says with noticeable sadness filling her voice. She's probably thinking about Gavin. Jerk.

"No problem," Sora replies and steals a glance at Meghan.

Meghan nods to Stephen and then walks toward the house. Stephen leans down so that he can look inside. "Um…hey, guys…I only live like two blocks over. I can walk from here."

"Okay," Sora says. She cuts her eyes to me. I purse my lips.

"Later," Stephen says, pushing the door closed. He follows Meghan to her porch.

"Hey," Gwen says quietly.

"What…?"

"Shhhh," she issues, putting her pointer finger on my lips. She tips her head toward Stephen and Meghan. I look at them. "'Oh, right…your jacket,'" Gwen says as Meghan reaches for the lapels of Stephen's jacket. "She's crying," Gwen explains.

"'That's not really why I got out here.'" Meghan shakes her head. "'I just wanted to make sure you were okay…and…um…'" Stephen motions toward the house and he and Meghan turn to face the front door. He puts his arm around her and they resume walking. "'Old school move but…I wanted to see you to the door.' Meghan just laughed," Gwen says with warmth in her voice. "'Sometimes, it's cool to go old school,'" Gwen says in place of Meghan.

Meghan pushes her front door open. "'Thank you,'" Gwen repeats as Meghan slips Stephen's jacket off her shoulders. Meghan passes it to him. "'Anytime, Megs…you know that,'" Gwen finishes with a smirk.

"Awwwwww," Kai moans from the front seat. Gwen reaches over to him and shoves him at the shoulder. Kai chuckles and bows his head.

"I don't think we should let him walk by himself," Sora says as Meghan's steps into her doorway. "The bear-dog already killed one human…maybe it goes on scent…"

"He seriously lives on the next block," I explain. "If we try to get him back in the car, he'll think something's up."

"Pull away," Kai says. "When we get to the end of the block, I'll hop out…follow him home. Stealth mode."

Sora nods. "Sounds like a plan," she says. She shifts the car into drive. "Oh…and you can get off Alex's lap now," she grumbles, pulling away slowly.

"Right," Gwen sighs, moving to the middle of the seat. She tries to slide further away, and I catch her hand. She smiles warmly then moves back in close to me. She lays her head on my shoulder at the same time the front door slams shut. Kai's already gone.

"You're next, fox-face," Sora says like it's a fact. She rolls her window down and drapes her arm out.

"Next for what…?" I grumble.

"Don't get your panties in a wad," Sora grumbles with all the articulacy that I'd come to expect from my dad's side of the family. She turns the wheel to the left. "I'm saying she's next to be dropped off."

"Oh," Gwen sighs. "I live at…"

"I know where you live, fox-face." We look at her in the rearview mirror. She checks us out. "We sniffed you out after our first run-in, fox-face."

"STOP CALLING HER THAT," I snap. Sora faux-pouts at us. "She's…" I look at Gwen's expectant face. "…my friend so you can stand to be a little nicer to…"

"Alex," Gwen whispers. "Call me that." She examines my dumbfounded expression and smiles. "Trust me," she breathes, putting more meaning behind those two words than I'm getting right now.

"Okay. Fox-face," I whisper.

"Now, call me 'your little fox-face.'"

I huff a chuckle. "My…little fox-face." Gwen smiles warmly, then leans into me more and peers up at me. "My adorable, little fox-face," I say as the corners of my mouth tweak upward. Gwen giggles and nuzzles her nose under my chin.

164

"Please stop," Sora complains with one hand on the wheel and the other over her forehead, massaging her temples. Gwen tips back and laughs. I laugh too, now that I get what she was doing. "We're here."

I take a quick look around Gwen's foster-parents' house. "Gavin," I growl as Sora shifts the car into park.

"Where…?" Gwen and Sora ask at the same time. Gwen glares at Sora in the mirror and my cousin returns the favor.

I point to his car in the Taylors' driveway, pulled far enough in to sit next to the house and in the shadows. "Not him…really." I return to Gwen to find her scrambling to get out of the car. Sora does the same. I open my door as Gwen…is already around the car and making her way toward the house.

I open the door. "STAY IN THE CAR," Sora and Gwen spit at the same time. They cut their eyes at each other again, staring each other down for a moment without saying a word, but I can almost see something passing between them. I slide out of the car. I slam the door behind me, drawing both of their attentions back to me. "What did I just say?" they snap in unison. They exchange awkward, annoyed glances again. I walk between them headed for the house.

I reach the stairs before Gwen finally manages, "Alex." I stop at the top step and turn to face them. They're both staring at me.

"You comin' or what…?" I ask. Gwen sighs before checking for Sora's response. Gwen nods and then rushes to the front of the house. I offer her my hand and help her up the stairs. "BTW, I'm ignoring you two whenever you're in agreement," I whisper once we're face to face. Gwen opens her mouth to reply but decides to let it go in the form of a laugh.

I look back to see why Sora isn't here yet and she's at the back of the car. She slips her leather jacket over her shoulders and zips it up to her neck. I guess she does have some modesty…even though the dress is still short enough to consider it a belt. She pops the collar on her jacket and turns toward us, while pushing the back of the car closed.

Gwen walks with me to the front door and freezes in place. "Kai," she mutters. I glance over my shoulder and find Kai, crouching in the yard. His eyes shift from gold to blue.

Kai yawns. "Stephen made it home okay." He looks at Sora walking up beside him. "Thanks for leaving the calling card." Sora nods. He looks back to us. "What's jerk-face doing here?"

I pull the storm door open. "We're about to find out."

Chapter 28: Wicked

"We're fine," I assure Gavin again through his open car door. I lift my pack higher up on my shoulder and it slides down again. Alex slips it off. I grin like a kid in a candy store and look down. I feel a rush of fox magic stream from the car. Two glowing blue eyes stare back at me. "Stop it." I slam the door in his face. I turn to Alex, and Gavin revs the engine. "We're just studying," I yell over his engine. I can practically hear him calling me out on losing the lying game. He pulls away quickly then roars up the street.

"So," Alex starts. "Have you guys been fighting since last night?" I stare at him with my mouth slightly agape. How could he possibly...? "Sora and Kai heard you after you stepped out of the room."

"He...just irritates me. You know what I mean?"

"No brothers or sisters remember?" He offers my bag. "...although, I do have two very intrusive cousins who won't leave me alone for more than five minutes." I take it with a chuckle. "Anyway, are you ready to 'study...'?" I nod once and turn toward the Baggett house. Alex catches my shoulder. "Hey," he whispers. "Are you really ready for this?" I frown. A breeze wafts between us bringing a swirl of recently cut grass and...sage and something else. Could it be the ingredients for a spell...? "I know she scares you."

"But not you. She always seems to back off whenever you're around." He reaches for my hand. I give it to him and he puts his fingers between mine. I look down and find something I never noticed before. His hands...they're stained with the different paints and various other coloring implements that he uses in his artwork. They give his hands character. They make them interesting. Those marks make them... "...pretty," I breathe aloud.

"Paint and grime are pretty?" he asks, lifting our hands for me to get a closer look.

"On you...yes," I return with a smirk. I hear the creak of a door opening at the front of the Baggett home.

"Are you two gonna stand outside and make out?" Jamie-Lynn begins. "Or are you gonna come in and ask me a buncha questions?" I swallow deeply, feeling a quiver of fear move up my spine. Alex tightens his grip on my hand. I look at him and he tips his head toward the house. I nod, and we walk toward Jamie-Lynn.

We walk up to the house that's a similar style to the Taylors' house. In place of red brick steps leading to a red paint-covered porch, the Baggetts have decided to leave the original gray stone coloring in place. The siding on the house is a butter-cream color with blue-green faux shutters beside all the windows on the first and second floor. The porch is cracked near the center...and there are runes...etched into the stone.

I gasp the second my foot falls on the porch. I feel my fox magic being drawn to the ground...no, downward into the now glowing runes. "Alex," I wheeze as my legs buckle.

"Gwen?" Alex puts his free hand under my arm and holds me up. "Gwen, what's wrong?" Alex looks into my eyes, as my life-force draws out of me like soda through a straw. I open my mouth, but my voice is lost. I wonder if this is how the old kitsune and Mrs. Turnipseed felt just before…the end… "Gwen?" Alex sounds muffled, like he's far away. My vision blurs… "Jamie, what's wrong with her?" I wish I had time to say good-bye to obāsan…and even Gavin…good-bye, Alex…I should've told you… "JAMIE!"

"Vita obice," Jamie-Lynn says calmly just as everything grows dim. I gasp. I feel my strength return, all at once. It slams back into me like a train. My back arches and my head whips forward. I look into Alex's eyes and see a pair of glowing green eyes reflected. "Cut the drama," Jamie-Lynn says.

Alex pulls me to my feet and makes sure that I'm stable. He caresses my right cheek. "You okay?" I nod. He releases me and turns to Jamie-Lynn. "WHAT THE HELL'S THE MATTER WITH YOU?"

"More drama," Jamie-Lynn points out, still maintaining her devil may care attitude. "Great."

Alex gets right in her face. "Jamie, I asked you a question," he growls between gritted teeth. "I've never seen you act like this. This cold…this…" Alex shakes his head out of frustration. "You've always treated everybody more than fair, since we were kids…"

"Everybody," Jamie-Lynn spits back. "Not every spirit…" She looks at me. "That thing…"

"Her name is Gwen," Alex barks. "And she kept your secret. She kept it from me. She kept it from her brother. She kept it and came over here despite the fact you scare the hell out of her and now I know why." Alex takes a step back from Jamie-Lynn. He points at her. "It's not right." He moves closer and offers me his hands. "It's not right," he whispers and holds both of my hands close to his chest.

"You actually care about her?" Jamie-Lynn asks with a hint of confusion in her voice. Alex nods but his eyes don't move away from mine. "And you, fox spirit…you actually care about him too, don't you?" I stare into his eyes and all that I think of is, *is it even possible for me not to care about him?*

"Yes, I do." I turn my attention to Jamie-Lynn. "Why do you think I've risked my life over and over again to protect him? Why do you think I'll keep doing that?" Jamie-Lynn laughs and bows her head. She nods.

"Included in the rune trap you stepped into," she starts. "…is a truth sigil. Neither of you could lie, right now, even if you wanted to." She steps to one side and motions to the doorway. "Come in, Alex…and Gwen," she says earnestly, stepping inside the house.

Alex looks at me for reassurance. I nod. He intertwines our fingers again. We walk over to the door. Alex holds the storm door open for me and I step inside. Just inside the door is the living room, unlike the Taylor's home that opens to the stairs. This room has an off-white living room set with a wood-grained coffee table and two matching end tables. A lamp sits on each end table, with pale white shades. The walls are ashen gray with ebon trim along the three doorways leading away from the room, around the floor, and around the ceiling.

I look around the room, filling my eyes with fox magic. There are runes everywhere. They're in the layer of paint underneath the top layer…along the

168

ceiling…they're even on the lampshades. "Gwen," Alex says. I look at him with my eyes still full of fox magic. He's so cute. "What's wrong?"

"Runes. Runes everywhere…" I glance around the room again. "…like the ones on the porch." I swallow deeply. "Each of these does something different though."

"They're mostly protection wards," Jamie-Lynn says from the doorway directly across from the front door. "Like the one on the porch." She walks into the room carrying a tray with a pitcher of lemonade and three glasses with ice on it. "Sorry about that, by the way." She places the tray down on the coffee table. "My grandma carved those and apparently," she starts sounding annoyed. "…with each generation of McCabe witches, they've gotten stronger."

"McCabe…?" She nods and pours a glass of lemonade. "I thought your family's name was Baggett."

"Yeah," she says with a contemplative face. "That was my dad's last name. My mom's maiden name should have been Fletcher."

"So, McCabe is the name of your original bloodline?" I suppose.

"Well, as far back as anybody bothered to keep records. Anyway, the runes on the porch were originally crafted to weaken a supernatural being that didn't have a shield up."

"Like the one you cast over me," I suggest. She nods and offers me the glass of lemonade. I stare at it.

"It'll help," Jamie-Lynn says, renewing the offer. I take the glass. "You're already down a star ball; you need all the help you can get." I frown. How could she possibly know that? "I see your tails," she states as her glasses slip down her nose a little. "One of them is dimmer than the other two." I nod and take a sip of the lemonade. It fills me with energy instantly. I look at the glass then at Jamie-Lynn. "It's a special brew. I came up with it myself."

Jamie-Lynn pours another glass and offers it to Alex. He looks to me and I confirm that he should. "Trust me, Lex," she pleads. He turns to her. "I'd never do anything to hurt you."

"Because you're in love with him?" I prod, hoping to get a rise out of her, but then realizing a second too late…I'm trying to prod a reaction out of a powerful, white witch. Alex stares at me out of shock then at Jamie-Lynn.

She laughs. "In love with…" She breaks off to release another bout of laughter.

"Okay, now you're just hurting my feelings," Alex whines.

"No, no…," she gasps between laughs and while waving her hand. "…no, it's not that." She wipes a tear from under her eye. "It's just…he's my friend. He's like a brother to me."

Alex frowns. "Like your brother…? I don't know what you're talking about Jamie, we…barely know each other."

Jamie-Lynn scoffs. "Oh, yeah…? Then tell me why everybody else at school calls me Jamie-Lynn, while you call me, Jamie." Alex seems at a loss. "It's because I've managed to erase most of your memories of us as kids…except that."

Alex shakes his head. "You messed with my head?" Jamie-Lynn nods. "Why?"

"Well, it started with my mom," she says, tucking a lose curl of her cinnamon hair behind her ear. She claps her hands together and exhales loudly. She motions to the sofa. "You should sit down for this."

"I think I'll stand," Alex says. He's furious. I sit and pull, tugging on his fingers still mixing with mine. He resists for a second, but I pull hard and he falls beside me.

"See...when I was a kid...I was as strong as I am now, but I didn't have any control over my powers," she explains. "And with your dad being who he was..."

"So, you knew?"

Her eyes press into a line. She grimaces as if she's in pain. "Lex..."

"So, you...and...and...Rex, knew my dad better than I did?" He places the lemonade down on the table with some force. "That's what you're telling me?"

"Alex," I sigh. He looks at me...and I'm hit with so much pain that it staggers me. Focus, Gwen. "Let her talk."

He draws his lips into his mouth. He motions to Jamie-Lynn with his free hand as if he were *opening the floor* to her.

Jamie-Lynn nods and keeps her palms pressed together. "...well, you saw me use my powers...a lot when we were little. You were never scared of me though." She nibbles her lower lip. "And that made me feel so good. My mom was scared though. She was worried that you wouldn't be able to keep it a secret...so..." Jamie-Lynn inhales deeply and swallows a massive lump.

"Go on," I say, caressing Alex's hand with my thumb.

"...so, my mom asked...your dad...if she could use a memory spell on you."

Alex huffs and runs his hand over his mouth quickly. He's trembling. His teeth clench. "And, he just let you?"

My mind races. I have to think of something to calm him down. I have to think of something to make him feel better. I stare at his tensed jaw and the vein that has appeared over his right temple...before I realize what's happening...my lips press against his cheek.

He gasps. "It's okay," I whisper, placing my lemonade beside his. He nods as a tear drops from his right eye. "It's okay," I repeat, pressing my forehead against his cheek and caressing his opposite cheek with my newly freed hand. "It's okay. It's okay. It's okay." He nods. I lean away from him. His eyes shut tight.

"So, tell me...Jamie," he groans. "What happened after that? What happened after my dad told your mom it was okay to mess with my head?"

#####

I can honestly say I have never wanted to stay close to and move away from one person so much in my entire life...at least, not at the same time. Every time Gwen touches me, I feel her take away some of my anger. It's like she's peeling an onion. With every touch, caress, and pat, she pulls off another layer of rage toward my father, Rex, and Jamie for lying to me all these years. I don't want her to though. I want to be angry. I want to be pissed. I look at Jamie. I want to take out my frustration on someone.

Gwen pulls me in close again. At the same time, I don't want to lose this feeling. The tingle that she gives me is like feeling the softest thing in the world, while staring at your favorite color, and eating your favorite flavor of ice cream all at the same time. "Well?" I say with a lot less anger than I wanted to use.

"My mom cast the spell," she says, like talking about casting a spell to alter somebody's memories is an everyday thing. "You forgot that you saw me make your basketball float in mid-air when you were six." I frown. Something in the back of my head tells me that that's true. "Then when you were seven, she made you forget that I made a ceramic frog hop around the backyard." True. "When we were eight…" She sighs. "…I made a tornado at the park." Also, true. "And then…"

"I get it," I spit downward to my chest. I tremble. "How…could your mom do this to me…?"

"Alex," Gwen sighs. "You have to understand…we, supernatural beings, have one rule that exists above all others." I look at her. "We keep ourselves secret from the *humans*." I suck air through my teeth. "In most communities, like kitsune, it's considered an unforgivable crime to bring attention to our race or any of the others." She looks away. "In fact, any kitsune found guilty of such a crime are subjected to anything from stripping them of their powers, to stripping their entire clan of their powers…" She looks at Jamie. "…or possibly being put to death."

Jamie runs her fingers through her hair. "Witches have similar rules…" She hugs herself. "…except death is a final option…only reserved for dark witches that threaten the balance of nature." She lifts her eyes. A tear falls away from her left eye. "But…having your powers stripped away…I think that'd be worse than dying."

"What?" I nearly shout. "How could losing your powers be worse than dying?"

"Witches aren't like any other supernatural beings, Alex." She looks at Gwen. "If Gwen had her powers stripped away, it would suck." Gwen's hand slips out of mine. She places one hand over her heart and the other around her waist. Somehow, I feel like the two are mirroring each other with this. "But after a while, she would start to feel like a normal girl. She would be able to go on living a normal life." Jamie shakes her head. "Witches aren't beings that have powers that make them supernatural, witches are supernatural powers."

Gwen cringes. I put my arms around her. "Are you okay?"

"I'm okay." Gwen huffs a laugh. "I thought I'd be comforting you by this point."

I smile. "You did. You're just too good at your job." She smiles. I come back to Jamie.

"Stripping a witch of her powers would be like tearing someone's soul out," she says with a deep swallow of air. "My mom told me about a witch that she knew once. The girl started using her magic to…for profit. She started by trying to use alchemy."

"Alchemy…?" I ask with a frown.

"Completely wrong…," Gwen growls.

"Exactly," Jamie agrees. "Alchemy is…was a practice used to combine magic and science…and create…"

"Abominations," Gwen sighs. Jamie and I look at her. "Sorry," she whispers.

"No, it's okay," Jamie says. "It usually ends badly. Most alchemists' ultimate goal is to convert base metals like iron or lead into silver and gold." Jamie goes over to the chair next to the sofa and sits. "Some people even try to create a philosopher's stone."

I look at Gwen. "Do I even wanna know?" She shakes her head. "Is it one of those things that usually ends badly?" I ask both of them. Gwen rests her head against my arm. I feel her nod. Jamie does the same and if the look on Jamie's face is the same as the one on Gwen's, then I'm glad I can't see her. "So, what happened to your mom's friend?"

"She…," Jamie starts, but breaks off. "…eventually tried to make a philosopher's stone…" Jamie plays with the black ring around her left thumb. "…she was, of course, caught, because it takes a lot of *material* to make the damned thing…and they stripped her magic."

Jamie stands and steps around the chair. She puts her hands on its back. "My mom said she went to visit her a few months after…" She shakes her head. "…she looked like a ghost of herself. She was bone-skinny and her hair was pale and thinning. She couldn't eat. She couldn't sleep." Jamie shakes her head.

"You saw her, didn't you?" Gwen asks. "You saw your mom's friend, that's why you're so shaken up by this."

"My mom…" Jamie laughs without any humor. "…she put the image of her directly into my head." Jamie's eyes go distant. She opens her mouth and no words come out. Tears start streaming down her face. She shakes her head and closes her eyes tight.

"That seems so cruel," Gwen moans, tears welling in her eyes.

Jamie shakes her head. "No, cruel would've been letting me try to follow in the woman's footsteps," she says bitterly and with a bit of disgust. "And then leaving me up to the decision of the Grand Council."

"Grand Council…?" I ask. Jamie arches her eyebrows and looks at me. She looks like I just woke her up from a dream or something. She nibbles her lower lip and looks away.

"Nothing," she whispers, sounding like her body and her voice are the only things still here with Gwen and me. The rest, her thoughts, her mind, and even her soul are far away. They stare at and take in something that Gwen and I can't and probably never will see. This expression on her face seems like I've seen it before, but at the same time, as if I've never seen it before.

"Memory magic," I moan thinking about how little I know about my own life, let alone about my dad's life. Jamie looks at me. I know this alien facial expression, too. She wants to apologize but doesn't know how. "I know you didn't want to do it to me, Jamie." I feel her and Gwen's eyes swell, staring at me. "It was a secret," I add, creating the apology for her. "It was this…big, huge, crazy-ass secret that you were born into and had to keep before you even knew you had to do it." Gwen and Jamie both release weighty sighs at the same time.

I look at Jamie, before settling on Gwen. She leans against me still, her eyes wandering to and fixating on a distant corner of the room, probably with thoughts of all the secrets she's had to keep. "It's not fair," I whisper. Gwen looks at me. An emerald-tinted tear rolls down her cheek, after falling from her softly glowing eyes.

"It's not fair," Gwen sighs in agreement, with a shake of her head that causes her entire body to shake. "I never…asked to be born kitsune." Jamie reclines in her chair as she brings her legs up and crisscrosses them under her. She seems especially interested in what Gwen has to say. "I never asked for my kitsune mother and my human father to be killed because of our insane spirit world rules."

Gwen shivers violently before collecting herself. More tears fall from her eyes though, each tiny little emerald seeming to tell a story of a thousand other tears just like it. "I never asked to be mistrusted by every other...supernatural being I encountered..." Gwen lifts her eyes to Jamie and more tears fall. "...including our own kind, just because of what I am."

Gwen has something in her voice at this moment that I only hear when she's arguing with her brother...true anger and disgust. Her voice sounds stilted...her words proper...she hardly sounds like herself. She sounded more like you would expect royalty to sound. "I...," she gnashes her teeth together and another tremor ripples up her body. "...I never asked to be looked upon like I was something..."

"...wicked," Jamie finishes with tears running down her face. Gwen stares at her and nods. Matching sullen eyes, matching tear streaks, matching pain caused by what they are. I can't help wondering if Sora and Kai feel even vaguely similar to this. I can't imagine Kai doing anything but loving what he is. Sora's different though. She's so reserved; she keeps such a tight lid on her emotions.

"I'm sorry," Jamie breathes staring at me, then moving on Gwen. "I shouldn't have done the things that I did to you..." Her eyes come back to me. "...and I should've told you...everything." She shakes her head, looks away and places the four fingers on her right hand over her lips...her thumbs twitching nervously.

"It's okay," Gwen pants. "You didn't know me from any other kitsune...I mean, my own brother's one of the best examples of the worst of us."

"You're wrong about him," Jamie breathes. Gwen frowns. "I've been watching him too. He's not nearly as bad as you think." Gwen sits up a bit, preparing to challenge Jamie's assessment. "Don't get me wrong, he should definitely stay the hell away from Meghan, but...the other one..." Jamie nods absently. "...he really seems to care about her."

"What other one?" Gwen and I ask.

"I don't wanna ruin the surprise," Jamie says with a bit of a smile and tries to wipe her eyes. Gwen tilts away from me so that she can see my face. I shrug, feeling just as lost as she is. "Look at us," Jamie pants. "We're crying like a couple of girls." She laughs.

"News flash," I say. She frowns. "You are a couple of girls...don't get me wrong, that's no excuse for the crying, but still." Gwen's jaw drops, and she shoves me at the shoulder. I laugh.

"I should've known you could handle it, 'Lex," Jamie says. She takes a tissue from the box on the end table next to her chair before tossing it to Gwen. I nod thinking, about how in the dark I was only a few weeks ago. How...Gwen and I...I look at her...weren't anything and now look at us.

"What?" I shake my head. "You were staring," she says in a hushed way as her cheeks turn bright red.

"You're cute. I can't help myself." Gwen moans an *aw* and her cheeks turn a darker shade of red.

"Okay," Jamie whines. "If you guys are gonna keep talking like that, I'm gonna have to go get a bucket."

"Make that two," a more mature version of Jamie's voice calls from the hall. Jamie's eyes swell to twice their normal size. Gwen goes completely rigid as she starts, then falls back against me. From behind Jamie's chair, in strides her mother, Daphne Baggett.

She stands every bit of five and a half feet if she stands an inch. Her hair is jet black and straight, where Jamie's is more of a browning, deep red and a bundle of curls. Her skin is a few shades darker than Jamie's. She puts her hands on her hips, exposing her white t-shirt under her brown corduroy jacket. She also effectively displays two other benefits that she passed down to Jamie…and I'm not talking about her big brown eyes.

"What's *he* doing here?" Daphne groans, sounding equal parts frustrated, angry and exhausted. Jamie opens her mouth to speak but no words come out. Daphne stares at the back of her daughter's head like the answer to her question might be written there. "Well?" Daphne snaps.

Jamie opens her mouth to speak again. Daphne snaps the fingers on her left hand, exposing a little black tattoo at the base of her thumb.

"Gwen saw me use my magic. I swore her to secrecy then I had to save Alex and Gwen from this powerful familiar after the dance. The memory of that thing was too powerful, and I didn't have time to do a proper memory spell on him so I told him that I would explain everything today and so he and Gwen came over and I told him everything," Jamie says. As she spoke she sounded as though she were trying to get all of it out in one breath. She's panting like a dog on a summer's day, so that might be true. Although, I can't help remembering that time that Gavin used that twig on me at the store. If Daphne just used a similar trick on Jamie, consider me officially pissed.

"Jamina Lynda Baggett," Daphne whines. I snicker involuntarily.

"Shut up," Jamie snaps.

"Of all the stupid…"

"Mom," Jamie moans as she stands up.

"…hare-brained…"

"Mom…"

"…irresponsible…"

"Mom," Jamie whines louder. Daphne stares at her defiant daughter and shrugs her shoulders as if to ask what she wanted. "Gwen's a…"

"I'll get to the fact that you let a kitsune in my house later," Daphne cuts her off. Gwen swallows deeply and shudders. Daphne's eyes move over to us. Her head tilts askew. "A kitsune that's down one star ball." She steps past Jamie. "Alex, did you trick this kitsune into giving one of her star balls to you?" I shake my head and look at Gwen expecting an explanation. She still seems paralyzed.

"No," I say. "She…gave one to her foster parents."

"Gave?" Daphne nearly chokes on the word. "You…gave up one of your star balls voluntarily to the Taylors?"

"How did you know…?" Gwen starts in less than a whisper.

174

"I would be a poor excuse for a Witch of Light if I didn't know the second a kitsune moved into to town and everything about their living situation, wouldn't I?" Gwen shrugs, unable to form any additional words. Daphne's eyes turn to me. She sighs and shakes her head. "So, Riley Garner's kid finally caught a clue," she says at me, not to me. I frown. "Yeah, I can imagine that my daughter..." She turns to look at Jamie again. "...filled in some of the blanks but, I'm guessing you've got a lot more questions." I sit up and nod. "So, kid...what do you want to know?"

"Everything..."

Chapter 29: Witches

It's amazing.

"Go and get me the purple crystal next to the sandalwood candle on my dresser," Mrs. Baggett instructs Jamie-Lynn, sending her running up the stairs.

From the moment I met Jamie-Lynn, I thought of her as an incredibly powerful, white witch that could probably destroy me with an afterthought. "Here you go," Jamie-Lynn chirps as she passes the crystal to her mother.

"Now, I'll need the *active life* rune with the black string connected to it," Mrs. Baggett requests.

Jamie-Lynn groans. "It's in your room," she whines. Her mother stares at her with her head canted to the left. Jamie-Lynn trudges upstairs. "I just came from there." Powerful white witch...right...lost my train of thought. Seeing Jamie-Lynn interact with her mother, I'm reminded of one thing that I have to keep reminding myself about...well, myself. *She's just a teenaged girl.*

"Now, are you absolutely certain?" Mrs. Baggett asks Alex for the fourth time now. He nods. "I have to warn you, it's not going to be pleasant."

"I don't care," Alex grumbles. "I want ALL of my memories back."

Mrs. Baggett's shoulders slump. "Okay, Alex. I have to warn you...your father didn't just get me to block your memories of Jamie from your consciousness...apparently, you've seen some pretty wicked stuff in your time, kid." She looks at him with so much compassion and caring that you'd find it hard to believe that she's a scary white... "You," she says to me abruptly.

"Yes, ma'am," I return with a suddenly stiff spine.

"You're gonna have to let him go." I release Alex's arm and inch away.

"Stay close," Alex says without looking at me. I stare at him and I see what he's trying to hide from Mrs. Baggett. He's afraid. He's afraid of everything that his restored memories will uncover. "I might need you to work some of your 'calming me down' mojo on me."

"Here you go," Jamie-Lynn says, still a little frustrated, as she extends the black rope necklace with a little gray stone attached by a silvery clasp.

"Thank you, baby girl," Mrs. Baggett sighs as she takes it. She drapes the charm over Alex's head and turns it so that the rune carved into the stone faces out. "Okay. Do not touch the active life rune," she explains. "That will help your mind keep track of where your body is right here in the now."

"What?" Alex snaps.

"Sweetie," Mrs. Baggett says. "We didn't just...erase your memory...we took the memories out of your head."

Alex frowns. "Took them out of my head...?"

"It would be like," I start. "If someone could take a scan of your memories, not your brain, but your actual memories...those parts of your memory wouldn't be gray splotches like something had been covered up...they just wouldn't be there."

"That is a very good way of explaining it, little kitsune girl," Mrs. Baggett compliments.

"Gwen," Alex growls. "Her name is Gwen."

"Oh," I pant. "It's okay. If you want to call me, *kitsune girl*," I whisper finding it hard to breathe let alone talk. "That's fine, Mrs. Baggett," I spurt, recognizing that I probably sound like an idiot.

"Gwen," Alex whines softly.

"No," Jamie-Lynn says over her mother's shoulder. "Mom, her name is Gwen." She drapes her arms over her mother's shoulders and gives her a squeeze. "And she's a good person." I smile.

Mrs. Baggett pats Jamie-Lynn's arm with a warm smile of her own. "I know, baby. I could tell the minute I looked into her eyes." She turns her attention to me. "And you can call me, Daphne, Gwen." I nod.

"Now, like I was saying, we took the memories out of your head. Mind you, that's some powerful magic, but we didn't mind doing it because that's the way your father wanted it." Alex nods. "So, to reverse that, we'll basically have to send your mind on a journey back through your life. Basically, you'll relive every moment of your life with a conscious mind."

She takes the purple crystal that Jamie-Lynn brought and places it in Alex's left hand. "And that's the other part," she continues while slipping a white crystal out of the left breast jacket pocket. "Since, you'll be getting every missing detail of your life, slammed into your mind basically at the same time." She breaks off to inhale deeply. "It's gonna hurt."

"Alex," I moan without trying.

Mrs. Baggett points the white crystal at him. "Are you sure you want to do this?"

"For the last time, yes," Alex grumbles. Mrs. Baggett places the white crystal in his empty hand and wraps his fingers around it tightly.

"Alright, alright, no need to get snippy." Mrs. Baggett looks at Jamie-Lynn still hanging over her shoulders. "Did you finish the incantation?"

"I think so," Jamie-Lynn supposes as she reaches into her back pocket. She returns her left arm to its draped position and passes her mother a folded sheet of paper.

Mrs. Baggett takes the paper, unfolds and reads it. She purses her lips and nods her. "That sounds pretty good, baby girl," she whispers. "Don't pour too much power into this one…we want him to see his past, not his future, okay?" Jamie-Lynn nods her head subtly, not taking her eyes off Alex. "Relax," Mrs. Baggett says, drawing another nod. "Ready?" draws yet another nod.

They both turn their attention to the sheet of paper. "Fletus infantia," they begin in unison. "Rideo risi risum parvulus. Validus vir. Sapientia Vetus."

The crystals in Alex's hands glow softly. "They feel warm," he says.

Mrs. Baggett and Jamie-Lynn ignore him and the crystals and continue. "Animadverto res incompertus. Curator de vicis concede. Ortus. Vita. Nex. Fio unus." They finish, and everything is lost to blinding alternating purple and white lights.

"Agh," I cry.

"Gwen," Jamie-Lynn yells over the swirling winds, filling the room. "Focus your fox magic into your eyes and ears…" I do and slowly the lights dim. No, they don't dim, they simply become more bearable. Also, the sound of swirling winds is replaced by…

178

"Alex's voice," I sigh. I look to Mrs. Baggett and Jamie-Lynn and they watch Alex with all the patient expectation of a mother hen hearing her chick's first pecks at its shell. Alex's voice fills the room in varying degrees. I hear him as he sounded only a moment ago. I hear him as a child. I even hear him crying as a baby.

"Here it comes," Mrs. Baggett moans. She leans back as if expecting a pop or another burst of light. Instead, the lights retreat into the crystals and the sounds of Alex's varying voices fade softly away. Alex's back seizes, and he arches wildly, his eyes roll, only exposing the whites.

He growls...actually, growls at us. Mrs. Baggett stands, taking Jamie-Lynn with her. The pair backs away from Alex slowly. "I have never...seen that happen before," Mrs. Baggett explains.

"He looks like he's fighting something," Jamie-Lynn explains. Mrs. Baggett nods in agreement. I reach for him. "Don't touch him," Jamie-Lynn shouts. "We don't know what's going on in his head right now. For all we know he could be seeing himself playing in the sandbox with me or he could be on the verge of being torn apart by a Sava daemon or something." I clench my teeth and nod.

Suddenly, Alex bolts from his seat. His pupils have returned, but they're different...not his usual chocolate color, they're paler...as if something tried to strip all the color out of them and just barely failed. He looks at Jamie-Lynn and Mrs. Baggett and leans forward. He bears his teeth and growls again. Veins seem to strain, containing the blood in his body. I force fox magic into my ears again and I hear it. His heart is racing. I stare at him as he takes an aggressive step toward them.

His heartbeat isn't accelerated because he's afraid...he's angry. Before I realize it, I step between the witches and Alex. "What are you...?" Jamie-Lynne starts but is cut off by a comforting hand on her shoulder. Mrs. Baggett nods.

"Alex," I say, taking his hands in mine. "Alex, listen to me...feel my emotions, I'm trying to calm you down...I'm trying to feel out your emotions, but all I'm getting is a swirl of violent anger." His head twitches and he leans toward me. He sniffs me. If I weren't so afraid, I'd be giggling like a schoolgirl right now. "Alex..." I release his hands and put my hands on either side of his face. "Alex, it's me. It's Gwen."

"Gwen?" he grunts.

I nod. "Calm down, you're scaring me." Alex relaxes a bit, but the color has not returned to his eyes. He places his hands on my shoulders and pulls me in closer. He continues to sniff me feverishly. I would complain, but with each sniff, he seems to calm down a fraction.

"Oh, enough of this," Jamie-Lynn groans. She shoves me aside and steps in front of Alex. She draws back and slaps him across the face as hard as she can. His head whips to the left violently. "SNAP OUT OF IT," she barks. Alex's head comes back around slowly. His eyes are closed, but his breathing is still unsteady. Jamie-Lynn's breathing becomes erratic as well. I think she doesn't know if that worked or if it is truly time to run in terror.

Alex's eyes open slowly, all color restored. He peers into Jamie-Lynn's eyes. "Thank you," he moans. He then collapses. I catch him with all the speed and strength at my disposal. I sigh.

"You're welcome," Jamie-Lynn whispers with a wobble that tells me she's about to…she falls, and her mother is there to catch her.

"What was that?" I pant, staring at Mrs. Baggett with wide eyes. "What was wrong with Alex? Was he…like that at some point in his past?"

Mrs. Baggett shakes her head as she moves a very cumbersome Jamie-Lynn over to a chair.

"No, I can honestly say I have never seen Alex act like that." She sighs as she positions Jamie-Lynn in the large comfortable chair with its inviting plush arms. "No. Jamina did exactly what I asked her not to do. She put too much of her own magic into the spell." I frown. "That wasn't a vision of Alex from his past that we just witnessed…it was a glimpse at his future."

"His future…?" I gasp, staring down at Alex. He sleeps soundly in my arms. He seems so peaceful…and so absurdly cute…that my mind wanders to thoughts of *keeping him for myself*. I frown a moment later. "*Keeping him for myself*," I mutter as I lay him across the sofa, what a horribly kitsune way of thinking about someone.

I turn my attention back to Daphne, who pours herself a glass of Jamie-Lynn's special lemonade. "I told her…," she whispers with exasperation before she takes a sip. "I told her…," she emits as she lowers the glass. "If that daughter of mine was a little more controlled with the use of her powers, she'd really be something." I frown. "She puts a tornado's worth of power into a spell to raise a gentle breeze."

"Mrs. Baggett," I begin humbly. She lowers her glass after another drink and moans a sound of acknowledgment before swallowing. "What would make…Alex act like that…I mean, what could happen to him in the future that…?"

She shrugs and takes another small drink. "That's the thing," Mrs. Baggett starts again, sounding frazzled. "That might not even happen. It's just one possible future. That's why he fainted. Sending someone's mind into the future is like rolling a pair of dice…only with dice that have an infinite number of sides that could land in an infinite number of combinations."

"Infinite…?"

Mrs. Baggett nods. "What we saw could happen…tomorrow…a year from now…ten years from now…or not at all. It's just his mind reacting to several dozen possible future outcomes." My eyes drift back to him. He looked so…different…so feral, but somehow, it felt like he still knew me.

"That's why true clairvoyants are such a rarity," she explains. "It's hard on any mind…be it human, witch, daemon…" Her eyes train on me with laser focus. "…or spirit," she ends with such absolution that it makes me feel unbalanced. I feel as if I could tip over at any minute. I peer down at my feet to make sure that they are both still firmly on the floor.

"That's not me," Mrs. Baggett says as a response to a question that I never knew I raised. I tweak one eyebrow. "That dizziness you feel, it's not me. Well, not totally me." She peers around the room. "Some of these runes are designed to keep the air fresh, but they're not working right for some reason."

I frown not getting her meaning. "There's a lot of ambient magic floating around the room…thanks to Jamina." I nod, understanding that sentiment.

Whenever Gavin and I would fight...really, fight...as kids, obāsan...grrr...grandma would have to come in and cleanse our auras from the air. She always said despite our few years that our auras were surprisingly strong. I infuse my eyes with fox magic. Tiny crimson and bright pink orbs of light slowly drift through the air. I inhale deeply. "Pretty," I moan.

"The red ones are mine," Mrs. Baggett explains. "The pink ones are Jamina's."

There are nearly twice as many red ones as pink ones. "You're that much more powerful than she is?"

Daphne frowns and shakes her head slowly. "You're looking at the number of hers compared to mine..."

"That and yours seem so much more intense than hers."

"Only to the untrained eye, Gwen," she replies as the fox magic leaves my eyes and only ordinary room tones remain. "First of all, there are more of mine than hers, because she basically powered the spell herself. Her magic literally forced mine out." I nod.

"Second, Witches of Light aren't like other supernatural beings, Gwen. The color of our aura doesn't just reflect our personalities, or how we use our powers." She pauses and takes in Jamie-Lynn, sleeping soundlessly in her chair. "It's as simple as this...the closer to pure white our power is...the more powerful we are." I fail at containing a pant. "And any Witch of Light with pure white orbs...they're considered a Grand Witch and are given protection of a corner of the world." Daphne swallows an uncomfortable and nervous lump. "And every year since she was ten...Jamina's orbs have gotten brighter and brighter."

Mrs. Baggett's eyes fill with tears. "Don't tell her, okay?" I nod. "I'm sorry to unburden myself on you like this...but I've wanted to tell someone...anyone for so long. I couldn't tell any of the witches because they'd be watching her from that point on...and of course, I couldn't tell any humans. And any other supernaturals around...well, there's always the chance they'd try to take her out for bragging rights."

"Then why...?"

"...tell you...?" I nod, drawing my lips into my mouth. "I can see it in your eyes...you can't help being good, can you, Gwen?" I bow my head, not knowing how to answer that. "It's okay, you don't have to answer. I know it's true."

I frown and look to Jamie-Lynn and suddenly, the pale pink orbs with bright centers, drifting through the air, come back to mind. "Wow," I utter breathlessly.

#####

Nightmares...the only word that I have that could describe what comes after me over and over again. Every year of my life, I saw more and more...*things*. I see things that live in the shadows...shadows that seem to come to life. People look normal one minute and then turn into nightmarish things themselves the next. I see horns, spikes, scales, claws, and sharp teeth...some like little bat or snake teeth...some like a shark with two rows...and still others like a piranha. There are people with fur, feathers or dolphin skin. Red eyes, vampire eyes, cat eyes...so many glowing eyes pass by.

Monsters are what I see, for lack of a better word for them. Through all these different nightmarish versions of almost humans, one thing remains constant. My dad's there. EVERY SINGLE TIME, he's right there. Sometimes he's encouraging me not to be afraid. Other times he shields me from someone or something. His anger and frustration with them all…constantly having to protect me or explain my fears away…telling me that everything will be all right.

I see…Grandma Garner…Grandma Garner laughs at…me…? My uncle is with her. Dad pulls me closer. "He'll show you," he snaps. I wrap my arms around his leg…I'm so young. He reaches down and rubs the top of my head. I look up at him and he forces a smile. "He'll show all of you." He sounds like he's frothing at the mouth mad.

"He'll show us what?" My uncle taunts. "He'll show us how stupid you are…? He'll show us how we were right to try to stop you from marrying into a powerless clan…?" *What powerless clan…?* Mom's family…?

"He's powerful," dad grumbles, sounding completely sure. "He'll show ALL OF YOU…he'll be strong one day…he'll be so strong that you'll beg him…BEG HIM to not just rejoin the clan…you'll beg him to lead it." Uncle Flynn bares his teeth and a tiny, little, white-haired Kai clings to his leg, mirroring me. "Kai won't be half the skinwalker that Alex will be."

"That's enough, Riley," Grandma snaps. "It pains my heart to do this…" …and judging by the look on her face, she's not lying. "…but I, as the eldest member of our clan, strip you of your title as alpha and banish you…" She chokes, tears filling her eyes. How did her mood shift so quickly? "…from this clan…"

My father roars at them, sounding more like a bear or a lion. His bellow is so loud and forceful that uncle takes a step back and Kai cries.

My father and I are alone now. He turns to me. "I'll have to get Daphne to make you forget everything that happened, but I hope you'll hold onto this, Alexander." He taps my chest, directly above my heart. "There's a wolf in you. He'll make you strong when you don't think you can go on. He'll make you brave when there is nothing but fear and wickedness around you." He puts his hands on my shoulders. "He'll make you feel safe…" He swallows deeply. "…when I can't anymore…" He bobs his head.

I nod obediently. A wolf…? A wolf…? My father was a wolf. He was the leader of our clan…? He threw all of that away to be with and marry my mom. They kicked him out of the clan after they had me. I was there to see it all. No wonder I've always felt weird around Sora, Kai, and grandma…why I never felt like I belonged.

The rest of my life passes in a blur. I saw the day I met Stephen and the first time we played with Rich. I recall meeting Jamie and her mom at the market…her mom and my dad realized who and what each other were instantly. I remember dad bringing me by whenever he needed help with something. I remember playing with Jamie…I see something weird, and then it's gone. I see every incident and occurrence that she mentioned, not to mention some that I don't think even she's aware of, like her setting fire to a hedge at the park. I see myself meeting Meghan for the first time…she was glowing…she was literally glowing with a bright golden aura surrounding her…like…a streak of red rushes past me…

"Gwen," I call. It's a memory, of course, so she doesn't react. I see every second from the moment I first saw her in the hall…but it's different now. I don't see her with an air of disbelief. I see her, as she is…her deep red, flaming aura wrapped around her like a cloak of fire. More than anything, I see how beautiful she really is. How I've been watching her even when I don't mean to and how occasionally, I manage to catch her doing the same thing. Those amazingly green eyes of hers probe every inch of me and through some bona fide miracle, she actually seems to like what she sees.

"Wait…what's going on?" I hear my voice echoing through blackness. I see Gwen, standing by a strange twisting turning tree. It has deep green…I'd say leaves, but it's more like a fur tree and I don't really feel like those things technically should be considered *leaves*. I guess that's not important now. She's wearing a white dress that hangs down in a straight line. She turns to look at me and she's crying.

"You shouldn't say that Alex," she moans through her tears. I step forward. She shakes her head and takes a step back. "I wish I had left…without saying anything to you…I…" Her expression deteriorates. She takes a step toward me. "I…can't be around you…"

My eyes flutter open…I'm staring at a ceiling. "I think he's awake," Daphne says. Gwen leans into view. She looks worried. "You kids are ridiculously angsty. One of you should probably say something."

"Are you okay?" Gwen whispers, moving her hair to one side.

I search through all my memories, trying to find some eloquent speech, some poem that would express how I feel about her, but my mind just keeps wandering back to the image of her in a white dress. "You were crying," I finally utter after she searches my eyes for some proof of how I'm doing.

"Only a little," she moans, wiping her cheeks.

I shake my head. "Not now," I whisper. "In my dream, you were wearing a long white dress and you were crying. You tried to tell me something, but I snapped out of it before…" And just as suddenly as I saw the vision…it's gone.

"Alex," she says with concern. I sit up and she moves with me. Her knees are on the sofa and her hands rest on top of them. "Before what?" I frown, whatever it was, it slipped away from me just that fast. I shake my head. Her arms slip over my shoulders. "I'm just glad you're okay."

"I'm better than okay." I wrap one arm around her waist and my other hand makes its way through her hair. "I remember EVERYTHING." She gasps and leans back a bit. She stares at me with a mix of joy and relief washing over her. Her eyebrows tweak a bit. "I see…everything too…" She frowns. "I see the runes that you were talking about…I see…" My eyes move to Daphne and Jamie sitting…no, sleeping in the chair next to her. "I see the bright red aura around Daphne…I see the pink one around Jamie."

Gwen looks to them. She and Daphne exchange a knowing look then she comes back to me. "You can see auras?"

"That's only temporary," Daphne assures me. "Eventually, you'll go back to having to focus to see them."

"To focus…?"

She nods. "At least, until you finally find your totem animal." I shake my head and look down at Gwen with both her hands clutching the front of my hoodie. "What? Did you already find your totem animal and just forgot?" I shake my head again. I sigh, take a deep breath, and explain to them the part of the dream when my grandmother kicked my dad and me out of the clan.

"That sucks," Daphne says and offers me another glass of Jamie's lemonade.

"Tell me about it."

"Maybe your dad was right," Gwen says. "I mean, he believed in you. He said that you'd be stronger than all of them, right?" I nod and sip the energy drink mixed with a double shot of espresso that Jamie's special brew is. "He believed in you. Maybe you should believe in him, too."

"That's true," Daphne piles on. "No matter what, he always said you were special, Alex."

I scoff. "He had to," Gwen continues. "I know you're mad at him for keeping all of this from you…"

"That's just it," I cut her off. "I'm not mad at him…or Rex or anybody anymore. I see why he kept it from me. Without being able to defend myself, all of this stuff would've scared the hell out of me as a kid." I laugh nervously. "I'm just barely handling it now." Gwen rubs my arm. "But I'm glad you're here to help me through it all." I stare at her and smile.

"What?" she asks with a matching smile.

"It's just…I see you. I really see you…"

Her cheeks turn almost as red as her hair. "And…?"

"…and you're beautiful…" The red on her face spreads to her forehead and across her nose. "In fact, you're the most beautiful, most perfect thing…I've seen in my entire life." She murmurs an *aw* and caresses my cheek. She leans forward until her forehead rests against mine. The energy passes between us. I tilt my head to the right and she mirrors me.

"Hey," Daphne snaps. "If you two are going to make out, please take it somewhere else." Gwen blushes all over again and so do I. We both laugh, and she wraps her arms around me again. I can't help but think that no matter how happy I am right now…something's going to come along and take her away…something wicked.

Chapter 30: Memory

Alex opens the door and steps onto the ash-gray concrete of the front porch. There's still no reaction for him. I pause and put my hand over my heart. He pulls his pack up on his left shoulder with his right hand…because he's holding my pack in his left. "Come on," he moans, still staring at me. He offers me his hand. "Protection spell, remember?" My eyebrows push toward the middle of my forehead. Memories of stepping onto the porch the first-time rush through my mind. "Jamie was just watching out for me, like you do."

I nod once, firmly. I put my hand in his and move my foot toward the front porch. "If the runes start draining me again…?"

"I'll carry you down the stairs and away from them."

I nod, put my foot down and…nothing happens. I breathe a sigh of relief. We walk across the small porch and it seems like there are more runes than when we got here. We make our way down the stairs and cross the small lawn. Alex peers down the block one way and then the other. "Guess we'll have to call your brother."

I retrieve my ruby red phone. He stares at it, paying special attention to the little clip part at the top. "Or we could call your cousins."

"Oh, no." He taps the right side of his head with his matching pointer finger. He smiles. Alex so rarely really smiles that when he does it's so….

"Pretty," I murmur. He tilts his head to the left, his finger still touching near his temple.

"After getting my memory back, I realized something." I arch my eyebrows in expectation. Alex leans in closer and places his hand next to his mouth as if whispering a secret. "My cousins are even more annoying than I originally thought they were."

"I heard that," Sora grumbles behind Alex. How did she and Kai get so close without me noticing? Alex didn't react at all, as if he was expecting them to show up. At least for once, they're dressed in appropriate layers for how cool the weather is. Sora wears her new form-fitting leather jacket over an even snugger ash-white sweater. She's wearing black boots that stop just below her knees and her jeans tucked down into them. Kai's wearing a charcoal gray t-shirt, but on top of that, he has a red hoodie that appears similar to Alex's. On top of that, he wears a sport coat that he's left unbuttoned. "Where have you been?" Sora snaps with a savage growl.

Alex tilts his head back lackadaisically and scratches his chin. He looks at his cousins with a more patient gaze. "We were studying English with a friend of ours. Working on our papers…"

"No," Sora grumbles and steps closer. She puts her hand on Alex's shoulder and turns him around to face them. It's not only that, she used her enhanced strength to force him. I steal a glance at Kai and can't help noticing that even he has a serious expression on his face. "I mean, where in the hell were you?" Alex frowns.

"We tracked your scent, cousin," Kai cuts in. "We tracked it to this spot exactly." Kai scratches the side of his head above his right ear. "After you got here…both of your scents just…disappeared."

I frown. "It's like he said," I start, recalling Mrs. Baggett's words while Jamie-Lynn was asleep.

"...while most of the supernatural community fears White Witches...that fear often leads to mistrust and animosity, more than respect. My greatest fear happens every day Jamina leaves for school. Despite how powerful Jamina is, her inexperience makes her a prime target for supernatural beings attempting to steal power or use her in some way."

Therefore, we promised that we would keep her secret, especially from Gavin... My eyes scan Sora's face that looks like she could kill me at any minute and Kai's that looks just as displeased with the situation. ...even from Sora and Kai. "We were working on our English papers."

"Why don't I believe the kitsune?" Sora grumbles angrily. "You two don't seem to get it. It wasn't as if you were in somebody's house and we lost track of you for a second because of some overwhelming smell. We lost you completely. Your scent made it here and evaporated. We couldn't hear you either. So, where did you come from?"

Alex arches one brow. "Like Gwen said, we were studying...working on papers." Sora growls to the point that her teeth show...correction, her fangs show.

"There's sage in the air," I offer. Sora frowns.

"Sage...?" Kai asks.

I nod once. Sora's frown becomes a full scowl. "Yes, sage is used in lots of spells and potions. It can be used to conceal things or uncover them. Maybe, it blocked your senses of smell."

"Sage is used by witches," Sora mumbles, still trying to contain her anger. "Were you two visiting a witch?" She looks back at Jamie-Lynn's house. "Does a witch live here?"

"No," Alex snaps. His expression has changed and become just as hard as Sora's. "We were working on our papers with my friend, Jamie. You know, Jamie?" Kai nods. Alex turns to Sora. "And sage is also used in A LOT of recipes. Her mom said she was marinating some rosemary chicken for dinner tonight and she spilled some stuff in the kitchen." He pinches his nose. "It made the house smell crazy strong. I'm surprised you can't still smell it on us."

"Rosemary chicken...?" Sora questions.

"Grandma made that once," Kai says, scratching to the back of his head. "She shooed me out of the kitchen because she said if I got any of the sage on me or anywhere near my nose, I wouldn't be able to smell anything for the rest of the day. Man, that would've drove me crazy as a pup."

Alex sucks in air between his teeth. Kai and Sora's expressions thankfully ease.

"You look funny with wet fur," Alex laughs at Kai. We all stare at him incredulously. "I don't know, for some reason, when you just said that I remembered coming to visit you guys in Seattle when I was six. It was the only day the sun was out that entire week. You got something on your arm and you went to towel off. You put the towel down, ran and jumped in the pool. When you came up, you were covered in matted orange and brown fur." Alex laughs. "You started moving your arms like a crazy person and crying. Sora had to push you out over to the edge and..." His upbeat humor gives way to a whimsical smile. "...and my dad pulled you out of the pool…you too, Sora." Alex taps the top of his head with his fist. "Sora clunked you on the head and your fur disappeared."

Sora covers her mouth, but if her eyes are any indication, she's laughing behind that hand. "That made him stop crying," she explains with audible humor in her voice. "…and gave him a whole new reason to cry." Sora and Alex both laugh.

Kai looks embarrassed and scratches his head again. "You remember that?" Alex bobs his head. "I thought you forgot all that stuff that happened when we were kids. Grandma told us not to be surprised if you didn't know anything about us."

"I guess all the weirdness that's been going on lately, jogged my memory," Alex says with a serious, but somehow light-hearted tone. "I know I don't always act like it…I mean, I act like you guys are a pain, most of the time, and let's face it, you are…" Kai smirks and Sora's usual stoniness comes back. "…but…I'm glad you guys are here. And not just because you guys have saved my life a time or two…but because you're family."

Kai steps over to him and quickly throws one arm around his neck. He pulls Alex down into a headlock. Alex laughs. "Geez," Kai utters between clenched teeth. "Don't get all Goth on us, just because you got some crappy memories back." They both laugh as they wrestle about in a cheerful manner.

Sora crosses her arms and shakes her head. She turns and walks down the sidewalk. "I'm gonna go get the car. One of you owes us lunch for the mini-panic you caused." Sora walks down to the end of the street and disappears around a corner. I glance back at the house and see Jamie-Lynn staring at us from the front window. She waves then disappears behind the curtain.

Alex and Kai stop wrestling. Alex managed to hold on to both of our bags. Kai gives him another playful shove before staring at him. "Something's different about you," Kai says. "I can't really put my finger on it."

"I just feel good, you know?" Alex returns. "I mean, I'm studying, trying to get my grades up." His eyes move over to me. He smiles.

A car rips up the street and screeches to a halt next to us. "Gavin," I moan. He opens his car door, looks around and then motions for me to come to him. I pause for a second and glance at Alex. My eyes dart toward Gavin and then back to him. He follows me as I move closer to Gavin's car. "What is it?"

"Could you send your pet away?"

"My cousin's not a pet," Kai snaps. Alex motions for him to stay calm. Kai grumbles under his breath and turns away.

"Kai's right," I start. "Alex is my…friend…" I stumble and feel a tweak of pain in my stomach thinking of Alex as *just* my friend. "…and besides, he knows everything. So, you can talk in front of him." Alex steps up beside me.

"Fine," Gavin says with a great deal of anger behind that one word. "I remembered something that Mrs. Taylor said once. She told me that she keeps a lot of mementos from you in her office at the school."

"Yeah, she took me there once. She has all of the pictures they took the day they agreed to be my foster parents and the paperwork…and…" Gavin arches his eyebrows. "…and…the first thing I gave them…my charm."

He nods. "How about we go take a look tonight?"

I frown and shake my head slowly. "We can't. We're supposed to go to the movies tonight…with Meghan and Stephen." Gavin scowls as if I told him I was preparing a goat sacrifice. "You remember Meghan, right? Pretty girl, blond, fierce blue eyes…I begged you to stay away from…"

"…that you dissed last night at the dance," Alex finishes. I smirk, still trying not to look at him. "The charm will still be there tomorrow. We can go get it then."

"First of all," Gavin returns. "What *we*? Second of all, I'm going to get it tonight, whether you come with or not, Gwenie." He tips his head downward. "Now, come on. I'll give you a ride home." I steal a glance at Alex. He smiles and extends my bag.

"Thanks," I whisper. "I'll call you." He smiles in that way that makes me feel like my entire body is one gigantic blush. I pull Gavin's passenger side door open and slide inside. I issue a finger-wiggling wave to Alex. Gavin climbs in and pulls away from the curb quickly.

#####

"So, let me get this straight," I start as Stephen pulls the car up to the curb.

"Yes, Alex…Meghan called me…I didn't call her. She asked me out, not the other way around. She recanted and asked Gwen to come and to bring you along so that it wouldn't be so…datey."

"Datey…recanted…?" I ask making sure that my tone tells him I'm poking fun. "Who are you? And besides, I thought you were hanging out with…?" I break off. Who did he tell me he was hanging out with tonight? It's weird…when I try to think about it, I think about how it felt when Jamie and her mom gave me my memories back.

"Nah, I didn't have any plans." Stephen gets the same confused expression on his face that I feel on mine. "At least, I don't think I did." He shakes his head and shifts the car into park. We file out of his mom's Nissan something or other and head toward the theater.

"What about you?" he starts again. "You invited your cousins. In case you didn't know, Meghan REALLY doesn't like Sora."

I shrug. "They overheard Gwen and me talking about the movie and said they wanted to come. Don't worry it won't be awkward."

"Don't tell me it won't be awkward, loser," Meghan whines behind us. She and Gwen walk over. "Hey Stephen," she says with her entire demeanor changing. She stares at him for a second before her eyes move to me. "Alex," she groans.

"So, are we ready?" Stephen asks.

"No," Meghan snaps. "Apparently, we have to wait on Alex's cousins, Kai…" She looks at Gwen as if she would cut her in half if she could. "…and Sora," she finishes adding so much venom that I feel like we should all head to the hospital for treatment.

"They don't…um," I begin, making an excuse for why they're coming. "…yeah, they haven't really made many friends since they moved here, so…"

"So, what…?" Sora asks with her arms crossed. She looks at Meghan and her smug sense of superiority practically becomes a flashing neon sign. She shifts her arms down to her sides…revealing a top that's cut so low I feel a little uncomfortable seeing her in it, being her cousin. I turn my head and frown.

188

"Nothing," I spit looking at the theater's sign.

"Let's go inside," Gwen murmurs stepping closer. She reaches down and takes my hand. I can feel her tension. "I think Meghan kind of hates your cousin and by extension me," she whispers. She looks back at the rest of our group. "Plus, I need to talk to you…" She peers at Kai and Sora. "…in private." She pulls me toward the box office.

She slips her free hand into her pocket. She pulls a folded bill out. "Um, which movie are we seeing again?"

I reach for my wallet. "Put that away."

"No, my…my foster-parents gave me money. Mrs. Taylor said that she could tell I really like you and she wanted us to have a good time." She rolls her eyes and puts her hand on her forehead. "…and I can't believe I just told you that."

I laugh. "Alright. Movie's on you, but drinks and popcorn's on me." She smiles and nods. She slides the money toward the cashier. "Two for…um…" I look up at the sign above the woman's head…thanking God that Mr. Hamish doesn't make me wear a vest at work…especially a maroon one.

"The romantic one," Meghan suggests. I groan. Gwen giggles and I laugh because she laughed.

"…*Fancy Flights,*" I mutter reluctantly. The woman collects Gwen's money, presses a couple of buttons and gathers a few singles then extends them with the tickets. Gwen takes the cash and tickets and passes me one.

"Um, give us a minute," Gwen asks Meghan and Stephen. "We'll be there in a second." Meghan gives us a curious look, but nods. "We'll be right back," she says to Sora and Kai. Sora looks at me. I tip my head to the theater letting her know that I'm fine. She steps up to the box office and buys her and Kai's tickets.

"What's up?" I whisper.

"There's a reason I picked this theater," Gwen explains. "There's also a reason I chose this jacket," she says, motioning to her definitely not pink jacket. I stare into her eyes…that look more and more concerned with every passing minute.

"Is it because…the elementary school is two blocks and a quick sprint through some trees away?" She draws her lips into her mouth and nods. "I'm coming with."

"Good." She tugs on my hoodie. "That means I don't have to ask."

"You never have to ask me to come with you, Gwen." She smiles. "Okay, we're definitely gonna miss the previews, but I did promise you popcorn so…we should hurry back."

She looks around then pulls me down the side street next to the theater. "Are you ready?" She slips her arms around my waist.

"Always," I whisper.

She smirks as her eyes glow and all I can think about is how beautiful she is. She exhales slowly, and flames appear on her shoulders and flicker through her hair. She takes a step and wind swirls around us. It was only one-step for her, but I can tell we're…she takes another step… "We're here," she says softly. …moving fast and really far. She lets me go and I step back. She looks around. The flames are gone, but her eyes are still bright. "I don't sense Gavin."

"Good," he snaps behind her. She jumps, then glares at him. "That's just how it should be…I'm so far ahead of you that you'll never catch up." He tips his head back. "Come on. I already found a way in."

"Makes sense," I say as she and I follow him toward the front of the school. "She's an elementary school principal…not exactly a lot of security needed, you know?" We reach the front entrance. Gavin walks over to the door. "Seriously, we're going in the front? Why don't we just go to the sheriff now and turn ourselves in?"

"Shut your pet up," Gavin snarls, pulling the front door open. "Or I will." He disappears behind the door. Gwen moves over to the door and holds it open for me. She gives me a pleading look. I groan and rush to the still open door. We head inside and round the tiny hallways, heading for the principal's office. Being here brings back a flood of memories. I remember my mom picking me up every day after school. My dad's face when he came for *Lunch with Your Dad* day and all the cafeteria served was PB&J sandwiches and orange slices.

"Alex," Gwen whispers. "Are you okay?" I nod. "Are you sure?" I smile. I wish Gwen had been here then…if for no other reason than I would've been able to get to know her sooner. I laugh to myself. Nah, knowing the reputation that kitsune have, my dad probably wouldn't have let her get anywhere near me. I look at her again…or rather, the big shadowy, bear-dog thing sneaking up behind her…

"Gwen," I moan, hoping that my wide eyes and pale skin give me away. Her eyes flick on like a switch. She nods subtly. She pushes me a few steps back as she swirls around and kicks the thing on the side of the head. It reels but recovers quickly. She wraps her arms around me before I even realize it.

"GAVIN," she yells as we make our way back to the main entrance less than a second later. Less than a second after that, the bear-dog is behind us. "No," she murmurs. She moves between it and me, pushing me behind her. I put my hand on top of hers and squeeze.

"We can do this," I whisper. She glances at me and quickly back to the bear-dog. "Don't be afraid to cut loose in front of me…like you did at the dance." She sighs and squeezes my hand back. She crouches and let's go…fire blazes up from her shoulders again…through her hair…and down her back. Three flaming, twisting tails rise from the small of her back. She exhales so loud that it seems to make the door's glass vibrate.

"Here I go," she states in an echoing voice. She pushes off and vanishes in a burst of bright red flames. She kicks the bear dog in the center of its face and it falls back. She springs off, lands, and disappears again in another eruption. She drives both of her feet into its side and it yelps in pain…

Weird. It never yelped in pain before. Did she hit it that hard or is something different this time? She bounces off again comes back down on its back. She buries her fiery claws deep into its back and it roars…something is mixed in the roar though. It sounds like a voice, like someone's voice screaming out in pain. Gwen appears in front of me again. She's on all fours, her tails whipping from side to side. A thin layer of flames covers her entire body.

The bear-dog struggles but rises to its feet. It takes a step forward and shutters. It sinks into the floor and the shadow that it left on the floor disappears around a corner. Gwen watches it warily. She takes a hesitant step forward. "Gavin," she breathes and then vanishes.

"Crap," I moan. I run as fast as my normal human legs can carry me around the corner and down toward the principal's office. Thankfully, the opposite direction of the bear-dog. I dart into the open office. I look around through the dark. "Gwen," I whisper. The door leading to the teacher's lounge flies open. Gwen and Gavin rush out in a blur of bright red and blue flames. The door slams behind them.

Gavin looks at Gwen. "Get your pet and go!"

"Did you get it?" Gavin nods. "Then we should all get out of here." They both look at me. "Come on, human and kitsune." Gavin nods again. They both leap the counter and Gwen grabs me. We're down the hall and out the front door before I realize it. I feel every jump when Gwen takes another step and I see Gavin's blue flames flair when he takes one next to us.

"This way," Gwen whispers. Gavin moves beside us until...we come to a stop on the side street next to the theater. Gwen breathes heavily. She takes several steps away from me, fire rippling off her.

"Gwen?" She shakes her head. She throws her right hand out to her side, a little fire flicks away and the rest leaves her body at the same time. She inhales deeply and turns her normal beautiful eyes to me. "Gwen," I sigh walking over to her. She shudders into a smile. "You did it." She nibbles her bottom lip and opens her arms when I get close to her. I open mine and she puts both of her hands on my chest.

She looks around. "Wait. Where's Gavin?"

"He took another step," I whisper.

"He did...?" Gwen gasps. I nod once. She looks behind her and I can practically see the frown on her face. "Come on," Gwen says before she runs toward the back of the building.

Chapter 31: Dating

Alex and I round the corner and find Gavin in the alleyway, crouched over…my charm. "So, you did manage to grab it?" I gasp.

"Yeah," he replies, still focusing on it.

"Well, give it to me." He ignores me completely. Fox magic flows to his hands. His claws descend. "What are you doing?" He ignores me. He carves Japanese kanji and kana into his forearms with his claws. I read star, force, and sever on his left arm as he moves to his right. "WHAT ARE YOU DOING?"

He glares at me. "What do you think I'm doing?"

"You can't," I gasp. Gavin returns to his writings. "You can't!" He finishes writing and moves his hands to either side of my charm. I feel an overwhelming rush of his fox magic and his hands erupt in blue flames. His flames engulf my charm and it glows. The symbols that he carved into his forearms glow, too. "Please…don't do this, Gavin."

Alex's hand reaches into the flames and collects my charm. He stands up and backs away. Gavin is on his feet instantly. "What the hell?"

"Gwen says not to do…whatever you were doing…so, we're not doing it," Alex says with a confidence I've never seen. That look in his eyes…I think Meghan would call that look…sexy. "What was he doing?"

I step between them, sensing Gavin's mood shifting to violence. I look at Alex. "He was performing a ritual." Alex cuts his eyes to Gavin then back to me. "That would forcibly remove my star ball from the charm."

"You mean it would take out the part of your…fox magic that you put in it…?"

"That's right, human," Gavin says, dripping with condescension.

"Yes," I concur. "It would. But, there is also a chance that it could ricochet or backfire during removal."

"You mean it could hurt you?" Alex supposes. Gavin scoffs.

I shake my head slowly. "If it does…ricochet…it will bounce back and hit the first human who came into contact with it…and destroy them." Alex inhales deeply. "It would kill my foster mom."

"There's no guarantee that'll happen," Gavin complains.

"Yes," I begin, annoyed by his arrogance. "But how many times has obāsan said that a ricochet hasn't happened when a binding is forcibly removed from an object? Huh?" Gavin inhales deeply through his nose and looks down. "Exactly, we're not doing it."

"Look at our options," Gavin starts with anger swirling. "You can let me finish the ritual and get you out of this town and out of danger until your fox magic returns in full. You can beg them to return the charm and release you from your binding, giving you back your full power but, as you said yourself, that's unlikely. Oooooooorrrrrrr, I could just kill your foster parents and free you from their bond."

"No," I snap.

"Those are the only ways to free her?" Alex asks solemnly. He lifts his eyes to Gavin, who nods. Alex nods along with him. "Then, there's really only one option."

I gasp and cover my mouth before I even realize it. Alex can't be siding with Gavin, can he? He can't really be suggesting we kill my foster parents or that we should try to remove the binding. Alex lifts his hand still tightly wrapped around my charm out toward Gavin. He is…a tear streams down my face…he does want to let Gavin kill her. I feel a horrible ache in my chest. How could he do this? I thought he and I were closer than that. I thought I was…I mean, I thought that we were…I try to speak but all I manage is a pant.

Alex's closed fist juts out to me. I gasp again. "I hope you can convince 'em to let you go," Alex says looking into my eyes. He opens his hand and the tiny sunflower charm falls into my waiting palms.

Gavin uses swift paw and is on Alex in a second. "WHAT DID YOU DO, HUMAN?" he roars with his fox magic causing his voice to boom and echo. He takes Alex, by the arm. I see it instantly…it was only for a second, but a bluish-silvery spark traveled between Gavin's hand and Alex's arm. They're staring at each other. Did Gavin feel it…he turns to me with a shocked expression on his face. He did feel it. I nod, confirming what he senses. Gavin, still in shock, releases Alex's arm.

Gavin takes a step back and exhales deeply. "Fine…Alex," he says, pointing one finger at me and another at Alex. "It's on you." He uses swift paw to leap upward and lands on top of the building to my right. "One week," he says looking over his shoulder. "You have one week to convince them, or I'll convince them…my way." With a burst of foxfire, Gavin is gone.

Alex continues, staring after him. He returns to me and…before I know it, my arms are already over his shoulders. I hug him…and it feels as natural as breathing. "Thank you…so much," I weep. Why am I crying? His arms slowly wrap around my waist.

"You're…welcome." His arms hold me tighter.

It takes me about s second to realize it. Alex has his arms around my waist. My arms are over his shoulders…and we're all alone. My left hand strokes the soft hairs at the back of his head. He pulls me in closer…our bodies touch and all the air rushes out of me. I try to collect myself. Breathe, Gwen, I command my body. It's not like Alex and I have never hugged before. We've just never hugged this tightly…or alone like this. I manage to take a deep breath but that just makes it worse, because I take in his scent and he smells so good. My breathing is become hectic, hurried.

What's wrong with me? Why is my body reacting to him this way? It's just Alex. Alex…who is cute and…funny…and who creates the most amazingly, beautiful things…and who just did the bravest thing ever. He releases me…no, he just loosens his hold on me. I move back so that I can see his face. That was a mistake. He's looking into my eyes. He leans forward until our foreheads touch. "I was so worried about you," he breathes.

My hands move to either side of his face. His skin is firm, but somehow soft…I just want…to hold him like this. What's wrong with me? "I'm fine," I return with a nod. "I'm fine. I'm fine." He nods gently moving his forehead against mine. His hands rest on my hips. That energy passes between us. The first time it was painful. The second time…there was nothing but an awareness that it occurred. Every time since then has been nice…pleasurable even…especially this time.

I open my eyes. When did I close them? His eyes remain closed. He's muttering something. I can almost make it out. "What?"

"Don't lean. Don't lean. Don't lean." The more he repeats it the softer it becomes until it is less than a whisper again. "Don't lean. Don't lean." I realize it now. I want to…I want to lean. "Don't lean. Don't lean." I want to kiss him. "Don't lean." I should kiss him. "Don't lean."

"What if I…want to lean?"

He swallows deeply. "If you lean, then I won't be able to stop myself…from kissing you."

"Then don't."

I lift my head and lean back. He leans back too. He looks at me with focused eyes that hide the slightest hints of shock. Yes, Alex…I feel the same way about you.

I inhale deeply. I swallow just as deeply, staring into his chocolate-colored eyes. His pupils widen briefly then shrink again. I frown and lean toward him, staring at his perfectly moistened lips along the way. I think he's moving closer, too. My eyes drift closed again. His breath caresses my lips. It's cool, soft, and sweet…and it causes me to tremble with anticipation…

"Hey, are you guys alright?" Kai asks, running up to us. Alex and I separate instantly. "You guys never came in, so we got worried and what was that?" Kai asks mockingly.

"I…," Alex begins.

"Kai," Sora says in that controlling way of hers. He looks at her and she shakes her head. She looks at me and frowns. Wait, it's not a frown. She's studying me. Why? She's actually making me nervous, almost as nervous as that hug with Alex. I steal a glance at him and come back to Sora. She's smiling, sort of.

"Gwen," Meghan yells from the end of the alley. She and Stephen run toward us. "Gwen, are you okay? Have you guys been out here this whole time and why do you look like that?"

"Look like what?" I ask rubbing the back of my neck with one hand while slipping my charm into my pocket with the other.

"Like that," Meghan says, cheerily and with a finger pointed at my face. "You look like you just got caught with your hand in the cookie jar…" Her eyes move to Alex. "…or something else."

"You too," Stephen suggests to Alex. He motions between us. "And why are you both blushing?"

"What…? I'm not blushing," Alex says.

"I-I-I'm not…either!"

"Yeah, you are," Meghan and Stephen both reply in unison.

"When I got here, they were hugging," Kai states in an exaggerated way. "And they looked like they were pretty close to kissing." Meghan opens her mouth, inhales deeply, and points at me. Stephen covers his mouth with his fist and scoffs.

"I didn't…," I stammer again.

"We didn't," Alex joins, moving his hand back and forth between us. "Why would she…I mean, with me…" Alex looks at me and I return his gaze while tucking a few stray strands of hair behind my ear. He smiles. I smile. Blood rushes to my cheeks.

"Oh my God," Meghan breathes while collecting my hand. "Come with me!" She drags me away. I look back at Alex. He looks down at the ground, still smiling. Sora crosses her arms and follows us.

We reach the sidewalk and go around the corner quickly. Meghan turns to me. She looks past me. "You can't claim to just be friends anymore. You are so totally crushing on Alex," she squeals. I frown. "I knew it…I knew it. I knew it. I knew it," she chants. "Don't deny it either, Gwendolyn Elizabeth Frost."

I open my mouth to speak and nothing comes out. Meghan opens her mouth and matches the tilt of my head, but with both eyebrows arched. I cut my eyes to Sora looking at us as if we're the most annoying things she's ever seen. Meghan looks at her. "You can't breathe a word of this to your cousin." Sora zips an imaginary zipper over her mouth and, as Meghan returns to me, rolls her eyes.

I sigh. "Okay, so I think he's a little…" My stomach rolls over a few times. "…totally and completely gorgeous," I whine. Meghan is really starting to rub off on me. I'm not sure if it's in a good way or a bad way, yet. "And then he just did the sweetest, most amazing thing," I gush. I'm gushing. What is wrong with me?

"What did he do?" Sora asks.

I cut my eyes to her and tilt my head back slightly. She nods getting my meaning. "My-my brother was being a jerk…to me…and Alex stood up to him for me. Nobody has ever stood up to my brother before."

"Wow," Meghan breathes. "Your brother's…so much bigger than him."

"Stronger, too," Sora adds with a bit of annoyance. Meghan turns to look at Sora. I mouth a quick, 'sorry.' She waves me off in a 'don't worry about it' kind of way. "You brought your car, right?" Meghan nods in return. "Could you give my cousin and Gwendolyn a ride home?"

"No problem," Meghan moans, feeling the weight of the situation.

"I…" Sora cuts her serious eyes to me. "…just remembered, I have something to take care of." If the look in her eyes didn't frighten me, the tone of her voice would've done it. She turns and walks away. "Tell my brother that I just remembered we have that thing."

"O-okay," I mutter. Alex, Kai and Stephen come around the corner as she walks away. Kai tilts his head in the direction that Sora departed. He points to Alex and I nod subtly. "Hey, we're…gonna get a ride home from Meghan."

"Stephen brought his mom's…I mean, his car."

"My mom and dad stopped by and picked it up," Stephen says, waving his phone in the air. "Apparently, they had to cut their dinner date short, because there was a break in at the elementary school." Alex and I exchange a glance.

"I'm kind of hungry," Meghan says cheerfully, taking us away from that awkward moment.

Stephen nods and pats his stomach. "We already skipped most of the movie. We could, at least, grab a bite, right?"

Meghan smiles with a nod. "I know the perfect spot." Meghan walks between us, heading in the direction of her car. Stephen follows her. Alex extends his hand to me. I stare at it for a moment. It looks like it was meant for me. It's where my hand belongs. I claim it and intertwine our fingers. He smiles and pulls me along beside him.

#####

We sit at La Hermosa Rosa, the little Mexican restaurant just off the square. I don't know about anybody else, but I can't remember feeling more awkward in my entire life. I look at Gwen to my left, wishing I could've talked to her about what happened in the alley…and what almost happened in the alley. I look across the table at Meghan and then to my right at Stephen. I can't believe they crammed the four of us around this tiny little square table.

Gwen puts her right hand under the table. She taps my knee with her pointer finger. I hook it with my left pointer before she can move it away. She smiles, her chin resting on her palm. She leans in closer and mouths a 'thank you.' I smile.

"Should we leave you two alone?" Stephen asks.

"Leave them alone," Meghan whines, drawing Stephen's attention. "They're in l…" Gwen makes a cutthroat motion across her neck, while staring at Meghan. Stephen and I laugh. "Well, anyway…I have to admit, you guys make much better company without Rich."

"Rich?" Stephen says. He looks at me. "Who's Rich?"

"Good way to look at it," she continues. Stephen turns back to her and arches his eyebrows. He shakes his head. "You're kidding, right? Pale, glasses, gangly…super creepy," she describes him in an especially Meghan way.

"Rich," I continue. "We've been friends since you introduced us at the sandbox in the park." Stephen frowns. Gwen squeezes my finger. I hate to admit it, but I forgot all about Rich too. This isn't even the first time either. Just earlier, I couldn't remember who Stephen made plans with tonight.

"Your server will be right with you," the hostess says to the table behind me. "Can I get your drink orders while you wait for her?"

"Champagne, dear," a familiar albeit nerdy older voice calls out.

It's Mr. and Mrs. Mortimer. His green tweed suit looks like something that his grandparents might have purchased near the turn of the century. His little, comical brown mustache manages to steal focus from his balding head, I'll give him that much. He wears glasses that are a few prescriptions thicker than Rich's are. Other than those few features and their ages, it'd be hard to find real differences between Rich and his dad.

His mom, on the other hand, makes me scratch my head and wonder how this marriage even happened. They're pretty much the definition of what Stephen calls a 'sitcom couple.' Not that I like older women, but it's still obvious that when Mrs. Mortimer was our age, she was ridiculously hot. She's taller than Mr. Mortimer and her long shiny chestnut-colored hair falls over her shoulders in waves. Her deep blue eyes are about the only thing that'll draw attention from her pearly white teeth.

"Alexander," Mr. Mortimer says in a way that no one has since I was eleven. "And Stephen. We haven't seen you boys around much lately." He looks from Gwen to Meghan. "And I see why, such lovely young ladies."

"Stop," Mrs. Mortimer exaggerates as if she's putting on a show. "You're embarrassing the boys and their dates." Mr. Mortimer puts his hand on top of hers and nods. "Is that…Meghan Powers?"

"Yes, ma'am," Meghan returns politely.

"Oh," she moans. "Now, I see why Rich has been so down lately."

"Wait…I thought…I mean, Rich told us that he was depressed…" I begin. They arch their eyebrows almost in unison. "…I mean, he said he was down because you guys…" I clear my throat. "…because you guys were fighting." They look at each other and shake their heads.

"No," Mr. Mortimer starts. "We…" He pats her hand. "…went through a rough patch there for a while, but we did some soul searching, went to couples counseling and we've been right as rain ever since."

"How long ago was this?" Gwen asks, taking the question right out of my mouth. The pair thinks collectively; mutter something back and forth before coming back to us.

"That was about six months ago," Mrs. Mortimer finishes.

"Just one question," Stephen chimes in. "Who's Rich?"

Mr. and Mrs. Mortimer both scoff a laugh. "He's joking. Right, Alex? Pulling our leg and all that?"

I shake my head slowly. "I think he hit his head or something," I whisper with a nod. "That plus what happened to Mr. Turnipseed."

"Oh, right, right, right," Mr. Mortimer murmurs while reaching into his back pocket. He retrieves his wallet and takes out a picture of Rich. They pass it to me.

"Thanks." I pass it on to Stephen. "See, Stephen! It's Rich, remember?"

Stephen takes the picture and studies it for a minute…like a literal minute. He stares at it like there's tiny words written across Rich's face and he's trying to read it all. He lifts his eyes from the picture, shakes it. "No, I've never seen THIS guy a day in my life."

He offers the picture back. Meghan reaches over and touches his shoulder. Gwen and I exchange a look and then stare at Stephen's perplexed face. I sigh and look down at the picture…I see soft chestnut colored hair and Mrs. Mortimer's blue eyes. Tan skin without a single blemish on a chiseled jaw and high cheekbones. Couple those things with the award-winning smile and fierce look of determination; I can only come to one conclusion…

"What's wrong?" Gwen murmurs, leaning closer. I shake the picture in the same way Stephen did, only for me, it feels like I'm trying to shake it until it changes back into what it should be. "Alex…?"

"He's right." I give the picture another look. "I've never seen this guy a day in my life either." I show her the picture. She frowns and takes it. She turns her back to the rest of us. She runs her hand over the picture and for a second, I swear tiny flames appear at the tip of one of her fingers.

"Can I get my picture back?" Mr. Mortimer says.

Gwen glances at him and nods. "Of course, Mr. Mortimer." She returns to the table. "Would you…give this back to Mr. Mortimer?" She extends the picture to me.

I glance over it. It looks like Rich again. I pant completely unintentionally. "One sec," I add while extending the restored picture to Stephen. "Give it one more look, Stephen. Maybe it'll clear up the fogginess."

Stephen shrugs in a 'what could it hurt' sort of way. He looks at it. I can tell he was expecting to feel nothing still but instead… "RICH," he shouts jumping to his feet. Stephen rubs the side of his head. "Rich…I remember Rich…I was supposed to hang out with him tonight. He-he said he wanted to have an Xbox night and…" Stephen gnashes his teeth together. He puts both of his hands up to his temples and his eyes become two lines.

"Stephen?" Mr. Mortimer says, rising. I stand up too. The entire restaurant turns to us out of concern.

"Stephen," I snap.

"…why can't I remember?" Stephen grumbles. He's having a panic attack. He looks at us, as if we could attack him at any minute. "Why can't I remember? What's wrong with me?" I reach for him and he knocks my hand away. "DON'T TOUCH ME!"

"Stephen," Mrs. Mortimer gasps. Stephen takes a step back and stumbles into the table behind him. The glasses on top rattle against one another. He turns and steadies himself on it, to the panic of the people there. His breathing doesn't slow down though. He's hyperventilating.

"Call an ambulance," Mr. Mortimer says.

"No," Gwen moans. She's looking at Meghan standing right next to her. "Meghan…you should try to calm Stephen down."

"Me…?" Meghan cries incredulously. "What can I do?" Gwen doesn't answer she just makes a shooing motion with her hands. Meghan nods. "Stephen?" She takes a step forward. "Stephen, it's me. It's Meghan."

"Stay away from me," he snaps, causing the couple at the table to do just that. Meghan looks at Gwen. Gwen tips her head toward Stephen again and motions as if she's putting her hand on him. Meghan shakes her head with a bewildered expression. Gwen just repeats the motions and then claps her hands together as if begging. Meghan purses her lips but obeys.

Meghan steps closer to Stephen. She extends her hand…palm down…out to his heaving back. Her fingers tremble in mid-air. "Stephen…" He growls breathlessly. "…Stephen…it's okay," Meghan sighs. "Whatever it is…it's okay." Her hand makes contact with his back. He wobbles, then looks at her. "It's okay," she whispers. He nods along with her. He takes his hands off the table and wraps his arms around her. She seems shocked…even afraid…for about a second. "It's okay," she whispers repeatedly into his ear, wrapping her arms around him.

I stare at the two of them, remembering the glow that surrounded Meghan the first day we met. I think about the way the lemmings and pretty much everyone else at school has adored her since we were kids…except me…well, Jamie and me. I've never really thought about it like this before.

Gwen steps up beside me. She sighs. "There's something supernatural about Meghan, isn't there?"

She shrugs. "I just knew that would work, because it almost worked on me when I was mad at her once." I nod. Gwen frowns. She looks at the floor. She collects…Rich's picture. "This…should be interesting," she whispers as she stands. She turns back to Mr. and Mrs. Mortimer and I do too. She holds the picture over her heart. "Mr. and Mrs. Mortimer, what do you see here?" They look at the picture and return with concerned faces to Stephen. Their eyes snap back to the picture.

"Who…who the hell is that…?" Mr. Mortimer poses, pointing at the picture. Gwen glances at it, mouths an 'oh, sorry', then moves her right hand over the picture. "Richmond," he says, staring at the picture. I steal a glance and its him, the way he really looks. Gwen gives the photo back to Mr. Mortimer.

Gwen takes me by the arm and turns me away from the table. She motions for the check from our waitress, then drags me toward the entrance. We stop at the vestibule, where the hostess would normally be if she weren't calming the patrons around our table.

"What's going on? I mean, I thought weird bear-dog would be enough drama for one night."

"It's a glamour," Gwen explains. "Someone or something has put a glamour…a really, big one…over Rich…not just over the picture…over his entire existence."

"How…? Why…?"

"I don't know." Our waitress gives Gwen the check. I slip it out of her hand. She sighs, probably too tired to argue with me. "But that explains the picture, why you and Stephen keep forgetting about him…" I slip two twenties out of my wallet to cover the bill. "…it even explains why he lied to you guys about his parents fighting."

"He's knows about it," I whisper and give the check to our waitress as she passes. "Keep it." She nods, then continues, on her way. "What does it mean though?" Gwen scowls and shakes her head. "Rich doesn't have any kind of magical powers or anything." I run through my restored memories. "No, he's as normal as anybody at our school." Her eyes drift closed lazily. "You're tired."

"I'm fine."

"Hey," Meghan says with her arm around Stephen. "Did you guys get the check? I think we're ready to go." Stephen nods like he's about to fall asleep on Meghan's arm. I nod. "Is it cool if I drop both of you guys off at Gwen's? I wanna make sure, he's okay," she says in a tone that is definitely not Meghan's. Her voice sounds like a song, causing Gwen and me to nod, as if we couldn't help ourselves.

Chapter 32: Goodnight

I tug at the collar of Alex's hoodie… at my bedroom door. "Thanks for letting me borrow this."

He holds my jacket up in front of me. "Well, you tore the sleeve on yours protecting me, so…" I reach for the zipper. "Nah, you can keep it," he whispers. I look at his dark t-shirt and frown. "I'll be fine. Promise." I nod and push my bedroom door open. I walk in.

"You…um…can come in for a minute," I start. "…to rest…if you want." He smiles. I move over to the daybed that seems to be calling my name. I stretch out across the soft comforter, letting my stomach rest on one pillow and my chin on another. My arms slide under the chin pillow and crisscross, giving me more support. The hoodie that I bought isn't nearly as cozy as Alex's is. I just want to wrap my entire body in its warmth and the fact that it smells like him doesn't hurt either.

Alex enters the room. I look at him over my shoulder. He moves to the bedside and hangs my coat from the nearest post. "You must be exhausted." He sits down next to me. His weight drags the bed down and I move with it, just to be closer to him.

"I'm fine," I lie, although my eyes half-closing lazily tells the truth for me. "Dinner helped a lot." He surveys me with more attentiveness than anyone else has in my entire life.

"Yeah, right. I can only imagine pulling a powerful glamour off drained you even more." In place of nodding, I lift my eyebrows and let them fall. He looks at me and a smile sneaks across his face. It's so subtle that if I had taken my attention away from him, I would've never seen the transition, not that I would take my attention away from him. He does not want to give up my attention either. He continues staring considerately, thoughtfully, in a way that tells me I'm one of the things that inspire him.

"What?" I ask in a breathless whine.

"You. You're so beautiful." My cheeks inflame…they feel warm and my forehead follows suit. I smile, pull my arms from under the now warm pillow, and place them directly under my chin, hoping to hide my face.

"You shouldn't say things like that," I flirt.

"Why?"

"You're making me blush."

Alex leans in closer to me. "What if I want to make you blush?"

He moves a stray hair from my face then lets his fingertips glide along my forehead. The spark…that beautifully, wonderful electric spark that he gives me…it feels different now…not painful again…not an awareness…not even pleasurable…it feels more like a want…like a desire. I crave that energy that passes between us.

"Okay," Alex starts, moving his hand away. He rises slowly. "You need to get some rest, so I'm gonna go so you can do that…"

"Alex, wait," I pant, catching his arm as he attempts to stand. I pull him back down to me. I breathe in deeply…the craving still moving along my forehead in a nearly straight line. It dances along my fingertips too. "Alex, have you ever…" I swallow deeply. "…wanted to kiss me…before tonight, I mean?" Alex smiles that flirtatious smile of his and that crinkle appears between his eyes…not that frustrated crinkle...the one he gets when he doesn't know how to say what he's really feeling...and just as suddenly, it's gone.

"Only every second of every day, since the moment I first saw you, Gwen," he admits. I feel dizzy, I'm so thrown by what he said. I knew that we've been attracted to each other and I've known we've come close to kissing before. "Why do you ask...?" I waiver. My head swims from the combination of exhaustion, shock and the thought of our lips meeting. "Gwen," he calls, sitting next to me...edging closer and regaining his original place on the bed. No, this time he's more on the bed than when he sat down initially.

"Why haven't you?" I query, sleepily.

He smiles again and laughs at some internal joke. "I really wanna tell you something like the time never seemed right or that we always seem to get interrupted, but the truth is..." He stares into my eyes. "...I was scared."

"Scared of me?" I ask raising my head with vigor I didn't know I had.

He shakes his head, never breaking eye contact. "Of course not." I lower my head. He caresses my cheek with the back of his hand. Touching me only makes the craving worse. Our contact is like the best and worst drug. "I was scared...that you wouldn't want to kiss me back."

"That's crazy...," I return without thinking about it. "I..." I break off. He leans in closer. I roll over onto my side. "I've wanted to kiss you...for so long," I whisper. He closes his eyes and presses his forehead against mine. He feels so warm...and his skin smells amazing. My eyes drift closed as well.

"So, what are we gonna do about this?" he whispers.

"Yeah," I return. "What *are* we gonna do about it?" His forehead rolls against mine until it breaks contact and his mouth moves closer to mine. Our lips touch...they graze one another first and then he presses his mouth against mine. His lower lip lands between mine. My mind instantly makes the comparison. If our touch is like a firecracker then, our kiss is...a firework. I grab him so tightly that I worry I might break him. He returns the favor, pulling me so close that our bodies touch.

We part...both breathing heavily and staring into each other's eyes. My left hand still tugs at his shirt while my right hand has found its way to the back of his head. Both of his hands are on my hips...his thumb brushes my skin just below his hoodie and above my jeans...and I am blissfully aware of its touch.

"That," he begins with a smile meant just for me. "...was worth the wait."

"It's a good thing we don't have to wait to do it again," I return...and he doesn't make me wait a second longer.

#####

Gwen and I are kissing...how is this happening...? Gwen and I are kissing and we're kissing on her bed no less. She rubs her hands against my stomach under my t-shirt. Her hands are soft and warm. They leave tingling trails across my skin. I nibble her bottom lip and she moans.

I hear a zipper. I sneak a peek...she's unzipping my hoodie. She sits up. I move with her, never breaking from kissing. She throws the hoodie off one shoulder then the other. I grab the bottom of my t-shirt and snatch it off over my head. She tosses my hoodie to the side at the same time that I throw my shirt on the floor. My hands

202

cup her face and hers run up my stomach to my chest. I stare into her beautiful green eyes. She pants, smiles then her bottom lip presses against her teeth.

We kiss again. She leans back and pulls me down on top of her. My thumbs caress her hips…not her shirt…not her jeans…her actual skin. Wow, I thought her hands were soft. I exhale loudly, and she moans again. The tingle…this impossible electric feeling that we get from each other, it's wrapping both of us up and taking us further…urging us on…warming us up…she's so hot…no really…she's starting to feel hot. I open my eyes.

"GWEN," I jump off her. She looks at me with half-panicked, half-confused eyes. I motion to the yellowish flames whipping around her bare arms. "Gwen, you're on fire!" Flames fume to her right and left. "Your bed is on fire, too." She scans the spots next to her.

"Ah," she yelps before claiming her pillow. She pounds the charred spot on her right. I grab another pillow and do the same with the spot on her left. The small fires go out fairly easily. "Open the window," Gwen says while running her left hand through her disheveled hair.

I hop off the bed and run over to the window. I undo the latch and it slides up smoothly. A cool breeze wafts in and the smoke clears out.

I turn back to Gwen, sitting on her knees. She's still breathing heavily. One hand remains in her hair and her other, judging by her shoulder and arm, is over her heart. Gwen's translucent white curtains blow inward, slightly obscuring my view of her. I'll have to memorize this moment…because I HAVE TO draw this later. She looks at me over her shoulder. She looks like she's on the verge of crying. I hurry to her.

"Are you okay?"

She scoffs a humorless laugh, causing a tear to fall. "I was just about to ask you that."

I wipe her tear away. "What was that?"

She shakes her head. She stares at her scorched comforter and frowns. "I don't know. I've never done that before…"

"I'm sure. If you did, you'd be replacing your bedding and stuff all the time."

She swallows deeply, hand still over her heart, and shakes her head again. Her eyes move to a distant corner of the room as if she's trying to stop herself from shedding another tear.

"No," she breathes. "I mean, I've never…" She looks at me, only to look down and bring her eyes back up immediately, nervously. "…done THAT…before." She fidgets while playing with her fingers absently. My mind tries to cycle through what she's hinting at but keeps skipping over the most likely scenario, because it can't be true. I mean, I'm sitting here, looking at her…and there's just no way that no guy has ever tried to…

"You've never made out with a guy before?" She shakes her head. "Not even another kitsune guy…?" She swallows deeply and shakes her head again, her eyes wandering away from me again. "Never…?"

"Alex," she moans and fidgets again. Her hands fall apart and land on top of her bed. She tugs at her singed comforter.

"No. It's…it's okay." She seems unconvinced. I claim her left hand. "Gwen," I call as that vibration of constant energy passes from my hand to hers and back again. She looks at me. "It's okay," I whisper. She smiles, despite the fact that her eyes still look like she's about to cry.

"Oh God," she moans with her eyes rolling upward.

"What…?" I ask looking around. "What? What…? What?"

Gwen bounces in place. "Now, I'm going to have to have the MOST AWKWARD conversation with my obāsan that I've ever had." I scoff another laugh. She grabs her pillow with her free hand and hits me with it as she giggles.

I laugh more. "Isn't there anybody else that you could talk to about this…?"

She shakes her head. "Like who? Would you rather I talk to Gavin about it?" An image of a blue flame motivated pummeling leaps into my mind.

"No, I would not." She laughs then I laugh again. Her amusement gives way to a gentle smile. I reach over and move some of the hair out of her face. She sighs. My thumb caresses her cheek and her eyes close. She nibbles her lower lip and I find myself leaning forward. She puts her hand on top of mine and draws both of her lips into her mouth.

"We…should probably hold off on that for a while," she whispers. I nod, even though my head feels like it might explode if I don't kiss her again soon.

"Gwen," Mrs. Taylor calls from the end of the hall. "Gwen are you home, dear?"

"Crap," Gwen spits between her teeth. "My foster-mom…" She looks around in a panic. "Quick, go out the window."

I look at her like the Martian she's acting like. "Gwen, we're on the second floor and I can't use swift paw or hunter's step."

"*Hunter's step*…? What's that?"

"Gwen?" Mrs. Taylor says again.

"I'm here." She jumps off the bed. "Um," she whispers. "Behind the door…" She tosses her comforter trying to hide the burned spots. I grab my hoodie and t-shirt from the floor and sprint to the door. I work to put my shirt on as it swings. I figure it would be a lot less…unpleasant for Gwen, and me, if I have a shirt on, at least.

"Gwen," Mrs. Taylor says as Gwen rushes to meet her. "We got home a little early, but I didn't expect you to be back so soon."

"Yes, ma'am. Stephen wasn't feeling very well, so we called it an early night," she partially lies.

"Oh, that's too bad. I hope he feels better." Gwen nods. "Are you sure you're not coming down with something too? You look a little flushed."

"Oh, I felt a little warm, so I opened the window," she fibs again, but mixes it with truth.

Mrs. Taylor's hand appears and touches Gwen's forehead, causing Gwen's eyes to bulge. That same hand moves to her cheek. "Uh-oh, you feel a little warm too." The hand withdraws. "I hope you're not going to end up sick again." Gwen pants and shakes her head. "I'm going to get you some aspirin and orange juice."

Gwen nods. "Thank you." Footsteps move away from the door and down the hall. Gwen pushes the door nearly closed and looks at me with guilt-filled eyes. I know exactly why…because in the short time I've known Gwen, I know she tries to be different from most kitsune. She always wants to be honest.

"It's okay, Gwen," I whisper. "You lied for our benefit, not yours. Most kitsune wouldn't do that."

Panic quickly returns. "We have to get you out of here. You can go out the window." I arch my eyebrows and fix my ruffled tee. "Well, I have no idea where Mr. Taylor is. For all I know, he could be taking the garbage out or in the living room, so you can't go downstairs. On top of that, Mrs. Taylor will be back soon, and she'll want to come in so…"

"Okay, okay," I say taking her hands.

"I'll help." She pulls me to the window. "I'll carry you down and then jump back up." I nod. She helps me put my hoodie on and zips it up slowly. "This should really be going the other direction." I smile. She shakes her head. "Sorry. Overtly flirty." She glances out the front window. "Come on." She wraps her arms around me.

I bend over and for a second, it feels like we're falling. My feet plant in the soil just under her living room window. "Be careful," Gwen whispers. "These bushes are thorny." I nod, thinking about how ironic it is that she didn't say 'be careful' before we jumped out the second-floor window. I bend to kiss her. She lifts herself on her toes to let me. At the last second, she changes direction and plants a peck on my cheek. I look at the awkward expression on her face. "Goodnight," she pants and then vanishes in a tiny burst of reddish-orange flames.

"Goodnight." Her window closes. I sigh. The cheek kiss made sense. I mean, we wouldn't want to burn down her foster-parents' house, you know?

I lower my eyes and… "Gavin," I snap at the sight of him, less than foot in front of me. He stares at me as if I'm something to eat. I imagine vampires stare at humans the same way.

He looks at Gwen's window. "What were you doing coming out of my sister's bedroom window, Alex?" He makes my name sound like it should have six syllables instead of two. I'd prefer him calling me Gwen's 'pet' compared to this.

"She-she…was exhausted after the…bear-dog…thing…fight," I stumble. "I-I wanted to make sure she got in okay…" He leans in closer. "…and-and…she…her foster-parents… came home…startled us…" His jaw tenses. "…startled her."

"Fine," he grumbles. "You can scamper home now." He pushes past me, driving my right arm into the thorny bushes. I follow him. He crosses the Taylor's lawn, heading toward the porch. He pauses on the second step and touches his forehead and tries to balance himself.

I run over to him. "Are you okay?"

"I'm fine," he snaps. "That second bear-dog thing, as you call it, is just tougher than it looks."

"Well, Jam-um, I mean, I think it may draw power from supernaturals. Cause Gwen fought that second one before and it's really strong…"

"Don't compare me to Gwen, Alex," his voice turns cold. "Even if she had all her star balls, she wouldn't be a match for me. That's why I'm here now, to see if she convinced her foster-parents to let her go."

"Give her time." He looks over his shoulder with that annoyed, *I'm tired of playing with this mouse so I think I'll eat it* expression. "She really likes the Taylor's, you know? And they like her. It's gonna be hard on all three of them when she asks them to let her go."

"It'll be a lot harder on everyone if she's dead because she was trying to save your worthless hide with only a fraction of her real power. That original bear-dog…it's a cake walk…this second one…" His jaw tenses again. I never thought I'd see it, but here it is. Gavin is nervous about something. If it weren't such a serious subject, I might enjoy it. Okay, I might enjoy it a little more. "…this second one is dangerous." He climbs the steps and rings the doorbell. I turn and walk away quickly. I hear the door open behind me and Mr. Taylor greets Gavin warmly.

I sigh and shove my hands into my hoodie pockets. "He's right, you know?" Kai says, rushing to my side. I nod. "Damn bear-dog thing is dangerous. Why didn't you tell us you guys fought it again?"

"We didn't. Gwen did." I can feel the smirk on his face even though I'm still staring at the ground. "What?"

"You really don't get it, do you?" Kai says putting his hands behind his head. I frown. "Sora and me…we're here to protect you…to watch your back…Gwen protects you, too…but she doesn't watch your back…" I look at him. "…she's too busy standing right beside you." I frown. I never thought of it that way. He rushes forward. "Come on. Sora should be pulling up at the next block soon…and if you want to talk about something being dangerous…keep Sora waiting." He laughs. I laugh and run to catch up to him.

Chapter 33: Couple

"There's something different about you," Meghan murmurs over her chai latté.

"Pfft, no there isn't," I reply, wiping down the table next to hers.

She stares…crosses her legs slowly…balancing her chin on her palm. Her eyes narrow as her silent study continues. I move away quickly so that she can't persist. She catches my apron and pulls me back. Who knew she was so fast?

"Yes, there is." She leans forward eagerly. "…and I want to know what it is." I shrug, trying to make my expression flat. Give her nothing. "Uh-uh, you might be able to fool someone else who just met you a few weeks ago, but you can't fool me Gwendolyn Elizabeth Frost." I frown. I hate it more when she calls me by my full name than when obāsan does it. "Come on, spill, loser."

The bell above the door jingles. Literally, saved by the bell. "Welcome to Jelly…" I freeze as Alex strides through the door. "…Bean," I finish breathlessly.

He smiles. "Hey."

"Hey." I can't stop myself from smiling…or blushing…or keeping Meghan from noticing me smiling and blushing. I shake my head. "What are you…?"

"Oh." Alex makes his way over. "Hey, Megs." She smiles, looks at me, and then back to Alex. He slips his hand into his hoodie pocket. "I…um…I'm on my break, but…I…um…stopped by the arts and crafts store to pick up some…um…some um…"

"Arts and crafts supplies…?" Meghan suggests.

He nods with a nervous laugh and motions to her. "Yeah, that's it. Um…anyway, I saw this…" He pulls an item from his pocket, concealed by his hand. "…and I thought you'd like it so…" He opens his hand. It's a tiny red and white fox…with a looped string coming from the top of its head. "…um…these things are big in Japan…or at least, that's what the guy at the register said, you know?"

I take it out of his hand with a gasp. It feels plush all over except for the tail. The tail is faux fur that comes down to an adorable, little white tip. "I love it," I moan, slipping my hand into my pocket. I pull out my cell and offer him both. "Would you put it on for me?"

"Sure." He goes to work.

Meghan instantly claims my arm drawing my attention to her. She mouths an over exaggerated, *'Oh my God.'* I wrestle my arm away from her, while shushing her.

"There." Alex offers my phone with my new charm dangling from its top left corner. "So, you really like it?"

"Nope," I reply flirtatiously. "Like I said, I love it."

Alex shuffles a bit and his cheeks turn red. "Okay. I should head back." He motions with his thumb. "Um…yeah, I promised Kai and Sora lunch so…" He backs away and bumps into the door. I cover my mouth to stop from laughing. He chuckles nervously "…I'll call you." I nod with a giddy smile, cradling my phone by my heart. "Okay, see you later, Megs." Meghan waves. "Bye, Gwen." He slides out the door.

"O…M…G," Meghan starts, rising from her chair the second the door closes behind him. I close my eyes, partially dreading the coming inquisition. "How did I not notice how totally cute Alex is before this very minute?" I sigh. "Maybe it's the two of you." I look at her. "That has to be it. It's the two of you as a couple…"

"We are not a couple," I protest.

"…that's it," she continues as if I didn't say anything. "You two make such a cute couple that he's cuter by being a part of said coupledom." She lifts her phone and gives it all her two-thumbed focus. "I have to post this."

"Please don't."

"Too late, I was halfway done typing before he even put the little fox thingy on your phone." She taps away. "What's that all about anyway, loser?"

"Inside joke," I whisper, trying to see what she's typing.

"There," she says with a big smile. "Posted…complete with pic."

"What pic?"

"The one I just snapped of you and him," she says as if I should've been aware of this. "Oh, and a couple of the ones from your front porch when we picked you up Friday night…oh yeah, and a few from when you two were dancing…" My jaw drops instantly. I had no idea that… "…oh and I snapped a few of you two last night when he gave you his hoodie after you realized your jacket was ripped. By the way, that was super cute."

I had no idea that she was chronicling Alex's and my relationship with such detail. How could I have missed the fact that Meghan is so into her phone and 'posting' things?

"Alright," Meghan continues. "You look like you could use a lunch break." My mouth falls open, but no words tumble out. "Hey," she calls to Emily behind the counter. "Emily, right?" she asks me quietly. I nod. "Hey, Emily…can Gwen take her lunch break a little early today?"

Emily shakes her head slowly. "Considering the fact that you've been our only customer since the breakfast and after church rush, sure why not?" She wipes down the counter. "But make sure you're back before the early evening rush."

"Early evening…?" I say. "But it's only one o'clock." Emily smirks then winks at Meghan. I look at Meghan and she winks back. Crap, they've teamed up against me.

"Come on," Meghan pants, dragging me toward the door. I look back at Emily hoping for a little help…some form of co-worker camaraderie…that hope quickly crumbles as Emily issues a finger-wiggling wave. Traitor. Meghan drags me to her car, parked at the curb. "Get in, loser." I remove my apron and climb inside.

"You should put the top up. It looks like rain."

"Yeah, whatever, loser." She starts the car. She presses and holds a button near her rearview mirror. The top lifts from behind the backseat. It emits a whirling noise just before it clicks into place. She looks behind her and backs out of the space slowly. "So, tell me, loser," she whispers. "What happened between you and Alex?"

I gasp and not just because she pulls away quickly. "What do you mean?" Meghan arches her eyebrows in a very *you have to be kidding me, by acting like I didn't just see that* kind of way. "He…he just made sure I got in alright…I wasn't feeling well so…he-he just…"

"Yes, you weren't feeling well," Meghan says. "That's why you're stuttering almost as bad as he was." I sigh. She rounds a corner and heads down a tree-lined road. I look around curiously. "Gwen…?" My stomach rolls over on itself. She never calls me Gwen, unless she knows she can make me spill…about everything. "We're friends, right?" I nod. She doesn't see it, but I know she's aware of it. "So, why don't you feel like you can tell me things? No judgments." The boredom has seeped out of her voice. In fact, she hasn't sounded bored since after Gavin left her at the dance.

"Well," I begin, confirming that she can make me spill my guts easily. "When he came in the house…we might have…gone up to my room…" Meghan audibly gasps. "…and then…I don't know, we might've…kissed…a little."

"You did?" she chirps, sounding and feeling honestly happy for me. I nod as that absent-minded smile returns. I put my elbow on the window frame and rest my head against my hand. "I'm glad."

"You are?" She nods. "Thanks." She smiles warmly, but it fades. For a second, I wonder if she's focusing on the drive, but there's more to it than that. "Where are we going?"

"There's this little mom and pop's place just outside town. I've always wanted to go there, but never had anyone to go with."

"What about…Stephen?" The corners of her mouth turn down and her eyes narrow. "What…? What's wrong? Is Stephen not okay…? You told me he was fine."

"He is fine. In more ways than one," she mutters under her breath. I can't help thinking if I weren't me; If I were any other girl, I wouldn't have heard that. Then again, she probably wouldn't be having this conversation with any other girl. Her eyes dart over to me then back to the road ahead.

"Cards on the table," she snaps. "I've kind of…sort of…had a crush on Stephen since… you know, forever."

I lean closer with my left hand behind my ear. "What's that? I can't understand you. You keep stuttering," I mock. She takes her right hand off the wheel and takes a swing at me. I laugh, and she does too. "So, how long is…*forever*?"

"Well, only since pre-k." I scoff into a laugh. "Stop laughing. He looked so cute in his Power Rangers t-shirt." She smiles absently. "But then he and Alex started spending all of their time with Captain Creepy…and even before the whole thing last night…" She frowns. "…in fact, since I met that guy, he's given me a bad vibe."

"What do you mean a bad…?" My thought cuts off due to a bad vibe striking me. "No," I gasp.

"No, what…?" I shake my head. It can't be. It's daylight. The bear-dog has only ever attacked at night…and never two days in a row. Maybe it's because there are two of them now. Whatever it is, I feel it, it's nearby, and it has that ravenous hunger again. I have to figure out a way to get Meghan to safety.

She leans forward gripping the wheel with both hands, staring through the windshield. "What the hell is that?" I follow her gaze to a massive shadowy blob in the middle of the road. Meghan slows down.

"Don't stop. G-go around it." She nods and drifts to the left side of the road. I look around, thankful that the road is empty besides it and us. Okay, so it would be a lot better if *it* wasn't here. The farther to the left Meghan maneuvers the car, the more the blob moves in that direction.

"What the hell?" Meghan barks. The shadow blob now covers the entire two-lane country road. I tense. It has the same feeling as the original shadow bear-dog thing. Deep, grassy gutters line the road on both sides so there's no way to get around it.

Meghan stops the car. "That thing looks freaky." I nod. She peers out of the back window. "I'm gonna back up." I watch the blob. It moves toward us as Meghan backs away.

"Hurry!" She steals a glance at it and her concentration slips...so does the wheel. The car cuts hard to the right and we move off the road and into the gutter. "Ugh," I groan when Meghan does.

She shifts the car into a different gear and presses down on the accelerator...hard. "Nothing's happening," she cries as the car does exactly as she claims. She presses harder on the pedal. The engine roars. The blob covers the car's hood. "Aagh," Meghan squeals and leans back in her seat. "What is this thing?"

I grit my teeth. I should tell her. I should use my fox magic to protect her. "It's..." Suddenly, the interior of the car darkens. The blob conceals the windshield. At the same time, parts of it spread over the passenger and driver's side windows. Fox magic fills my eyes. There's no holding back now.

"Gwen," Meghan shrieks in a panic. "Your eyes are glowing!"

"I know. Now, I'm gonna get us out of here."

"WHAT DO YOU MEAN, GAVIN CALLED YOU?" I shout at Sora, rounding a corner doing fifty-five and I'm sure we're up on two wheels.

"What part of *Gavin called me* is hard to understand?"

"Will you guys stop fighting so that maybe we can get there to see if he's lying or not," Kai barks, bracing himself between the roof of the car and his seat.

"What I'm trying to figure out is how you got Gavin's number...and vice versa," I say. I catch Sora's eyes in the rearview. "When did you guys even meet?" I think back over the last two weeks. "That night after the second time the bear-dog attacked me. You came home muddy and with your jacket torn." She scowls and speeds up.

We come around a wide, winding curve and...

"What the hell is that?" Kai snaps.

Gavin crouches on top of a large black, slimy rock on the side of the road. Sora goes faster. Blue flames cover Gavin's shoulders and back. He claws at the rock. The car screeches to a stop next to the slimy thing. Sora's out of the car before I can get my seatbelt off with Kai right behind her.

I climb out. Sora and Kai phase into furry stripes. "What is this thing?" Sora demands.

"Feel it out," Gavin says, not breaking his assault. "It's the familiar that's been attacking Alex."

"Familiar's can change shape?" I ask, stepping closer.

"Stay back," Kai says as he and Sora tear at it, too. "It might be a blob now, but it might turn..." I nod and grit my teeth. "...ew..." Kai spits, pulling something away.

"I thought you said Gwen was in trouble," I say.

Gavin bares his teeth, showing his sharp canines. "Who do you think I'm trying to get to?"

I step forward before I can stop myself. "Gwen's in there?" Gavin nods while digging his claws in deeper. He pulls back, ripping a chunk and tossing it away. I look around, not knowing what to think. I find a big, sharp rock. I spot another one, almost as big, half buried in the grass. I pick up the first one and pry the second one loose. Weapons in each hand, I run and jump onto the blob.

"What are y-?" Sora starts.

"Shut up," I snap and pound with the rocks. After about the fourth hit, I hear glass cracking. I hit it again to be sure and it cracks more.

"Keep hitting," Sora says, grabbing something solid. She yanks another part of it away. "Gwen says she and Meghan are away from the windshield." I scowl. "Smash it!" I nod and wail on the windshield. A hole appears in the blob. One red flaming left arm reaches through it. Gavin catches Gwen's hand. They clutch each other…and their flames swirl together into bright purple fire.

"Get back!" Gavin growls.

Sora leaps down. Kai grabs me and jumps back. Gavin puts his free hand down near the hole. The purple flame moves up his right hand then his arm, before making its way down his left arm. The bright violet fire intensifies and spreads across the blob. The black shadow shreds with a ripping noise and a burning tar smell. Tattered pieces of it peel away from Meghan's car.

I crunch on something underfoot. It's a part of the shadow, a part with…a tooth. I jump back. "Ew!" All the pieces slowly evaporate. The bear-dog in blob form still had its teeth and claws. The driver's side door opens. "Meghan!" She stumbles out, in a gasping, wheezing panic.

She looks at me, then at Sora and Kai. She screams and wobbles back against the car. Gavin stands, blue flames covering his shoulders and arms. Meghan falls. She crawls up the hill past the gutter, mud and grass staining her dress.

Gavin leaps down and growls, revealing his sharp teeth. I run to Meghan's side. Gwen climbs out and moves between her brother and Meghan. "Leave her alone!" Gavin takes a step forward. "I'll handle it." Gavin takes another step forward. "I said I'll handle it," she barks, her voice booming.

Gavin sighs and the flames vanish. His eyes stop glowing too. "Fine. I'm going to check for any sign of that thing." Gavin turns away.

Gwen turns to a sobbing, shivering Meghan. "Meghan, it's me. I'm still the same old Gwen." Meghan shakes her head and tries to move further up the hill, digging her fingers into the damp soil.

"Meghan, it's okay," I say, remembering that I'm the most normal person in the group. Meghan's eyes dart to me. "You're okay. Just breathe."

Meghan inhales deeply as more tears fall. "What are they?"

"Well, my cousins are skinwalkers," I begin honestly. Gavin turns and practically roars. Gwen extends her hand to him. The rumble subsides. "And Gwen and her brother are kitsune…or fox spirits," I explain in as even a tone as I can manage.

"Fox…spirits…? Skin…walkers…?" Meghan asks, hyperventilating. "What does…? What are…?"

"Breathe, Meghan," Gwen orders. "If you don't get enough air, you're going to…" Meghan's eyes roll back, and she passes out. Gwen checks Meghan over with glowing green eyes. "She passed out…but what are we going to do…? She knows everything and…"

"Yeah and why is that…?" Gavin grumbles.

"Not now," Sora says. Gavin clenches his jaw and frowns. "What are we gonna do?"

"Jamie," I whisper. Gwen's eyes light up without the fox magic glow.

"Who or what is a *Jamie*?" Kai poses.

"Isn't that the *friend* whose house you two went over to yesterday *to study with*?" Gavin says. I nod. "So, you lied to me?" Gwen frowns and busies herself with Meghan. "I'm actually a little proud." Gwen rolls her eyes. "I actually believed you."

"Why Jamie?" Sora asks.

"She's...she's a Witch of Light," I explain.

"Memory spell," Sora moans, putting everything together just that fast. "That's why you've started remembering our childhood memories." I nod.

"Kai," Sora starts. "Get Meghan into the car. Meghan's seventeen, right?" Gwen nods. "We've got about an hour, if we're lucky, before the memory spell won't work on her." Kai nods. He slips one arm under Meghan's legs and another behind her back. He lifts her effortlessly.

"I'll grab her stuff," Sora continues. She collects Meghan's bag and several other items. She moves out of the car. "You," she says forcefully to Gavin. "Do something about the car." He frowns. "Make it look like *more* of an accident than it currently does."

Gavin nods and his shoulders and hands erupt in flames. He reaches under the front left wheel. He pulls up, bends and puts his legs into it. He hefts the car, sending it flipping through the air. It careens to a stop a little way down the hill.

"Holy crap," I moan and look at Gwen kneeling. "If he's that strong...how strong is this second bear-dog thing...?" Gwen sighs and extends her hand. I pull her to her feet.

"Too strong." She looks at her hand, turning over in mine. "You're bleeding."

"I am...?" There's a gash in my palm. "I must've cut my hand against the rock." Gwen places both of her hands around mine. Her eyes glow and red flames surround my hand. They don't burn. No, in fact, they feel good. She inhales deeply.

"There. I stopped the bleeding, but it'll take a little time to heal fully." I nod. "We need to get Meghan over to Jamie-Lynn's...and pray that she forgives us for..."

"She cares about Meghan," I say, turning to Sora's car. "She'll help." Gwen nods, but her mind seems to be working through all the possibilities. "It'll be fine."

She sighs. "Gavin...?" Gwen looks around.

"He went to look for the summoner," Sora says from her door. "Come on." Gwen grabs my hand, carefully intertwines our fingers and pulls me toward the car. As her arm extends, I notice bloody streaks moving down it.

"You're bleeding," I snap. She shakes her head. She runs her free hand along her forearm and the blood disappears, revealing no wounds.

"See? I healed myself before I got out of the car."

"Come 'ere," I whisper. She steps closer, nibbling her lower lip. I unzip my hoodie and slide it off. I drape it over her shoulders.

She slips her arms through. "Thanks." I nod. She walks backward, pulling me with her.

212

Chapter 34: Dangerous

"JAMIE, COME ON," Alex shouts, pounding on her front door feverishly. He looks at the windows on either side of the porch, before examining the door and giving the runes imbedded in the concrete a once over. He takes a step back and turns to us. He walks down the stairs, tossing his hands in the air powerlessly. "They're not here, or at least, they're not answering. Are you guys getting anything?"

"No," Kai replies.

"Between the sage in the air," Sora continues. "And whatever muting wards she has on this house, we can't see, hear or smell anything."

"And we can't even get near the place," I add. "Given the runes she has carved into the front porch there's no telling what's going on around back." Alex purses his lips and nods. He crosses his arms, matching Sora's posture. Kai scratches the back of his head. "What are we going to do?"

"Gwen," Meghan moans from the backseat. She opens the backdoor and slides out, clutching her head.

"Megs how are…?" I pause, looking her over. Her disheveled hair has streaks of mud and a few grass clippings. Her hands leave muddy prints wherever she touches. I sigh. "How are you feeling…Meghan?"

"Calmer," she moans lifting her tear-filled, blue eyes. "But still so confused." I nod. "Gwen be honest with me…what's going on?" I take a step forward; Meghan leans away. I wrap my arms around myself, my eyes brimming with tears.

"I'm sorry. I didn't mean to trick you."

"Meghan," Alex says, stepping forward. "How long have you known me?"

"Pretty much all my life," Meghan replies.

Alex nods. "Trust me, when I tell you…" He looks at me. "…you can trust Gwen. She's never wanted anything from you, but to be your friend." Meghan's eyes dart to me then back to Alex. "And, I think she'd be the best one to tell you…everything."

Meghan sighs. "You had to keep everything a secret, didn't you?" I nod as tears fall. "Why…?" Her lower lip quivers. I shiver. "Tell me," she snaps.

"I'll tell you everything…but not here."

"I'm not going anywhere with you," she says angrily.

"Maybe you can sit in the car…and chat," Alex suggests.

"Do I have any say in this?" Sora asks.

"Come on," Alex says. "My break ended twenty minutes ago. It'll probably take us another ten minutes to walk back to the store."

"Walk?" Kai poses with arched eyebrows. "Why do we have to walk…?" Kai motions to Meghan and me with his thumb. "They're the ones who need to talk."

Sora rolls her eyes and emits a cheek-puffing sigh. She shoves her hand deep into her pocket. She retrieves her car key and tosses it to me. "When you're done talking, have blondie drive you back to the coffee shop. I'll stop by and get the key from you later."

"Thank you." She nods. She looks at Alex and Kai and throws her thumb in the direction of the square.

Kai groans but starts walking. "Blondie…? We have blond hair, too."

Alex stares at me. I gasp and start unzipping his hoodie. "Keep it," he says softly. I smile and so does he. Meghan swallows deeply and looks at Alex. He spots her watching him. "You'll be okay. I promise." Meghan nods.

I walk to the car and open the front passenger door. I extend the key to Meghan. She hesitantly claims it and walks to the driver's side. Meghan climbs behind the wheel and I take the seat next to her.

"So..." She looks at her muddy hands before rubbing them together, trying to clear away some of the reddish-brown mud. "...you're a...fox...spirit...?" I nod. "What was that...other thing Alex called you and..." She swallows a deep, dry lump. "...Gavin...?"

"Kitsune. It literally means 'fox' in Japanese." She bobs her head unevenly, still grinding her palms together. "I'm going to tell you everything," I state plainly, trying to keep my voice sympathetic and tender. "Okay, Meghan...?" I take a deep breath and dive in.

I start by telling her how my parents, the fox spirit, Aoi and the human, Delwyn fell in love. ...how they married, relatively young, and had two children...Gavin and then two years later, me. ...how they died when I was still very young because my mother broke our laws to marry my father. ...how Gavin and I went to live with our obāsan in Japan.

"Obāsan...?" Meghan interrupts.

"It means 'grandmother'...sort of. Actually, I think it means 'honored older woman.' I just know that my obāsan preferred Gavin and me to call her that." She inhales through her nose and nods. Next, I talk about how our grandparents trained the two of us to be proper kitsune. Surprisingly, she has no questions about our upbringing.

Finally, I reach the part of my story when I convinced my obāsan to let me come back to America on my own...to try to live my life as a normal teen.

"Wait," Meghan interrupts again. "Really...?" She turns so that she faces me at less of an angle. "You gave up using all that power...all those things that you could do as a...kitsune...to try and be...normal...?"

"To be honest, I never thought of it as giving anything up...I was too busy thinking about the things I'd gain."

Meghan frowns and shakes her head. "Like what...?"

"Well," I say, looking away to ponder my response. "Just thinking about what I've gained since I got here...the Taylors...and I gained you as a friend...and..."

"Alex?"

I smile whimsically and before I realize it, I start playing with my hair. "Yeah," I breathe, unable to stop smiling. "And I'd trade every kitsune trick and power that I have, for them...and you."

"Aww, loser," she murmurs, starting to sound like her old self. "That's so sweet." She puts her dirt spattered hand on top of my dirt and blood-spattered hand.

"There's more," I say softly, putting my other hand on top of hers. From there, I tell her about how the bear-dog attacked Alex the night that we started decorating for the dance. I describe all the subsequent attacks and even the second bear-dog; up to and including the attack we just escaped.

I explain what happened to Stephen and Rich's parents last night at dinner and how a glamour seemed to have wiped Rich from everyone's memory. I end by telling her the reason that we're parked outside of Jamie-Lynn's house.

"So, do you understand why I kept all of this from you…from everyone really?"

Meghan purses her lips. Her brow moves into an expressionless position. She sighs heavily. She tries to process everything that I've told her…and it's too much. It's too much to ask anyone to accept. The reason that it was so easy for Alex is that, on some level, he already knew all of this. Her eyes lift…new tears welling in them.

"Don't ever lie to me again," she snaps. "You got that, loser?" I nod. She smiles and throws her arms around me. "Good. I hate being lied to."

I put my arms around her. "I'm so sorry, Megs." She pats my back. "I'm actually kind of glad that we had to tell you." She nods against my shoulder. "Given the fact that we were attacked in broad daylight, it was probably getting too dangerous for you to be kept in the dark."

"Yeah, I can understand th… Wait," she cuts herself off. "What are you guys doing about Rich?" I shake my head. "Someone or something put a…glamour…?" I nod. "…on him to wipe his existence, right?"

"Yes."

"Well, have you guys looked into why that is?"

I frown and fidget. "Well, Alex and I had to work today. Plus, Sora and Kai had to watch his b…"

"Seriously…? You guys are like the Avengers or something and you're worried about work?" My head slumps. "I get it. I get it, loser. It's all a part of keeping up appearances, right?"

"Yeah, that's it exactly."

"Then why not have me and one of Alex's cousins go with Stephen to check up on Rich while you guys finish your shifts?" I open my mouth to respond. "Nope. Don't say it's too dangerous, because I'm in it now. That thing ran us off the road and trashed my car. I want payback." She bobs her head unevenly and puts Sora's key in the ignition. "Or at least, I want to help you guys figure this out." She starts the car. "But first, I want a shower before I get you back to work."

#####

"Absolutely not," I growl, I actually growl, at Gwen and Meghan. "It's too dangerous."

"She wants to help," Gwen whines, motioning to Meghan in her weather-wise, inappropriate tiny little sundress.

"No. We agreed, we'd all go together Monday after school."

"Why put off until Monday what you can investigate today?" Meghan hums. Gwen and I look at her. "What? You weren't expecting me to say that, were you, loser-boyfriend?" Gwen's jaw drops immediately. "What? Too soon…? You guys haven't exchanged possessive pronouns yet?" I frown. Gwen does too. "Yes," Meghan says before either of us can answer. "I'm actually very smart. My beauty seems to make people think otherwise."

I shake my head to snap out of whatever it is that Meghan was doing. "If the weird-bear-dog has anything to do with what's going on with Rich, they'd be in danger."

"And…" Gwen starts.

"And, Stephen really wants to go check on Rich," Meghan cuts her off. "Ever since that…" She looks at Gwen for confirmation. "…glamour…?" Gwen nods. "Yeah, ever since that glamour came down, he's been worrying himself sick, practically pacing a trench in his bedroom." I stare at the floor. "Yes, I've been in Stephen's bedroom."

"That didn't take long," Sora snips. Meghan tweaks her head to one side and glares at her. Sora returns the favor.

"It's not that," I interrupt, their staring contest. "It's just…he didn't call me or anything. I figured he would've called…I'm his best friend."

"He felt awkward," Meghan says. "You didn't forget about Rich…he did."

"Okay," Sora chirps. "Enough with the teen drama, what are we gonna do?"

"Sora," Mr. Hamish calls from the back.

"Yeah, Mr. H," she says.

"Could you come help me move this shelf back here?"

"Sure thing, Mr. H." She walks away. I look at Gwen, who has one finger pointed after Sora and her mouth hanging open.

"Mr. Hamish figured that if Sora and Kai were gonna be hanging around all the time, he might as well give them something to do and pay them under the table."

Gwen nods. "That's a little weird." I shrug.

"Well," Meghan starts again. "Are we gonna do this or not?" She points to her dress. "Just in case of weird-bear-dog attack or even weirder-bear-blob attack, I wore cheerleader shorts under my dress and I have my stun gun in my purse."

I scowl and tweak my head. "She acclimated quickly," Gwen quips.

"I couldn't help it," Meghan says, wrapping her arms around Gwen and reminding me that she's almost a head taller than Gwen is. "I mean, who has the cutest kitsune bestie ever? I do, that's who," Meghan adds, giving Gwen a squeeze that causes her to blush and giggle. "…but look who I'm telling, loser-boyfriend."

I shake my head. "The problem isn't that I don't want to know what's going on with Rich…it's that Stephen still doesn't know about this." I look at Meghan. "He might not handle this as well as you are, plus it'll still only be one of my cousin's against the bear-dog…so far they've only been able to beat it together."

"Details," Meghan says confidently while patting her purse with her free hand. "Stun…gun…"

I open my mouth to protest. "Why don't you just get Gwen's jerk brother to watch you guys' backs here," Kai says. We turn to find him perusing the quick sale candy by the counter. "And then me and Sora can give Stephen and Meghan a ride over to…" He makes air quotes. "…Captain Creepy's."

Gwen and Meghan both point at Kai with curious expressions. "Kai eats about as much as he and Sora earn." Gwen nods. "And I still think it's dangerous…but that sounds like a better plan."

216

"So, let's do that then," Sora says, returning from the back. She smacks her hands together. "Gwen, call your brother and let him know the plan. Meghan," she continues, saying her name hesitantly. "Key," she snaps making a *give me* motion with her hand. Meghan quickly fishes the car key out of her clutch and tosses it to Sora. "Also, call Stephen and make sure he knows we're on the way." Meghan produces her phone from her still-open purse.

Kai walks past me with both hands behind his head and what looks and smells like a Blow Pop in his mouth.

Sora follows him and smacks me on the shoulder as she passes. "Call us if anything happens." I nod. I look at Gwen as Meghan, Kai and Sora walk out of the store. Gwen's staring at her phone.

"Crap," she groans with a concerned expression. "Emily needs me back at Jelly Bean. I gotta go. I'll call Gavin on the way and tell him the plan." She backs toward the door. I follow.

"So, I won't get off work until nine tonight," she says with her back pressed against the door. Has she been talking this whole time? She looks at me. "Well, like I said…I gotta go."

I step up to her. Her eyes feel like they're saying something to me…asking…demanding. I answer. I cup her face and press my lips against hers. Her words trail off into a string of mmm's, followed by a deep inhale. She places her hands on top of mine. Her warm hands…her really warm hands…I open my eyes and there are bright orange flames on either side of my face. I take my hands from underneath hers quickly and place them on top. The flames go out as her shocked, frightened eyes snap open.

"No," she moans with tears replacing the shock.

"No, no, no, no," I whisper. "It was my fault. We…knew this might happen, but I couldn't help myself…I had to kiss you."

"Had to?" I nod. She cranes her neck and brings a pained expression back with her. "I know the feeling."

"At least give me a real smile before you go," I ask. She giggles into a smile. "There it is."

"Okay, I'm going. My jacket is at the shop so, I'll give you back your hoodie when you come over." I nod. "Oh, and be careful. If something happens between here and there, just yell for me and I'll come out." I nod again. "And…and I hope the rest of your night goes okay." I nod again. "Oh, and I'll call…Gavin on the way over there, but knowing him, he'll keep his distance and keep watch without us knowing."

"I don't know," I say light-heartedly. "When you and Meghan were trapped inside the bear-dog-blob, he looked really worried."

She smiles. "I know. He's my brother after all." She pushes the door open. "Okay, I'm really gone this time." I smile and wave. She takes a step back, sighs and slumps her head. "Sometimes I like being a lying kitsune."

"Wha…" before I can finish, she puts her hands on either side of my face and presses her lips against mine. She inhales deeply, and I hold perfectly still. She lowers herself a bit and huddles her forehead against mine.

"Don't burn him," she mutters. "Don't burn him. Please don't burn him." She opens her eyes slowly.

"You didn't." She smiles and gives me one more peck before bolting out the door. I smile, watching her the entire way as she crosses the square.

"Very sweet," Mr. Hamish says from behind the counter. I half-turn to see him. "But, there's no necking in the store, kid. That kind of thing tends to turn some customers away."

"Sorry about that, Mr. Hamish." He nods and opens a magazine. I turn back to the door as Gwen walks into Jelly Bean Coffee. "I'll remember that."

Chapter 35: Combined

Alex flips another chair over onto a table as I mop along behind him. He's fast. If not for him, I'd still have at least another half hour before I finished. "Thanks again...for helping, I mean."

"Don't worry about it." Alex moves on to the next to the last table. "Do you think they're okay?" He flips another chair. "Stephen and Meghan, I mean."

"I think so," I answer, not even able to convince myself fully. "Sora and Kai are with them and they'll protect them no matter what, right?" He nods, although he doesn't seem convinced either. "Can we...talk about something else? If I start thinking about it too much, I'll start to worry and that won't help anybody."

"Okay. Why don't you finish telling me about your uncle? You said he came in here tonight?" I put the mop into the soapy water and nod with a sigh. "I thought he was only in town for business."

"He told me that he would be staying in town for a few more days. He wants to get to know me and Gavin." Alex arches one eyebrow quizzically. "Exactly my thoughts. I mean, I met him once when I was six and then..." My heart sinks. "...I mostly know him from pictures and stories that my mom told obāsan, when she would write home." I break off.

Alex moves to the last table. "I'm sorry."

I shake my head. "I don't really remember them. I mean, I get flashes...only images...the sound of their voices... I know that my mom had the same color hair and eyes that Gavin does and that my dad had green eyes and red hair like I do. My obāsan says that I look like my mom...but there aren't any pictures of her for me to compare for myself." I wring out the mop, using the lever on top of the bucket. "My obāsan says that she feels like my mom is still with her when I smile."

"I like your smile too," Alex says, flipping the last chair.

"Very sweet, coming from the guy who hardly ever REALLY smiles." I'm trying not to flirt and failing miserably. I mop under the last table and return it to the bucket. The entire room smells vaguely reminiscent of the pine trees surrounding the school.

That familiar crinkle appears between his eyebrows. "I don't?" I shake my head, undoing the knot of my apron. He sighs.

I walk over to him. "Don't get down about it." I toss the apron on a table. "I mean, you try to smile...you want to smile and...be happy, but it's like something's stopping you. It was worse before you got your memories back, but now...I don't know it seems more intense." He looks away. "Alex..." He turns back. "If you don't wanna talk about it, we don't have to." He smiles...that fake smile. I smile...really smile.

"There it is." I laugh. "When you smile..." He pauses for effect. "...the room lights up."

I snicker. "That was really bad." He laughs. "I mean, please tell me you don't ever plan to say that to anyone else."

"No, I wouldn't and anyway, it's not like that." He looks into my eyes. "When you smile...you smile with your entire body." I frown. "And it's warm and it's real and your entire body seems to just glow with this energy that makes everyone around you more content…happier even." He nods. "That's what I mean when I say your smile lights up a room."

I huff a laugh…that cuts short at a lost breath. I inhale deeply trying to catch it again. I stare into his mahogany eyes. Even without my fox magic, I can see that his brown eyes hide little flecks of hazel and deeper browns. They draw me in and I lose another breath.

Before I know it, I'm leaning toward him with my hands pulling at the front of his hoodie. He reciprocates by putting his hands on my forearms and slowly moves them up my elbows toward my shoulders.

My eyes drift closed, and I swallow deeply. I shake my head. "We shouldn't be doing this," I moan, still tugging at his hoodie, pulling him closer with every handful of its warm, dark fabric. "We shouldn't…"

"No, oh, no," he replies, just as breathlessly. "You're right. We shouldn't…" He leans closer. His hands hold my arms, drawing me to him. I hope he doesn't stop. I hope he doesn't come to his senses. "…we're being so bad." He's not. Good.

"Right," I whisper. "Baaaaaadddddddd Gwen and Alex…" I murmur flirtatiously as our foreheads touch. When we press our foreheads together…like this, it increases the tingle…but not like kissing him, kissing him gives me a more amazing feeling than anything I've ever imagined. I expect to feel his eyelashes brush mine, but they don't. He closed his eyes, too. His forehead rolls against mine. We're so close now that I can feel the air escaping his barely parted lips…on mine.

"What the hell's going on?" Gavin barks over my shoulder. He uses swift paw to take Alex out of arm's reach before I can react. Gavin pins Alex against the wall…knocking several tables and chairs over along the way. Alex glares into Gavin's eyes that, I'm sure, are still glowing from the ripple of his fox magic.

I use swift paw to move over to them and separate them instantly, shoving Gavin away. "Leave him alone." Fox magic causes my voice to echo. Gavin asserts himself and our auras collide. Flares of red and blue flames spark from the point of intersection. Soon after, there's a tiny purple spark of electricity. Alex tries to step forward and I put my hands out to block him from Gavin.

Gavin looks at me then Alex and back to me. "You don't even see it. You're willing to fight me…your own brother…for him."

"He's my friend."

"Maybe you do see it and you're just lying to yourself." I inhale deeply.

"What are you guys talking about?" Alex asks. I glance at his patently confused expression. "Gwen?" I try to answer but my mind goes numb.

"Tell him," Gavin snaps with a flicker of blue fire escaping. I stare at my brother…and shake my head. "Fine…then I will…"

"You can't…"

"Tell me what?" Alex asks with a desperate ring to his voice.

"Your obsession with this…mortal…," Gavin starts, pointing at Alex. "…will be the death of both of you."

Alex takes me by the arm and pulls me around to see him. "What…is he talking about, Gwen?" I open my mouth again and this time something comes out…all the air inside of me. I hyperventilate. "Gwen?" Alex takes my other arm and that shared

220

energy pulses through me. Is that what this has been this whole time? "Gwen, you can tell me anything…you know that, right?" I nod blankly.

"Well, tell him about this," Gavin grumbles. Alex turns his attention to Gavin at the same time I peer over my shoulder.

I return to Alex and our eyes meet. "I told you that my mother and father…died because they were bound together…and were forcefully separated, right?" Alex nods. "Well…" I swallow deeply. "…obāsan…I mean, my grandmother…told Gavin that as they…fell in love, their bond…their binding…it kind of…created itself."

"Fell in love?" Alex asks with a shocked expression and furrowed brow. His bewildered eyes examine every inch of my face.

"That's your take away?" Gavin roars.

"Shhhhh," I shush him with my hand outstretched.

"You're falling in love with me?" Alex asks.

"I didn't say that," I breathe quickly. "Are you…falling in love with me?"

"I didn't say that," Alex returns just as fast. I smile. He smiles in return.

"You grinning idiots are going to die," Gavin says.

We all jump as someone pounds on the front door, causing the glass to rattle violently. We turn to find a panicked, frenzied Meghan. Oh no, did something happen to Stephen? Gavin uses swift paw and appears next to the door. He unlocks the door and throws it open.

"Meghan," I gasp as Alex and I run to her. "Meghan, what happened?" I take her by the shoulders and pull her into the coffee shop.

"Th-that thing…attacked us…," she says with a panicked expression. "We didn't even get into Rich's house and it appeared out of nowhere." She shakes her head. "I hit it with my stun gun…it shook for a second then just shrugged it off." She pants. "If not for Sora, I wouldn't be standing here." She shakes her head. "Oh," she moans and pulls away. "Bring her in," she yells out the door. "No one else is here." *Her*…? "There's no one else here, right?" I shake my head slowly. Kai and Stephen carry Sora in quickly with her arms draped over their shoulders. Meghan moves to one side and they hurry in with Sora.

Gavin becomes pale instantly at the sight of her. "Sora," Alex moans before Gavin can. "What happened to her…?"

"Come on," Kai groans. "We'll lay her down in one of the booths near the back." Stephen nods and carries Sora along with her brother to the back of the restaurant.

"Close the door," Stephen says. Meghan, seeming more in control than I thought, pulls the left door closed and then the right. She bolts them quickly. I rush to catch up with Kai and Stephen as they lay Sora across one of the tables near the back.

I reach her side and gasp. "Oh my God, her arm!" I take in the stream of blood and torn flesh that used to be identifiably her left arm. Her mid-section shows signs of tears and punctures in random places and she still bleeds profusely, even with her accelerated healing.

Despite the excruciating amount of pain, she must be in, she's conscious. She grits her teeth and covers her eyes with her right arm. Her eyes clench shut, but tears manage to escape and roll down the sides of her face. Her breathing is shallow and sporadic, at best.

"Gavin," she moans and squeezes her right hand into a tight fist. Is she…actually calling for Gavin over her own brother or her cousin…?

I snap with the realization. "Wait, in my dream about you two…" I turn to Gavin. "You healed her with your fox magic, the same way that you healed me."

Gavin scowls. He shakes his head slowly. He still appears to be staunch white and nauseated. "I…I don't know if I could heal this much damage."

"You have to," Alex pleads.

Gavin looks at him…really looks at him. His eyes move to Sora. She moans his name again between clenched teeth. His resolve solidifies instantly. He nods.

"Okay," Gavin says, removing his jacket. "But I'm probably going to need some of your fox magic too, Gwenie."

I nod. "Whatever you need, take it."

Gavin nods. "Kai, right…? She's your sister. I need you to stay and be an extra pair of hands if we need them." Kai nods. "Meghan," he continues. "Find her something else to wear, if there's nothing here…" He tosses Meghan his car key. "…go and buy her something." Meghan nods and runs toward the back.

"YOU TWO," Gavin snaps at Alex and Stephen. "TURN AROUND…NOW…!"

They both obey instantly. Gavin, infusing his arms with fox magic, grabs the remains of Sora's shirt and jacket at the same time. He stares at her for a moment. She moves her right arm away from her eyes and returns his gaze. She nods firmly and Gavin proceeds to rip her shirt and jacket open, leaving only her bra to cover her top half. He moves to her arm and tears the remnants of her sleeve away as well.

"Hands," Gavin snaps as he moves to the other side of Sora. I hold my hands out over her mid-section. He reaches under my hands and pulls her tattered arm over her body. She groans in pain, emitting a sound reminiscent of a wounded animal and a moan mixed. Gavin places his hands on top of mine. "Focus," he says calmly, staring into my eyes with bright blue flames licking behind his pupils.

I flood my hands with fox magic…giving him all that I have at my disposal. Our flames blend into a swirl of purple. Sora grits her teeth more and her back arches in one fantastic spasm as the flames move over her abdomen and seep into her wounds. Gavin tenses…the muscles of his mid-section flex underneath his snug-fitting t-shirt…he feels it…I feel the emotional pain that she feels…but he feels the physical pain. Are these the hidden gifts our mother passed down to us that obāsan mentioned…? Or, are they more like hidden curses…?

"Live damn it," Gavin mumbles, staring at Sora's face. "Live. If you die, I swear I'll kill you myself." He pours more magic into her. Her back eases and she slumps back down. She remains motionless.

I gasp. "Is she…?" The flames around Gavin's hands dissipate. The fox magic in my arms wanes as well.

He inhales deeply and looks down on her with a solemn expression. He shakes his head. "She's sleeping," he whispers. He looks at Kai. "You should get something to clean her up with."

Kai nods. He turns to walk away but returns. He puts his hands together in a praying fashion and bows to Gavin. "Domo arigato gozaimasu, Gavin," he whispers.

Gavin closes his eyes and nods. Kai rushes off in search of something to clean up his sister.

"You two just keep looking in the direction that you're looking," Gavin grumbles at Stephen and Alex. Gavin places his jacket on top of Sora to cover her top half.

"Gavin, your coat…?"

"It's just a jacket," Gavin quips, resting his hand on the table next to hers. "Where is that human with something for her to…?"

"I found a shirt and some jeans in Emily's locker," Meghan says. She runs over with the items in hand. Kai comes back with several damp towels and even a few dry ones.

Gavin moves away from Sora. "Gwen." He clenches and unclenches his left hand. "Help Meghan clean her up and get her dressed." He looks at Kai. "You can tell us what happened as they tend to your sister." Kai nods firmly and exchanges the towels for the clothes with Meghan.

#####

"You two can look now," Gavin says. Stephen and I turn to find him laying Sora, in fresh clean clothes, across one of the couches. Stephen and I walk over to a table nearby and take down chairs. As I put my chair down, I swear I see Gavin caress Sora's cheek and whisper something to her. That's crazy though. Anybody who would try that with Sora is likely to lose a hand.

Gwen and Meghan stand nearby, wrapping Sora's clothes in a towel. "What happened?" Gavin grumbles at Kai as he takes a seat on the backrest of a chair.

Kai sighs and sits near his sister. He watches her, then turns to us. "I don't know. We picked up Stephen and headed over to Captain Creepy's." Stephen scowls. "Sorry…and headed over to Rich's. Sora asked me to check the grounds since she didn't sense anything. So, I did." He shakes his head. "I heard a noise and ran back to the front."

"Stephen," Gwen says, sitting down at the table with us. Stephen lifts his eyes to Gwen and then Gavin. He trembles and shakes his head. Gwen purses her lips and sighs.

"We walked up to the front door," Meghan starts walking over to our table. She takes a seat next to Stephen but angles herself so that her back isn't to Gavin. "Stephen said that something seemed off about all of it. He said that the grass looked like it hadn't been cut in weeks and that a couple of the plants hanging from the front porch looked dried out, like they were dying."

"Those are things Rich usually handles," I add.

Meghan nods. "Sora asked Stephen if he noticed anything else. He shook his head. Sora rang the doorbell and waited. Nothing happened, so she rang it repeatedly. Nothing."

Meghan tilts her head from side to side unevenly, then looks at me. "We decided to leave, maybe come back and try it later…as soon as we stepped off the porch…Sora started…well…growling." Stephen makes a noise somewhere between a grunt and a whimper, causing Meghan to break off.

Stephen stands, takes a few steps away from the table, rubbing his palms against his jean pockets. Meghan sighs. "She yelled at us to get back…run," she exaggerates for the story. "Before we knew it, something was rattling around in the bushes between the Mortimer property and the next yard. Then this thing...just came charging at us. It was the size of bear but charged like a rhino. Stephen and I tried to run...but I could hear it gaining on us. Sora shoved us down, but the thing...gored her.

"It knocked her a few feet away and kept driving her into the ground. I screamed for Kai..."

"...that's when I came running and phased on the way around..."

Meghan nods. "Sora finally managed to kick the thing in its...I guess, eye because it reared up and started stumbling around blindly. Sora got to her feet, covered in black and white stripes. She charged the thing while it was still staggering around. She kicked it in the face at the same time Kai showed up and kicked it in the side...but it changed..."

"Changed?" I ask. Meghan nods.

"Yeah," Kai says. "It got bigger...and had bigger, sharper teeth and horns on its head and spikes down its back...and claws, too."

"I suppose next you're gonna tell me it breathed fire," Gavin jokes.

"So, you've seen it too?" Meghan returns.

"Oh, come on," Gavin groans. "There's no way that's true."

"It is," Gwen says. "When we fought the second bear-dog thing..."

"The second one...?" Stephen snaps near the door.

Gwen gives a shoulder slumping sigh. "The second one shot fireballs at us."

"Yeah, but...at first, this one felt like the original bear-dog thing," Kai says. "When it changed...everything about it changed...how it felt, how it fought...how it moved..."

"A different master," Gavin suggests.

"What?" I say.

"Same familiar, but it has two different masters, the difference being the power level and the skill of each of its masters. Think of them like my car," Gavin continues. "The original bear-dog is the design that the first year auto-engineer came up with...basically an engine, four tires, doors and a roof. Designed to do exactly what a car does, get you from A to B, or in this case, whatever it is that bear-dogs do. And then you've got the guy who's been designing cars for years, he comes in and gives you a moon roof, tinted windows, heated leather seats...you know, the works."

"Is that possible?" Gwen asks. "Two masters in control of the same familiar and on top of that, you guys fought the one bear-dog while Alex and I..." She looks at me. My lips become a straight line and I nod. We've come this far. "...and Jamie-Lynn fought off the second."

"JAMIE-LYNN," Stephen barks. He shakes his head and paces. Meghan watches him.

"So...," Gwen continues. "I don't think it's one bear-dog with two different masters..." She touches her chin.

"And given Gavin's car analogy," Meghan jumps in, slowly moving her eyes away from Stephen. "I doubt if two of these shadow bear things..."

"Bear-dog," I correct her.

224

"Bear-dog things…I doubt that one person is controlling both of them."

"Right," Kai breathes. "I mean, 'cause even after the thing basically dragged Sora across the lawn in her human form, she was still okay enough to keep fighting." He fidgets. "It wasn't until after it changed that things went downhill."

"They fought it…hard," Meghan explains. "I mean, even with the claws and spikes and fire…they still were doing pretty well…until the thing broke away and came after me. It was about to chomp down on me when Sora…" Meghan breaks off. "…shoved me out of the way…that's when it happened. It bit her…and slammed her to the ground. Then it pounded her with one sharp clawed paw." Meghan sounds angry and disgusted. "It started to take another bite out of her…until Kai jumped on its back and started ripping out its spikes."

"I lost it," Kai admits. "I wasn't thinking straight…I just saw Sora and all that blood…" His eyes go distant. He puts both hands over his face and slowly pulls them down.

"That's when I hit it with the stun gun," Meghan says. "It staggered and fell."

"A stun gun…?" Gavin says.

"Yeah," I start. "And Rex used a gun that night outside his house. It seems to me that the bear-dogs are vulnerable to whatever their masters are vulnerable to."

"Hm, that actually makes sense, pe…I mean, Alex," Gavin says.

"After that, Kai said we should make a break for it," Meghan continues. "I fished the car keys out of Sora's jacket pocket and tossed them to Stephen. Then, I helped Kai get Sora into the car. The thing was already on its feet again before we even got out of the driveway. It chased us to the border of the yard and then just disappeared."

"Actually it…," Kai starts. "The shadow followed us for a few blocks."

"REALLY…?" Meghan asks. Kai nods. "Wow." She stands and turns toward Stephen, who's clearly panicking. She moves to his side. "And that's when we came here."

"I'm so sorry that you guys had to go through that," Gwen says.

"You should be," Stephen grumbles. "It's your fault."

"What?" Gwen asks.

"Take it easy," I snap. He looks at me then focuses on Gwen.

"Meghan told me why you came here," Stephen continues. "If you hadn't, none of this would've happened, you…fox…thing…whatever you are."

"They're kitsune or fox spirits," Meghan says calmly, motioning to Gwen and Gavin. "And Kai and Sora are skinwalkers." Stephen huffs.

"Don't even get me started on the tiger people," Stephen snaps. "If not for all of you coming here, Rich would be okay and not…who knows what with some scary ass shadow monster…" Tears stream down Stephen's face. "If not for you…" He points one trembling finger at Gwen. "My godfather would still be alive…" He shoves the table out of the way and walks toward us. I'm on my feet and standing in his path. "If not for you…monsters…that *thing* would've never come here…and…"

Meghan steps between Stephen and me. She slaps him. His head whips around.

"Meghan," Gwen gasps. I fall back into my seat and I swear Gavin chuckled.

"Stop it, Stephen," Meghan snaps with a stern tone that doesn't even sound right coming from her and a sterner finger pointed at his face. "You're not being fair. Gwen didn't ask for any of this to happen…and she's not the one who killed your godfather…or did whatever that thing did to Rich…in fact, she's been trying to get to the bottom of this whole mess since it started…AND BTW, it started when the first bear-dog thing attacked Alex…not Gwen."

Stephen stares at the floor. "Stephen," Meghan continues with a softer tone. "You're one of the best…nicest people I know…and this isn't you. You're scared…and you're sad, heartbroken really…and you're worried about one of your best friends…and you're letting all of that affect the things you're saying." Stephen clenches his jaw and a thick tension vein pops out over his right temple.

Meghan pulls a chair off the table next to him. She fumbles it. He catches it and helps her put it down. "Sit," she snaps. He does. She takes a seat…in his lap. "You guys talk it out," she says with her forehead touching his temple. "We'll listen from over here."

"Bullet dodged," Gavin whispers.

"I don't know about that," I whisper back. "We're still no closer to figuring out what happened to Rich…"

"Not exactly," Gavin says confidently. "We know that the twin uglies are guarding his yard…now we just need to figure out why."

Gwen shakes her head. "No way. I'm not letting what happened to Sora happen to anyone else."

"How can you say that?" Sora asks, sitting up. Kai moves to her side and crouches next to her. "I'm fine, baby bro." Sora lifts her exhausted face. "You can't say that…when you don't even know what happened…"

"They told us what happened," I say.

Sora shakes her head. "No, they didn't." She tries to stand, and Gavin is there to offer her a hand. She stares at him. "Thank you," she whispers, her eyes drifting closed on the '*you*.' She stands. "When the first bear-dog attacked me…while it was pushing me…it felt like it was draining my energy…"

"Like in my dream," Gwen sighs, clutching my hand under the table. I pat her hand, partly to comfort her and partly because my fingers are losing feeling under her grip.

"…but when it changed, and it bit me…it felt different…" Sora touches her forehead and Gavin helps her into a chair at our table. "…it took…nearly everything out of me with just one bite." Gavin's hand rests on her right shoulder. Sora stares at me and taps his hand. Gavin removes it instantly.

I frown. "So, now not only is the bear dog acting like a guard dog for Rich's yard…"

"Or Rich," Stephen says behind Meghan's hair.

"What's that?" she murmurs.

"Think about it," Stephen starts, tapping Meghan's leg. She stands, and he does too. "Sorry about my mini-freak earlier." Something seems to have changed in him. "But like I was saying…think about it…the first night the thing attacked…it attacked you…" He points to me. "…at the school, right?" I nod. "But the next day the only real evidence that it was really there was…"

226

"My trashed locker," Meghan whispers. Stephen nods. "And that was the same week that I..." She groans and touches her forehead. "...it was the same week that I treated him like a pile of poo in front of some of my so-called friends."

"And every time since then," Stephen continues. "It's attacked Alex when he was with Gwen or Gwen when she was with Alex..."

"The dibs," I guess. Gwen's disapproval comes in loud and clear through her eyes... I groan. ...and even more so, through her vise grip, crushing my hand. "...never mind. It was stupid. Stephen?"

"Well, yeah, that was my guess, that he felt cheated and lashed out at the two of you," Stephen continues. "In fact, it probably only attacked Sora when she was at his house, because it sensed she was the strongest...and even then, when it saw a chance, it went straight for Meghan."

"Yeah...but," Gwen cuts in. "That was the second bear-dog, not the first one."

"But the second bear-dog," Stephen says. "Formed around the first one so..."

"Maybe their masters'," Gavin supposes. "...emotions got mixed at the same time as their...meaning the familiars...bodies did." Stephen touches the tip of his nose and points at Gavin. "It's insane how much of a knack you mortals have for this stuff," Gavin complains, his eyes moving from Stephen to Meghan and then settling on me.

"So, what do we do now?" I ask.

"We break for now," Gavin says, sounding certain. "Half of us are exhausted, beaten, and drained...and the other half is a bunch of humans, no offense."

"None taken until you added the *no offense*," Stephen admits. Gavin smirks and shakes his head.

"We probably shouldn't completely go our separate ways...division of powers and all that," Sora says.

Gavin and Meghan nod. "Stephen, can you sleep over at my house tonight?" I ask.

"Are you kidding...? My parents have treated me like I'm so emotionally fragile lately that I could probably get away with anything right now."

"Meghan," Gwen calls. "Do you think you can sleep over at my place tonight?" Meghan holds her phone up. "Just got a text from my mom...," she starts with annoyance and sadness peppering her voice. "She's bummed about my car but understands if I want to stay with a friend until she gets back from the Gulf with her boyfriend."

"Gavin," Gwen says quietly. "I think you should stick close by...and by close by, I mean, you should sleep in my room tonight." Gavin must be exhausted because instead of giving her some jerky comeback, he just says...

"Okay."

"Wait," Meghan starts. "Why don't the three of us just stay at my place?" Sora's jaw drops as she scowls. Oddly, Gavin has the same look. "I mean, my mom's out of town. We have a guest bedroom where jerk-face can sleep, and my bed's huge, so you can crash with me without getting into each other's space." She touches Gwen's shoulder.

"I'll have to convince my foster-parents, but...yeah, I think that could work."

"Fine," Gavin says.

Sora growls immediately after his response. Everyone looks at her. She shuffles uncomfortably and her eyes dart away. "Sorry, it's just...," she tugs at the flannel shirt's collar. "Whose shirt is this?"

"My co-worker, Emily's," Gwen offers lightly. "Why? Is something wrong with it?"

"Well, on top of it not being my style. It's also kind of...small." I look at the sleeves hanging loosely around her arms and take in how the bottom falls below her waist. I shake my head. "It's small," she repeats in a sterner voice with her eyes bulging. Kai shrugs. Gwen stares at Sora with her mouth in an 'oh' shape.

"I don't get it," I moan.

"It's squeezing my boobs, okay?" Sora snaps. Gavin and Kai laugh. Gwen and Meghan soon join in. I look at Stephen and Meghan and notice that she has one hand covering his eyes...and the other hand...wrapped up in his hand.

Chapter 36: Hidden

"Here," Meghan says, offering me a pink on white toothbrush, still in its original packaging. I stare at it. "It's my back-up." She looks down her pale-yellow hallway at Gavin, heading toward the bathroom, a towel draped over his shoulder and phone in hand. "Here." She throws a second unopened toothbrush at him. He catches it in stride and without looking.

"Thanks," he moans, stepping into the bathroom, closing the door with his foot. Meghan growls.

"Are you pissed that he's here?"

"It's not the most ideal arrangement, but it is a necessary one," she hums, making her voice sound as prim and proper as mine does unintentionally. "Plus, as long as you're here, I can manage." I smile. "Your fosters were really okay with you sleeping over…? I mean…" Her eyes roll. "It's a school night," she finishes with a mocking adult tone.

I laugh. "Yeah, I told them about your 'accident'…minus the part where I was in the car with you…"

"…and the part about the shadow monster trying to swallow us, car and all."

"Yeah. Well, Mrs. Taylor sounded proud that I wanted to stay with you tonight. She would've been happier if I'd agreed to get you to come to our place, but…I convinced her that you'd probably be more comfortable at your own house, surrounded by your own things."

The bathroom door jerks open. Gavin stands shirtless in the doorway. "Wow," Meghan breathes.

"It's pink!" Gavin snarls holding up the toothbrush.

"Guys can use pink things!" I say. "Heck, guys can even wear pink."

"Not this guy!"

"Then use your finger for all I care," I grumble. He steps back into the bathroom. "Sorry about that, Megs." She doesn't respond. She has the nail of her left pointer finger between her teeth. She stares down the hall…at the bathroom door. "Meghan?" She stays in whatever daydream has her. I snap my fingers. "MEGHAN!"

"Wha…?" she moans, coming out of whatever fantasy she was having about my brother. "I'm sorry, I spaced…what were we talking about?"

"Gross!" I push past her, heading toward her bedroom. She follows.

"Gwen?" I sit on the edge of her pink comforter with my head in my hands. "Are you tired…?" I sigh. "Hungry…?" I lift my head and stare at her. "What…?"

"My brother…still…? Really, Megs…?" She sighs and crosses her arms. "Did you forget how he abandoned you at the dance? I mean, I warned you…?"

"I'm not." She sits next to me. She snatches the toothbrush back. I gasp. "Hey, if you're gonna accuse me of things…I get to take my toothbrush back." I laugh.

Meghan stares into space. "I don't know," she complains. "He's…just so…dangerous…so…hot…" She looks at me. "He's like you." I scowl. "Not like that, I mean…he doesn't look at me…like I'm some idol to be worshipped," she explains. "Like you. He argues with me. No one's argued with me in nine years, Gwen."

"I know…how it feels to be different…"

"No, you don't!" Our shoulders slump simultaneously. "I like…liked Stephen and he liked me." Her eyes water. She scoffs an exhale. "But I couldn't tell…I couldn't tell if it was me…" A tear rolls down her cheek. "…or if…or if…"

"…or if it was whatever makes the lemmings the lemmings…" She nods and sniffs, tipping her head back, trying to stop more tears from coming. "…he's not like that," I whisper.

She reaches up and swipes at her right eye. "Yeah, right. You're just saying that to get your toothbrush back." She laughs as she returns it.

"Seriously, I've seen the way the lemmings look at you…" I pause. "…in fact, I've seen the way everyone looks at you. Stephen doesn't look at you like that."

Meghan scoffs and turns away. I climb down and crouch in front of her. I gaze into her frightening blue eyes. "Really," I continue emphatically. "He looks at you like…um…like…" I draw my lips into my mouth.

"…like…Alex looks at you?" Her lower lip puckers as she watches me intently, waiting on my answer.

I try to form words…again, but nothing comes. "H-how does Alex look at me…?" I ask…more like a plea, with my forehead furrowing and my eyebrows moving toward the middle.

"Like…" She shakes her head. "…like you're the only thing in the world that matters."

"He does?"

"He tries to hide it, like most guys do, but like anybody…guy or girl…who really likes somebody, he can't. Since the day he met you…"

"…he hasn't been able to take his eyes off me," I whisper through a smile. Meghan does too. I put my hand on her knee, and she puts hers on top of mine. Suddenly, I feel like one of the lemmings. I don't know what it is, but everything about Meghan tells me that she's human. The influence that she has over people…like Gavin and my gifts…it's clearly a blessing and a curse.

"He said something similar to that, but he…wait," I break off, stumbling over a realization and take my hand out from under hers. "How did we start talking about you and my idiot brother and then move to talking about me and Alex?"

Meghan laughs. "I'm very good," she explains dripping with confidence.

"No, you're not," Gavin says from Meghan's open door. He leans against the doorframe with a towel covering his lower half. I put my hand over Meghan's eyes. "Oh please," Gavin starts arrogantly. "If she sees something she's never seen before she's more than welcome to throw money at it." He scrutinizes Meghan's pale yellow tinted room. "Nice room. What…is it decorated in early canary…?"

"I'll have you know," Meghan starts, trying to curtail her anger with a modulated, proper speech pattern. "That the color of these walls maximizes the sunlight that comes in through my east window and…"

"Do not engage it," I grumble between clenched teeth. I hold my hand up in front of her mouth but make sure that I don't touch her. "That's what it wants…attention."

"Whatever," Gavin says casually, walking away. "These sheets better be soft. I don't sleep on anything less than one thousand thread count."

230

Meghan scoffs and shakes her head. "I can't believe I ever wanted to go out with it."

"Then go for the nice guy. Go out with Stephen." She sighs and arches her eyebrows in an '*I'm not sure*' sort of way. "Or you could just keep banging your head against a wall trying to sort through my brother's lies, double speak and empty promises."

Meghan's lower lip vanishes into her mouth. "No, thank you."

I smile. "Good."

#####

"Man," Stephen groans, plopping down on the sofa next to me, rocking my dad's Foo Fighters t-shirt and my pajama bottoms. "It's been forever since I spent the night here."

I shove his shoulder. "Yeah, I think the last time was when we were twelve." Sora comes out of my bedroom. "Kai and Sora were visiting then, too." Stephen smiles. "Rich, too."

Sora sits on the coffee table and stares at Stephen. She leans forward in her tiny-strapped, skin-tight, low cut tank top. "How are you dealing with all of this, Stephen?" His eyes immediately get big. "What's wrong? Are you scared of me since you've seen me transform?" Stephen shakes his head slowly, still…staring. "Then why are you staring like a goon?"

"It could be," I grumble. "…because you're practically showing him your chest."

Sora sits back, looks down, pulls out her top a little and frowns. "No, I'm pretty well covered."

"You guys are lucky," Kai says, stepping out of the bathroom, toothpaste surrounding his mouth. "She usually walks around naked back home."

"Naked?" Stephen mutters. I punch him in the shoulder. "OW! What was that for?"

"She's my cousin," I say. "Be grosser, please." Stephen covers his mouth and snickers. Sora's eyebrows arch.

"What I don't get," Kai continues. "…is how you can have that little blond hottie sitting in your lap one minute and then drool all over my exhibitionist sister the next?"

Sora grabs a magazine and flings it at Kai. From the sound of it flopping against the wall, she missed. Kai raspberries her. She jumps up, wearing tiny black boy shorts and runs after him.

Stephen follows her with just his eyes. "That would've been my next point," I say. "You…Meghan…you guys seemed pretty tight tonight."

"Adrenaline from almost being eaten by a weird shadow bear thing. Seriously, man I…" He looks at me and his entire argument deflates instantly. Sora chases Kai into my room and slams the door. He comes back with a serious face.

"What's going on, man?"

He shakes his head. "How are we doing this? I mean, I was seriously almost killed by that thing today…and the thought of it coming from Rich…" He shudders. "…and it…killed Mr. and Mrs. Turnipseed."

"How did you…?"

"Kai told me." His right hand clutches into a fist. "How did all this happen?" I shrug. "And is this thing with Rich something new or is it something he kept hidden from us for years?" I shake my head again. I wish Sora wasn't trying to give us space to talk. She's better at explaining this stuff than I am. Maybe if Gwen were here… "And then we're just sitting around talking about Meghan Powers of all people…"

"That's it," I whisper. "The reason I'm able to handle all this…well, before I got my memories back…the reason I was able to handle all of this was Gwen. I mean, she's been there with me every step of the way, you know?" Stephen frowns and lets his eyes wander. "Maybe you just have to find something that helps you keep everything in perspective, you know?"

"Like my best friend's constant 'you knows'?" We laugh.

"Nah, man," I smack him across the leg. "I was thinking more along the lines of the pretty girl who you've been crushing on since we were all in the sandbox together. The same pretty girl who…when everybody else started looking at her completely different, the way you saw her stayed the same." Stephen stares into space again, but this time he wears a goofy grin. "The girl who makes you get that look on your face."

"It's that easy, huh? Just make a play for Meghan Powers, right?"

I nod and Gwen flashes through my mind…her smile, her beautiful green eyes…the sound of her voice…the way she talks…even her fire. The thought of her makes me wear the same goofy grin Stephen has. "Yeah." He purses his lips and leans back. "And do yourself a favor." His eyes come back. "Stop staring at my cousin. She'll literally rip your heart out." We laugh again.

He puts his hand on his chest. "She won't really do that, will she?"

232

Chapter 37: Relationship

I spring from a tree branch and land on another. Swift paw propels me from one to the next. I don't even know where I'm going, why I'm going, or why I left without telling Meghan or Gavin. Ugh! Clearly, I'm lying to myself now. Something inside me tells me that he wants to see me. I want to see him, so here I am, darting from tree to tree, from shadow to shadow trying to reach him. The air is strangely cool around me, despite the flames covering my arms. Although, under the flames, I'm wearing a tiny, soft pink tank top that Meghan proclaimed was too small for her. At least, my legs are covered. Capri pants on Meghan make for regular pants on me. Thankfully, they're soft enough to sleep in.

I perch on a tree limb. At least I managed to grab some of her little *feety* socks, as she called them, and my shoes before I bolted out her bathroom window. Alex's apartment complex is across the street. I can practically feel him or is that just my imagination? I place my hand over my heart. He's calling for me…he's not in a panic or worried…he just wishes he could see me…like I want to see him.

Get it together, Gwen. You're here. You want to see him. He wants to see you. You've shared a few kisses with him and they were amazing…minus burning things. I frown and nod, a moment later. I push off the limb. I make it across the street and to the top of lamppo- "No," I moan as my foot slips against dew-covered lantern. I correct in mid-air and land on my feet. "Idiot," I snarl angrily. "Just because you're kitsune doesn't mean you're perfect."

"Not by a long shot," a voice says from a nearby tree. I gasp. How did someone get this close without me noticing? I leap back. "Did I scare you, Gwendolyn Frost?"

"How do you know my name?" I bark at the shadows, expecting to see the shadow-bear at any moment. …nothing… "Who are you? Are you Rich?" An echoing laugh fills the air and it sends a tremor of fear up my spine. My eyes fill with fox magic and I catch every particulate, every dust mote and every moist droplet in the air. I tremble, still not seeing anything. Alex, where are you?

"Get her," the voice demands. The shadow takes shape and the original bear-dog charges. I don't ponder fighting, instead, I jump over the car behind me and make a run for it. I use swift paw and dash through the parking lot. The roof of a car crunches under the bear-dog's massive paws. *You have to get to Alex*, repeats in my head…and a few of the lessons obāsan taught me creep in as well. I have to get to higher ground. If this thing is a true "bear-dog," emphasis on the dog part, it can't possibly climb, right? I spot a tree near the next apartment building and jump up into it. The bear-dog nips at my heel just as I slip between two branches.

I wedge myself into a split in the trunk and stare down at it. It jumps, bares its teeth, and snaps at me again. Luckily, it doesn't jump nearly high enough to reach me. I sigh. Now, I just have to think of a way to signal Alex or maybe his cousins. I forgot to grab my phone. I look around, hoping to find some way that I can get away without moving lower.

The leaves shuffle above me. I don't see anything even with fox magic eyes. I look down and… WHERE DID THE BEAR-DOG GO? A branch above me cracks. Something crashes through the plumage. Before I can move, the bear-dog falls on top of me, knocking me down. I hit a branch on the way. "Argh!" It spins me around…

"Ugh!" ...finally, crashing, landing on the back of my head... "Hmph!" ...the bear-dog, and all its impressive weight, smashing into me and driving me into the mud a second later. "Oof!"

I struggle to push it off, but I can't get any leverage. I open my mouth to scream, but before I can, a massive, black paw slams into my head. My teeth gnash together and my mouth fills with blood.

"Hold it," the shadow voice says. The bear-dog breathes on my neck. It was that close to biting into me. I shiver. "Aw, poor Gwendolyn, she thought she was so pretty...so talented...so smart...soooooo," he breaks off mid-hiss. "...perfect."

"Not perfect," is all I manage from under the paw and after expelling the blood from my mouth.

"Well," the shadow says as a shadow figure steps out from behind the bear-dog. "You won't be anything after tonight." He smiles...or at least, I would call it a smile if his teeth weren't black shadows, too. I swallow deeply and tears stream from my eyes and across my face. "Oh, no," he moans attempting to sound sympathetic. "Don't cry, Gwendolyn. I promise. I'll make it quick. One bite and your head will be gone."

"Screw you, buddy!" A tree limb flies through the shadow figure. He dissipates and at the same time so does the bear-dog. I lift my head as much as I can. I couldn't recognize my savior's voice with one ear full of mud and the other covered by a paw.

Alex reaches for me. "Are you alright?" I nod and take his hand. He pulls me to my feet and wraps his arms around me. "We should probably..."

"It's gone," I say as he pulls me toward his house. He looks at me, then the immediate area, refusing to relinquish his grip on his makeshift weapon.

"Are you sure?" I nod. He steps back, holding the limb with two hands. He moves to one end and uncoils a suede string, with a stone attached. He drops the tree limb, shoves the stone and string into his pocket.

"What's that?"

"This..." He pats his pocket. "...is a warding charm that Rex gave me, while you were...um...asleep."

"Unconscious, is more like it." He nods and draws his lower lip into his mouth, which reminds me. I quickly wipe my mouth on the back of my hand.

Alex watches me clear the excess blood from my chin and I'm thankful that I healed the inside of my cheek with fox magic. He tugs his right sleeve over his hand and gently wipes my chin. He moves to my cheek, staining his sleeve with blood and mud. I stare at him, being so attentive...and I melt...my legs feel weak.

"Rex told me to be careful with it." He pulls his sleeve back up. He reaches up with his right hand and picks leaves out of my hair. "...because it's only good for a few uses." I nod.

"You scared the hell out of me," he says, making it sound more like a plea than a complaint. I swallow, not realizing how dry my mouth had become. "Look at you. You must be freezing." He takes his backpack... Why is he carrying a backpack...? ...off and places it on the ground. He takes his hoodie off. He's only wearing a gray t-shirt underneath, although it's more than I'm wearing.

"I'm fine," I lie meekly. "Really, I am."

"Liar." He drapes his hoodie over my shoulders. "What are you doing here?"

234

"I thought you wanted to see me," I answer with disappointment.

"That might be true, but that still doesn't explain why you're here, you know?" I shake my head and purse my lips. Why am I here? The bear-dog almost mauled me, and no one would've known if Alex hadn't come along.

"Why are you out here?" I counter.

"I live here."

"You live in the parking lot?" He laughs. I laugh.

"Come with me," he says simply. I start to ask where, but he takes my hand in his and collects his bag before I can. We quickly cross the street; watching out for the bear-dog.

We approach a small building, similar to the apartments' shape and design. "Keep an eye out." He kneels in front of a garage door. He takes a lock off at the bottom, shoves it into his pocket and raises the door handle. It slides upward with surprisingly little noise. Inside, a collection of dust-covered boxes and random miscellaneous items stand.

I point inside. "What is this?"

"Wait and see." He collects my hand again and pulls me inside, flicking on a light switch. We work our way between the boxes' narrow pathways. We reach the back of the garage-made storage bin, and there is a large thin object, covered by a paint-spattered sheet. He releases my hand and moves over to the sheet.

I slip my arms into his hoodie's sleeves. "What is this?"

"This…" He grabs the sheet. "…is something I've been working on for a few months, but I got stalled out. After our visit with Jamie, I got inspired again."

He tugs. The sheet falls away, revealing a large canvas with a painting of a man and woman embracing, on the verge of kissing. I step closer and get a better look at the man, dressed in a black tuxedo, and the woman, with long jet-black hair, wearing a white mermaid-style dress. The woman reminds me of someone…

"Is…is that your mom?" He nods. "And that's your dad?" He nods again, rubbing the palms of his hands together. "This is their wedding photo?"

"Yeah. My mom sent me to see three different therapists after he…died. One of them actually said something useful…" He pauses and shoves his hands deep into his pockets. "She told me that I should find a healthy way to say goodbye to him." He returns to the painting. "And I picked this."

I place my hand over my mouth as tears stream down my face. "It's beautiful," I murmur.

"Thanks. I still have a lot of work to do on it. I never really used brushes in my artwork. I was just coming out to work on it, because…" He pauses again. "…I was thinking about you and since I couldn't see you, before I knew it, I was on my way out here."

"Are you…still going to work on it?" He shrugs. "You should." He looks over the painting. "Can I watch?"

He smiles. "Of course." He moves over to a stack of boxes. He grabs a drum with a handle near the top, filled with…I sniff…paint...and places it in front of the canvas. He motions for me to sit…and I comply, placing both hands in my lap. He opens his backpack and pulls out various small tins and tubes of paint, an assortment of brushes, several small paper cups, and a lidded Mason jar with water in it. He mixes some of the paint and I watch him attentively.

#####

"…and that's when the Taylors took me on as their foster-child," Gwen finishes. She looks absently through the bland, bluish-gray painted railing, surrounding our tiny patio.

"So, what'd you do over the summer and the start of fall…you know, before you came to school?" She pulls the blanket higher up on her shoulders.

"Mostly trying to re-acclimate to life in America," she explains in that overly explanatory way that's so adorable. "So, different than living in Japan with my obāsan…you know?" She smiles, then draws her lips into her mouth. I bob my head along with her, getting our inside joke.

"School with kitsune is so different than high school with humans. At least, there I knew that there was a good chance that the other students I was talking to were lying to me." She looks at me. "Meghan and present company excluded, of course." I bow my head. "It's just that…I feel so…awkward everyday…there and here."

"I'd've never guessed. On your very first day, you made friends with *The Great Meghan Powers*." She covers her massive smile. I put my arm around her and pull her closer. "I thought you were a superhero right then and there…just turns out that I was right." She leans against me and giggles.

She lifts her head suddenly. She points, staring at the dark purple sky trailing off into slowly brightening light blue just above the tree line. "Is that…is that the sun?" I nod. "Have…" She comes back. "…have we been talking all night?"

"I guess so."

"I guess so, too," my mom says, stepping out onto the patio. Gwen and I look at her. Mom crosses her arms. She's pissed. "What's going on here?"

"Mrs. Garner," Gwen breathes, sounding flustered. "I…"

"She got into a fight with her brother," I blurt out.

"What?" my mom says, sounding confused, which is better than mad.

"Yeah," Gwen joins in. "My brother was giving me…" She looks at me and then her eyes dart back to my mom. "…he was giving me a ride back to my foster parents' place…we got into an argument…shouting match really and…" She sighs. "…I jumped out of the car and ran away from him at the first stop sign. I was close by, so I figured…"

"Did you call your foster parents and your brother to let them know where you were? That you were safe?"

Gwen nods. "He's…my brother is on his way to pick me up now."

Mom nods. She points at me. "We'll talk later," she says with her serious tone. I nod. She steps back into the house.

My head bows as the door closes. "I'm so dead."

Gwen covers her mouth with both hands. "I'm sorry."

I stare into her beautiful green eyes. "I'm not. I'm sorry you had to lie again to cover for me."

236

"I'm not. Besides, not totally…a lie…" I frown. "…'how can you tell if Gavin and I are about to get into an argument?'" I shrug. "'If we're talking to each other, we're about to get into an argument.'" I laugh. "Obāsan came up with that one."

"Seems legit. Well, to be honest, the guy's not too bad, right?"

She scoffs into a frown. "What…what has he done to make you say that?" I shake my head. "Then why would you say…?"

"Oh well, I…have met his sister."

She points at me with bright red cheeks. "You set me up for that one."

I lean toward her. "Guilty." She reaches over and scratches Max between his ears. I had forgotten he was even out here with us. "He really likes you."

She looks down at the little furry rascal and grins. "I…never thought I'd say this, but yeah…I like your dog, too." She leans over Max's head. "But…I have to admit, Max." She glances at me. "I like Alex a little bit more than you." Max whines, as if he knew what Gwen was saying.

I try to suppress a chuckle. "That's cool. I've already had the talk with him about it…" She laughs infectiously. "…he was heartbroken at first, but I think I talked him down off the ledge." Max looks around with just his eyes. We laugh, and she leans in my direction again, letting her pale emerald eyes take in every inch of my face. Gwen poses a soundless, 'yeah?' I nod inching closer. "Yeah."

She tilts back and away from me. "Hmm," she moans, as she places her hand against my chest, closed into a fist…with her fingers on me. It's weird. It's almost as if she meant to grab me but changed her mind. "We can't," she pants. "We might…" She swallows deeply. "…I…might set fire to your whole patio."

"I don't care."

"Your mom might be watching."

"Tempted to slow down, but still, I don't care."

"I haven't brushed my teeth, I'm covered in dried mud, and I just feel gross."

"Not gross…Gwendolyn Frost, you could never be gross," I whisper and move a strand of her mud caked hair back. She giggles adorably. "Besides everything you just said about yourself applies to me, too."

"Oh yeah," she breathes again as her hand sweeps across my chest.

"Yeah," I answer with my fingers tracing down from her hair and then following the line of her jaw. "Well, except the mud…but I have paint on my hands, so I figure we're still even." She moans a positive response, just before she presses her lips against mine and tugs at the front of my t-shirt. I caress her cheek as her lips part and come together again around my lower lip. A horn blares from the parking lot.

We separate and her shoulders slump instantly. "That's Gavin. I can tell by how annoying the honk is." I laugh. I stand up, take both her hands and pull her to her feet. Max lifts his head and watches Gwen. She pulls the blanket off her shoulders and folds it neatly.

"Your brother's waiting…"

"He can wait." She passes me the folded blanket and turns toward the patio door. She stops and comes back to me. "What are we? I mean, I know we've been telling people, since the day we met, that we're just friends, but…" She breaks off, sinks a little and then takes a step forward. "…but we've kissed…a few times…and I want to know…" She puffs as if she's running out of air. Her shoulders move up and down quickly and I can tell her heart is racing. "…what does that mean to you? Because…it means something to me and if it doesn't mean anything to you…" She puts her hands on her hips then quickly switches so that her arms cross over her chest. I drape the blanket over my left arm. "…then I should know now, so that I won't…"

I cup her chin in my right hand. I tilt her head up slightly, lean in, and kiss her. I step back, her eyes remain closed and her lips still puckered. She is so amazingly, breathtakingly beautiful. "It means…a lot to me, Gwen." Her eyes open slowly. She smiles. "And, going back to your first question, we can…be whatever you want us to be…" She nods. "…but if I have any say so in it, and I hope I do, I'd really like you to be…my girlfriend."

She grins and emits a noise somewhere between a squeal and a shout that makes Max jump to his feet. She throws her arms over my shoulders and squeezes so tightly that I think a couple of bones in my back crack all at once. "Ugh," I moan.

"Sorry," she returns as the horn blares again. "I gotta go." I nod, reach past her and push the door in. Max scurries into the house before we do. Gwen steps inside and I follow. Kai and Stephen are *sleeping*, although they both just closed their eyes.

"Uh-huh," I moan as we tiptoe past them. I drape the blanket over the sofa and walk with Gwen. She pulls the front door open, turns, and opens her mouth to say something. "I'll walk you down."

"Not a good idea. I'm covered in mud and I spent the night at your place…Gavin's already gonna be at threat level blue."

"Did…" I motion to her. "…did you just make…a joke, Gwendolyn Frost?"

"Maybe," she replies, pushing the word together, making it smaller than its five letters.

"Well, it was a good one." I bend down to kiss her. She arches on the balls of her feet and pauses. She looks past me and her eyes widen. She moves to my right and kisses me on the cheek.

"Good night…I mean, day, Alex."

"Good day, Gwen." She walks away and waves as she heads down. I sigh and push the door closed behind her.

I turn to my mom, standing near the kitchen entryway with her 'mom arms' folded across her chest. "It wasn't what it looked like," I explain, shoving my hands in my pockets. She glares. I feel like the head inquisitor of the Spanish Inquisition stares me down. *This little factoid brought to you by Gwendolyn Frost. Gwen, making Alex remember things for almost a month now.*

"Alex," my mom says, stepping closer. "I don't make many rules for you, because I know that despite the fact that it's been four years now, you're still grieving your father's death." I sigh and try to exhale a breath that almost chokes me. I always feel like this when mom brings up dad, because all she ever does is talk about my grieving…never hers. "But one of my rules was that I don't want you here alone with Gwen." She turns to the sofa. "And I'll say it again for the two boys pretending to be asleep. NO GIRLS OVER WHEN I'M NOT HERE." Kai and Stephen both lift their heads groggily, as if they really had just woken up.

"Actually," I start knowing that I'm going to regret this, but not able to stop myself. *Damn you, teen angst.* "You told me that I couldn't study in my room with her...not that she couldn't be here..." She arches her eyebrows in a way that tells me if not for the facts that I'm her son and that she'd go to prison, and not necessarily, in that order of importance, I'd be dead right now. "I'm gonna shut up now."

Mom watches me, never breaking that expression. I try to squeeze by her without touching her. She turns when I finally manage to wiggle past. "We're not done talking about this, Alexander Bryan Garner," mom says, instantly reducing me to a four-year-old who just wrote on the wall with a charcoal pencil.

I scratch my head like Kai does. "Sorry, ma..." I toss my hand, trying to find a way to apologize. "...I was worried about her and I didn't want to just send her home." Mom slips her hand under the blanket and grabs her jacket. She pulls it on quickly. "It's just...her brother...he's..."

"That guy's a jerk," Stephen and Kai say. I motion to Kai and Stephen. Mom pulls her hair out of her jacket and grabs her purse off the tiny nook overlooking the kitchen.

"...ma, it's just that..." She sighs. "...I care about her, ma." She walks over, and I feel like I should put my guard up.

She puts her arms around me, instead of attacking. "I know you do, baby," she whispers. "Just one of the million ways you remind me of your father." I inhale deeply and put my arms around her. She releases me and touches my face. She smiles warmly with watery eyes. "I have to go back in, but you kids should get ready to head out too or you're gonna be late." She turns to Kai and Stephen. They both wave at her. "Bye." She heads toward the door.

The door slams behind her. "Dude," Kai says rising to his feet. "Your mom works way too much." I nod. "And I think I should just say..." Stephen and I stare at him. "...I'm going first in the bathroom." He walks away. We laugh. "Wake Sora up," Kai says from the bathroom. "Oh, when you do, protect your groin."

I go over to Sora's...dang it...I mean, my bedroom door and knock in a non-too-subtle fashion. She jerks the door open. "WHAT?" Her hair is tossed in wild, wavy curls all around her head and she's wearing a faded gray t-shirt with blue lettering that says, *Navy Football.*

"Sun's up...means it's after six and we need to get to school." Sora gives me her bewildered, *Are you insane* face. "Hey..." I point at her t-shirt. "You changed clothes."

"Shut up," she snaps, tugging at the collar. "Why do you smell like something just burned you?" I frown. "Yeah." She points to the center of my shirt. "Right there." I pull my shirt away and there's a small scorch mark, about the size of a thumb. I pull my shirt up. "Ugh," Sora complains, covering her eyes. "I don't want to see that."

"You're one to talk." My skin's a little red right underneath the burn. I purse my lips. "Great."

"What?"

"Nothing," I say, shaking my head. It's just that my new girlfriend has a chance of burning me to death every time we kiss.

Chapter 38: Confrontation

"Oh…my…GAWD!" I moan, walking to my locker, Meghan behind me. I work the combination.

Alex leans against the locker next to mine. "What's wrong?"

I pull my locker open, shaking my head and trying to articulate something beyond *oh my gawd*.

"It was brutal," Meghan says.

Alex's eyes take on a concerned glint. "What? Did…" He looks around. "Did you guys get attacked again?" I utter a mixed whine and a whimper. I toss my Algebra book in my locker and take out my Biology textbook.

Meghan leans against the other locker beside mine. "She and Gavin actually made me glad I'm an only kid." A thin, pale-skinned boy with brown hair walks over to Meghan, looking at the locker behind her. "You can get it later," she says casually. "We're talking about something important here, so go away." The boy nods and departs.

"Don't you have to go to your locker?" Alex asks Meghan.

"Crap, English is my first class, isn't it?" She walks away. Alex laughs. I smile.

"So, what's the bear-dog saving scoreboard looking like?" he asks. "Because after last night, I think I've finally caught up."

"No way. I'm still up four to three." He laughs. "You got my mind off my argument with Gavin." He nods. "I can't believe we're laughing about this."

"Hey, we can laugh about it, or we can sit around crying about it." He moves the curly strand of hair that Meghan left out of my ponytail to the side. "Me…? I'm just…exceedingly happy that you're alright."

"Well, I'm exceedingly happy that you saved me."

"Well, I'm exceedingly happy that you're my girlfriend."

Huge, blushy smile. "I'm …" I break off to tug at his backup hoodie, since his other one is at my house in the dryer. "…so exceedingly happy that you're my boyfriend." I lift myself on the balls of my feet. He leans forward and pauses. "What's wrong?"

"Um," he moans and his eyes dart to the left…his left, my right. A collection of students watches our every move. "Yeah…according to Stephen, the buzz on the Twitter-verse is that there are about a million and one pics of you and me on Instagram and thanks to the video of us at the dance, we're the current *it* couple at J.A.H."

"I'm sorry most of your last sentence consisted of words and then there were some things that I just didn't get." He laughs off my comment. "But us being the new…" I groan softly and bob my head from side to side. "…*it* couple, reminded me of something." I move back to my locker and open it quickly.

"I managed to get off work tonight," I say, trying to pass the time. "Did you still want to…you know, really study…with me…tonight…you know, English and…um…" I feel my cheeks blush and I smile.

"…Biology…," he whispers. "English, yes. Biology…" He rubs my back. "…hell yes." I giggle. I pull my locker door open, attempting to hold off the flirt and desire to kiss him. He takes my Biology book from me and holds it.

"Thank you." I open my backpack and retrieve the item that I came back for.

He frowns. "What's this?" he asks about the pink object draped over my arm.

"This." I excitedly unfold it. "I figured the bear-dog seems to attack us only when we're near each other and since we're…" I bob my head and drop down into a whisper. "…boyfriend and girlfriend…I mean, I don't know if we're really telling anyone or if we're going to keep on playing the roles of two friends for the masses or not but…"

"Rambling, Gwen." He smiles, stepping closer.

"…right. Rambling…" I hold the garment up for him…

"…it's a pink hoodie?"

I flash a large smile and nod with giddy energy. "Well?" He looks at me curiously. "Nothing says 'couple' like taking on each other's likes and interests, so…"

"So, my interests equal 'hoodie enthusiast'…?"

"No." I try to reclaim my enthusiasm. "But…" I break off and my shoulders slump.

He takes my hoodie. "I think you…will look…adorable…" He drapes the hoodie around me. "…in this." I unzip my jacket and slip my arms out of it. He continues holding my hoodie around me and then helps me into it. Then he claims my jacket and pack, places them in my locker and reclaims my book and notebook.

He pushes my locker closed and looks me over. I extend my arms to my sides. "Yep." His eyes half-close dreamily. "Adorable."

"I prefer to think of myself as beautiful," I flirt.

"Yes, you are." He tugs at the pockets of my hoodie and I feel wobbly standing close to him.

"Gross, now you two are dressing alike," Kai complains, stepping closer. I laugh. Sora and her ever-present scowl maintain their distance. She crosses her arms. Her scowl…scowls. "Congratulations," Kai whispers. I frown. He points at me. "Girlfriend." He points at Alex. "Boyfriend."

"How…?"

He points at us. "I was awake, and you guys weren't even trying to talk softly. Have you told the besties?" He lowers his hand. "'Cause I told yours." He motions to me again. "Did you tell yours?"

"Kai, are you always this annoying?" I ask.

"Yes," Sora and Alex return. I look at her with arched eyebrows. Her façade crumbles a little and she laughs. I do, too.

"Guys," Meghan stage whispers as she and Stephen join us. She looks me over. "See, I told you he would like the hoodie."

"Megs, focus," Stephen says in a stern tone.

"Right. He's here."

"Who…?" Sora asks.

"Rich," Meghan answers. "I heard it through the…lemmings. I told them to keep an eye out for him and they came back and said Captain Creepy…" Stephen clears his throat. "…that that poor, sweet victim of magic…" Stephen nods. "…was at his locker this morning."

"So, what are we gonna do?" Stephen asks.

All eyes turn to Sora. "Why are you guys looking at me?"

242

"You're usually the one barking orders," Alex answers.

"I don't bark," she says plainly. She fidgets uncomfortably. Why do I get the same sensation from her now that I get whenever she's around Gavin? "Barking is for dogs. I'm a tigress." She pouts. She's actually pouting. Disemboweling. Maiming. Tearing to bits. All those things I expect from Sora, but never pouting.

"Fine," she grumbles. "We should talk to him...hopefully since we're in school he won't try anything." We nod almost in unison. "Alex and Stephen should go. Gwen and Kai, I want you two sticking close by in case he does decide to try something..." She motions to Meghan. "...and I'll keep an eye on Blondie here."

"What...why...?"

Sora turns to Meghan. "Because...the bear-dog's primary target has always been you. Its secondary target is Alex and Gwen and even then, only when they're together." Meghan nods. "Plus, I'll call..." Sora grumbles and rolls her eyes. "...Gavin and see if he'll stick close to the school." I nod.

"Okay," Alex breathes. "We've still got a couple of minutes before first. We should go now." Stephen moves to his side.

"Be careful," Sora warns. They turn to walk away and my heart leaps into my throat. What if Sora's wrong? What if Rich does try something?

"Wait," Meghan says. She catches Stephen's right hand. "Let him know..." Meghan clenches her jaw. Tears well in her eyes. "...let him know that I'm sorry...for what I said to him in the restaurant that night. It was mean...and...petty...and I didn't mean..."

"What'd you say to him?" Stephen asks.

"She said..." Kai starts, but Meghan's snaps her fingers in his face.

She inhales deeply. "He asked me if I wanted to go out with him sometime. A couple of...the lemmings showed their disgust and I piled on..." She touches the spot directly under her nose. "...I called him a pathetic, skeevy loser..." Stephen's jaw tenses this time. "...and..." And...? There's more. "...that he was such a blip of a nothing. That he could disappear tomorrow, and no one would even notice...not even Stephen." A tear escapes her eye. Stephen nods, understanding why Rich took this so hard. Clearly, Rich knew how Stephen felt about Meghan and how she feels about him.

Meghan sniffs. "So, I guess this IS my fault. I mean, I'm the one who set him off."

Stephen takes her hands and holds them near his heart. "No. This is my fault and Alex's..."

"And we might've egged him, too," Kai submits.

Stephen nods. "There's plenty of blame to go around. We could've been there for him, more than we were."

Alex pats Stephen on the shoulder. "Come on." Stephen follows.

"We'll be right behind you," I whisper. Alex nods. I cringe because I want to kiss him, and I should've kissed him...and...

"Hey, where'd you go?" he whispers from directly in front of me. I shake my head. He swipes the four fingers of his right hand across my left cheekbone and kisses me. I drop my biology book and notebook and put my arms around him.

I moan as we part, wishing it were longer. "Be careful," I whisper. He nods and releases me. My hands tremble and feel warm. I have to fix this. I don't know what I would do if I ever burned him.

"Muy caliente," Meghan breathes. My head bows and I laugh.

Kai offers my biology notebook and book. "Ugh," he groans. "You guys are gonna be one of those couples, aren't you?" I shrug. "Come on. Remember we're supposed to stay close but not too close." I nod and follow him. I steal a glance at Meghan. Sora walks over to her, arms crossed and scowl intact.

#####

"How are we gonna do this?" Stephen asks. I shake my head. We stop walking. "Come on. You've been doing this longer than I have. What are we gonna do?"

I shrug. "I've been doing this for about a month longer than you." Stephen nods. He looks behind him and finds Rich rifling through his locker. "Dive in?" I suggest. He frowns. "It's something Jamie's dad used to say all the time." He inhales deeply and turns in the direction of our former friend, who I hope is still our friend.

Rich's decked out in the best...or, the worst Goth gear. A long black coat, big, black boots, black cargo pants and a black with white writing *Black Sabbath* t-shirt. At least, he got one thing right with his outfit. If I didn't know better, I would swear he was wearing black eye make-up, but I know that's just dark circles. On top of that, he looks thinner and paler than I've ever seen him and I've seen him down with the flu.

The closer we get, the more I feel weirded out. The best way I can describe it comes from Mrs. Bustamante...he makes me feel *ill at ease*. His hair looks greasy, slicked to one side and disheveled and not in a way that looks like he secretly took an hour to get it that way. His glasses are missing too. That's weird. He wears bifocals and he's not even squinting.

"Rich," Stephen says. No response. Stephen's eyes dart to me and back. I shove my hands deep into my pockets and rock on my heels. "Rich," Stephen repeats louder.

Rich lifts his head and turns it eerily slow, kind of like an owl swiveling its head. He smiles showing off his dull, graying teeth that I could swear were white only three weeks ago. He sees us...taking us in like a bug collector would look at a couple of butterflies in a glass case.

"Well," he starts, puffing his rank breath. "If it isn't my best friend..." There's a weird, exhausted creak to his voice. His eyes focus on me and it sounds like gravel shifting as his pupils move. "...and the lying, no good freak who pretended to be my friend." I frown.

"Rich," Stephen cuts in. "We know what's going on with you, man."

"And what's that?" Rich snaps. "That the lies of this 'sleepy little town' have been removed from my eyes." He's getting jitterier. "Because now..." He's practically yelling. Stephen and I look around nervously at the people watching. "...now..." He points one trembling, spastic finger at me. "I see you..." Angrier. "...freaks...I see ALL of you for what you REALLY are. You...Gwen...Jamie-Lynn...Meghan..." ...*Meghan*...? So, she really is supernatural. "...and your cousins..." He's seething. At least, the crowd started moving on for the most part. "You're all trying to infect us normal people...us human beings with this...this..."

Gwen and Kai appear between Rich and us. Rich stumbles back, running into his locker door. "Gwen?" I breathe. There are a few students still standing around, staring at us. "You guys just…"

"Relax," she says softly, but with a serious tone and glowing bright green eyes. She holds up two leaves, clenched on either side of her middle finger. "Everyone just sees the three of you talking and Kai and me, walking over to join you."

"Oh good, your…" He makes air quotes. "'…girlfriend' came to your rescue."

"Only because you wanted to escalate the situation," Gwen explains.

"You're steady callin' us freaks," Kai says. "But you're the one who signed a blood contract with a familiar." Rich looks at Kai as if he just spoke German. "You know. The blood ritual that lets you summon your shadow dog."

"I didn't need any ritual, you freak." He lifts his right hand, palm facing up. A shadow rises from his hand and swirls. Kai and Gwen both take a step back. Is he summoning the bear-dog, right here in the hall? Will Gwen's fox magic be able to cover that, too? The shadow gets smaller and rounds out. It takes the shape of a crystal about as big as his thumb. He takes it between his pointer and thumb. "All I need is this to get rid of your kind."

"Ugh," Gwen moans and leans away. She takes a step back and stumbles, crashing into me. I catch her. "What…what is that…?"

"It's a crystal," I whisper. "Didn't you say something about the shadow man using a crystal when he killed that kitsune in the woods?"

She nods slowly. "But not like that one…it was bigger than this one." She trembles. "Also, I didn't get any sensation from the crystal in my dream. This one…" She shivers again, turns to me, and buries her face in my chest.

"What are you doing to her?" I snap. Rich shakes his head slowly. I've never wanted to punch him in his face as much as I do right now. I put my arms around Gwen and pull her close.

"I'm not doing anything to her…yet." Stephen steps beside Kai. Rich pauses. Stephen grabs him by the shirt and pulls him nearly off his feet. "Get off me," Rich complains.

"What the hell is wrong with you?" Stephen snaps. "Can't you even see what this…this thing is doing to you?" Rich struggles against Stephen's grip. "Listen to me. I'm your friend…damnit, I'm worried about you! Alex is, too!"

Rich resists Stephen's grip. "I can't believe you're siding with these…freaks against your own kind."

"What's going on here?" Principal Stanford snaps.

Stephen releases Rich, who curls his hand around his crystal fragment. "Nothing," Stephen says to Principal Stanford, who seems unconvinced. "Just a…um…disagreement between friends."

"Yeah," Rich adds, his stench even causing Principal Stanford to pause. "Just a disagreement…among former friends. I don't really care for the company Stephen's been keeping lately."

"I don't care about the specifics, boys," Principal Stanford grumbles. "I just want to make sure you're not causing a disruption in my hallways." He looks at Gwen and me. "What's wrong with her, Garner?"

I shake my head. He arches one eyebrow. "Feeling a little...queasy," Gwen moans on the verge of vomiting. "I need..." She swallows a massive choking lump. "...to get some air," she finishes while tugging on me as if she were about to fall. "Can...can Alex...take me outside...?"

Stanford looks her over. He nods. "Go ahead." He returns to Rich and Stephen...and where has Kai gone? "And you two, get to class. Right now." Rich turns on his heel with more swagger than I thought him possible and walks away. Stephen moves to follow him. Stanford puts his hand up in front of his chest. "No. You can go that way," Stanford says, tipping his head the opposite direction. Stephen watches Rich leave and then does as he was told.

I carry Gwen to the nearest exit, which takes us to the back of the school. She lets go of me as soon as we step outside. She holds onto one of the poles holding the white awning up. She inhales deeply and repeatedly, bent over, holding on with both hands. Her breathing slows a little.

"Better?" She looks exhausted. She nods with half-closed eyes. "Good."

"What's going on here?" Gavin asks. Gwen turns, leaning against the post. She swallows deeply and extends her hand to me without looking. I step closer; she instantly intertwines our fingers and pulls me to her. "Seriously," Gavin continues. "What's wrong with you?"

"We confronted Rich," I explain.

"I know. Your cousin called me and asked if I'd come hang around just in case. That doesn't explain what's wrong with my adorably, pink-hooded little sister."

"I saw it," she moans. "The crystal or, at least, part of the crystal that the shadow man used to kill obāsan's friend. Rich had it with him."

"Okay, but what's wrong...?" I moan. "We figured that if he was part of this whole thing then..."

"No," Gwen whispers. She pulls on my hand. "Come 'ere." I step forward and she leaves the post in favor of wrapping her arms around me. Gavin groans. She looks at him. "He's my boyfriend! Get over it!" I frown while looking at Gavin over Gwen's shoulder. He shrugs and shakes his head slowly.

"It's not what I expected," Gwen continues. "It doesn't just steal powers like we originally thought."

"What do you mean?" Gavin asks. "The Creep drained the old kitsune's power...losing her power killed her, right...?"

"That's what we thought...it might even be what killed her...but that wasn't all. That wasn't the end. When she died, a part of her...maybe all of her was trapped inside of it." Gavin scowls and trembles with rage. He has murder in his eyes. I don't blame him. "And not just her," Gwen sobs before burying her face in my chest again. "There were so many inside it."

I stroke her hair. "And that was only a small piece."

"We have to stop him...now," Gavin snarls and for the second time since I met him, we're in complete agreement. "No matter what we have to do."

Chapter 39: Shadows

"…but why did we have to wait until after sundown," I ask Alex as we stand at the edge of Rich's yard.

"He's braver at night," he returns. "If there's ever a time to make him bring his A-game…" He looks at my brother on my right side. Gavin nods firmly, shadows half-covering his face. He looks to his left at Sora and Kai…standing at the ready.

"Okay," I reply. "But…" I peer at Meghan and Stephen behind us. "…I want you three to stay back."

Stephen frowns as Meghan rubs his shoulder. "You can't expect me to…"

"Can and do," Sora says to Stephen without looking. He frowns. "This thing has nearly killed me, Gwen and even Gavin…" She turns to see him. "…what do you think you'd be able to do against it?" She smirks. "You don't even have a stun gun." Meghan smiles.

"So," Gavin starts. "What's the plan, Sora?" All eyes turn to Sora. She smirks. Alex looks just as confused as I am.

"Why don't you go up to the front door…?" She looks at Gavin. "…and ring the doorbell…?" she finishes in a mocking tone…or is it…? Is she…flirting with Gavin?

Gavin returns her gaze and grin with the same playful glint. "Is that a dare?"

"Yes," she says confidently, her eyes fixed on Rich's front door. Gavin strides forward with the same bravado.

"Gavin," I pant. Sora catches my arm before I can take another step. "What are you two doing…?"

"The four of us have never fought this thing together, have we?" I shake my head slowly. "Your brother is going to be bait…knowing him, he's not going to hold back, which means he's going to thrash Rich's familiar effortlessly…" Gavin, his shoulders squared, marches toward the door. "…and when he does that…the three of us will crush the other one…once and for all…" I nod.

"You're sending the invites out," Alex says calmly. "Don't you think you and Kai should put on your party clothes?" Kai laughs and slips his hand into his pocket. Sora smiles and does the same. They both phase into their tiger-selves. He looks at me and takes both of my hands in his. "Your turn."

I nod, warmth coming from his hands. The fox magic flows through me…unfettered by doubt…fear…shame…or anything other than the longing to put an end to this madness…to protect the person who I've…fallen in love with… My shoulders erupt in flames…moving down my arms and my claws descend. Moving down my spine and my three tales emerge. Flowing up to my head and my fox ears and fangs appear. I look into Alex's eyes and see my glowing jade pupils reflected.

"You're so hot," he breathes. He taps my chin with the side of his right pointer finger. I tilt my head up slightly and he kisses me. "Go get 'em."

I feel a swirl of malevolence all at once. Gavin is fighting the original bear dog already. Sora wasn't kidding…Gavin is fighting it all out, throwing all his power into crushing it. He puts the bear-dog onto its belly with a downward punch to the head. He spins, throwing blue streaks of fire off, coming to a stop to drive his foot into the side of the creature's head. The bear-dog tumbles. Gavin does not relent…he is already on top of it. He tears at it from the center. The bear-dog sinks into the ground and rushes back to the house.

"CATCH IT BEFORE IT GETS BACK INSIDE," Sora snaps.

"IT WON'T MAKE IT," Gavin barks. Kai steps forward.

"Not yet," Sora orders and Kai becomes as still as a stone.

Gavin drives his fist into the front porch and a blast of blue flame flares up around him. A squealing shriek fills the air. The bear-dog...or more than likely its owner cries in pain. Gavin stands slowly...his shoulders moving up and down rapidly either from anger or breathlessness, I can't tell from here.

Gavin pulls his right hand back and from the porch to his curled fingers is a long streak of black inkiness. He pulls harder and jumps off the porch, dragging it with him. "Come out here and face us, coward," he bellows at the open doorway.

A figure appears in the darkened space. He looks ghostly pale against the gloomy entryway. Rich staggers to the threshold...the dark circles under his eyes look black now...not purple...black...his head slumps forward, his black hair falls in greasy clumps in front of his forehead.

"You freaks," he spits, frothing at the mouth. "You come to my house..."

"Why not...?" Alex shouts. "You came to mine..." I look at him...how could he hear Rich from there?

"What are you talking about?" Rich snarls back. "I didn't..." Rich's next word is cut off by the sound of thunder...rolling toward us.

"Get ready," Sora whispers, looking right. Kai and Alex turn too. "We're on," Sora shouts and she and Kai are off.

"I'm going, too," I say. Alex nods. I use swift paw and meet the Garner siblings at the edge of the Mortimer yard. They stare at the high bordering hedges. "Be careful," I warn them. "This is the one that absorbs your powers."

"We know," Kai says.

"No," I murmur. "I mean, it absorbs your powers..." They look at me. "The first time Alex and I fought it, it shot fireballs at us...using my fire."

"Gwen," Alex says softly. I glance in his direction. He seems so far away. Meghan moves to his right. Stephen stands on his left. They watch my brother and Rich. "Remember what Rex told us. You don't beat the familiar, you beat the master." I nod. "And here it comes."

I turn back to the hedge just in time to see the horned, spike-covered, sharp-toothed second bear-dog leap over them...complete with its fresh coat of black-on-white fur.

"Crap," Sora groans, while using swift paw to move away from it. "It copied me."

"Gwen," Kai says from behind the creature. "Your senses are as good as ours, right?"

"Is this really the time?" I ask, watching bear-dog number two go after Sora.

"Yes. You should go and find the summoner like Alex said. We can hold this thing off until then." I shake my head. "The only reason he beat us last time is because he got the drop on us. We can do this...trust us." I frown because Kai is being logical.

248

I nibble my lower lip because he asked me to trust them. I scoff because he's right on both counts.

"Don't die," I whisper. He nods and rushes off in a blur to help his sister. I peer at Alex.

"Go," he says. "Follow that thing's trail back to the summoner." I nod. I use swift paw to leap up into the nearest tree and dart from sturdy branch-to-branch, following the path that the creature used. I stretch out with my physical senses to track the summoner...but I stretch out with mother's gift to feel out my friends and brother. I still sense Alex as if he's right here with me. My brother is still fighting the remains of Rich's familiar. Meghan stands next to Alex...but she's moved over to Stephen and clutches at him for support.

"Keep going, Gwen," I whisper. Stop the summoner, not the summoned, I order myself. I pause... "Ugh," I groan before I can stop myself. It's that same nauseatingly malevolent feeling that came from Rich's fragment. Only more intense...there are more of them in his...so many, too many. I feel them all. They're in pain. Frightened. Losing heart. I have to save them. I have to find a way to free them.

I move through the rushing leaves and branches as fast as I can. I leave the cover of foliage surrounding me, landing in the backyard of a plain white house with a white picket fence around it. It has low-cut grass and it is open with only a few small trees around. The trail ends here. This place is strange. Lawn gnomes, rose bushes, a birdfeeder, even a birdbath...nothing about this place suggests evil lives here. "Ugh," I whine. The malevolent feeling is getting closer.

I crouch, left arm crossing over my right, my foxfire braying upward like fiery hairs standing on end. You have to end this, Gwen. You have to end this...for Alex's sake...for Meghan and Stephen's sake...for Kai and Sora's sake...for the sake of the Turnipseeds' memory...for the sake of my brother...and God help him...even for Rich's sake.

I find strength in my desire to protect them all. The backdoor opens slowly with a slight creak and a whoosh of in rushing air. Whatever...whoever appears in this opening...I must crush them...to protect my new life here. I rush forward...don't think...attack... He steps out of the shadows and I freeze. I slide to a stop, my Converse skid across the dew dampened grass. "No...," I gasp as my mind seems incapable or unwilling to wrap itself around what stands in front of me. "No...," I sob as a tear streams down my face.

#####

Sora and Kai kept true to their word. They're handling the new bear-dog. I have to admit...they both look more cat-like than they normally do. They're even moving on all fours.

"Alex," Meghan whispers. "Do you think Gwen's okay?" I nod with my hand over my heart. "Do you really think so...?"

"No, Meghan..." I look at her. "I know she is." She smiles and then gets a puzzled, concerned look on her face. "What is it?"

"Stephen...?" I follow her gaze and catch Stephen running across the yard. "What's he doing?" she practically screams and starts running before I can stop her...and then I'm following her before I can stop myself. The spiked-larger bear-dog staggers and tumbles over after a double-double dropkick by Sora and Kai. Stephen moves behind it. The thing is on its feet a second later but ignores Stephen. It turns to Meghan…fire billowing from its mouth.

"Meghan," I yell as the bear-dog opens its mouth wider.

"Meghan," Stephen shouts from somewhere. I can't see him. It fires, just as Kai comes down on its head.

"NO," Kai growls.

"ALEX," Sora shrieks and pulls me out of the way.

"MEGHAN," I snap, reaching for her as best I can…as the fireball lands in the spot where I used to be. A smoldering crater marks the space where Meghan and I stood.

"Meghan," Stephen yells cheerily. I frown.

"I'm up here," she shouts from a tree branch near the front of the yard. How did she…? She cups her hands around her mouth. "KEEP GOING!" Sora and Kai smile and dart at the still-recovering familiar. Stephen rushes toward Gavin and Rich again. I follow him, taking the long way around the familiar versus skinwalker smackdown.

"What are you stupid or something…?" Gavin snips at Stephen, who ignores him entirely.

Stephen moves over to Rich and grabs the front of his shirt. He gives him a good shake. "WHAT'S THE MATTER WITH YOU? Can't you see what this thing is doing to you…? You look and smell like you could fall down dead any minute…"

"Don't you get it?" Rich counters. "It's all their fault…the reason for everything bad in this world is because of freaks like them." He looks at me. "Because of our so-called friend…"

Stephen shakes him again. "You've been brainwashed. I mean, what about Mr. Turnipseed? What did he ever do to you? What did he do to deserve what happened to HIM…?"

"He married one of them," Rich snarls. Stephen and I gasp. "That's why I had my pet rip that old bastard apart."

"No." Stephen releases Rich as tears stream down his face. "You did…what…?"

"That's all I needed to hear," a velvety voice with a distinct Spanish accent says. Rich looks behind him and finds, Mrs. Turnipseed. Red surrounds her deep blue pupils…sharp fangs glistening …

"You're dead…," Rich breathes, sounding shocked and horrified.

Mrs. Turnipseed claims his face and pulls him closer. She bites into his neck. She makes a noise, reminding me of Max slurping from his water dish, mixed with his growl. Blood spurts from Rich's neck and runs down his back. Whatever screams he might have had are lost to gurgles in his throat. His arms fall to his side. She releases him. Rich wobbles for a second and then falls to the left as lifeless as the ghost that he resembled.

"No…" She wipes her blood-covered mouth. "…that's you," she brags to Rich's body.

"Mrs. Turnipseed?"

250

Her eyes move up to Stephen's face as the blood drains away and the whites of her eyes return. "I'm sorry," she whispers, her eyes moving from Stephen to me and back again.

"You're alive...?" Stephen sighs. She nods, staring into his eyes. He puts his arms around her and holds her tight. She seems shocked and then settles into his hug. She puts her arms around him and strokes the back of his head. I stare at Rich. His pale skin almost glows in the moonlight...his eyes seem to have lost their natural shine. Aside from that and the blood, he looks the same as he did a minute ago, but at the same time, he looks completely different.

Meghan sighs. She stands beside me and looks down on Rich. "How did you...?" I ask, motioning to the tree that she was in a second ago. She shakes her head. I pause when I realize something else. "Where's Gavin...?" I look at Kai and Sora, still fighting the newer bear-dog. "And why is that thing still here...? Gwen..."

"The trickster with the blue aura," Mrs. Turnipseed starts. "...ran off in that direction." She tips her head in the direction that Gwen ran off.

"He went to help Gwen. Will you protect them?"

She looks at Stephen and nods. "It's what my Jordan would've wanted."

I nod and run toward...Gwen, I hope.

"Alex," Stephen says. I turn. "Be careful."

I nod and run to follow the bear-dog's trail back to Gwen. I dart through the opening in the hedge that's been there since we were seven. I've known Rich, played in this yard since forever and now he's...don't think about it. Just run. Focus on the warm feeling in the center of your chest and follow it to her.

I hop a chain-link fence and rush across a darkened backyard, ignoring the little rat-dog nipping at my ankles. I leap over the other side, passing through a wide-open yard, getting closer and closer to a white picket fence. A white picket fence...with flairs of bright red and blue flames on the other side. I jump the fence and freeze...Gavin then Gwen fall back with a bolt of lightning.

"Gwen," I pant, running to her side.

"I'm fine." Red flames cover her entire body and give her the appearance of a fox made of fire.

"I'm fine, too," Gavin complains, rising in a similar blue flames state.

"Two freaks or three, it doesn't matter to me," an angry voice snarls. A red swoop of hair and a large, bushy red beard covered pale face steps forward. "You'll all be inside of this soon," he continues, extending a dark, oblong crystal.

"Gwen am I crazy, or is that...your uncle...?"

"You're not crazy," Gavin growls.

"He's behind all of this," Gwen explains. "He only pretended to just get to town for Mr. Turnipseed's funeral...when really he was just coming back..."

"So, he really killed the old kitsune while Rich...really...killed Mr. Turnipseed."

"The loss of even one *human* life was regrettable," Mihangel groans. "I knew that that kid was a little unpredictable...a little broken when I found him crying in that alley." He looks at us. "But I was willing to take that risk...besides he did exactly what I needed him to do...he threw you all off my scent."

"Why are you doing this, uncle?" Gwen sobs.

251

"Don't call him that," Gavin snaps.

"My thought exactly," Mihangel grumbles. "I've hated your kind ever since your father told me what your mother was."

"What...?" Gavin roars.

Mihangel smirks. "Yes, and I'll let you in on a little secret," he gloats. "The other kitsune didn't kill your parents..." Gwen seethes. Gavin's been seething since he first mentioned their mother.

"No," Gwen cries, shaking her head.

"...it was me," Mihangel brags. "I didn't know that I'd kill my brother mind you. I mean, how was I supposed to know that Delwyn had bound himself to..."

"SHUT UP!" Gavin roars from directly in front of him. Blue flames fill the entire backyard with Gavin as its center...like its sun...

"Concustidio," Mihangel says in a panic, extending the crystal. Gavin claws and scrapes against a semi-transparent purple octagon.

"Shut up! Shut up! Shut up!" Gavin repeats, attacking repeatedly.

Gwen vanishes in a burst of red flames, growling the entire way. "Suffoco," Mihangel spits and Gavin falls, clutching at his throat. Gwen appears behind Mihangel, ready to rip into him. "Cohibeo," he says aiming the crystal at her. Her hands snap to her sides and she falls.

Gavin writhes, gasping for air. Mihangel focuses on Gwen. He smiles and marches over. He switches the crystal from his right hand to his left. His right hand palm up, glows. He half-turns to me. "I'll be with you in a moment, whatever you are." He puts his hand, palm down; on the ground, a circle burns into the grass, forming around Gwen. "A member of the Order, bearing abominations," he snarls. "...unthinkable."

"No," Gwen sobs.

Mihangel places the crystal at the top of the circle, next to Gwen's head. "Omnia mea tua erunt," he starts in a weird echoing voice.

I hear a growl and Mihangel looks at me...because the rumble is coming from my throat and I'm already running as fast as I can. He turns and punches me in the face...I fall and hit the ground hard.

"I don't even need the crystal to beat you," he snarls, kicking me in the side. He kicks me again and something snaps, but he doesn't even let up long enough for me to scream. He kicks me repeatedly. The pain is blinding. My vision blurs and then the feeling from the rest of my body goes next until all I feel is his foot colliding with my cracked ribs.

My eyes come back into focus just in time for my mouth to taste like pennies. My ribs are screaming bloody murder. My left eye's nearly swollen shut. Mihangel spits cuss words as he continues kicking me. I look at Gavin. barely breathing. I look at Gwen, no fire...not even a flicker of a flame. Tears pouring down her face as she takes in my appearance. I have to help her. No, not just her...them. If we stop Mihangel, Gwen and Gavin and even Sora and Kai will be safe. I have to help her. Help them! I have to... He kicks me again, only this time, I turn onto my broken ribs and wrap my arms around his leg.

252

"Let go," he barks, trying to pull it back again. I shake my head, clutch tighter and shut my eyes. "Let go!" He punches me in the top of my head. "Let go!" Another punch. This one hits me in the ear and everything rings.

"ALEX!" Gwen shrieks after a sixth and seventh punch come down. I open my eyes again as the eighth one nearly crushes my skull.

"GWEN," I shout back. "We'll ALWAYS be uneven, because…" …another fist… "…because I LOVE YOU! AND I'LL DO ANYTHING TO PROTECT YOU!!!" Another fist comes down and suddenly… everything… tastes… like… purple… horseshoe… clouds…

Chapter 40: Blue

He loves you…

"I know that," I reply aloud…or did I?

He really and truly loves you, my darling Gwendolyn.

"I love him, too."

Then get up and protect the one who is dear to your heart as he tried to do for you.

"I can't…"

You can, and you will, Gwendolyn, the voice says with authority. *I'll lend you my power!*

"You will…?"

Of course.

"Why?"

I would happily give anything to protect you and your happiness.

My eyes open to the purple crystal, glowing soft blue, and somehow I recognize instantly…

"Mom?" The blue light moves to me. My body burns with purple fire and suddenly, Mihangel's spell no longer restricts me. I stand.

"What are you doing?" Mihangel growls. He kicks Alex off his leg. I stare at my heart laying on the ground. His chest rises and falls erratically, but better than not at all. My eyes dart back to my…uncle…

"You killed my father," I murmur. "You killed your own brother, because he loved my mother. You killed my mom…you nearly killed my brother because he was enraged by this. You nearly beat Alex to death because he tried to protect me…"

Mihangel's eyes move from me to the crystal. He gnashes his teeth. I step to my right, obscuring his view. "I'm sorry. Blood or not, on behalf of them and all the others you've hurt with this cursed object, I can't forgive you. I can't." Purple fire explodes from me, streaming upward, threatening to scrape the heavens. "And I wouldn't, even if I could."

"Are you going to kill me?"

"No, she's distracting you," Gavin says casually behind Mihangel. Gavin seizes his head. "I'm going to kill you." He snaps Mihangel's neck as if it were a twig. Gavin shoves him. He lands with a thud. Gavin's eyes still glow pale blue.

"Gavin, why did you…?"

"Because you shouldn't," he whispers. "…especially when you look and feel so much like mom…" I look down at my hands, burning pale blue. I gasp.

Protect each other…always, the tender voice echoes on the wind. *…my darling children…and know that your father and I love you and we're very proud of you.*

"Okāsan," Gavin sighs as a tear rolls down his cheek. It's strange, but somehow, he feels the way he felt when we were little kids. The blue flame moves away from my body and floats in mid-air.

"Momma," I sob, staring at it with tears streaming from my eyes. The blue flame fades and I no longer sense mother's aura. Gavin stares at me. I take a step forward and I'm in his arms. "It was momma."

He nods against the top of my head. "I know." He takes a deep breath. "Now, we should probably focus on healing your p…" I lean away and glare at him. "…your boyfriend." I smile. He laughs into a groan of "shut up."

I roll Alex onto his back. Blood covers his head, matting his hair. I moan. "He'll be okay," Gavin reassures me, which is strange in and of itself. We crouch over Alex, holding our hands above his chest, Gavin's hands underneath mine. I feed as much power into him as I can…purple flames erupt from our combined effort. The fire moves across Alex's chest, up to his head and out to his arms. I feel drained, like the flames may be taking too much. The seconds tick by.

"He's not healing," Gavin grumbles.

"What…?" My eyes fill with fox magic and look down at Alex. The largest gash at the top of his head still drips blood…his breathing remains labored…erratic.

"He's not healing," Gavin repeats, sounding angered. Alex coughs up a spatter of blood from his barely parted lips. My heart stops. "He's got a punctured lung…" I shiver. "…his ribs must be broken…one must have punctured his lung! He's drowning in his own blood if the things not collapsed!" Alex makes a loud sucking noise before he falls still.

"Alex…?"

Gavin growls and is on his feet. He stalks away. I rest Alex's head on my lap. He's not moving. He's not breathing. I still feel a tingle emanating from him, but…

"What's wrong?" Sora asks. I half-turn to her. The second I do, what little resolve I had crumbles. Tears pour from my eyes. Sora's head tilts awkwardly and her stoic façade evaporates. "No," Sora sobs. "No," she repeats with a whine, stepping forward. Gavin is already there with his arms around her. She struggles against his hold but submits and falls to her knees. "No," she wails, tugging at Gavin's jacket.

"Alex?" Stephen moans and runs over. He drops to his knees on the other side of Alex and gives him a shake. "Come on, man." He shakes him again. "Come on, man. I lost one best friend today. I can't lose two. Alex…?" Meghan places her hands on Stephen's shoulders. "No, 'cause…'cause Alex can't be." Meghan massages his shoulders. "No, see…no…"

I look at Kai and Mrs. Turnipseed. Kai whimpers like a scolded pup…and she covers her mouth. I nod and turn my eyes to Alex's still face. His angelic…blood-spattered…still face…

"Alex," I whisper as calmly and evenly as I can. "We're even. We're even because I love you, too." I rock back and forth, cradling his head in my arms. "I love you so much that the thought of losing you is causing me…pain…" I wipe some of the blood away from his mouth and then move on to his forehead, turning my pink hoodie sleeve crimson.

"You promised. You promised that you would never hurt me…" I lean in closer, pressing his forehead against my heart. "…and seeing you like this, it hurts. I feel like I'm dying without you…" I gasp an inhaling sigh. "I can't go back, Alex. I can't. I can't go back to a life that doesn't include you. Do you hear me? I can't." Two of my tears fall to his cheeks. "Don't die," I breathe. "Don't die. I'm a selfish, selfish kitsune. I can't be without you. What we have, our love, it's my prettiest possession." I press my lips against his…and I get nothing. There's no reaction from him. No breathing. No tingling. Nothing.

I cry unfettered tears. I cry with reckless abandon and hold him close. My fox magic erupts from me involuntarily. My bright red flames cover me and Alex entirely. I can't breathe. I can't…not without him…I can't…

"Too hot." I pant and lower Alex's head from my chest. I stare into his barely open eyes. "…you're too hot to be with a loser like me," he says gruffly, but with a smile.

"You're alive," I wheeze, staring into his eyes…that aren't brown anymore. They're amber-colored, like when he…

"What?" he asks. "You're looking at me weird."

"Am I looking at you like someone who's in love with you?" He nods as best he can. I kiss him.

We part. "That's cool but if you wanna press my face against your chest again that's cool too." I shove him off with a laugh. He groans. "Ooh, ribs…ribs…," he spits between clenched teeth. I wrap my arms around him again and hold him close. "Never let me go again, fox-face."

"Never," I whisper. Only…I have to because Sora takes him out of my arms. I manage to hold on to his right hand. She crushes him against her chest. Alex emits some noise that is lost in the slightly weathered flannel of her shirt.

"YOU IDIOT," she snaps. "I thought you were dead." Alex makes another noise. "What…?" He pushes against her stomach and gets some separation.

"I can't breathe," he snaps. She frowns. "You were smothering me with your boobs."

"Sorry," Sora whispers and hugs him more gently. Kai walks over and puts his arms around them. Alex cringes and brings his knees up toward his body.

"We should," Gavin starts, letting his words hang in the air. "…probably finish healing him, before his cousins' puncture his lung again." I nod.

Sora turns Alex so that he's lying on his back. He groans a complaint and then rests his head on her knees. Gavin and I move to either side of him. We combine our healing foxfires and it washes over Alex's body. He winces at first and then settles in. Meghan walks over and kneels beside me. She looks at Alex and smiles. Stephen kneels beside Gavin and extends his fist to Alex. Alex smirks and taps it with his own.

"Boys," Sora grumbles and wraps her arm around Alex's neck. She rests her chin on his forehead and closes her eyes. "I love you, cousin," she whispers. I don't think Alex even heard her. He pats her forearm just the same.

"Done," Gavin exclaims and removes his hands. The four of us stand and give Alex room, except Gavin. He steps forward and offers him a hand. Alex takes it and arrives on his feet a second later. "What you did for my sister," Gavin says, drawing Alex closer. "I'll never forget that…Alex." Alex nods.

Sora walks over to the pair. "What you did for my cousin," she begins with a flirtatious tweak of her eyebrow. "I'll never forget that."

"You'd better not," Gavin flirts back.

"Ugh," Kai growls. "Did I just log on to gross dot com forward slash sister hook-ups?" We all laugh.

I step between Gavin and Alex and throw my arms around him. "Alex, I never got a chance to say this to you…well, not to conscious you…I mean, I hinted at it but I…"

"Gwen…rambling…" I nod. "…don't get me wrong, adorable, but…"

"…but, I love you." My heart thuds, waiting on his reaction.

"I know. I heard you. It's the reason I came back…"

"Ooooooooo," I moan at the same time as Meghan.

"Well, that…" He caresses my cheek. "…and this…" He kisses me. I move my hands away from him…I don't want to burn him, but I will not let fire cut this kiss short. He wraps his arms around my waist, resting his hands on the small of my back. We part and I breathe heavily…my heart pounding. I stare into his amber highlighted eyes and see bright green reflected back at me. "I love you too, Gwendolyn Frost."

#####

"This is the spot," Gavin says, taking one last step up the hill. I puff, coming up behind him. Stephen does, too. Gavin looks at us. "Lightweights."

"Well," Stephen starts. "Forgive us for not being supernaturally blessed with crazy amounts of stamina and strength."

Meghan drapes her arms around Stephen's neck. "I managed okay." Stephen and I stare at her ridiculously high heels.

I breathe heavily. "Yeah, but you do have crazy tree climbing skills." She pokes her tongue out. "Seriously, I still want to know how you got in and out of the tree."

Meghan shrugs. "I told you, I don't know. One minute I was in the tree, the next I wasn't. I figured Kai saved me then came back and got me."

"Wasn't me," Kai says.

Meghan smiles, shrugs, and pulls Stephen closer.

"We'll worry about it later," Sora says. You would think that a girl wearing a short skirt in thigh-high grass would be a little uncomfortable. Not Sora, she looks at home, like she's been out here her whole life. She crosses her arms, looks at me and Gwen then at Gavin. He grins and she looks away.

"So," Gavin says, staring at Sora. "You guys are coming back, right?" Kai groans.

"Yeah," Sora replies. "We're going back to pack our stuff. After I told our grandmother what happened, she insisted we make this move permanent." Kai groans.

"And you're okay with that?" Meghan asks. "Packing up your whole life and moving cross-country?" Kai groans again.

"Not like I had a lot of friends or even a boyfriend back home," Sora returns. Kai groans again. "Kai, I'm sure Stacy will understand." Kai lets out something that sounds like a cross between a groan, a whimper and a howl. "He'll be okay."

"What about you?" I whisper to the strangely quiet Gwen, clinging to my arm this whole time.

"Pretty," she whispers. I frown. She points at the sunset. This hill overlooks the town and the sun is just plunging below the taller buildings. It reflects off the inlet behind them, giving everything a content orange glow.

"Yeah." I sigh. "Are you going to be alright?" She shrugs. "I mean, are you sure you're going to be okay, moving here permanently…to be with me?"

"I've never been surer of anything in my entire life."

"Aw, that's so sweet," Gavin and Meghan moan. Gavin does it sarcastically.

"Ignore him," I say.

"I always do."

"So, you managed to convince your foster parents to let you go?" She nods. "And you didn't even need them to return your charm to stop the bad guy."

"Oh, don't think I haven't been rubbing that fact in Gavin's face all week." I laugh. Gwen smiles. "Now, I just need permission from one more person before I can leave."

"Who?" She arches her eyebrows. "Oh. Me...?" She nods again.

"Yeah," Gavin says. "Turns out you two are bound...that's how she was able to pull you back from the brink...it's how she was able to channel our mom from that crystal, too."

I nod. I hold her hands close to my heart. "Gwendolyn Elizabeth Frost...I release you." She inhales deeply, heartbreak in her eyes. She didn't want to be unbound. "With one stipulation..."

"What?" Gavin snaps as Gwen asks softly.

"That you promise to come back to me one day."

"I promise." A tear rolls down her left cheek.

"Come on, Fox-face. You can't do that."

"I can't help it. I'm going to miss you so much."

"Then...hurry back," I whisper. She nods and tilts her head back as if she wants a kiss. I lean forward, happy to grant her wish. She pauses and looks away. "What...?"

"It's here," Gavin says. A circle burns into the grass behind him. Lines appear in the circle and carve out an octagon. Inside the octagon, a square appears. The empty space between the circle and the octagon and the octagon and the square fill with Japanese kanji and kana. "Step back." A huge pale white flame erupts. "It's time to go," Gavin murmurs. He looks past Gwen and me. Sora scowls.

"It's been...real," Stephen says, sounding unsure if that's the right word.

"More like it's been supernatural," Meghan corrects. She pulls Gwen out of my arms. They hug. "Now you hurry back, bestie."

"I will."

"I have to admit, fox-face," Kai starts. "You're not half bad, for a lying, no-good kitsune."

Gwen laughs. She looks to Sora. Sora bobs her head and that's it. Gwen smiles and tips her head.

"No goodbyes for me?" Gavin asks, and silence covers the hill. "Wow."

"Fine. It was nice...*fighting* with you," Sora says in a way that makes my stomach turn.

"Yes," Gavin returns. "The *fighting*...was nice." My stomach churns. "I'll try not to do anymore *fighting* until I get back."

"You'd better not," Sora says with deadly clarity. Gavin smirks. I try to shake off the eerie feeling.

Gwen puts her arms over my shoulders.

"Watashi wa," she whispers. "Watashi wa subete no watashi no kokoro de anata o aishiteimasu. Watashi wa anata no kokoro to karada to tamashī o aishiteimasu.

259

Watashi wa futatabi watashi no ude no naka de anata o hoji shite made, watashi wa futatabi anata no nyūsatsu no kisu o ajiwau koto ga dekiru made, watashi wa, futatabi anata no koe o kiku made, watashi wa sūbun o kaunto sa remasu."

"What?"

"I'll tell you when I get back." She perches on her toes and kisses me. For a second, her hands heat up on the side of my face and then the sensation is gone. I'm only left with the amazing tingling sensation that passes between us and her soft, supple lips on mine. We part. She presses her forehead against mine.

"I hate saying goodbye," I say. "So, I'll just tell you, see you later. I love you, Gwendolyn Frost."

"I love you too, Alexander Garner."

"Come on," Gavin says. She steps back…and one of the hardest things I've ever had to do ensues, I let her go. She sighs as she approaches the blue flames. "Alex." Gavin steps closer. "I hate to admit it, but it turns out that it was a good thing that you and my sister were bound." He offers me his right hand. "You saved her life and I can't express how grateful I am for that."

"Of course." I take his hand. We shake firmly, and I try to let go, but he grabs my forearm with his left hand. He stares into my eyes and his glow. Intense heat comes from his left hand, even through my hoodie. I groan.

"Sorry about that," he says, letting go. "I guess sometimes I don't know my own strength." I nod and rub my arm. "Let's go." He steps into the fire, looks over his shoulder, and sighs. He takes one more step forward and vanishes.

Gwen moves backward, staring at me. I nod. She smiles. "Watashi wa anata o aishite," she whispers just before she disappears. The flames die out a second later, leaving only a charred circle.

"Come on, cos," Kai says, draping his arm over my shoulder. "She'll be back."

"I know. It's just gonna be a really suck-ish December without her."

"Well, that just means," Meghan chirps. "…you need to buy her a kickass Christmas present." Stephen laughs, causing me to laugh. Meghan and Kai join in, even Sora chuckles. We head down the hill.

"Hey, what did you and Gavin mean about *fighting*?" Kai asks.

End.